Carol Rivers, whose family comes from the Isle of Dogs, East London, now lives in Dorset. *East End Angel* is her seventh novel.

CAROL RIVERS

EAST END ANGEL

**SIMON &
SCHUSTER**

London · New York · Sydney · Toronto · New Delhi

A CBS COMPANY

East End Angel, my seventh book, is dedicated to Joe
and Esta, Wendy, Jason, Ella and Jessica, and
Vicki and Terry, with all my love.

First published in Great Britain by Simon & Schuster, 2010
This edition first published by Pocket Books, 2010
An imprint of Simon & Schuster UK
A CBS COMPANY

1 3 5 7 9 10 8 6 4 2

Simon & Schuster UK Ltd
1st Floor
222 Gray's Inn Road
London WC1X 8HB

www.simonandschuster.co.uk

Simon & Schuster Australia, Sydney
Simon & Schuster India, New Delhi

A CIP catalogue record for this book is available from the British Library

ISBN: 978-1-47117-676-0

Typeset by Hewer Text UK Ltd, Edinburgh
Printed and bound by CPI Group (UK) Ltd, Croydon, CR0 4YY

To Maxine, Emma, Gráinne and everyone at Simon & Schuster, a big, big thank, you. To Dorothy Lumley, once more and with heart, thank you. And to my dear Chris, for your hard work online, thank you. And Kate, I haven't forgotten that it all began with you.

For the many online resources I have used to help me bring *East End Angel* to life, I am so grateful. To the wonderful Ali, Ade and Nathan, you're fab! To my Facebook friends, Diane Allen, Janine Pulford and the indefatigable mags4you, to the ever supportive Judith and musical wizard Steve Harrison, and to Kate Flynn – my thanks and affection.

For Jill at Gladys Court for reading over and over again, to my very first readers Jacqueline Richards and Pamela Burridge, to the amazing Daisy Woodward and Eve Hostettler of the Island Trust and to the Romantic Novelists' Association (RNA), which keeps authors in touch with everything writerly and works so hard to sustain us, this is my opportunity to thank you for everything.

And lastly to you, to the readers of Rivers novels everywhere, the biggest thanks of all!

Part One

Chapter 1

June 1941, Isle of Dogs, East London

Pearl's breath caught in her throat as, through the parted blackout curtains, she saw a tall figure standing outside the house. Dressed in naval uniform and wearing an officer's peaked cap, he smiled at her sister, Ruby, who hurried out to him.

Even before he swept off the cap and tucked it under his arm in order to greet Ruby in a warm embrace, Pearl had recognized Ricky Winters. Looking twice as handsome in uniform as ever he had in civvy street, he pulled Ruby close as she went on tiptoe to kiss him.

Pearl kept her eyes fixed on the couple, hoping there was some mistake. But with every movement of his body, a physique that still had the power to turn her knees to jelly, it became clear to Pearl that Ruby and Ricky were an item. Struggling for breath, Pearl's trembling fingers found their way to the soft satin folds of her dress, reminding her that this was her wedding day.

'You all right, sweetheart?' It was her husband's deep voice that brought her back to the present and Pearl swung round to look into Jim Nesbitt's concerned blue eyes. The deep crease between his fair eyebrows and shock of sandy hair, which had been cut rather too short, were a reassuring sight. All she wanted to do was throw her arms around him and tell him how much she loved him.

'Yes, I'm fine,' she nodded. 'Just nervous, that's all. Well, s'pose I should be; a girl don't get married every day, does she?'

Pearl felt the sweat bead her top lip as a thousand

3

questions rushed through her mind, all for Ruby, who hadn't said a word about seeing Ricky. With an effort, she listened to the conversation between Jim and her mother, who had come to join them. Amy Jenkins was very fond of her new son-in-law and between them they were in raptures over the wonderful service.

The church ceremony had been everything Pearl could have desired. Even the little things she would remember, like the cut on Jim's chin that he'd made with the razor as he'd rushed to dress this morning. The sight of it had prompted her to reach up and kiss him as they'd stood waiting to sign the register. Quietly she'd teased him at the tightness of his white collar and tie. In wartime, it was make do and mend, and Jim wasn't a fussy dresser though he always looked smart. His major expense had been her solid gold wedding ring, and Pearl's heart gave a little flutter as she gazed at her finger. Not a two-bob piece of tin from Woolworths, but a solid gold band from up West. They hadn't had time for an engagement, though Jim had told her he'd buy her an eternity ring after they were married. They'd make a Saturday afternoon trip of it and go round all the best jewellers.

Pearl's gaze softened as she thought how lucky she was to have a husband in a reserved job. His engineering skills had exempted him from the call-up. She would never have the heartbreak of seeing him go off to war like so many other brides. And when they'd walked down the aisle and out of the church, Jim had found her hand and squeezed it, telling her with his eyes how much he loved her and would always be with her.

There was no confetti but there were pats on the back and cheers, and Ruby, looking a picture in her blue brides-maid's dress, waving madly from the church porch. Had she been waiting for Ricky then?

Pearl was suddenly aware that Jim and her mother were

staring at her. 'Think I might get a breath of fresh air,' she stammered, adjusting her veil. 'Matter of fact I wouldn't mind taking this off. It's hanging on by a wing and a prayer.'

'Give her a hand, son, will you? Take her out to the yard for a breather.' Amy Jenkins clasped Jim's arm with affection. 'Her dad and me will hold the fort till everyone else comes. We sent the car back to fetch your mum and then me sister and Syd's brother. The others will have to walk, but it's not far from the church. Then when you come in we can start on the food and drink.'

Jim nodded obligingly. 'I could do with a smoke an' all.' His eyes twinkled as he slipped his arm around Pearl's waist. 'And a little cuddle with me wife.'

'Talk about young love!' Amy nervously patted the collar of her dove-grey suit. 'Off you two go and make the most of a few minutes of peace. And that reminds me, if there *is* a raid, God forbid, I've put a few things in the Anderson to tide you two lovebirds over: a couple of blankets, the new oil lamp and a flask. All you'd have to take with you is a few nibbles from the table. The rest of us would go to the public shelter, but I really don't think we'll be put to the trouble.' A sigh escaped her lips as she added hesitantly, 'I don't wish Jerry on me worst enemy but now Moscow is their new target, the bombers ain't such a danger to us.'

Jim nodded emphatically. 'Winnie warned 'em, didn't he? Now they know a leopard don't change its spots, especially one as bloodthirsty as Hitler. But you're right, Mrs Jenkins, for me and Pearl it was perfect timing.'

Everyone was relieved the Luftwaffe was busy elsewhere. The past nine months of Blitz had almost taken the heart out of the city. On 11 May the Luftwaffe had returned to Germany leaving London shattered and burning after the heaviest raid ever. And it was then that Pearl had decided she was going to grab every ounce of happiness she could

for the future, including accepting Jim Nesbitt's proposal of marriage. Yet now, on what was supposed to be the happiest day of her life, it was not the German bombers that Pearl was most afraid of but someone much closer to home.

'Anyway, we ain't going to think about the war today,' her mother decided, resuming her bright smile and patting her short fair hair, curled overnight to within an inch of its life. 'This is your special day, my loves, and no one, not even Adolf, is going to spoil it!'

As she hustled them through the kitchen Pearl made up her mind that somehow she had to prepare Jim for Ricky's appearance. It was on the cards that Ruby would invite him in. Ricky wasn't a stranger to Jim, as the two men were the same age – twenty-eight. Both had been members of the Dockland Settlement Club, a meeting place for the youth of the Isle of Dogs, and it was where, at sixteen, she had first met Jim, a keen rower and swimmer, and much in demand on the dance floor.

'Blimey, your dad opening a scrap yard?' Jim's voice brought her back to the moment as they walked into the backyard. 'Reckon this place needs a bit of a tidy.'

Pearl smiled wistfully. Those were her mum's sentiments entirely. The Blitz had given Syd an excuse to be his natural disorderly self, and as Pearl gazed round, she felt a deep affection for her dad. She was so lucky to have a husband who thought the world of his father-in-law.

Suddenly Jim's strong hand grabbed hers as he pulled her into the shade of the Anderson. A few dandelions, sprouting from the turf on the shelter roof, scattered their seeds around them. 'Fairies', she and Ruby had called them as kids. The sky above was as blue as Jim's eyes and the only reminder of war were the silvery barrage balloons floating high above the island.

'Here, let's take this off.' Jim's gruff voice was filled with tenderness as he lifted the yellowing veil from her shoulders.

Pausing, he smiled as she slid out the tiny pins that held the headdress in place. The whole ensemble, from the long, invisibly darned veil to the even more re-upholstered white dress, had been her mother's and safely preserved in a bottom drawer. Altered overnight to meet the demands of a 1941 fashion-conscious young woman, it had graced Pearl's slender five foot eight inches with elegance. And in wartime, when silk was almost unobtainable, the dress, old as it was, had proved a treasure.

'There, that better?' He tipped up her chin. 'Do you know how much I love you, Mrs N?'

His words felt like a dagger to her heart. 'Jim, there's something I have to tell you.'

He laughed. 'It's too late to change your mind now. You ain't Pearl Jenkins any longer, you're Mrs Nesbitt and, left up to me, will remain so till we pop our clogs.' Pearl swallowed on the lump in her throat at his words of love as he took her hands. 'I want you to know you're the best thing that's ever happened to me, sweetheart. I want the world to know it. If I could shout it from the rooftops I would.'

'You'd be lucky to find a roof that ain't been bombed,' she teased, but saw the hurt on his face.

'I'm not much good at expressing meself, am I?'

'Oh, Jim, you're the best.'

'It's all up here.' He tapped his head. 'But it don't come out right. I want to say things about your eyes, like they're the greenest I ever seen. Emerald, they are, like them big fields in the country. Yeah, that's it – that's what your eyes remind me of – fresh air and little houses with straw roofs.' He held her face between his hands, smoothing his rough thumbs over her cheeks. 'And then there's your nose. It turns up a bit at the end, gives you this ladylike look till it does a twitch just before you start nagging me.' He laughed self-consciously, clearing his throat as his hands slid down over her shoulders. 'I

7

want to say so much. I just wish I had the old dickybirds to say it.'

Pearl fought back the tears. 'You don't need words, Jim. You're ... everything to me, everything.'

For a moment they were silent, content with their world and the thought of their future together. Pearl couldn't bring herself to spoil it. Why should she? This was a day she wanted to remember, a day that she could tell her children about.

Jim cleared his throat. 'It's hard to believe it was the bombing that brought us together. The Blitz, I ask you! Who would have thought you'd have got a job with the council, same as me? Monday, September the second it was, five days before the raids started. There you was as I walked in your office, the girl of me dreams, sitting at this desk all prim and proper, bashing away at them keys and you didn't hardly look up. But I knew it was you all right. Pearl Jenkins, little sweet sixteen, who'd stolen me heart all them years ago, then 'eartlessly given me the order of the boot.'

'Jim! I never did!'

'Well, a tap on the arse then.'

'I was young,' she fumbled, the dark spectre of Ricky overshadowing her again. 'I didn't even know you fancied me.' She had given the cold shoulder to Jim even though she hadn't wanted to hurt his feelings, but had never explained the reason. Why, dear God, on this day of all days, was she having to face this part of her past she would rather forget?

'You was too good for me then, just like you are now,' Jim said earnestly, bringing a cry of protest from her throat. But once more he stopped her from speaking. 'It's true, you could have had anyone you wanted, you was so pretty. All the blokes were after you, I didn't ever get a look-in. But I'll tell you something for nothing. You was not nearly as lovely then as you are now.'

A tear wrestled its way down her cheek and he frowned in confusion. 'Hold on a minute. What have I gone and said now?'

'Nothing. I'm just happy.'

'Blimey, what do you do when you're down in the dumps?'

Pearl couldn't help but smile. Jim's easy humour was one of the things she loved and admired so much. Her husband held her close, managing to entangle himself with her veil. Clumsily he attempted to unravel her long blonde hair that had been swept up into a glossy roll and pinned under the lace. His big hands, those of a hard-working engineer, were no match for the delicate arrangement, and Pearl's own fingers reached up to intervene. As she lifted her arms, his eyes went hungrily down to the swell of her breasts. Suddenly he brought her against him in an embrace, pressing his mouth hard over hers and kissing her passionately. Pearl responded, and when they finally broke apart, they were both breathing hard.

'Jim, you do love me, don't you?'

'Now what sort of question is that? Ain't you heard a word I've been saying?'

'It's just that we've only had a few months to get to know each other again. With the bombing, we've not had much time for ourselves.'

'Couldn't agree more,' he nodded. 'And starting from now you've got me undivided attention.'

She put her hands round his neck. 'I really do love you, Jim.'

'Does that mean we can have another cuddle?'

She smiled, clutching his arms so hard that he made a face.

'Blimey, you're tough for such a little thing.'

'I just want you to know that I've never wanted anything more than to be your wife.'

9

He licked his dry lips. 'Say that again Pearl, 'cos I wanna remember those words all me life.'

She whispered it again, never more grateful for the fact that their love had grown out of friendship and trust. Unlike her past experience, this was a love that was whole and healthy. Her husband would come home every day for his dinner, play with his kids and would be faithful. The kind of man her dad was. A man of all seasons, her mum said. Spring, summer, winter and autumn alike, Syd Jenkins never missed a night in his own bed cuddling up to his wife. And when his boilermaker's job had allowed, he'd walked his two young daughters to school in the morning and given them each a kiss goodbye at the school gates. That was just the kind of husband and father Jim would make, and as Pearl felt Jim's strong, warm body close to hers, she knew she had made the right choice.

'Come on, you can do better than that, Mrs N,' Jim prompted, his fingers fumbling not in her hair but at the tiny buttons between her breasts.

'Jim, Mum's in the kitchen. She could be out at any moment. She only told you to take me veil off, nothing else,' Pearl teased.

He let go of her instantly. 'Blimey, you know how to kill a man's ardour, gel.'

'There'll be plenty of time tonight.'

'All right, I'll be a good boy.' His sparkling blue eyes told her that he was, as always, prepared to do anything to make her happy. And that included waiting until after they were married to make love. She hoped and prayed that he would be so passionate in his need that he would never ever guess that things were not as he assumed.

If Pearl had been her usual happy-go-lucky self, she would have seen that rationing hadn't noticeably limited the spread that her mum and dad had put on for the guests.

She would also have remembered that the black market butter for the baps and sandwiches, and the cucumber and cheese that were virtually unobtainable in wartime, were all courtesy of Jim's ingenuity. Nor was there any sign of the Spam that haunted the larders of working-class Britain. For Jim had worked a miracle with his mates at the works canteen. But Pearl wasn't aware of the wedding breakfast being greedily devoured by their guests. Nor was she listening to the non-stop verbal from her aunty May and her husband, Ron, with their teenage daughters, Betty and Jane. Nor could she have said exactly what comments had passed between her and Aunty Till and Uncle Ted, her dad's brother and his family, now living in Barking. As for her friends from school, Laurie Smart and Sheila Barton, and Moira Bush from work, she'd been in a daze when she'd spoken to them.

When would Ruby and Ricky walk in?

The answer came as Ruby appeared in the hall. Behind her stood a tall figure in uniform. Pearl felt Jim's body tense. Slowly his hand lowered the mug of ale that seconds before had been glued to his lips.

'Christ, Pearl, is that who I think it is?' His tone was one of disbelief. Pearl closed her eyes in distress. When she opened them, his face had washed a ghostly grey. Then, sensing the fact that she was not as shocked as he was, he demanded, 'What's he doing here?'

But Ruby was there before Pearl could reply. Throwing herself into Jim's arms, she hugged him. 'I've got meself a brother-in-law at last!'

Jim was silent as Ruby stood back. 'You both remember Ricky, don't you? From the club?'

Pearl glanced at her husband and searched his face. She knew that the two men had always competed fiercely at sport and there had been no love lost between them. Jim had been popular amongst his team mates but not so Ricky,

a loner, though Jim had never possessed any of Ricky's smooth charm, which had seemed to set him apart from the others and had turned all the female heads.

'You could say we were acquaintances, yes,' Jim muttered coldly.

'It's been a long time,' Ricky nodded. 'Congratulations.' His eloquent tone had Pearl's heart banging against her ribs as his gaze travelled slowly towards her.

'You two was much older than us,' burst out Ruby, seemingly unaware of the tension. 'I was only just left school when you rowed for the club, Ricky. Pearl, you must've been what – sixteen?'

Pearl nodded. 'Yes, about that.'

'We used to watch the boys in the gym, remember?' Ruby giggled, nudging Pearl's arm. 'Those other two girls liked a good gander through the window too. That Stella Burns and her mate. They was always throwing themselves at anything in trousers. Dunno what happened to her. Someone said she got …' Ruby looked embarrassed. 'Anyway, that was a long time ago now, but how strange that me and Ricky met up at the pictures again? Remember that film *Captain Fury* we saw last year, Pearl? Well, it was showing again a few weeks ago and Ricky was on a weekend's leave with one of his mates. I was with Irene Naylor from work. Don't know how he recognized me but it was that flashy gold band on his arm that caught my eye.'

Pearl had already noted the sub-lieutenant's gold braid and it was clear that Jim had too.

'So you've joined the reserves?' Jim said icily.

'The Royal Naval Volunteer Reserve,' Ricky corrected in the same tone.

'Yeah, the Wavy Navy,' sneered Jim, and Pearl cringed at the derogatory expression.

She was not surprised when Ricky retorted, 'And you, Jim? No uniform?'

'You better help yourselves to something to eat before it's all gone,' Pearl suggested quickly, giving Ruby a little nudge.

'Good idea,' Ruby nodded as she slid her hand through Ricky's arm. 'And I want to introduce Ricky to Mum and Dad. Dunno if they'd remember him, but they might.'

But when they were alone, Jim turned on Pearl. 'What did you do that for? I can speak up for meself.'

'I didn't do anything.' Pearl was shaken. 'And don't bite me head off, Jim. I was only telling them about the food.'

'They could see the grub clearly enough, couldn't they? There's enough to feed the five thousand. Didn't you see he was having a go at me? And I certainly don't need you to fight me battles.'

'You started it, Jim,' Pearl retaliated. 'Saying about the Wavy Navy.'

'Are you taking his side?'

Pearl went scarlet. 'Course not. But I don't want a row on me wedding day.'

'Wedding or not,' growled Jim, 'I'm fed up with every Tom, Dick and Harry thinking a man in civvies has no backbone. It's people like Winters that get me goat. A bloody reservist, I ask you! They think they're God's gift to the country. And what the heck is he doing here anyway?'

Pearl shrugged dismissively. 'I've no idea.'

'You didn't know she was seeing him?'

'No, she never said.' Pearl wondered why her sister had not told her about Ricky. They spoke about everything and had shared the same room since they were kids. They'd gone to the same school, had the same friends and only gone their separate ways when Pearl started her job in the council offices. Later, Ruby had joined Brewer's, the wholesalers on the wharf. When war broke out, Brewer's was requisitioned by the War Office and Ruby had stayed on and joined the assembly line.

13

Ruby was her best friend. They had no secrets, except, it seemed, for Ricky.

'Well,' continued Jim irritably, 'she should have said she was bringing a guest. It took us a month of Sundays to sort out who was coming and who wasn't.'

Pearl thought it unwise to correct him. But it was her mum and dad who'd written all the invitations and arranged the wedding. Oh, they'd got a nod out of Jim now and then, but he'd been too busy at work after the bombing to take much part in the preparations. As for Mrs Nesbitt, sitting in her ivory tower and sniffing at most of their plans, well, they wouldn't have been married today if it had been up to her.

'Don't let's get upset over nothing,' Pearl said softly.

'Nothing it might be to you, Pearl, but turning up at me wedding without an invite is a bloody big insult to me.' He stiffened his shoulders. 'But what's done is done, I suppose. Anyway, I'm going over to talk to Mum. She wasn't feeling too bright this morning. Kept going on about Pride Place and how it would be cheaper to live with her.'

'Oh, Jim,' Pearl sighed heavily, 'we've been over all that before.'

'I know. I know. Anyway, she's on her own. Sitting there like a bloody wallflower.'

'I'll come over in a minute.'

Jim cast her a grudging smile. Pearl watched him make his way across the room to sit by his mother, clad in her widow's weeds, perched stiffly on a wooden chair by the window. Pearl knew that this day must be a lost battle for her. Jim had refused her offer of their living with her when Pearl had found the rooms above a corner shop in Pride Place. It needed doing up but it wasn't far from her parents in Roper's Way. And Jim would have done anything to win her, including finding them a home of their own.

Pearl watched as Jim tried to jolly along the conversation. The going was tough. Mrs Nesbitt's face was easy to read. How could her son have been so unwise as to marry beneath him, marry a person whose family lived in Roper's Way, a three-up, two-down terrace blackened by the chimneys of the Millwall factories and within spitting distance of the nearest public house? Her son was destined for far greater things in life. Jim's dad had been an engineer also. His job had brought ownership of their detached house in Villa Road. Their neighbours hadn't been costermongers or dockers, but piano-playing spinsters and retired businessmen.

A smile touched Pearl's lips as more guests filled the room and Jim and his mother were lost to sight. Marrying into the Jenkins family was one fight that Jim had won, but it was clear there would be many more ahead. Pearl was still smiling at the thought when there was a light touch on her arm.

Her heart jumped as she turned and gazed into the dark eyes of Ricky Winters.

Chapter 2

Ricky smiled and time stood still. Pearl thought how the naval uniform gave him an authority he hadn't possessed before, a dangerous attribute for someone already as self-possessed and arrogant as he.

'Could we talk?' he asked.

'There's nothing to say,' Pearl shrugged, glancing quickly round to see if she was being observed.

'I'd like to explain why I'm here.'

'I don't want to know,' Pearl answered, shifting her position so that she was well hidden.

'Pearl, I completely understand, I really do. But I'd like to put the past behind us. I know it's a lot to ask. But for Ruby's sake I think we should.'

She could hardly believe he'd said that. 'You've got a damn cheek, Ricky!'

'Please – give me another chance.'

'What for? A chance to do to Ruby what you did to me?'

'I know how bitter you must feel—'

'You don't know anything,' Pearl retorted, her mouth dry and cheeks hot. 'You've got a nerve to say that on me wedding day!'

'Please don't get upset. I only want to see you happy.'

'Then leave. Tell Ruby you have to go somewhere. Tell her a lie, if you have to. You're good at those.'

He looked at her with dark intensity. 'I admit I deserved that – once – and I've lived to regret every moment of deceiving you. But time's gone by and I've changed. I'm not the man you once knew.'

Pearl shook her head slowly. 'You expect me to believe that?'

His black eyelashes fluttered on his handsome cheeks. 'I didn't mean to hurt you.'

Pearl swallowed tightly. 'I don't even know why I'm standing here listening to you. You lied to me and it wasn't just once, it was time and again. Until you got found out.'

'They weren't lies. Not real lies meant to hurt,' he protested. 'I didn't mean to let you down. It was that stupid girl Stella Burns – she was the cause of the trouble, and I couldn't make you see, you were so young.'

'Yes, I was,' Pearl nodded, her green eyes filled with regret. 'And I trusted you, believed you. Now, please, Ricky, go away and stay out of my sister's life too.'

16

'But, Pearl, I think too much of Ruby to make the same mistake again.'

'Get out, Ricky.'

'Not before I tell you my side of things.'

She pushed past him, but he caught her arm. 'Please, I'm begging you, Pearl. Could we go somewhere quieter? For Ruby's sake, if not for your own. And if you don't like what you hear, then I promise, you won't ever see me again.'

His grip was firm and Pearl glanced around anxiously, knowing that she would have to do as he asked or they would draw attention. Reluctantly she nodded and, making her way through the crowd, she slipped quietly out into the hall.

'What did you mean, for Ruby's sake?' she demanded as she spun round and found him behind her, his dark eyes full of urgency.

'I'm falling in love, Pearl.'

'What?'

'I mean it. Ruby's good for me – uncomplicated ... a breath of fresh air in my life, and I know I can make her happy.'

'But you've only just started taking her out.'

'I know what I want now and if I'd not been such a fool, I would have known when you and I were together that I should have settled down and married you. I regret losing you, but I can't turn back the clock.'

Pearl shook her head in disbelief. 'And you're saying you're in love with Ruby?'

'Yes, I believe I am.' He paused. 'Pearl, does Jim know about us?'

Pearl felt her legs go weak. 'That's none of your business.'

He smiled. 'Neither does Ruby. So isn't it in our mutual interest to be friends? I mean, we love two people very dearly – we wouldn't want them hurt just as we no longer want to be hurt. Doesn't that make sense?'

When she didn't reply he continued, 'And you won't be seeing much of me anyway.' He looked down at his hands, twisting them together and flexing his fingers. 'You see, I'm expecting a posting. We've already been kitted out with cold weather gear.' His eyes met hers. 'No doubt we'll be part of the Atlantic runs to Archangel and Murmansk. The chances are ... well, need I say more?' His smile was suddenly forced. 'Ruby may never see me again if my luck doesn't hold out.'

Pearl knew all too well of the many British lives that had been lost at sea during the war so far. The newspapers and wireless broadcasts told frequently of the tragic losses in the icy, U-boat-filled North Atlantic, and she could see the fear in his eyes, despite his smile. For one brief moment she felt hope that he too might suffer such a fate and then in the next, a deep guilt that she could ever think such a thing.

He nodded slowly as if reading her thoughts. 'If I don't get through, then for you, nothing is lost. This conversation, my reappearance in your life, will be just a memory ... but let me assure you of this: my feelings for Ruby are sincere and if I should return, I would consider myself the luckiest man on earth if she will have me.' He held out his arm and the wavy gold band glittered. Without warning, he took her hand. 'Pearl, let's agree that this is for the good of the people we—'

'What the blazes?' Jim's voice cracked in the air. He leaped towards them and crashed with Ricky into the banister. He had Ricky by the shoulders and pushed him into the kitchen. Ricky's oath was audible as he broke his fall on the table. Syd and Ruby rushed out from the front room.

'What's going on?' Syd demanded.

'Nothing, Dad, nothing!' Pearl protested as she pulled Jim back.

'It was just horseplay,' muttered Ricky, putting distance between himself and Jim as he straightened his tie.

Pearl held on to Jim's arm and felt him shaking. The anger in his eyes and his clenched fists made her very frightened.

Ricky put his arm around Ruby. 'Perhaps we should step out for a breath of fresh air,' he said and, with a wary glance at Jim, took Ruby through the front door.

Syd frowned at his son-in-law as they stood in the kitchen. 'You all right, Jim?'

Jim nodded. 'Yes,' he muttered, shrugging his jacket back into position across his shoulders. 'Sorry about that, Mr Jenkins.'

Syd's smile returned as he slapped Jim on the back. 'It's a wedding, ain't it? And a wedding ain't complete without a bit of a dust-up.' He turned to his daughter. 'You've got a honeymoon waiting for you, gel; your mother's just gone out to tie me old boots on the bumper. So hurry on upstairs and get on your glad rags.'

Pearl did as her father said, but she felt sick inside. Her dad had managed to restore calm but she knew Jim's temper was simmering very close to the surface.

Pearl sat in the passenger seat of their borrowed car as Jim drove them to Margate. She had dressed hurriedly in her new green suit and had abandoned her plan of a Veronica Lake hairstyle before rushing back downstairs.

Why had Jim attacked Ricky? He hadn't spoken since they'd left the island. His jaw was set and his gaze fixed on the road.

Instead of her enjoying the scenery, the ugly scene replayed itself in her mind. What had her dad really thought? If only Jim hadn't lost his temper.

Pearl gazed out of the window. She wanted to enjoy her honeymoon. It was a once-in-a-lifetime occasion and

she and Jim should be laughing, enjoying themselves and excited at the prospect of their wedding night.

'Let's stop,' Pearl said after a while, 'and have a cup of tea in one of them little shops.'

'Time's getting on,' Jim replied, not even looking at her.

Pearl felt desperate. A honeymoon in Margate and a whole week to be with each other. Jim had spared no expense to make her happy. And now he wasn't even speaking to her.

'Jim, I'm sorry about what happened.'

'What were you doing alone with him?'

'He was just saying he wished us the best.'

'It looked more than that to me.'

'Well, it wasn't. Jim, what's got into you?'

He looked at her and the anger still oozed from his face. 'I don't trust that bastard.'

She put her hand on his arm. 'I know. But don't let it spoil our honeymoon. Let's forget about everything except us.'

'The man's a philanderer,' Jim continued heatedly. 'A rogue. Just because he's got himself a uniform he thinks he's bloody Clark Gable. He's not changed from what he was, full of codswallop and the women daft enough to fall for it.'

'Is that reason enough to hit him?'

'In my book, a man looks after his own right from day one. And that's just what I was doing. I'm sorry I caused a rumpus, but he deserved all he got and more.'

'Can we forget it now?' Pearl had never seen this side of Jim. He was like a dog with a bone; he wouldn't let go of his dislike of Ricky. He was such an easy-going man usually, and this seemed very out of character. She pouted miserably. 'You haven't even said how I look.'

He gave her a brief smile. 'You look lovely. You always do.'

20

Pearl was deep in thought as they continued their journey; she didn't want to think of Ricky, or Jim's reaction to him, but she couldn't help but wonder if Ricky had really been telling her the truth. Could he be falling in love with Ruby? But all she wanted to do now was to enjoy the wonderful things that were happening to her and Jim.

She thought of the clothes she had brought with her. Even though there was a war on, she had managed to buy underwear that was soft and feminine. Her shoes had taken for ever to find. They were a soft green and very expensive, from the Co-op. She would never have had enough coupons if her mum and Ruby hadn't saved up theirs too. With a wonderful week ahead of her, there was so much to look forward to. Slowly a curl of excitement began in her stomach.

Half an hour later they reached Bay View, the hotel that Jim had chosen. It had a pretty pink door and brown tiled roof, and looked so romantic that Pearl wanted to cry. Taking a deep breath, she waited for Jim to open the door of the car, her heart beating fast with excitement.

Pearl lay in bed beside Jim, staring at the shadows reflected through the lace. The blackout curtains were still parted; she hadn't the heart to pull them together. The sky was studded with stars and the smell of salt and seaweed blew in through the open window. Pearl thought how wonderful tonight was. She had felt a thrill as Jim signed the register for them as a married couple. He had even arranged flowers to be in the room with a message on them: 'To My Darling Wife. These flowers aren't as beautiful as you. Love forever, Jim.' After a delicious fish-and-chip supper they had come up to their room. But now her nerves were getting the better of her, for she knew the time had come when they would make love and she wanted it to be perfect. Ever since Jim

had asked her to marry him, the niggling thoughts of her past with Ricky had preyed on her mind. She wasn't a virgin, as Jim expected her to be. Would he know or was it possible for her to pretend during their lovemaking? What if he suspected that it wasn't her first time?

In the moonlight she saw his face. It was filled with tenderness. 'I love you, Pearl. I'm sorry about nearly spoiling our day.' He brought her into his arms and kissed her passionately. 'Don't be nervous, sweetheart. I won't hurt you.'

He began to slide down her nightdress straps. Oh God, please don't let him guess, she prayed. She loved him so much that, to her, he was the only man she had ever been with. And the only man she would ever want. His lovemaking was wonderful, slow and tender, and then as he entered her, she gave a gasp. Her mind seemed to fly away, her body shuddered and together they lost themselves, uniting in a shared joy.

When it was over, Pearl held his strong body tightly. Had he guessed anything? But he took her in his arms and kissed her, telling her how beautiful she was and making her thrill all over again.

When he had fallen asleep and Pearl lay contentedly beside him, she understood for the first time what it was like to feel truly satisfied. When Ricky had first taken her, she had been too young to know that he was an inconsiderate lover, and the feelings of emptiness afterwards were down to Ricky's selfish and uncaring actions. Jim's gentle coaxing and tender passion were all that any woman could want. She felt fulfilled and wanted, unlike before, when Ricky had taken what he wanted, leaving her feeling ashamed and guilty.

As Jim stirred, she nestled closely against his warm skin and tried not to let the thoughts taunt her. Why was Ricky still on her mind? The thought of him with Ruby made

her feel sick. Had Ruby given herself to him already? Pearl shuddered yet again. Ruby hadn't even mentioned they'd been going out together. Was it because the wedding had come between them? Perhaps it was her fault, she should have taken more interest in Ruby lately. Pearl closed her eyes as if to try to squeeze out the vision of her sister in his arms. Ricky had insisted he'd changed, that he was a different man. Had meeting Ruby changed him? Could that be true?

Finally sleep came, but her dreams were filled with shadows.

Chapter 3

Jim was asleep when Pearl woke. One arm was flung across her, the tiny hairs that grew over his muscles gleaming gold in the early morning sun, the blackout curtains still undrawn. Pearl lay still for a moment, remembering every second of their lovemaking. This was what true love was about: two people becoming one; something she thought was an impossible dream.

Carefully she moved his arm to one side. Slowly she stood up on the warm, thick carpet, a true luxury after the linoleum at Roper's Way. She took her wraparound cotton gown from the chair and slid it on. Every inch of her seemed to glow as she walked to the window. Their lovemaking had been wonderful, with whispered words of love so sweet and tender that Pearl felt sure he couldn't have guessed that he wasn't her first man.

She jumped guiltily as a pair of strong arms slid round her. 'Who's an early bird then?'

She nestled into his chest, hiding her suddenly hot cheeks. 'I tried not to wake you.'

'I knew you wasn't there, even in me sleep.'

'That's a lovely thing to say.' She slid her hands over his strong shoulders and round his neck.

'What were you thinking? Looked as though you were out there, on the blue horizon.'

'Isn't the sea wonderful?'

'Dunno. Not till we swim in it.'

She laughed. 'Didn't bring me swimming costume.'

'You don't need one. Not for me.'

'Jim!'

He pulled her against him. 'Come back to bed, Pearly-girl.'

'What about breakfast?'

'I've got mine.' He began to nibble at her neck.

She giggled as she wanted him all over again. 'Breakfast's in with the price.'

'So am I.'

They laughed as he threaded his hands through her tangled blonde hair. 'We've got all day for ...' She trailed off as he lifted her into his arms.

They fell on the bed and soon she was naked.

When Jim had asked her to marry him on Saturday 17 May, at exactly half-past two in the afternoon as they were walking in Island Gardens, she'd accepted without hesitation. And now here she was, married and so happy. She'd never forget that day. 'I love you so much, Jim.'

'And I love you.'

'Now I don't want to get up.' She wrapped herself round him. 'Let's stay here all day.'

'Thought you wanted breakfast?'

'I've got you.'

He laughed, tilting her chin. 'Every time I look in your eyes, I lose me train of thought. Me brain goes to mush.'

Pearl giggled. 'What if the siren goes?'

'We'll pretend we didn't hear it.'

Pearl thought she would be happy to die in Jim's arms. But for now she wanted to forget the rest of the world. And she knew that Jim did too.

'See that old pile of rubbish?' said the clippie, who wore a man's uniform, issuing their tickets with a little 'ting' on her machine. 'It was one of our best cinemas until September last year. All art deco and pink and gold inside. Then, in the blink of an eye, it was gone.'

Pearl looked down at the half-demolished building from the top floor of the bus. 'What a shame.'

She clutched Jim's hand as they sat side by side enjoying the sun's heat shining through the window. She had worn a cardigan over her frock as she had got sunburned yesterday on the beach. Jim, who didn't like the sand much, had sat on a deckchair with a handkerchief tied over his head. He'd laughed as she'd paddled at the water's edge and got the hem of her dress all wet. Today they had taken the circular bus tour to Broadstairs. It cost only one and six and if there was a raid, the clippie announced, the driver would pull over and everyone must run to the nearest cover. Today was only their third outing in daylight. They had stopped at a coconut shy and Jim had knocked three coconuts from the stands. He'd won her a little green china ashtray with 'Margate' written on the side. The rest of their time they'd spent in their room making up for lost time. In the evenings they'd gone out, strolled arm in arm through the darkened streets and exchanged kisses on the seafront benches. Tomorrow they were going home and Pearl was wishing their holiday could go on for ever.

'It was called the Astoria,' continued the clippie, holding on to the seat rail as the driver pulled away from the kerb. 'Before it was bombed, me and my old man used to go

25

there. The seats were lovely, covered in soft material and nice and roomy. All three cinemas were built in the thirties, this one and the Regal and the Dreamland. I saw me first film at the Regal. *The Camels Are Coming* with Jack Hulbert, it was.' She sighed and pushed back her uniform cap. 'Now I've only got a pile of rubble to remind me. I lost me husband last year, at Dunkirk.'

'Oh, I'm so sorry,' Pearl said sadly.

'Rotten luck,' nodded Jim.

Pearl clutched Jim's hand even tighter. If it wasn't for his job he too could have been at Dunkirk, or even up in the air during the Battle of Britain. Or he could have been in a ship somewhere, in danger of being torpedoed, like Ricky. The thought of him had intruded again, and determinedly she put him out of mind. She had her Jim beside her and that was what mattered. His work on bombed sites and underground was dangerous, but the chances of survival were much higher than being in the services. They had everything to live for, a future mapped out.

'Still, you two young things look happy enough,' said the clippie with a mischievous smile. 'You on leave, son?'

'It's our honeymoon.' Pearl blushed.

'That don't take much guessing,' the woman smiled. 'Well, make it last as long as you can. String it out before your bloke has to go back.' She gave them a wink and made her way to the seats at the front where two soldiers sat. It was clear they were rookies as they were talking about the camp close by.

'She thought I was enlisted,' Jim groaned as the bus picked up speed and he stared at the two soldiers. 'I feel rotten when I think I ain't on me toes for Britain. Blokes like them are risking their lives for the country.'

'But so are you,' Pearl insisted, pushing back the wave of hair that fell over her face. 'Like them flats you was on a couple of weeks ago. You had to make sure they didn't

collapse. If I'd known you were climbing all over them, I'd have had kittens.'

'Not the same as fighting, though.'

Pearl looked worried. 'Jim, don't keep talking like this. You're doing your bit for the war effort.'

'She assumed I was on leave,' he mumbled under his breath as if he hadn't heard her.

'Jim, I don't want you drafted away,' she insisted. 'With your job as an engineer, you can stay at home. You said that was what you wanted too.'

He put his arm round her. 'Thing is, I fight with me conscience,' he admitted, rubbing his chin. 'Any man could do what I do with a bit of training.'

'No, they couldn't,' Pearl objected. 'And I should know, as I type out all the papers that are relevant to your work. There ain't many engineers with your experience. When a call comes through from the LCC, it's you and your blokes they want, because they can rely on you to put London back together again.'

He kissed her forehead lightly. 'I'll pay you later.'

She smiled wistfully. 'You can joke, but it's taken you ten years to learn your trade. And what about all the stuff you did before the war? All those diagram things you helped to put in the Underground.'

He laughed. 'Diaphragms, you mean.'

'Yes, those.' Before the war he had been involved in the works to safeguard the underground system from flooding. Special flood gates and diaphragms had to be installed for use should a direct hit land on any of the lines. Jim had been called in by the LCC to work with the Chief Engineer's department. Pearl didn't understand much of what he'd described, but she'd read in the newspapers that it was work of vital importance.

'I can't help but wonder if I should've joined up,' he murmured, lost in thought.

A shiver went through her. 'You know how I feel about that.'

'You're right. This is our last day,' Jim agreed, sliding his arm tightly around her. 'What mischief are we gonna get up to?' He eyes were full of teasing and Pearl shivered as his hand went on her knee.

'Can't wait to get off the bus now,' she giggled.

'Mrs Nesbitt, you're a naughty girl.'

'And we've got the rest of our lives to be naughty in, thank God,' Pearl nodded as she squeezed even closer.

For the next hour Pearl tried to enjoy the coastal ride, but each time the bus stopped, more soldiers got on. She knew that Jim was feeling uncomfortable. He was the only man in civvies apart from an elderly man at the back. But Pearl didn't care.

I'm never going to end up like the clippie she told herself firmly, with only memories to keep me going. I'm never going to be one of these women who say they're proud of their dead husbands for giving their lives for their country. I'm going to be selfish and make certain that my man doesn't die. I'm going to make sure we'll have our lives in front of us. That we'll have babies who grow up with a dad.

At last the soldiers got off. Pearl felt Jim relax. They began to talk about their new home. It was only four rooms above Hemsley's, the corner grocer's shop in Pride Place. A month's rent had been paid in advance and some bits of furniture moved in.

'It's been a wonderful honeymoon, Jim,' Pearl sighed, snuggling up. 'I'll never forget it.'

'Nor will I.'

Pearl breathed out a grateful sigh, thinking how every moment was so precious. And when they went home, unlike many couples, who had to live with their parents, they had a home of their own. Life was good. Even the

memory of Ricky had faded. Life was taking on its rosy glow again.

She laid her head on Jim's shoulder. Tonight she was going to wear her new nightdress. It was silk, bought from a black market trader at Cox Street. He'd told her it was the last bargain he was likely to get, as the docks were so quiet with no merchant ships coming in. Instead of wearing it on their first night, she'd saved it for their last. She couldn't wait to see Jim's face.

Soon the promenade was in sight. Tonight they would be in each other's arms once more.

'Well, ducks, how are you two lovebirds getting on?' Gwen Hemsley, their landlady and owner of the corner shop over which they lived, returned Pearl's ration book over the counter.

'We're going to decorate, if you don't mind.'

'Not at all. I'll bet you make it nice.'

'I've got lots of ideas, which is more than I can say for our dinner.' Pearl looked at what she'd bought. Spam, potatoes and dried egg. Last year, meat including bacon, butter, cooking fat, sugar and tea had been put on the ration, and this year, Jim's favourites – eggs and cheese – had gone the same way. The Ministry of Food was responsible for the fair sharing of food amongst the public, and at a price everyone could afford. But people were noticing that the weekly rations were beginning to vary as foods became more and more scarce.

'Sorry, love, but if you'd have come earlier, you could have had a piece of fish.'

Pearl hated queuing. There were always complaints from the long lines of women standing outside the shops. Although potatoes and fish, as yet, were not rationed, the fish was unpredictable. There was only so much a person could eat of potatoes. The Dig for Victory campaign had interested

Jim, but time prevented him from keeping an allotment like her dad. Number twenty-seven A, Pride Place didn't have a garden to grow vegetables in. No space either for chickens or rabbits. At the back there was just the lav and a sheet of corrugated iron to put over the coal. Their back window overlooked the flat roof of the Hemsleys' storeroom and the exterior stairs leading up to their rooms. The iron railings had been taken as all the metals had gone into the war effort. Every street had suffered its losses. Jim was good with his hands and had made the staircase a rail as Fitz wasn't as good at woodwork. When they'd first seen the rooms, they were in a very poor state. But the rent was only twelve and six a week. Jim had suggested they search for a better place, but Pearl said she liked it. She was afraid Jim's mother would persuade her son they should live with her at Villa Road.

'What about some more veg?' suggested Gwen. 'The Spam can be hidden by a few spuds.'

'Yes, s'pose that will have to do.'

'You two must be living on love,' chuckled Gwen, rolling her eyes. 'Oh, I'd trade all me own coupons for a good cuddle once in a while. But Fitz is too dog tired of an evening to do anything more than fall asleep in his chair.'

Again the colour filled Pearl's cheeks. She was getting plenty of cuddles, all right. She and Jim were tired too, but that didn't stop them having fun. They couldn't leave each other alone.

Pearl lowered her eyes to the counter. Three weeks after returning from Margate, she was well and truly back to reality as far as the housekeeping went. She tried to make Jim's meals interesting but they weren't like their breakfasts at Margate. How the hotel had managed to produce them she didn't know. They had given them a real egg each morning, said to come from the chickens kept next door. The bread had tasted as though it had been fried in real fat. The bacon had been delicious.

Cooking had never been of interest to Pearl; she liked being with people more. Before the war she had taken under her wing one or two of the older neighbours in Roper's Way, especially the Sampsons, next door. She liked to run errands for them and do a bit of housework if they weren't feeling up to the mark. There was a true community spirit on the island and Pearl liked to be part of it.

'You'll be able to knock up something,' said Gwen, pulling her crossover pinafore across her flat chest.

Pearl didn't want to admit just how useless she was with food. Gwen and Fitz Hemsley were a hard-working middle-aged couple who'd lived all their lives at Pride Place. Fitz's parents had lived in the four rooms above the shop. After they had died the rooms had been left empty. But now there was a war on, every penny was needed.

'Now don't go overdoing it,' said Gwen with an affectionate pat on the back of Pearl's hand. 'I saw you and Jim coming in late again last night. I was just closing the blackout curtains and there you were walking up Pride Place in the dark. Fire-watching, was it?'

'No, Jim had a big job on and worked late. So I met him over his mum's. I thought I might be able to do a bit of tidying-up for her.'

'Oh dear, no wonder you both looked all in!'

Pearl grinned. Gwen had met Mrs Nesbitt during the first week they'd moved in. Jim's mother had given the little corner shop the once-over immediately. Wasting no time, she had demanded if any smells were likely to drift up from the storeroom. The enquiry had not been well received. The Hemsleys were scrupulously clean. Jim had apologized afterwards for his mother's lack of tact but it was still a sore point.

'Downright rude,' was Gwen's observation. 'My Fitz nearly showed her the door. In fact, he would have if she wasn't Jim's old girl.'

Pearl had to explain that Mrs Nesbitt had wanted them to live at Vale Road. Since their refusal, Mrs Nesbitt had given Pearl the cold shoulder, even though she'd done everything to be friends.

'The best refusal you ever made in your life, love,' observed Fitz, pushing his spectacles to the bridge of his long nose. 'She'd have driven you up the wall.'

'I'm trying me best, anyway.'

'It's all you can do in this life.'

When Pearl got in, she felt exhausted. Holding down a job and being married wasn't like being single. And now she knew how hard her mother had worked to keep everyone happy.

Jim had wanted her to give up work and become a lady of leisure. But she liked her job in the Borough Surveyor's department. Mr Hedley, her boss, was very nice and so were all the girls. But after coming back from her wonderful honeymoon, she could see the housework wouldn't get done by itself.

Pearl loved her new home. The kitchen, one large living room and two bedrooms were modest, but they were also a safe distance from Villa Road, though she could walk to Roper's Way in under ten minutes.

Pearl was eager for Ruby to call but she too was working hard. Brewer's was now an armaments factory and busy helping the war effort. Ruby was also learning first aid in her spare time, a fact that brought a smile to Pearl's lips as Ruby didn't have a strong stomach.

Pearl lowered her groceries to the kitchen table. Last night she'd hung yellow gingham curtains in the kitchen-cum-scullery, and Jim had painted the brown larder a shade of blue. There was a drop-down work surface on the tall cupboard and underneath, space for crockery. Next to this was a stove. It was old but still worked well. A set of heavy lidless pans stood side by side on the shelves by the door,

and four battered ones Gwen had left still hung on the wall. Pearl's dad and mum had given them their old wireless set and it stood on the shelf beneath.

Jim had distempered the dark walls a soft green. He'd stuck back the loose flowered tiles around the fireplace, and the wooden mantel shelf had come up shiny with a polish. An old-style wind-up gramophone had been left in the corner, but the needles were worn out. Jim had bought Pearl a very nice beige settee and two armchairs. The suite wasn't new but it was clean and looked elegant beside the maple bookcase.

Pearl went to change her clothes. Their bedroom was her favourite place. She shivered in delight as she thought of the wonderful nights she and Jim had cuddled in the big double bed. They had bought it from one of the girls at work who had evacuated. The shiny maple headboard squeaked a little but Jim had managed to oil it.

Pearl thought how lucky she was as she threw off her shoes. A wonderful husband and beautiful home, all to her taste. Even the dressing table with triple mirror reflected a woman's touch. A frilled curtain hung round it under the glass-covered top. On its surface were her personal effects: hairbrush and comb, hand mirror and her most prized possessions, three little frosted-pink jars in which to keep her jewellery. Jim had given them to her as a wedding present.

She hadn't yet thought about what to put in the small bedroom next door. There was just a camp bed in there and boxes. But in time, it would convert to a small bedroom or nursery.

Would she get pregnant soon? Would she be able to carry a baby after what had happened to her? Dr Cox had said he couldn't see why not.

Pearl sat down on the edge of the bed. Suddenly the memories came flooding into her mind as though a dam

had burst. It was just before her seventeenth birthday when she met Ricky at the club. For her it was love at first sight, or so she thought. Because of their age difference he'd persuaded her not to tell anyone they were going out; they were too much in love, he'd insisted, to allow anyone to spoil their romance. At first he'd paid her all the attention she could want. Taken her up West and to Lyons, walked her along the Embankment and bought her small gifts, telling her how beautiful she was. But as soon as she'd given in to his demands, he'd treated her indifferently, making her do things she disliked so that she felt ashamed of what she had at first thought was the romance of her life. Then she'd missed her monthly, and another, and had felt sick, too sick not to know that she was pregnant. Pearl pushed her hands over her face as she couldn't stop the memories from tumbling back, along with all the pain of losing that little life inside her.

There was a tap on the door and Pearl stood up shakily. She had been lost in a nether world, where the past and all its emotions had become alive again. Unguardedly she had let it all in and now her legs felt like jelly. Pushing back her hair and trying to compose herself, she went to the kitchen door. It was a shock to see Ruby standing there. She looked very smart and pretty.

Ruby threw her arms around her. 'Oh, I've missed you, Pearl.'

'And I've missed you. Come in, come in.'

'Did you have a nice honeymoon?'

'Wonderful. I've been longing to tell you about it. But you haven't been round.'

Ruby looked away. 'I wanted to give you a chance to settle in.'

'We've been home three weeks. I called at Mum and Dad's and they said you were on another course.'

'Yes, more first aid, though I can't say I'm Florence

Nightingale.' Ruby looked round the kitchen. 'Oh, Pearl, you've done this up lovely. Just look at them curtains!'

'I ran them up by hand.'

'Is that a new settee?'

'Yes, do you like it?'

'Better than our old one at home.' Ruby walked round, giving little oohs and ahs.

Her strawberry-blonde hair was turned under and tucked behind her ears. The light-coloured jacket with padded shoulders looked new. It was then that Pearl had a pang of nostalgia as, being the same bust and waist size they had always shared their clothes. They suited the same colours, both having blonde hair and green eyes. Clothes rationing had started on 2 June. Pearl decided that Ruby must have used a lot of coupons on the jacket.

'Was this expensive?' Pearl asked, touching her sleeve.

'Don't know. It was a gift.' Ruby sat down on the settee. Looking at Pearl she gave a small shrug. 'From Ricky.'

Pearl sat down quickly. She felt her tummy turn over as she looked into her sister's eyes. 'So you're still going out with him?'

'As a matter of fact, that's why it's been difficult to get round. We spent all the time together that we could, before he was posted.'

Pearl looked down in her lap. She was trying to disguise her disappointment and Ruby saw it.

'I take it you still don't approve?' Ruby said, her tone rising. 'Is it to do with what went on at the wedding? Why Jim took such a dislike to him? To be honest, Pearl, I'm baffled. I mean, Dad thinks it was just high spirits, and Ricky says they'd just had a glass too many. But even so, I don't understand what went on. Do you?'

Pearl knew if there was ever a time to share her secret with Ruby it was now. But shouldn't she have told Jim first, a little voice inside her head demanded. *He's your husband,*

he has the right to know the truth. How could she tell Ruby about the past and not tell Jim? What would Ruby think of her? She looked up at Ruby and knew that she couldn't find the courage. Lowering her head, she shook it slowly. 'It was just a misunderstanding.'

'Well, it must have been a big one. Jim had Ricky by the collar.'

'It was like Dad said, a bit of horseplay.'

Ruby was silent, then said in a husky voice, 'Pearl, I want you to know that I love him.'

Pearl bit her lip hard, trying to calm herself. How could Ruby love him? He was the one man on earth that she shouldn't be loving.

'I can't understand it,' Ruby pressed again. 'Are you upset with me?'

'No, course not.'

'What is it, then?'

'I just want you to be happy.'

'Then give me a hug – please?'

As she pulled Ruby against her, Pearl felt the tears fill her eyes. Why was this happening? She wanted to be happy for Ruby but how could she be?

Ruby was just leaving when Jim came up the stairs.

'Hello, Jim. Pearl said you've had a wonderful honeymoon.'

He kissed her cheek. 'You bet.'

'She told me all about it.'

'Not all, I hope.'

Ruby smiled. 'Only the best bits.'

Jim looked her up and down. 'So where are you off to, the Savoy?'

Pearl saw Ruby blush. 'No, I'm going to my first-aid class.'

'Go on, pull the other one. Bet you're being wined and dined.'

'No, not till Ricky comes home.' She looked at Pearl and before Jim could reply, she ran down the stairs.

Jim turned, his expression dark and angry. 'Did I hear right?'

'Yes, but please don't get upset.'

'Of course I'm bloody upset.'

'Come in, we don't want everyone to hear us.' Pearl closed the kitchen door. 'Jim, you haven't even kissed me.'

'Listen,' he said, throwing down his lunch box in an angry gesture, 'your sister is playing with fire and, God help her, she's going to get burned.'

'Jim, she's all grown up. There's nothing I can do to change her mind.'

'Yes there is, if you tried. You're like two peas in a pod. She always takes notice of you.'

'It's different this time,' Pearl protested. 'She thinks she's in love.'

'That's ridiculous! And you should put her right on the subject.' He took hold of Pearl's arm. 'Sit down. I'm going to tell you something. And perhaps after what I've said, you'll come to your senses.'

'What about your dinner?'

'It can wait. Now sit down.'

Pearl sat on the kitchen chair. She felt her happy world crashing down around her. Ruby wouldn't listen no matter what she said, and Jim was angry with her for something she had no control over.

Jim loosened the straps of his overalls and sat on a chair. 'Winters and me were members of the Dockland Settlement Club as you know. We was at each other's throats from the off. He did everything for show, and me and the lads couldn't stomach it. Our company wasn't good enough. It wasn't until he chucked in the Docklands Rowers for the Essex Flyers that people began to see he didn't give a toss for the club, or the island, for that matter.

He wasn't born here, just worked for the PLA and lived in digs. No one knew him and he only joined the club 'cos there was nothing else around.'

'But I thought you always won the rowing,' Pearl said helplessly.

'Not against the Flyers we didn't. They had better boats, good men and the time to train. Sounds like green-eye, don't it? But he is a rat. One of the worst.'

'I've never heard you talk like this before.'

'And I don't want to now, as I promised a mate I'd never tell a soul.' There was a long silence. 'Danny's family and hers wanted it hushed up and I gave them me promise that they could count on me.'

'Danny's family?' Pearl whispered.

'My cousin, Danny Shorter, lived over Blackwall.'

'I didn't know you had a cousin on the island,' Pearl said, bewildered.

'Danny was Mum's nephew – her sister's boy. Mum didn't have much to do with her sister as she married into trouble, apparently. The two sisters never spoke and Mum don't know about this – but I was friendly with Danny. We didn't have no grievances, in fact I like him a lot. He was a good kid, a bit rough round the edges but he was solid enough and worked on the roads for the council. When Aunty Madge died, Danny took up with Gladys. She was a bit of a daft moo, but Danny was saving up to get spliced. Then Gladys had a bit of a fling with guess who.'

Pearl swallowed. She knew the answer without Jim saying.

'Yes, lover boy. He got her up the duff, then gave the poor kid the boot. She jumped off one of the bridgers. Lived over Ebondale Street. Surprised you don't remember that.'

Pearl felt as though someone had hit her. She didn't remember Gladys but she could remember her dad reading out a sad article in the newspaper. 'Wasn't it an accident?'

'It was made out to be, for the family's sake. But it was his fault.'

'Ricky's?'

'Danny came round my house the day he found out she was pregnant. Gladys's dad thought Danny was responsible, but Gladys admitted who the real culprit was. Had to really, as she and Danny hadn't done nothing. So her dad and Danny goes round to Winters and he laughs in their faces. Said Gladys was up for it and more fool them and they can't prove a thing. So they give him a good hiding, don't they, but a hiding don't mend the damage he'd done to an innocent kid. Gladys's parents never said anything because they didn't want their girl's name dragged in the mud.'

Pearl shivered. She knew how Gladys must have felt with a baby on its way. But she must have been desperate to jump into the river and end her own life.

'So you see, there's no love lost between Winters and me. I don't know how he had the gall to walk in your parents' house. He hates my guts and I hate his.'

Pearl listened to Jim's voice filled with bitterness. 'But what can I do?' she asked. 'Ruby thinks she's in love.'

'Then you'll have to snap her out of it.'

'Jim, how can I?'

'You've always looked out for her. Can you really stand by and let her make such a mistake?' He stood up and pushed his hand through his untidy hair. 'If Ruby gets tangled up with him, she's not the sensible girl I thought she was. Though it has to be said that most women seem to be fools where he's concerned. Her heart will be broken, I guarantee it. I want nothing to do with him, Pearl, and I don't want him near you.' He held out his hand. 'Now, give me that kiss we haven't had.' He took her in his arms and kissed her. But it wasn't with the same passion they usually shared. Once again Ricky had come into their lives and poisoned it.

Chapter 4

All through July, Pearl listened with dismay to the reports on the wireless. The Russians were fighting bravely and resisting the Germans but what was to become of all those poor people caught in the crossfire? To Pearl it seemed as though everyday a new conflict had been added.

One August evening Jim came home with not one but two newspapers. He was intrigued by world events and would sit and pore over the news. 'Listen to this,' he said as his dinner grew cold and he buried his head in the newspaper. 'Winnie and Roosevelt have met in secret. They've made a pact. They ain't gonna let the Nazis walk all over us any more.'

Pearl sat down at the table. 'All it says,' she frowned, tracing the line of text with her finger, 'is that they met on a fishing trip to discuss the situation . . .'

Jim gave a howl. 'Read between the lines, love. Take my word, we'll soon have the Yanks on our side.'

Pearl gazed into her husband's bright eyes. 'So, if the Americans are with us, that's good, isn't it? They'll frighten Hitler off.'

'Not without us, they won't.'

'As long as you aren't involved.'

He took her hand. 'Pearl, me heart is involved already.'

'What does that mean?'

'No bloke worth his salt will stay at home.'

'Don't say that!'

'If things come to a head, I've got to put me hand up.'

She froze as tears filled her eyes. 'Jim, you're scaring me.'

'Do you want us to win?'

'Yes, but I don't want to lose you.'

'Who says you'll lose me?' He smiled, that lovely white

smile that had the power to light up her insides. 'Anyway, I'm not gone yet.'

She threw her arms round him. 'I won't let you go.'

'Oh, Pearly-girl, I love you so much.'

'If you love me you wouldn't be talking like this.'

'I've got to. The war is coming closer.'

'I know, I know, I hear it all the time. I listen to the girls at work, to where their husbands are, or were, or they don't know where they are, or they wait for letters, they dread the telegrams, they can't eat or sleep because of their men and – oh, Jim – I don't want to be one of them!' She clutched him tight, pressing her face into his rough collar and smelling the metal smells and dust and oil that were ingrained in his overalls. She loved everything about him. Even though they had their tiffs, it was wonderful making up.

He patted her back. 'You mean everything to me, sweetheart, and I think you know it. But after this war I want to live in a country that's free and not ruled by a crazy dictator. A world where you can speak your mind without being chucked in a concentration camp for your beliefs.'

'But we don't have them in England!' Pearl protested weakly.

'Only because we're a democracy. We've a ting-a-ling on the throne, and freedom of speech. We can vote in every election. We take it all for granted, but it will all disappear if Hitler has his way.'

Pearl twisted out of his grasp. Her heart was thumping. 'I know all that. I'm as patriotic as you or anyone, but I don't see the sense in you joining up when you can do as much – if not more – for your country at home.' She wrung her hands. 'Seems to me this isn't about the call-up, it's about you wanting to put on a uniform like Ricky Winters.'

As soon as the words were out she regretted them. Jim's lips turned down slowly at the corners.

'So that's what you think?'

She hung her head. 'I didn't mean it.'

'But you said it.'

'Jim—'

Rising to his feet, he snatched up the papers and stuffed them under his arm. Without a word more, he left. She listened to his boots on the stairs. What had she done?

Going to the landing, she looked over. 'Jim! Jim!'

Fitz Hemsley came out from the storeroom. 'You after Jim, love?'

'I – no, not really.' She didn't want him to know they'd had a row.

'Done a bunk, has he?' Fitz chuckled. 'Escaped to the pub?'

'Yes, I should think so.'

'You two fire-watching tonight?'

'Yes.' Though the bombing wasn't as bad, they still had to do their part.

'Gwen saved two rashers for you today,' Fitz shouted up. 'They'll do nice for Jim's tea.'

'All right. I'll be down.'

Fitz returned whistling to the storeroom.

Pearl sat at the kitchen table. Why had she mentioned Ricky? Why had she said such a thing? Is that what she truly thought? Was Jim envious, even jealous of Ricky? Oh, she knew he hated him because of Danny, but was there something deeper?

She glanced at the clock and sighed. She'd go down and get the bacon; Jim would enjoy it, although there was nothing to fry it in but marg. Would it taste as good?

But by nine thirty the bacon was burned to a cinder and Jim still wasn't home. Pearl set off alone for her fire-watching duty. She left Jim a sandwich and a note saying she was sorry.

★

It was a very warm afternoon in late August, and Pearl thrust open the small window of the Borough Surveyor's office. But instead of a reviving breeze, only the noise of the traffic came in. The small room was stuffy as three tables had been squeezed in for the staff. Pearl lifted her hands and wiped her fingers on a cloth she took from her drawer. In the air-deprived conditions her speed on the typewriter was slower. Mr Hedley, her boss, had gone early, leaving her and Moira Bush to complete the outstanding paperwork. They were one clerk short and had to finish it all before going. Mr Hedley liked all the contractors, removers and tradesmen's bills up to date. Head Office required duplicate copies, and the ink from the blue paper had smudged in the heat.

'I'm melting,' sighed Pearl, fanning herself with an envelope. 'Even my blouse is wet.'

'The council should improve our working conditions,' nodded Moira, pouncing on Pearl's unguarded comment. She hit the roller of her typewriter and snapped out the sheet of paper. 'Don't know what it must be like for your poor husband, crawling over some of these bomb sites in all the dust and dirt and now this heat as well.' She tapped the paper she was holding. 'This sounds like a deathtrap. The roof's caved in where the incendiary went down the chimney in May. Last month the whole lot collapsed. By a miracle the terrace next door is still standing and people live in it, despite the six-inch crack in the wall from top to bottom. The poor sods mustn't be able to sleep at night for fear they'll crumble away too.' Moira paused for breath. 'And look at this, they've sent your Jim to assess the risks. That's a laugh. It's the risk to his life they should be assessing.'

After listening to Moira for the last four years, Pearl merely shrugged. 'He can take care of himself.'

But Moira ploughed on. 'All these places still on fire and

falling into the wharfs. Not that our engineers take unnecessary risks, of course.'

Pearl looked back at her typewriter.

'I suppose the worst things are unexploded bombs,' Moira tried slyly.

Pearl drew the damp hanky across her forehead. The eau-de-Cologne was refreshing. 'I don't think about that. I know he'll come home at the end of the day.'

'Course you do,' Moira nodded. 'Working for the council is better than fighting Jerry.'

Pearl began typing again. Moira would be a nice person if she wasn't full of woes. And it didn't help that Pearl was thinking about Jim. Although they were speaking again and, more importantly, cuddling, there was a stony silence on the subject of Ruby and Ricky.

'A bloke don't know when he's well off,' Moira continued relentlessly, 'but your Jim does, I'm sure.'

'We'd better get finished.'

Moira lifted her hand in an arc around the room. 'Makes you dizzy, don't it, seeing all this paperwork? Years and years of it. London is falling to bits and the LCC have to stick it back together. We've got our own work well and truly cut out, as well as the engineers. Let's hope the war will be over soon.'

'If only,' nodded Pearl, quickly reminding herself she was lucky to have a husband at home and, no matter what the dangers of Jim's job, they could never be as threatening as those overseas.

'You all right, Pearl?'

'Yes.'

'You seem a bit down. Get your husband to take you to the pub. The beer's not dried up yet. Be thankful for that.'

Pearl smiled; it was a long time since they'd enjoyed a night out. Their fire-watching duties kept them busy, as did calling in to see Jim's mum.

'I'm glad I'm young, free and single,' said Moira, banging on her typewriter once more. 'I can enjoy meself.'

But Pearl wasn't listening. She was wondering if perhaps one evening they might go to the cinema, or treat themselves to a nice tea at Lyons. Perhaps she'd suggest it to Jim after they'd paid a visit to Villa Road tonight.

Pearl walked unhurriedly along Villa Road and felt the curtains twitching on either side. It was considered a respectable area, and, amazingly, most of the houses were undamaged. One or two chimneys had fallen away, and several windows blown out, but on the whole, the Luftwaffe had failed to make much impression. Pearl was smiling as she walked up to the front door, amused at the irony of Jim's mother's insistence throughout the Blitz that the German air force were deliberately targeting elderly spinsters and respectable people. If Germany was waging war on Villa Road, it had failed miserably, Pearl decided as she reached up to lift the polished brass knocker.

'Oh, it's you.'

Pearl's smile remained in place. She entered the dark hall, which was never lit, even in the depths of winter. To her left a flight of brown carpeted stairs were lost in the gloom. The parlour door was open and she walked in. No windows were ever opened, even in summer. The crisscross tape on the windows had been sealed not once but twice over and the thick curtains were drawn almost together in anticipation of the blackout.

One small light was burning in the parlour. It spread thinly over the dark green upholstery of the couch and the stout metal guard in the fireplace. Above this was draped a mantel curtain and on the shelf were photographs in ornate frames. Jim as a baby, as a toddler, as a young man, but none of the wedding. The dear and departed Mr Nesbitt, complete with handlebar moustache, frowned out

from a sepia impression, a younger Thora Nesbitt standing beside him.

Pearl was shown to the uncomfortable wooden nursing chair, where, still in her coat, she sat down, a ready smile on her face despite the cool reception.

'I've had a very bad few days,' complained Jim's mother, unsteadily taking her crocheting from the chair and dabbing her nose with her handkerchief. It was a quite remarkably long nose, Pearl decided, thankful that Jim's didn't follow suit. Over her grey head Mrs Nesbitt was wearing some sort of black cap, which made her look very severe. Her clothes were deadly dull, calf-length and shapeless, though Pearl always had the impression they were well-preserved quality.

'I'm sorry to hear that.' Pearl shed her coat only because it was so warm in the room, full to the gunwales with heavy, ornate furniture. She didn't want to give an indication she was uncomfortable, so she kept her perch on the edge of her chair.

'The doctor tells me I'm overdoing it. Faint spells and such like, with a terrible head. He said I could do with a holiday.'

Pearl leaped in fearlessly. 'Where would you like to go?'

'By myself? It's unthinkable.'

'With a friend, then?'

'No one quite understands . . . not like your own.'

Pearl felt the cold chill of the pointed finger. Not at her, but at Jim, and almost rose to the bait. Then remembering that she'd fallen into this trap before, she began to talk about the one topic that was common to them both, and that was Jim. Nevertheless, when Jim's whistle at the door came half an hour later, Pearl hurried to greet him, relieved that he'd managed to leave work early. Jim took her in his arms and kissed her. She kissed him back so passionately that he laughed.

'Hey, what's all this about?' He glanced over her shoulder and frowned.

'I'm just pleased to see you.'

He eased his big frame from her arms and again glanced into the darkened hall. 'Mum in?'

Pearl nodded, reflecting that her mother-in-law never went out after midday, just in case of a raid.

'Blimey, it's like a furnace in here,' Jim muttered as he pulled at the back of his dungarees. Pearl could see the 'V' of sweat under his braces. She loved him all the more for the hard work he did in a long and gruelling day and the effort he was making to keep his mum happy.

Soon came the change of note in Mrs Nesbitt's voice as her son walked into the parlour. Knowing Mrs Nesbitt enjoyed time alone with her son, Pearl went to the kitchen where she busied herself with a little cleaning before she made the tea.

In contrast to Villa Road, number twenty-four Roper's Way could have been on another planet, Pearl decided as, one sunny late afternoon in September, she hurried up the path of her childhood home. Threading her fingers through the letter box, she pulled up the key and let herself in. Her spirits lifted immediately at the sound of pans clattering and the mouth-watering aromas that flowed from the kitchen.

'Mum? Ruby?'

'We're in here!' her mother called. Pearl hastened along the brightly lit passage. As a child, she and Ruby had rushed home from school to their favourite meals, even though, like the rest of the island, her parents were poor. Despite her dad's regular boilermaker's job at the factory, it wasn't well paid. When war was declared and the government drew up new laws on austerity, it had no meaning for islanders. Even clothes coupons had been a joke, as everything they wore was second-hand.

'Hello, love!' Amy Jenkins, dressed in her pinny, lifted her flour-covered hands. 'Don't want to dirty that lovely frock,' she grinned. Ruby, also in a pinny, was sliding a tray of potatoes into the oven. She looked up in surprise. 'On your own, are you?'

'Jim's on a call-out.'

Amy rolled her eyes. 'Poor love.'

'Either that or he's got a bit on the side,' laughed Pearl, taking care to keep her dress clean and slide her chair back a few inches from the table.

'Your Jim has only got eyes for you,' Ruby admonished as she closed the oven door. 'That's a nice dress. Is it new?'

'It was from that little shop in Poplar near the Queens. I had a few clothing coupons left.' Pearl had been extravagant, but the dress was just her size and not too expensive. And hadn't Ruby had that lovely new jacket? Anyway, Jim had given her the money for the dress and forbidden her to spend it on groceries.

'So what's the emergency?' asked Amy.

'Up at the Aldwych. Remember St Clement Danes church last year when it was bombed? How the tower stood after the bells all fell down? Someone's reported a pipe sticking up near the bombed site. Jim's got to make sure it's not dangerous.'

'On his day off too,' said Ruby.

Pearl smiled. 'I don't mind. I thought we could all go down the market.'

'You girls go and enjoy yourselves,' Amy said as she took off her apron. 'I'm popping along to see your dad. He's at the allotment, digging me up a few nice veg. If you're still here when he gets home, Pearl, you can take some spuds with you. What've you got Jim for tea?'

Pearl was ashamed to admit that she had nothing. 'Gwen's saved a tin of sardines for me,' Pearl ventured hesitantly.

'Have you got any coupons left?' Ruby asked curiously.

'No, but the dance isn't till November.'

'You might get something on the old girl's clothes stall at market.'

'I don't know,' Pearl shrugged, imagining the new bolero she had in mind. 'She won't have anything like I want.'

'Hark at it,' pouted Ruby mischievously. 'You'd think there wasn't a war on.'

'Well, I reckon a girl should take pride in her appearance. Have her hair trimmed and wear nice underwear,' said Pearl casually, 'so even if she wasn't accomplished in the cooking department, keeping attractive for her man was something she knew about.'

Ruby burst out laughing again. 'Oh, Pearl, you ain't never gonna change.'

'I hope not.'

'So when's the dance?' Ruby asked as they rounded the corner.

'Saturday the twenty-second. Can you come? Jim can get the tickets.'

'And play gooseberry? No, thanks.'

'But it's a works do! There's bound to be a few blokes there.'

At this Ruby's face dropped and she stared at Pearl. 'What would I want a bloke for?'

'To dance with, of course.'

'As long as you don't try palming me off.'

'Why would I do that?'

Ruby shrugged. 'As long as you understand I don't want no one but Ricky.'

Pearl looked away. 'You're old enough to know what you want.'

'He's not a five-minute wonder, you know.'

'I never said he was,' Pearl murmured guiltily.

'I had a letter yesterday. Ricky writes so lovely, just like

'That's nice,' Amy nodded. 'Sardines are very versatile. Now tell me, what are you going to do with them?'

Pearl didn't know. Other than squeezing the disagreeably smelly fish out of the tin and holding her nose at the same time, she didn't have a clue what to do with them.

Both Amy and Ruby burst out laughing.

'What's so funny?' Pearl went scarlet.

Amy waved her hand. 'The look on your face, that's what. Don't worry, I was only teasing.'

Pearl grinned. 'I dunno why Jim don't complain about me cooking. I think he's even lost weight since we got married.'

At this they all laughed. But Amy patted Pearl's shoulder. 'Your hubby looked all right to me; in fact, I'd say he was in the peak of health.'

Pearl knew Jim was happy but it certainly wasn't because of his stomach. She was only too willing to forget about housekeeping and leap into bed. Any time they had spare, they were at it like rabbits, as the old saying went. Tiffs aside, or perhaps because of them, their lovemaking was very exciting. She'd heard girls at work say they had to lie back and think of England when it came to sex. But England was the last thing *she* thought of when in bed with Jim.

'Even so,' said Amy, adjusting her scarf, 'I know you won't take your husband's good nature for granted. If that boy needs feeding up, then you are the one to do it.'

Pearl made a face. 'Yes, Mother.' And grinning at Ruby, she shared the joke.

Later, as they were walking arm in arm to market, Pearl and Ruby discussed anything but food. It was all fashion, make-up and hairdos, and Pearl was pleased to announce the works' Christmas dance. 'I've got me eye on this little bolero,' she said dreamily as they approached West Ferry Road. 'It's in the same shop as I bought this dress.'

he speaks,' Ruby said eagerly. 'You can read it, if you like.'

'No, thank you. It's private.' It made Pearl feel ill to think that Ruby was following in her footsteps. Ricky had charmed her, just like he was doing to Ruby, but what could she do to stop it?

'Then I'll tell you what it said,' insisted Ruby as they approached the market. 'He couldn't write where the ship was or what he was doing on it or when he'd be home, because of the censor. But at the end he asked me to wait for him and the minute he got home he'd come round. But the best thing was at the end. He signed it, "With all my love, R." And there were three kisses at the bottom.'

Pearl walked the rest of the way to market feeling very upset. She had managed to persuade Ruby to come to the dance. But what use would it be if she wouldn't look at anyone but Ricky?

Chapter 5

The weather changed in October and, along with the struggle to cook, clean and share in her duties of fire-watching, Pearl was now faced with the problem of damp. Their rooms were unheated except for the living room. Although she'd seen her dad light the fire many times, getting damp coke to light was a new experience. Her dad had seemed to do it effortlessly. But then they'd had a coal bunker, keeping the nuggets dry. Here, there was nothing more than a piece of corrugated metal in the corner next to the outside lavatory.

Pearl was accustomed to going outside for the toilet, but heaving a scuttle up the stairs was no fun. And if Jim hadn't

covered the coal, then she hadn't thought to, either. Jim insisted she leave lighting the fire to him. But he worked late and she was the first to be home. Pearl didn't like the coal dust over her clothes or the sharp splinters of the kindling. Her newspaper balls lit very well, but died rapidly – unlike those that her dad had made, which soon had the fire blazing as she and Ruby had stood the wooden horse in front of the hearth to air their clothes. No such luxury now!

It was on a dull Monday morning in the middle of October when Pearl realized that winter was beginning to set in. The draughts were lifting the checked curtains from the windows and the kitchen smelled musty. She sipped her cup of tea thoughtfully as she sat listening to the wireless. How could she brighten the day? Looking around the kitchen, she was amazed at how dreary the place looked. In summer their new home had seemed like the perfect love nest. But then she'd had the door wide open and a soft summer breeze had blown the smell of dampness away.

Turning off the wireless, she prepared for work. Day-to-day life went on, whatever else was happening in the world. Wearing her heavy coat for the first time, and taking her umbrella, she set off. A few spots of rain fell and the bus smelled of camphorated oil. Pearl smiled as the bus conductress took her fare. The ting of the machine now brought back happy memories of Margate.

When Pearl arrived at work, the talk was all of Russia. 'Dad says the Russians would cut their throats rather than being taken by the Nazis,' Moira Bush said the minute Pearl walked in. 'I suppose you've heard? Or are you still on cloud nine?'

'As a matter of fact I am,' Pearl replied breezily, sliding into her seat and brushing the sleeves of her immaculate white blouse for minute specks of dust. It had taken her almost an hour last night to press her clothes properly. The

old iron that had to be heated on the stove dated back to the Ark. Thank goodness Jim didn't need his overalls and dungarees pressed. Taking her compact from her drawer, she raised it to hide the spectacle of Moira's pinched face. Pearl tweaked into position the glossy wave that fell over her eye. She went to great lengths to maintain her Veronica Lake hairstyle. Should she have it cut? Bobs were popular. But Jim liked her hair long.

Pearl smiled at Em, the third clerk in the office. At thirty she was the oldest, yet still living at home with her dad. She wore unflattering utility clothes and lace-up shoes. Most of the girls wore heels and drew seams down the backs of their legs, as there was a shortage of stockings.

'Are you both going to the dance next month?' Pearl asked as she replaced the compact in her drawer.

'I suppose so,' said Moira dully.

'I will if I can leave Dad,' said Em quietly.

'Doesn't he like being by himself?' Moira's eyebrows shot up.

'It's not that, exactly.'

'What is it then?' Pearl and Moira asked together.

Em looked down at her desk. 'It's just that—'

Just then Mr Hedley walked in and Em went scarlet.

'Good morning, ladies,' said Mr Hedley, scrutinizing each desk.

They all replied, 'Good morning, Mr Hedley,' then began to type very quickly. As he walked slowly round examining their work, Pearl wondered what it was that Em had been going to say.

The Christmas dance was scheduled early in the hope that the Luftwaffe would be absent on the night of 22 November. Last year, celebrations had been called off because of the Blitz. But this year Pearl had every intention of showing off her husband to all her friends and colleagues, and dancing

53

the night away. Everyone anticipated a big event. All the departments had contributed towards the expenditure and the grand total had provided for the hire of the popular Ray James and His Band, and a wide selection of raffle prizes, together with a comprehensive buffet and plenty of drinks. Despite the shortages, the night promised to be an exciting one.

At the beginning of November Jim came home with a present of black market clothes coupons. He knew how much her appearance meant to Pearl. And she'd hinted for some while about a black dress with sequins sewn on the bodice. He'd even sported out on a new shirt for himself, although the utility cut was, in Pearl's opinion, a little staid.

As for shoes, she'd found a reasonable pair, with high heels and black straps with little black bows. Then something horrible happened. It was a damp Thursday evening and her thoughts were again on the dance as she walked home from work. She needed a new coat to go over the dress. But she didn't have any coupons left and anyway, a coat would be far too expensive. With her attention taken, she didn't hear the newspaper vendor's cry. Then coming to an abrupt halt, she stood still as she stared at the board.

'*Ark Royal* sunk! Read all about it. Torpedoed by Italian U-boat.'

Pearl bought a paper. 'Is this true?' she asked the old man as he cuffed the drip from his nose.

'It ain't no false alarm,' he nodded. 'They got her this time. Eighteen of our lads are missing. S'pose we got to be thankful it ain't as bad as the *Hood*. Nearly fifteen 'undred went down on her.'

Pearl remembered only too well the heart-dropping morning in May when news came through that the German battleship *Bismarck* had sunk the prestigious *Hood*. So many lives had been lost. Jim had come round to Roper's Way with the news and they'd all sat in silence as he'd read out

the gruesome details of the battle cruiser's demise.

Pearl could hardly bring herself to read on. But there it was in black and white. The *Ark Royal* had been torpedoed and sunk just off Gibraltar. So many claims had been made by the Axis forces before, but now she had finally gone.

'Our navy ain't gonna find that sub,' pointed out the vendor angrily. 'Not like they cornered the *Bismarck* after chasing her for two days. Crippled by a torpedo bomber attack, she was. Didn't have nowhere to run with our navy and airforce at her heels. But a sub! Who's gonna know what one it was? Long gorn by now, anyway.'

Pearl walked away with a heavy heart. Not only for the loss of the great aircraft carrier and crew but for all their families. It was a terrible tragedy, and just before Christmas too. Then she remembered Ricky, on a ship in the Arctic. Was it bad of her to wish that he too would go down on his ship? Ruby hadn't said she'd heard from him lately. The U-boats were picking off the convoys' escorts and then the merchant ships. The papers said that the German submarines had our navy at their mercy. Any survivors from the sunken ships were often left in the ocean to die. She thought of Ricky slipping below the freezing waves, but then felt ashamed. How could she wish someone dead? It was a dreadful thing to think.

When Gwen and Fitz beckoned her into the shop, Pearl knew that it would be to discuss the tragic happening at sea. Fitz was very upset and put up the closed sign. They stood listening to the Home Service news on the wireless. Pearl and Gwen had tears in their eyes. Half an hour later, as she climbed the stairs and stood on the landing outside her door, the mist was thickening around the yard. There were fog horns sounding on the river. Slowly the roof tops disappeared under a yellow fog. The strong smell of smoking chimneys was mixed with an undercurrent of disinfectant. That meant the bugs were rampant. The use

of naphtha was an attempt to kill them as they hugged the wet patches on walls. Pearl shivered.

Quietly she said a prayer for all the souls who had died at sea, then let herself in. The kitchen smelled of mould. Despite all Jim had done to improve it, the walls were spawning a fungus. The yellow gingham curtains were stained at their hems and she looked cautiously round for scuttling black bodies.

Suddenly the door opened and Jim stood there, his broad shoulders buried under his donkey jacket. He rammed the door shut, giving a sigh of relief to be inside.

'Christ, love, you gave me a shock, sitting there in the gloom. Why don't you put the light on?'

'Have you heard the news?' she replied half-heartedly.

'The *Ark Royal*?' He nodded and flicked down the light switch.

Pearl felt an uncontrollable sob in her chest. She put her hands up to her face.

In a moment Jim was beside her. He took her in his arms and pushed back the lock of hair on her face. 'What's up, Pearly-girl?' He held her so tightly she could hardly breathe.

'War does such terrible things,' she mumbled, leaning in to him. 'All those poor sailors and their families . . .' She still felt guilty about secretly wishing Ricky was dead.

'It's something we have to live with, love.'

'But how long will it all go on?'

'Come on, now,' he said, holding her away from him and wiping a tear from her cheek with his thumb. 'This ain't like you.'

She nodded. 'Daft, ain't I?'

'Now, there's nothing that can be done, and I don't know about you, but I wouldn't mind a little light relief from the day?'

'There's no dinner ready yet,' she said, feeling even more guilty.

He laughed. 'That's not the kind of relief I meant.'

'Oh, Jim, I love you so much.' She threw her arms round his neck. 'You always say the right thing.'

'Dunno about that, but I'm bloody freezing. Let's go where it's warm.' He lifted her into his arms and carried her to the bed.

'What about me clothes?' she laughed.

'Leave them to me. Get under.'

In no time at all they were making love and he was kissing every inch of her body. Pearl forgot her misery and guilt as Jim made her forget the world and Ricky too.

Later they sat together beside the fire and Jim spoiled her with slices of bread and dripping, and, thanks to Gwen, an extra helping of sugar in their tea.

She had no regrets about buying a new dress now. What did it matter? You had to live every minute as though it was your last. She might even go to market, where coupons weren't necessary, and look for a coat. Ruby was right: there were bargains to be had if you searched hard enough.

Before long they had run out of coal. Rather than go down in the foggy dark to get some, they climbed back in bed. Feeling happier, Pearl linked her arms around her husband's waist and smiled. They had the whole night to lie in each other's arms.

By the time the dance came round, Pearl had bought a new wardrobe, including a grey second-hand astrakhan coat with a velvet collar, which looked out of this world. Parading around the living room with only her bra and French knickers on underneath, she'd had a very positive response from Jim. He hadn't cared a fig that she'd broken into the housekeeping. Instead he'd assured her that he was a lucky man to have such an adventurous wife.

On the afternoon of the dance, Pearl prepared well in advance. Jim had said he would be home by four o'clock

and she managed to leave work before twelve thirty. The bus brought her home in ten minutes and she hurried to drag in the tin bath. But in her haste she forgot the fire. She was freezing by the time Jim came home.

'Blimey, did I take the wrong turning? Is this the North Pole?' He rubbed his gloved hands together.

'I had a bath and forgot the fire,' Pearl admitted as she shivered in her towel.

Jim threw down his things and laughed. 'I'll soon warm you up.'

Pearl giggled through chattering teeth. 'Trust you, Jim Nesbitt.'

'Don't say I ain't obliging.'

'I've got me hair to dry yet.'

Jim kissed her. 'I like you just the way you are.'

'I'm a dope, that's what. Fancy forgetting the fire.'

He lifted the strands of her wet hair. 'You know what, you're just like a playful puppy. And that's what makes me love you. I wanna look after you and see those sweet lips turn up in a smile.'

Pearl giggled even though she was freezing. And it wasn't long before they were kissing and cuddling. By the time they thought about going out, they were starving. Jim's tummy was rumbling as he tried to loop his tie in the mirror. Pearl felt excited despite her hunger as she smoothed down the skirt of her black dress.

When Jim turned round she took a breath at the sight of her handsome husband. He'd definitely lost weight since they'd married. But it suited him better than when he stuffed himself full of his mother's cooking. Not that Jim had lived at home much before they'd married, as he'd travelled round a lot and lived in digs. She straightened his tie. 'That's better. It's the woman's touch that counts.'

'I'll have your touch any day.'

'You're a lemon, you are.'

'Gonna squeeze me, then?'

'Don't start that again,' she giggled. 'We're late already. We'll have to have something to eat at the dance as I ain't got time to cook.'

'I can live on love,' Jim teased her. 'Can I kiss you?'

'No, I've just put me lipstick on.'

Laughing, he caught her wrist and, running his gaze over her, he said huskily, 'My God, Pearl, you're an eyeful. I still don't know how I managed to make you me missus, but somehow I did. Are you happy, Pearly-girl?'

'Course I am.'

'Tell me you love me.'

'I'm always telling you that.'

He smirked. 'And if you dance with anyone else tonight, tell them to behave themselves or they'll have Jim Nesbitt to deal with.'

Pearl was still smiling as she put the finishing touches to her hair. She couldn't wait to dance and enjoy herself at a real do. At least Ruby had agreed to join them, even though she said she didn't feel like dancing as she hadn't heard from Ricky. Once again, Pearl's guilty thoughts came back. Would Ruby really be broken-hearted if he didn't survive? Or would she get over him quicker than she thought?

Pearl sighed, shaking her head as if to dispel all the irrational thoughts. The dance hadn't come a moment too soon; after last year's bombing, everyone needed a good Christmas.

Pearl hadn't ever been inside the hall of the Friends' Meeting Place where the dance was held. But she knew the Victorian building had served many purposes in wartime. During the Blitz it had been bombed several times. After being hastily repaired, the large wooden floor and wide stage, with its heavy curtains, were often in use. Tonight there were Christmas decorations pinned from

wall to wall and a large Christmas tree stood just inside. There were chairs and tables set out along the perimeter for refreshments, and a small anteroom next to the kitchen had become a bar.

'There's a wonderful turn-out,' Pearl said excitedly, breathless from their brisk walk. She clutched both Ruby and Jim's arms and they joined the long queue. 'I'm gonna dance you off your feet tonight, Jim.'

'Now then, gel,' chuckled Jim, 'don't forget you're a married lady.'

Pearl laughed. 'That don't make any difference. Not when you haven't been out for months.'

The only reminder of war seemed to be the row of gas masks hanging on the wall in the lavatories. No one ever bothered about masks after the first weeks of war. The cumbersome apparatus was more of a hindrance than a help. Ruby and Pearl giggled as an elderly lady, reluctant to leave hers unattended, asked the cloakroom girl if it would be safe.

When they'd handed over their coats, Ruby and Pearl squeezed in front of the mirror. Ruby looked lovely, Pearl thought, as they attended to their make-up. She wore a lime-green, slim-fitting evening gown. It was more thirties than forties, but the green matched Ruby's colouring perfectly. Her cheeks were flushed and her blonde hair, unlike Pearl's shoulder-length style, was clipped up into a glossy roll. Pearl wondered if she'd heard from Ricky yet, although nothing had been said. At least she had agreed to come to the dance. So was there hope she was forgetting him?

Before long they were hustled out of the way by other girls eager to look in the mirror.

'Is that another new dress?' Ruby asked Pearl as they walked out.

'What do you mean, another one?'

'Well, you're always buying something.'

Pearl grinned. 'I like to keep me husband's interest.'

Ruby grinned too. 'You manage that all right. He only has eyes for you.'

Pearl felt proud. She was so lucky to have an attentive man at her side.

'What about Jim? Don't he ever want a new suit?' asked Ruby as they made their way through the big doors.

'He's got a new shirt,' Pearl teased. 'I had to hide his overalls tonight so he couldn't find them.'

They were still giggling as they found themselves inside the hall, with the tables and chairs arranged down either side. The band was warming up at the far end and Ruby clutched Pearl's arm. 'Look, there's Em and Moira.'

They waved and went to join them. As Pearl looked round she could see a few familiar faces. Amongst them were one or two young men. There would be no excuse for Ruby not to dance. Perhaps tonight she would meet someone who would make her forget all about Ricky.

The four girls were talking when Jim arrived with the drinks. 'I got in a round early,' he told them as he lowered the tray. 'Shandy it is, girls – not much in the way of choice, I'm afraid, but I count meself a lucky man tonight, having four lovely ladies to entertain.' His eyes twinkled and a big smile stretched across his face. Pearl liked to hear him flirt because she was proud of him and knew she could trust him. Sometimes she couldn't believe this handsome man was her husband!

The band had been belting out music all evening – Glenn Miller, Joe Loss, Ted Heath, Jack Hylton and even George Formby. The jitterbug, from America, had been the most popular dance. All the young couples had swung themselves up and down the floor, including Pearl and Jim. And though Jim hadn't quite thrown Pearl over his head,

as some of the male dancers did their partners, they had joined in as energetically as the others. Pearl thought that even Ruby looked as though she was enjoying herself. It hadn't taken long for a young man to ask her to dance and she hadn't refused.

The good-looking singer of the band had attracted some admirers. He was dressed in a white jacket, black trousers and black bow tie. The small group of young women from the typing pool stood watching him. He crooned out the old favourites as he stood in the spotlight; 'I'll Be Seeing You', 'We'll Meet Again' and 'Run Rabbit Run', followed by the sentimental tunes like 'Dinah', 'Say It (Over and Over Again)' and 'Whispering Grass'. Ray James, the leader of the band, a small man with a moustache, kept the three saxophone players, two trombonists, one drummer and pianist playing without a pause. But when the food was served at nine o'clock the band took a break.

Pearl was amused to see that Arnold Raven, a cook from the canteen, had taken a liking to Moira. He sat at their table, a big, cheerful young man who, Pearl thought, looked as though he'd eaten too many of his own pies. Em, too, had found a nice dancing partner, a tall young man from the rent department, called Colin.

When the men went out for a smoke, the gossip started. Moira was the first to suggest that someone was on the fiddle in the canteen. 'Arnie saw a jam roll he'd made this morning turn up in the refreshments,' she whispered.

'How did he know it was his jam roll?' asked Ruby.

'Oh, he can tell,' Moira assured her, and everyone hid their amusement.

'Colin's nice,' said Pearl to Em, who was quietly sipping her lemonade.

Em went scarlet. 'Yes, but I've got two left feet.'

'If you have,' said Ruby, 'he's not noticed.'

'He's too polite to say anything, I expect.' Em looked

62

even more embarrassed. Pearl thought how pretty she was in a blue suit, which made such a change to her preferred utility wear. Her hair was newly waved, and once or twice Colin had put his arm around her. Was there a budding romance?

'These are delicious,' said Em, changing the subject quickly as she nibbled a biscuit. 'I know it's not chocolate but it tastes the same.'

'That's 'cos you've forgotten what chocolate tastes like,' sniffed Moira. 'I saw some jellies in the kitchen. Bet there won't be any left for us as the front tables went up first.'

Pearl and Ruby glanced at one another. Pearl had to smother a giggle as, without Moira seeing, Ruby rolled her eyes.

Suddenly a young man came to the table. Pearl knew him only as Blackie, a friend of Jim's who worked in the vehicle maintenance department. 'Hello, Pearl.'

She smiled. He had called in a couple of times to see Jim on his way to the pub. 'Hello, Blackie.'

'You enjoying yourselves, girls?'

They all nodded. Blackie looked at Ruby. 'I was wondering if you'd like the next dance?'

Pearl hoped she would accept. Blackie wasn't handsome, but he did have lots of very nice wavy black hair.

Ruby smiled hesitantly. 'I'm getting me breath back.'

Pearl knew Ruby wasn't impressed. Blackie stood no chance against the likes of Ricky.

'So how are you, Pearl?' Blackie said politely.

'Very good, thanks.'

'Jimmy is happy as Larry since he got hitched. Considering he was a bit of a lad.'

'Was he?'

'Not now of course, no,' Blackie hurriedly added. 'Not with a missus like you to come home to.'

Pearl knew that Jim had had two real girlfriends before

her. The first one was when he left school, the other he'd met in Dagenham when he was working away.

'In fact,' continued Blackie, 'I wouldn't mind settling down meself. But I ain't found the right girl yet.' He glanced quickly at Ruby, who looked away.

Pearl smiled encouragingly. 'Your dreamboat is bound to come along.'

'I hope so. I'd like someone to write home to if me number comes up.'

'You're not enlisting?' asked Pearl quickly. 'You're in a reserved job, aren't you, like Jim?'

'I volunteered when they asked me,' he shrugged. 'The enlistment board came round and told us volunteers are needed on them desert tanks.'

Pearl stared at him. 'But couldn't you refuse?'

'Dunno,' said Blackie doubtfully. 'It's hard being a bloke at home. People think you're a conchie.'

'I'm glad they didn't ask Jim,' she said firmly. Then she saw Blackie's expression. 'Did they?'

'Wouldn't know.' Blackie smiled and said quickly, 'Well, nice to see you again.'

After he'd gone Pearl sat thinking about what Blackie had said. Had the enlistment board approached Jim?

'Miss me?' Jim whispered later as he took his place beside her.

'Jim, I was talking to Blackie just now—'

'Nice bloke is Blackie. Damn fine mechanic.'

'Yes, but he said—'

'I'll get a round in before the next dance, shall I?' Jim interrupted, pecking her cheek and hurrying off.

Just then Colin and Arnie returned. They all talked for a while and as the lights went down, the music struck up. Ruby got up to dance with Pearl's boss, Mr Hedley, who was politely asking his staff in turn for one of the foxtrots or quicksteps.

Pearl forgot all about Blackie after that as Jim whirled her round the floor, making her laugh and telling her how beautiful she was in her new dress. Pearl thought once again how lucky she was to have a husband who was so attentive and generous. He'd bought all the drinks without a murmur, and though they'd eaten the small supper that came with the price of the ticket, he hadn't complained about not having a hot meal. Her mum had said that the way to attract a man was through his stomach. But fortunately for her, Jim was the exception.

'Here you are, lovelies, don't swallow it all at once,' he teased as he placed yet another drink in front of her and Ruby. 'I don't want to have to carry you both home.'

Ruby smiled up at him. 'You spoil me, Jim.'

'Why not? You're a smasher. But don't let me wife hear.' He winked at Pearl. 'Now, you gonna tell me who's given you the eye tonight?' he asked as he sat down and sipped his beer.

Ruby just shrugged. 'There's no one here for me, Jim.'

'You've had a lot of dances, though. And the next dance is mine. I'm gonna make all the young blokes jealous.'

Ruby grinned. 'All right. As long as you don't throw me over your shoulder like you was with Pearl. I don't want to show me knickers.'

They all laughed but Pearl wondered if Jim would look so happy if he knew that Ruby had eyes only for Ricky. As her sister hadn't mentioned him, he was unaware of her strong feelings.

'Come on then, twinkle toes.' He held out his hand and Ruby took it, a big smile on her face.

Pearl watched Jim whirl Ruby round the floor. He wasn't the best dancer, but he had an old-world courtesy that made a girl feel secure in his arms. He always got Ruby laughing if she was down.

'Your Jim's a good laugh,' said Moira, narrowing her

eyes at Arnie, who was now propping up the bar. 'Wish Arnie was more energetic. Likes his wallop and his food too much.'

Pearl studied the red-faced young man who was drinking from a big tankard.

'How long have you known him?'

'When he got taken on at the canteen last year.'

'Have you been out with him before?'

'A few times. But I keep him at arm's length. I'm saving meself for Mr Right.'

Pearl smiled as she looked at Jim dancing. 'Sorry, but Mr Right's taken.'

When her boss came over and asked her to dance, Pearl dutifully accepted. He puffed and panted his way through the foxtrot, and she was relieved when it was over. Mr Hedley mopped his brow with his handkerchief and looked at his watch. 'Very nice, Mrs Nesbitt, thank you.'

'Thank you, Mr Hedley.'

She was smiling as she made her way back to the table. Moira was just leaving with Arnie. They said good night but Jim barely replied. His face was set like stone.

'What's the matter, Jim?' Pearl said as she sat down.

'Ask your sister,' he growled.

Pearl looked at Ruby. 'What's wrong?'

Ruby took her handbag from the chair. 'I'm going now.'

'Why? The dance ain't finished yet.'

'I'm catching the bus.' With that she was gone.

Pearl looked at Jim. 'What's going on?'

'Why didn't you tell me she's still seeing Winters?'

Pearl shrugged. 'You've never asked. Anyway, she's not, he's at sea.'

'She told me she's crazy about him.'

Pearl looked away.

'You knew then?'

'I told you before that she thought she was in love.'

66

'And I told you she should know better.'

'Jim, don't let's argue over Ricky again.'

'Christ!' He banged his fist on the table. 'Can't you see she's asking for trouble? Didn't what I told you about Danny and Gladys make any impression?'

'Don't shout, Jim.'

'I'll do what I bloody like.' He swallowed the last of his ale, then stood up. 'You'd better understand this, Pearl. Winters and me have never got on and never will. If that louse ever shows his face around me or mine again, there'll be hell to pay.'

Pearl remembered the tears in Ruby's eyes. 'You didn't say that to Ruby?'

'I spoke me mind because I'm not bloody soppy like you, encouraging the kid to write daft letters and moon over a waste of space like him.' He turned and walked away.

Pearl felt physically weak. His words hurt. Not because he said them in anger but because she knew they were close to the truth. But what could she do to stop Ruby?

Chapter 6

By the time the music ended, Jim still hadn't come back. Pearl was worried about Ruby. She got up and looked outside, then went back in and took her coat from the peg. There was no point in staying. Jim had a temper and he was probably cooling off at home.

Em bumped into her at the door. 'Are you leaving?'

'Yes.'

'Where's Jim and Ruby?'

'He's walked her home,' Pearl improvised. 'She had to be back early.'

'I'll get my coat and Colin and me will walk with you.'

Pearl would have liked to be on her own, but she didn't want to sound rude.

Colin met them outside. 'Lucky there's been no raids tonight.'

'Yes, it was a wonderful evening.' Em dug her hands in her pockets. 'I really enjoyed myself.'

'What about you, Pearl?' Colin asked.

'I'm going because my feet are killing me.'

He laughed. 'Jim and you are good dancers.'

'We danced at the club. They used to have good dances there before the war.'

'It put a stop to a lot of good things,' nodded Em. 'Still, we all made up for lost time tonight.'

Pearl listened to Em and Colin talking. Colin said he'd been turned down because of his bad sight.

Suddenly Pearl yearned for Jim. Whatever their differences she should have been dancing in his arms this minute. He was only being protective towards Ruby.

'I hope Dad's all right,' Em said as they turned the corner of Pride Place.

'Why?' asked Pearl, suddenly remembering that once Em had been about to tell her and Moira about her dad but Mr Hedley's appearance had put paid to that.

Em's voice was soft. 'He's got this spine disease and the hump on his back frightens the kids. They even throw stones at him. And one night a lit rag was pushed through the letter box.'

'That's dreadful,' said Colin, pulling up short.

'Around where we live they don't know better. Dad was very upset. It was at the time you got married, Pearl. That's why I couldn't come to your wedding.'

'No wonder he don't like being on his own,' gasped Pearl.

'Yes,' agreed Em hurriedly. 'So I'd better be going.'

'Thanks for walking me home.'

'It was a pleasure,' said Colin quietly, wheeling his bicycle beside Em.

Em walked off with Colin, his bicycle wheel squeaking as they went.

How could those kids do that, Pearl wondered as she went down the alley. The poor man must be terrified. For all her problems, she was lucky that a deformity wasn't one of them.

Pearl came to the top of the stairs. There was no light in the kitchen. Letting herself in, she found only darkness. The fire was out and she sank down on the bed. It was half-past eleven. Where had Jim got to? And Ruby? Was she all right?

She kicked off her shoes and found a blister. She was too cold to take off her coat. Pulling the cover over herself, she curled up and soon was asleep.

Pearl suddenly remembered it was Sunday. Turning to look at Jim's side of the bed, she found it empty. Then last night tumbled back. How had such a wonderful evening turned into a catastrophe?

Pearl slid her feet to the floor and pulled her crumpled coat round her.

'Jim?'

The fire was alight and she rushed to the kitchen. He was sitting at the table dressed in his baggy trousers and jumper. The saucer was full of dog-ends. How long had he been there? She threw herself into his arms. 'Oh, Jim, I was worried about you!'

He slowly disentangled himself. 'You got home all right?'

She squeezed herself on his knee. 'I walked with Em and Colin.'

'Sorry. Me temper got the better of me.'

'And I'm sorry too. Where have you been?'

He looked at her with sunken eyes. 'Walking. Thinking. Go in by the fire and I'll make the tea.'

'I don't want tea. I only want you.' The next moment she was kissing him and he was kissing her. Pearl felt her upside-down world return to normal. Nothing mattered, just each other, and she wanted to tell him so. She wanted to be made love to, to be reassured and know that everything was as it used to be. 'Let's go to bed.'

But he took her hands. 'Pearl ... please.' His voice was weary. 'Just do as I say for once. Sit by the fire.'

Reluctantly she obeyed. Her hair was all over the place and her teeth needed brushing. No wonder he didn't want to cuddle her! Quickly she pinched her cheeks in the mirror.

He soon appeared with two cups of tea. A great wave of love enveloped her. Why did they have to quarrel?

Placing wood on the fire he stood up slowly. 'We need to talk, Pearl.'

'We can talk in bed.'

He sighed. 'Before I know it, you'll have sent everything else out of me brain.'

'Jim, I know I spend too much and I'm selfish and I ain't a good cook, but I can change—'

'Pearl, it's none of those things,' he cut her short. 'I don't care how much you spend or where you spend it. And food is the last of me worries.' He sat heavily on the chair. 'As I've said, I've been walking all night, thinking things through.'

'You could have thought them through here,' she pouted.

'We'd have ended up in bed.'

'Is that such a bad thing?'

'No, course not,' he shrugged, raking a hand through his hair. 'When we make love it's wonderful. There ain't nothing like it, in my book. You're a beautiful woman and

70

I can't get enough of you. You've got this, like, knack for good taste, like the way you look – you're always turned out top notch. And this place, you've done it up real nice, like you see on the films, even with your little touches, but ... but ...'

'But what?' Pearl had a sinking feeling. What had he been hiding?

'There are things in a marriage that are just as important as sex. Like talking – and sharing.'

'I thought we did all that.' She gazed into his eyes. 'I love you, Jim. I try me best.'

'Pearl, answer me honestly.' He held her hands. 'Did you know how serious your sister is about Winters?'

Pearl gave a hesitant shrug. 'What do you mean by serious?'

'I went round to Roper's Way this morning to see if Ruby got home all right. Your parents had just left for church. I wanted to apologize for my outburst. You know what she said? She said it was none of my business and that she had no intention of giving him up.'

'I only knew about them writing, I swear it.'

'You knew about them writing?'

The sinking feeling came back as she nodded.

'Just look what it's led to,' he burst out. 'Do you really want to see your sister go the same way as Gladys?'

'Jim, she'd never kill herself.'

'How do you know?' His eyes were hard. 'Are you willing to take the chance?'

'That's not a nice thing to say.'

'And Winters ain't a nice bloke. I told you what he did to Danny and Gladys. He's responsible for the ending of a life that should have been lived much longer. My God, Pearl, isn't that proof enough?' When she didn't answer, he drew back. 'Or is there more to this than meets the eye? Something I don't know about?'

'Course not,' she protested, going scarlet. 'What could there be?'

'You knew him once, at the club.'

Her heart gave a guilty lurch. Jim had never put these questions to her before. He was like a different person, as though he distrusted her. 'You sound like you're jealous,' she flung back.

'Jealous?' he repeated, looking her intently in the eye. 'Maybe I am. Have I got reason to be?'

'Jim, that's another rotten thing to say.'

He stood up, staring at her as though he was searching her face for an answer. 'I don't know ... I don't know,' he murmured, pushing his hands in his pockets. 'I just can't put me finger on it. Something's not right ... there's something I don't understand. Why he's come back. It's just too much of a coincidence.'

If she told him *everything* now – admitted to the truth – she was sure she would lose him. He would never want her after what she'd done with Ricky.

'You're accusing me,' she heard herself bravely saying, 'but what about *you*? I don't go on to you about all these girlfriends you've had.'

He tilted his head. 'What girlfriends?'

'Blackie said you were a bit of a lad once.'

He shrugged. 'So what? I've always told you the truth. The girls before you meant nothing. All young blokes sow their wild oats.'

'You say you've always told me the truth. But what about the enlistment board?' she demanded, just remembering what Blackie had said.

'Who said about that?'

'Blackie,' she replied, pleased to see that going on the attack had worked. But her satisfaction was short-lived as he threw the last piece of wood on the fire.

'I was going to tell you after the dance.'

The words filled her with terror. 'Oh God, Jim, no!'

He kept his eyes averted. 'I'm sorry, Pearl.'

It was then the bottom of her world really did fall out as she realized that, like Blackie, he had enlisted.

Pearl sat in the chair, her arms clutched around herself. Her heart had only just stopped pounding. She could hear the rattle of china in the kitchen and feel the warmth of the fire. The newspapers were in the rack by the hearth, the clock ticked on the mantel next to the ashtray, a souvenir from Margate. Everything was as normal in their love nest, but it wouldn't ever be the same again.

Jim was leaving in a week. Seven days. Packing his bags and leaving. Well, she wouldn't let him go. They couldn't take him away from her, whoever *they* were.

'Drink this.' Jim's tone was tender. He was trying to make amends. But nothing was going to mend this – unless he said he wouldn't go.

'I don't want it.'

'Come on, love, for my sake.' He made her take the hot drink. The cup rattled in the saucer.

'Are you cold?'

'No.'

'I'll get a blanket.'

'Jim, a blanket ain't gonna do any good. You've just told me you've enlisted. That behind my back you had it all planned.'

'It was the *Ark Royal* that did it.'

'The *Ark Royal*?' She had thought it odd that Jim hadn't gone on about the sinking. But as they'd made passionate love, she'd assumed that he didn't want to upset her. 'So you've been keeping this secret since then?'

'Not secret. Not like that.'

'It's all right for you to accuse me of living in a fantasy world. But this takes some beating. I suppose you'd have said goodbye the night before you left?'

'I told you, I was going to after the dance. I didn't want to spoil your fun.'

Pearl's eyes widened. 'But you walked out on me anyway!'

'I was angry. Upset.'

'And you don't think I'd be upset?' Pearl demanded. She could hardly contain herself. She felt indignant, angry and terrified. No matter how she carried on, he seemed to have decided.

He sat down in the armchair. 'Let me explain.'

'I wish you would.'

'Me and Blackie were interviewed along with another two blokes at the council. Me and Blackie got picked.'

'But Blackie only mends engines!'

'He's a top-notch mechanic, love.'

'And I suppose you're a top-notch engineer?'

'Engineering and mechanics is what the government is interested in at this moment. I'm not allowed to know the details, but I can tell you where I'm to be trained.'

'Trained?' she repeated in a daze. 'So you really are going?'

'It's my duty.'

'What about your duty to me?' she burst out. 'Or have you forgotten we was only married in June.'

Once more he was beside her, comforting her. 'Come on now, gel, buck up.'

'Don't go,' she pleaded. 'Tell them you've changed your mind.'

'I can't do that.'

She began to cry.

'Come here . . .' He tried to hold her but she pushed him away. 'Don't do this, sweetheart.'

'I can't help it,' she sobbed.

He spread his fingers through his hair and down the back of his neck. 'Do you remember in August of last year, when they bombed the factories at Luton?'

Pearl shrugged. 'S'pose I do. What's that got to do with us?'

'It was just before the Blitz. They used to make cars at the Vauxhall factory but now it's tanks. Special ones, called the Churchill.'

'Jim, I—'

'Listen a minute. I'm trying to explain. See, Britain was so short of tanks after Dunkirk — we only had about a hundred left — that Winnie goes to Vauxhall and asks them to dream up a new one. Well, that's just what they did. The first batch are out next month. The rub is, we've got to account for the terrain they cover. The desert ain't all sand dunes like you see at the flicks; it's rocky as well. That's where the engineering comes in, creating ways for our tanks to get through.'

'Desert? Do you mean in Africa?' she screeched.

'I don't know exactly. But that's my guess.'

'All that sand!' she gasped. 'You didn't even like it at Margate.'

He smiled. 'I'll have to get used to it, won't I?'

She could see the fair hairs on his knuckles. She loved his hands so much. She didn't want to think of a gun in them. 'But Africa's thousands of miles away,' was all she could think of to say.

'And Africa is very important to us,' he said gently. 'The Axis forces have got Western Europe tucked up and now they're gonna try for the Suez Canal. This will give them your old carrot blanche to the oil fields. If they get these, they'll starve us of oil. Not to mention cut us off from India, part of the British Empire.'

Pearl was too ashamed to admit that she didn't know much about oil or the Suez Canal. All that was important was Jim.

'So you're really going?' she whimpered.

'Pearl, *think*, love. If Britain don't go out to meet the

war, it will come to us. We've fought off one invasion. But another? Could we do it again? And at what cost?' He looked into her eyes and that was her undoing. The tears overcame her anger. He wrapped her in his arms. She knew she couldn't change his mind. The war now had them in its grip.

Chapter 7

Pearl sat in the front room of her parents' house. She'd called in after work, needing to talk. Em had been very kind and listened to her troubles but now she needed her mum and dad. There were two days before the 29th and Pearl hadn't slept a wink.

'I don't suppose he had a choice, love,' said her mother calmly. 'You can't be angry with him.'

'But he *wants* to go.'

'He doesn't want to leave you, obviously,' reasoned her father, folding up the newspaper and sticking it down the side of his chair. 'A man's got his duty to do.'

'But he was doing it at the council,' Pearl protested. Everyone saw Jim's point of view and not hers.

'I read all about them new tanks,' her father said. 'Not details, of course – no, they don't give those. But they sound pretty formidable. And Jim knows his onions when it comes to engineering.'

Ruby sat beside her. 'I'm sorry, Pearl.' She seemed to be the only one to understand.

'I won't let him go,' Pearl said fiercely. 'I'll think of something to stop him!'

'Now, now, ducks,' reproved Amy as she got up from her

chair and closed the heavy curtains. 'There's no use getting cross and wasting your energy. Jim has done what he thinks best and you must come to terms with it. If your father had gone into the services in the last war, I would have had to do the same.'

Pearl sighed, knowing that was true. Her dad's job, making and fitting parts for ships, had kept him at home in the Great War. But she had no doubt that if he'd had to go away, her mum wouldn't have been the baby her daughter was.

'You're going to be ill if you carry on like this,' Ruby said quietly. 'I've never seen you without make-up on before.'

'I keep crying it off.'

'You don't ever cry.'

'I do now. I hope it will make Jim change his mind.'

Ruby grinned. 'That's just like you.'

'Is Jim calling by before he goes?' asked her mother, retying the straps of her pinny round her waist. 'Your dad and me would like to wish him well.'

Pearl smiled weakly. 'Yes, after he's seen his mother.'

'How has she taken it?' Amy enquired, eyebrows raised.

'I tried to talk to her yesterday,' Pearl sighed. 'I said I'd go round just the same whilst Jim's away. That she could rely on me for the shopping and I'd do the cleaning and even the washing if she wanted. But all I got was that it's my fault he's going. A real wife would have known how to keep her husband at home.'

'The old witch!' cried Ruby, but Amy put up her hand.

'She was just upset, I expect.'

'But why should she blame Pearl?' demanded Ruby angrily.

'Don't take it personally, love,' said Syd. 'She'll come round.'

'I don't know, Dad.'

'Did you tell Jim?' asked her mother with a frown.

Pearl shook her head. 'Course not. He'd have been upset.'

Her mother smiled. 'You did the right thing.'

Just as Pearl was about to say that she was always trying to do the right thing where her mother-in-law was concerned, but it hadn't got her very far, the air-raid warning went.

'Blimey, it always catches you out unexpected,' said her dad, jumping to his feet. 'You girls, grab your coats and go out to the Anderson. I'll make a flask of tea whilst Mum finds the blankets and candles.'

'I'm staying put, Syd,' said Amy resolutely, adjusting her turban as if it was a helmet. 'The enemy can do what they will. Under the stairs is cover enough for me. At least it's warm and we've got a lamp in there.'

'I'm not going in the shelter either,' said Pearl, looking at Ruby for support. 'The last time the warning went, me and Jim got under the table. Anyway it might be a false alarm.'

'Don't forget July,' her father pointed out gloomily, 'when the Co-op wholesale was hit. There was fifty-three people killed around Hill Place and Broomfield Street.'

'Yes, and it was a shelter in Broomfield Street that caught it,' Amy reminded him. 'So thank you very much, love, but the answer is no. I've got all me bits and pieces under the stairs, and to my mind it's just as safe as the Anderson. You girls coming?'

'No, we'll go under the table,' said Ruby nudging Pearl's arm. 'Sorry, Dad, but you're outvoted.'

Syd Jenkins scratched the top his head. His blunt features and pockmarked skin around his cheeks and mouth wrinkled into a grimace. 'Women. I'll never understand 'em.'

'You weren't meant to, love,' chuckled Amy, but with the low hum of the bombers, their laughter died. Syd ushered his wife to the cupboard whilst Pearl and Ruby crawled under the table. They pulled the sofa cushions with them, and a tartan rug. Soon even the tassels on the tablecloth shook.

'Hope Jim's all right,' whispered Ruby as she wriggled next to Pearl.

When it all went quiet, Pearl looked at Ruby. 'Jim told me he apologized for losing his temper at the dance.'

'Yes, he did.'

'I was worried about you that night.'

'I just don't understand what he's got against Ricky.'

Pearl didn't want to talk about Ricky. All she had on her mind was Jim. 'Remember when we used to play under the table?' she asked Ruby. 'Me, you and Betty and Janey? We'd tell ghost stories and listen to the grown-ups. They were always gossiping about each other, mostly in whispers, but we could hear everything.'

Ruby giggled. 'Yes, I know.'

'Course, Aunty Till and Uncle Ted, and Aunty May and Uncle Ron hadn't moved out to Barking then. We were a big family then.'

'And now there's only us.'

'I miss all that.'

Pearl found herself wishing they were back in the Blitz. Though it had been dangerous, it had also been exciting as Jim saw her every day, and before the war life had been very different.

The moment arrived that Pearl had been dreading. Blackie was coming to meet Jim and they would catch the bus to the station. In the thin, grey light of Saturday morning, Pearl and Jim sat together at the kitchen table. It would be the last cup of tea they would share. As he lowered his cup and slid it away, Pearl knew he had become stronger as the week had gone on. He'd maintained a quiet resolution whilst she had done everything in her power, from tears to tantrums and back again, to stop the hand of fate. Nothing had worked. The war had lured Jim away from her.

'Now don't forget our savings,' Jim told her patiently

again, as he had done so many times over the past week. 'With your wage and my army pay, you should be comfortable.'

'I know. I know. But it's not the money.'

'According to my calculations,' Jim went on insistently, 'you should have roughly thirty-six bob each week to cover the rent and electricity. And you won't have me to feed.'

Pearl smiled. 'You might even put on weight.'

'You'll write, won't you?'

'I won't have much else to do.'

'And if there's a raid, go to your mum's.'

'Jim, I told you, don't worry.'

He held her hand. 'After I've left, go back to bed.'

'How can I sleep without you?'

'Don't make me feel bad.'

Pearl traced her thumb over his skin. All the blond hairs sprang up under her touch. How long would she have to wait before she could do this again?

He pushed back the chair. 'I've got to go.'

'Please don't, Jim,' she begged for the last time. 'It's not too late to change your mind.'

'It is, love. I've signed on the dotted line.'

'We could say you were ill.'

'Pearly-girl, you ain't half making this difficult.'

'Why should I make it easy? They're taking you away from me and I don't even know when I'll see you again.'

He pulled her into his embrace. 'Stubborn as a mule and all mine.'

He kissed her long and hard whilst her tears ran down between their mouths and she could taste the salt and longing in them. The pain was like a knife in her ribs.

He slung his duffel bag over his shoulder. Then, in the early light, he was out of the door and gone.

From the front window she watched him join Blackie.

Step for step, almost as if they were marching, they strode down the road. He didn't even look back. She knew he didn't want to see her crying.

Pearl went to work each day, came home again and went to bed each night. She felt like a sleepwalker. She couldn't eat – food tasted like rubber. She tortured herself with fears, sunk into self-pity. One minute she was angry, the next afraid. And he wasn't even at war yet.

The bed felt empty without him. For the first two nights she hardly slept. For the third and fourth she managed a few hours. On the fifth night she slept on the couch. In the cold and gloom of the early morning, she felt a slow resignation. She'd fought all she could. Now she had to accept, like millions of other women, that her husband was gone. It wasn't as though he'd left for ever. It wasn't as if he was sick and wouldn't get well. He was only doing his training.

That night, there were no fire-watching duties and she made up a fire. It fizzled once or twice, but finally caught. Suddenly she was hungry. Opening a tin of Spam she ate it, cross-legged by the warmth. As it was Friday she brought in the tub from the landing outside and boiled three sauce-pans of water. It was shallow but hot. She even washed her hair afterwards.

The following morning, the first Saturday of December, she went to work with make-up. A week had passed since Jim had gone and she had survived.

At work, Moira relayed the news: Japan had refused Roosevelt's olive branch; the Nazis shot people in Paris as a reprisal for resistance; the temperature in Russia was twenty-seven degrees below freezing.

'We ain't doing too bad here, then, are we?' Pearl said when Moira finally took a breath.

'Oh, you're back in the land of the living, are you?'

Moira commented. 'I was beginning to think you'd lost your voice as well as your husband.'

Pearl managed to smile. 'At least I have got a husband, Moira, and he ain't lost. I'm proud to say he's a soldier and fighting for his country.'

Em nodded. 'He's very brave to have gone when he was in a reserved job.'

'Jim is a man of action,' Pearl agreed. It was a new feeling to be the wife of a soldier. She was proud in a way she hadn't been before.

Em sneezed and blew her nose. 'Think I've got a cold.'

'You want to watch it,' Moira warned. 'This weather could bring on the flu. You don't want to be bad for Christmas.'

Em looked downcast. 'I don't want me dad to catch it. There's lots of germs about.'

Pearl wanted to know if Em's romance with Colin was still on. But she didn't want to ask in front of Moira.

When Mr Hedley came in at twelve, he enquired after Jim.

'I haven't heard yet, Mr Hedley,' Pearl answered quietly. 'But I'm sure he'll write soon.'

'Well, give him my best, won't you? He's doing a grand job. We're all very proud of him.'

Once again Pearl felt a glow of pride. So many in the department had asked after him.

On her way home she splashed out. From Gwen she bought dried egg and a tin of corned beef. Both Gwen and Fitz were eager to know of Jim's progress.

Pearl climbed the stairs and opened the door. She was beginning to get used to being single again. As she did the housework she listened to 'Boogie-Woogie Bugle Boy' and managed a chorus or two of 'White Cliffs of Dover'. That afternoon she was going to tea at Roper's Way. Pearl smiled ruefully to herself. She hadn't paid a visit to Jim's

mum. But she could always say she'd had a cold. As Em said, there were lots of germs about. And Mrs Nesbitt didn't like germs.

'So you've heard nothing from Jim?' asked Ruby as they strolled to the market. They were walking down the after-effects of their tea.

'No, nothing.'

'He'll have to be careful what he writes. The censor vets every word.'

Pearl shrugged. 'I only want to hear how much he misses home.'

'He can't fill up two pages with that.'

'Yes, he can. If he doesn't, he'll get it in the neck when I see him.'

They laughed as they walked arm in arm. It was a mild December afternoon, with a hazy sun. The winter hadn't been cold so far, more dull and dreary. Christmas decorations and trees were as rare as bananas. It was a year when the public at large were tightening their belts to the last notch.

'I've heard from Ricky too.' Ruby smiled dreamily from under her plum-coloured scarf, which she'd wound round her head.

Pearl wished Ruby wouldn't go on about him. She tried to think of something else to say but Ruby was determined.

'Even Ricky can't guess how long the war will last. It could be over in a year. Or four or five. I want what you've got, Pearl: a man of my own. And not just any man. One as good as Jim. And I know that man is Ricky.'

If only he was one-tenth the man that Jim was, Pearl thought, but kept quiet. It seemed that being parted from Ricky was making Ruby even more eager to have him. Could love really change a man so much that, in Ricky's case, he was really serious about Ruby?

'Let's go to the clothes stall,' Pearl said as they came to Cox Street. 'My astrakhan coat was a real bargain. She might have something nice for Christmas.'

'You mean you're not buying new?'

'No, I've got to save.'

'Some hopes,' Ruby giggled.

Pearl grinned. 'I haven't got Jim to feed and I don't like me own cooking.'

'So when Jim comes home he could find a new woman in the kitchen?'

'As long as it's me. Look at these passion killers,' chuckled Pearl as she held up a pair of extremely baggy drawers.

'They're enough to put you off having a bit of the other.' Ruby screwed up her small nose. 'When Ricky comes home I'm going to buy a pair of silk knickers like you had for your honeymoon.'

Pearl froze where she stood. 'What do you mean?'

'You know what I mean. I want to know how to please him. After all, one day he'll be my husband. And don't give me that old-fashioned look. This is the nineteen forties, not the fourteen hundreds.'

Pearl was horrified. 'But you might – you could get pregnant.'

'It's a chance I'm willing to take,' Ruby reasoned calmly. 'Who knows what could happen? I don't want to think the worst. But I may not have much time with the man I love.'

Shocked at this turn of events, Pearl wished more than ever that she could speak honestly to her sister, as they had always shared everything, but now Ricky was creating a chasm between them and Pearl was powerless to prevent it.

Chapter 8

It was six o'clock on Sunday evening and Jim was lying on his bunk in the Nissen hut. He was trying to compose a letter to Pearl but the words weren't coming easy. He'd written all sorts to start with. First just 'Dear Pearl', then rubbed it out and put 'My darling'. When he'd reread it, he knew it wasn't him and settled instead for 'My dearest Pearl'. Now he'd exchanged that for something with a lighter touch, and begun, 'Dear Pearly-girl, are you missing me? I'm missing you. The weather isn't cold here and our digs are comfy and warm. Living with a bunch of blokes is all right, but I'd prefer to be with you. How's your mum and dad and Ruby? How's Mum? Tell her to keep her pecker up.' And that was it, more or less. He wasn't allowed to say where he was or anything about his training, or the fact that he now knew where he was headed.

He and Blackie had been issued their kit. Blackie had been sent to the armoury, whilst Jim was in engineering. Each day they learned more about the desert. Some were simple things, like survival; making meals of bully beef and dog biscuits, and using protective gear so you didn't get sunstroke. But the other part, the exciting bit, was the mock-ups of the desert, the minefields, the boulders that had to be shifted to get the tanks through. This was Jim's line of work, his niche; the hastily built camps, the roads, the drainage and water systems. There was so much to learn about North Africa.

Licking the end of his pencil he added a full stop and a comma to his letter, though unfortunately they didn't take up much space. Perhaps he'd leave writing till tomorrow when he could think of something else to say.

Suddenly there was a shout and the commanding officer

and their sergeant strode in. Everyone jumped off his bed and stood to attention. Jim felt his heart pound as the CO stood there, his eyes hidden under the peak of his cap.

'Good evening, men. Stand at ease, will you?'

Everyone relaxed though Jim felt a high air of tension in the room.

'Sergeant Docker is about to read a bulletin fresh from Headquarters. The information it contains will mean a great deal to all of us. It may, in fact, accelerate our plans and certainly changes the shape and dimension of the war.' He paused. 'Sergeant Docker?'

The tall, burly man with a walrus moustache stepped forward. Glancing at each man and then at the document he held, he began; 'Today, December the seventh, nineteen forty-one, the Japanese have attacked the United States of America's naval base at Hawaii, Pearl Harbor.'

There was an intake of breath from every recruit. Jim knew this meant only one thing. The Yanks would finally join the war.

'The news so far,' continued the sergeant, 'is that the United States navy's battleship force was taken by surprise and unable to mount an effective defence. The Japanese have now effectively removed any obstacle previously considered to be in their way of expanding their empire southwards. This catastrophic strike to America will end the long struggle of the United States to stay out of the war and Congress will shortly give President Roosevelt the authority to join Britain and pursue the conflict, all-out.'

Jim felt a wave of elation. America was now in the war, which meant the Allies would have a much better chance of winning it. Nothing could stop them now.

'Mum, Dad, Pearl, come and listen!' shrieked Ruby and they all ran to gather round the wireless.

Pearl sat beside her sister on the couch and Syd stood

with his elbow on the mantel. Amy hurried to perch on the arm of the fireside chair. In a sombre voice the commentator described the attack by the Japanese on Pearl Harbor. Other US bases in the Philippines had been targeted too. There were many casualties to the American naval fleet, and troops and civilians. To make things worse, it had all happened whilst the Japanese envoy in America had been in peace talks with President Roosevelt.

'The Americans were duped,' said Syd in a low voice when the broadcast was over. 'They fell hook, line and sinker for the bait.'

'But what will happen now?' asked Ruby in alarm.

'God only knows.' Her father lit a roll-up. 'There's no stopping the Japs, it seems. Hong Kong will be next. We've got only a handful of troops there. I don't like to think what might happen, I really don't.'

'Will America join the Allies?'

'If their congress gives them the nod, then yes.'

'Jim says that America has been sitting on the fence,' said Pearl, trying to remember Jim's words exactly.

'A massacre like this changes everything,' Syd muttered, blowing smoke from the corner of his mouth. 'The US of A has to retaliate. There's a lot at stake. The Pacific and South-East Asia is crucial to our success. We still hold Malaya and the northern Philippines but only just.'

'Syd, I really wish you'd smoke outside.' Amy made a face.

'All right, all right, I'm going.'

'Dad?' Pearl followed her father outside. 'If America does come in, will it be to Africa as well?'

'Could be. America's armada has been sunk in one day. She'll have a tough time recovering from that. But Japan has made a big mistake in crossing Roosevelt. They've underestimated the Yanks, just like Hitler did with the Russians.'

As they turned on the wireless once more, the drama of

Pearl Harbor began to unfold. The casualties were in their thousands. It was now clear that Japan had planned the raids well in advance. They had deceived the Americans into believing Japan wanted peace in order to strike the fatal blow.

Pearl and Ruby remained glued to the wireless. Pearl knew that every move made from now on would effect Jim in some way. She guessed that Ruby was thinking the same about Ricky.

Pearl read Jim's letter a dozen times. She was disappointed as it was full of Pearl Harbor. Only four lines were about how much he missed her. He did write that he hoped to see her soon. As he hadn't said when, she assumed he meant Christmas.

After such shocking news at the weekend, the office was in uproar on Monday. All the girls in the typing pool, Mr Hedley and the other bosses, *everyone* was talking about Pearl Harbor, and she listened with interest to their views. Her husband was now part of the war machine and so was she. She'd got married believing Jim could avoid it, but the reality was, the war was closer than ever.

But if Pearl had thought Monday was bad, Wednesday brought a real blow. News came in that the British navy had also suffered a terrible loss. HMS *Prince of Wales* and HMS *Repulse* had been sunk fifty miles off the coast of Malaya. '"Two of our greatest warships were torpedoed and bombed yesterday by Japanese warplanes,"' read Moira from the newspaper. '"The loss of life is the greatest in one incident. Over eight hundred officers and men are now either killed or missing in action."' Moira stopped and put down the newspaper. 'Me dad said the Japs were going to give it to Britain next,' she whispered hoarsely.

'They couldn't fly all the way over here, could they?' exclaimed Pearl, chiming in for the first time.

'No, but they've got a navy,' replied Moira immediately. 'And there's a lot more of them than there are of us.' Moira lifted the newspaper again. 'It says here that the *Prince* was crippled, hit in the stern and its propeller shaft twisted, so it couldn't move. They finished her off and went for the *Repulse* . . .' Moira gave a little choke. 'I can't read any more. Here, you read it.' She threw it on Pearl's desk.

Pearl couldn't either; it was too upsetting. Thank God Jim wasn't at sea. What would she have done if she'd read that and had a husband, father, or brother on board? What must be going through Ruby's mind about Ricky?

There was one more week until Christmas and Pearl hadn't heard from Jim. Why hadn't he written? She wanted to meet him at the station, throw her arms around him like in the films, and kiss him until he was black and blue. But she'd heard nothing and she felt abandoned. She told Ruby so when she called round that evening.

'They wouldn't have posted him already, would they?' said Pearl in the middle of *ITMA*. Even Tommy Handley hadn't been able to make her laugh.

'Course not,' said Ruby as she turned off the wireless.

'It was awful about the *Prince of Wales*.'

'I'd die if it happened to Ricky. And I haven't had a letter.'

'Could be the Christmas post,' said Pearl, hating herself for feeling secretly pleased.

'Looks like it'll be just us and Mum and Dad round the Christmas table.'

'And Mrs Nesbitt, of course.'

'I forgot about her,' Ruby groaned.

'I don't want to leave her alone at Christmas.'

'Jim's time will be precious on leave. Especially if it's only a weekend pass. Or even twenty-four hours. Some of the sailors Ricky knows haven't seen their wives in a year or more.'

'But Jim is only training at Luton,' Pearl protested, adding quickly, 'I think.'

Both were silent. Ruby sighed as she sat in the fireside chair, her cheeks red from the fire. Her striped knitted waistcoat and baggy trousers made her look very young. She kept herself very smart, Pearl thought, considering the utility designs that were forced on people by the government. As for herself, Pearl did everything possible to avoid the restrictions and was now a good customer of the clothes stall at the market.

'Pearl?'

'Hm?'

'You know we was talking about ... well, getting together with a man?' Ruby sat forward with her hands on her knees and Pearl's heart sank. She had tried to convince herself that Ruby wasn't serious, but looking at Ruby's flushed face, she could tell that was a vain hope. 'I decided to go to the clinic at Stepney.'

Pearl was truly shocked. 'You didn't!'

'After you saying about getting pregnant, I gave it some thought.'

'You mean you really are serious?'

'Yes, course.' Ruby sat stiffly, her expression offended. 'You should be pleased I took your advice.'

Pearl hadn't suspected that Ruby would go to such lengths and it was a big shock to her. If only she could think of a way to really dissuade Ruby, but the subject of Ricky was making them grow further apart.

'They were a bit snooty about it at first, as I'm not married,' Ruby continued in a cool tone. 'They tried putting me off by telling me about how some girls go for these backstreet operations to get rid of a baby.' Ruby shuddered. 'I must admit they did scare me. But all these old wives' tales like soaking sponges in vinegar and putting them up there really don't work, even though some women believe they do.'

'They told you about that?' asked Pearl in dismay.

'Yes, and drinking gin in a hot bath.'

Pearl shook her head disbelievingly. 'I never thought I'd be hearing this from you.'

Ruby stuck out her chin. 'I wouldn't have done that anyway. And don't look so disgusted, Pearl. You and Jim must have done it.'

'We didn't!' exclaimed Pearl in alarm. 'We waited till we got married.'

'So you didn't know anything about sex?' Ruby stared hard at her and it was then that Pearl realized what she had said. Guilt flowing over her, she tried to stop the mental pictures in her mind of Ricky kissing her, making love to her, and even worse . . .

'Look,' Ruby continued in a persuasive tone, 'I might have been a bit wild when I was younger, Pearl, and Mum and Dad did spoil me a bit after keeping a close eye on you. And I did get away with a lot you couldn't, but at the same time I'm not daft – or ungrateful. It was you that made me think about getting pregnant and that was why I went for advice. Babies ain't just something you stick in a pram and feed, they need a lot of looking after. So do you want to hear what they said or not?'

Pearl didn't want to hear but she couldn't offend Ruby. If it had been any other man than Ricky, Pearl was sure it wouldn't seem so bad. In fact, she would probably be telling Ruby she'd done the right thing by going to the clinic. But even the thought of Ricky doing to Ruby what he'd done to her made her feel quite ill. Pearl nodded her head dejectedly.

After a moment Ruby went on, 'Some women use pessaries, something I can get from the clinic. They're not a hundred per cent effective, but then nothing is. Not even the Roman Catholic way where you only sleep with a man on certain days. And then there's the other way, where the man must stop in time.'

Pearl shivered.

'What's wrong?'

'Nothing.'

'Or of course I could do what you do. But as you're not speaking much to me, I don't know what that is.'

Pearl went bright red. 'I don't do anything.'

'But you haven't got pregnant.'

'It just hasn't happened,' Pearl said embarrassedly. She didn't know why she hadn't conceived. They had made love enough times. Was it the worry of that other, more dreadful thing, that was always at the back of her mind?

Ruby crossed one leg over the other, patting Ruby gently on the arm. 'Is that what's been worrying you? Not being able to have a baby?'

'No ... no,' Pearl insisted.

'Only you'd tell me if you was worried, wouldn't you?'

'I'm not worried, Ruby.' Pearl knew she was going even redder.

'The nurse at the clinic asked me if not conceiving was in our family and I said no. After all, there was you and me and we've got our cousins, Betty, Jane and Howard. We're all perfectly healthy, so I'm sure you and Jim will have the tiny patter of feet soon.'

Pearl jumped to her feet. 'Ruby, I don't want to talk any more about this.'

Ruby stood up and said gently, 'Sorry. It must be a sore subject. Trust me to put me big foot in.' She hugged Pearl close, but there were tears in Pearl's eyes. Why was she so upset?

'Listen,' Ruby whispered as she held her. 'Please don't worry about me. I'm not going to get into trouble. I'd rather kill meself than that.'

Pearl thought of Gladys. 'Don't *ever* say that!'

'I didn't mean it.'

'Never say it again. Promise me?' She hugged Ruby tight.

'Course I won't.' Ruby laughed. 'You're daft, Pearl Nesbitt.'

'I care about you.'

Pearl loved her little sister so much. If only she could stop Ruby from loving Ricky. But love was blind.

Later, when Ruby had left, Pearl sat alone, the thoughts tumbling through her mind. Ruby had sensed her worries, but she couldn't tell her the truth. The real truth. And even if she did, it would only be her word against Ricky's. He would never admit to the fact that on the night she had told him that she might be expecting, they'd quarrelled and she'd fallen down the club stairs. It was just after she'd found Stella Burns in his arms and he had been saying the same words of undying love to her. To hear them and see them together had been a big enough blow.

But then he'd heartlessly told her she meant nothing to him. She'd began to cry and he'd laughed at her. Pearl felt the tears streaming down her cheeks now as she remembered the scene so clearly. The snow, on that winter's night, covering the buildings and the ground in a pure white blanket. And the tiny patch of blood that was the end of their baby's life.

Chapter 9

Christmas passed without any news from Jim. Even though her dad had managed to bring home a rabbit for Christmas dinner, as he'd won the boilermakers' raffle, she and Ruby had to put on brave faces. Neither of them had received letters. Nor had Mrs Nesbitt agreed to any of Pearl's requests to join them for Christmas dinner.

When the news came over the wireless that Hong Kong had fallen to the Japanese, it felt very gloomy. Pearl counted herself lucky she could wear her slippers and Jim's plaid dressing gown and mope by the fire. Poor Ruby had had to see out the day with their mum and dad.

The following week a letter dropped on the mat. Jim told her how much he missed her and how upset he was at not getting Christmas leave. He hoped to be home for the New Year before his posting.

Pearl sank down on the chair. She would be seeing him soon. But he was being posted. Where were they sending him? Would he know?

When she got to work, there was only her in the office. Em had asked for time off to be with her father, and Moira had a week's holiday. Pearl thought about Jim all the time. It was easy without Moira's interruptions.

Jim's heart was in his mouth as he strode down West Ferry Road. He was going to see Pearl at last. He couldn't wait. But he also had to call on his mum. The old girl had written and told him she wasn't so good after food poisoning at Christmas.

With only two days' leave, he had to see his mum first, as when he and Pearl were reunited, they wouldn't be getting out of bed. When he finally arrived at Villa Road, he gave a hearty knock on the door. He had a key, but for the life of him couldn't think where he'd left it. The door opened slowly.

'Mum?'

'Oh, son! Is that you?'

'Course it's me. Happy New Year.' He went to walk in, lowering his kit bag to the floor. He swept off his cap with a proud flourish, but he didn't get far before his mother

began to stagger. He caught her in his arms and sat her slowly down on the stair.

'Blimey, Mum, what's up?'

'My legs have gone.'

'Must've been the sight of my ugly mug. Sit there and I'll get you a drink.'

When he returned, she was waving a small black fan in front of her face.

'Drink this.'

She held out a shaky hand. 'Why didn't you write you were coming?'

'Thought I'd give you a surprise.'

'Have you seen Pearl yet?'

'No, I made a beeline here.'

She smiled. 'You're a good boy to put your mum first. Now help me into my chair.'

He helped her to the fire. It was full with big black nuggets. 'So what's been up then, Mum?' he asked warily.

'I had a bad attack on Christmas Day.'

'What was wrong?'

'I've got a delicate stomach and being all on my own—'

'On your own? Wasn't you with the Jenkinses?'

'I didn't like to trouble them.'

'But it would have been no trouble. Pearl wrote she was having you over!'

His mother folded her hands together and sighed. 'I know she has more than enough to do with her work and people of her own to see. I was quite happy here – and what's Christmas, after all, without your nearest and dearest? You and your father meant everything to me and just the sight of you now makes up for all the loneliness.'

Jim undid the buttons of his tunic. He leaned back and tried to listen attentively. But he was out of the picture and seemed to have lost the gist of things. He was surprised Pearl hadn't had his mother over for Christmas, though.

The old girl needed a bit of cheering up and he would have thought a couple of hours at the Jenkinses wouldn't have gone amiss.

'Does Pearl visit you?' he asked, wiping his sweating forehead with the coarse sleeve of his uniform.

'Occasionally, dear. But I don't want to put on her.'

'What about your neighbour? Still come in, does she?'

'You know how independent I am. Since your father went, I don't like to be a burden to others. After all, they've got their own lives to lead.' She coughed delicately and Jim leaned forward to pat her back. 'Better up than down, eh?'

'I've a weak constitution. But I do what I can for myself. The doctor is very good, but he's got his patients to see.'

'One good thing,' began Jim earnestly, 'there ain't been no bombs gone off round here. All the houses are still standing.'

'Yes, I'm grateful for small mercies. Now, you must be hungry. I'll get you something to eat.'

'No, I must get home.'

'Just a small snack while you keep me company?'

'Go on, then. Nothing fancy, mind.'

'I've got a nice chop in the pantry. You're in luck, dear, as I haven't had one since before the war, and there's no better person I'd like to cook it for.'

'But, Mum—'

'You're welcome to it. I can't tolerate meat at the moment. I eat very simply and don't spend a lot on myself. Now, sit back and put your feet up. Here's a newspaper. Your father used to enjoy the *Gazette*. You take after him in so many ways.'

Jim gave a resigned sigh. He wondered how long a chop took to cook. Taking off his jacket, he lifted his feet to the stool and picked up the paper. Lulled by the warmth and comfort of an easy chair, very soon he was asleep.

★

Pearl rushed into his arms. 'Jim, oh, Jim, I can't believe you're home.'

'Did you get my letter?'

'Yes. And I couldn't wait to get home from work today.'

'Miss me, did you?'

'You don't need to ask that.'

'Happy New Year, sweetheart.'

'I am happy now. Come in, it's freezing.'

Jim stamped his feet, blowing on his rough red fingers. 'They say we're gonna have snow.'

'I've lit a fire. But it's burned down as I thought you'd be here sooner.'

'Don't need a fire. You're enough to keep me warm. Give us a cuddle, you little cracker.'

She ran into his arms, feeling the unfamiliar rough cloth of his army greatcoat under her touch. He smelled the same, though; he was still her Jim. She drew her fingers over his cold cheeks. 'You've put on a bit of weight.'

'I'm glad to say you haven't.'

Pearl wriggled out of his grasp and turned round, showing off the suit she was wearing. It was a soft fawn, with pleats at the waist, and the jacket was lined. She'd bargained for half an hour at the market in an effort to purchase it, finally knocking the price down by half. New suits cost anything upwards of four pounds if they were good quality and she had been tempted to pay the full second-hand price of two guineas as it had very little wear. There was a small hole on the hem, easily hidden if you knew how, and so she'd got it for twenty-five bob.

'Well, do you like it?' she asked, batting her long eyelashes and making a pose.

'I like it. But I like what's in it, more.'

Pearl raised her eyebrows. 'Are you hungry?'

'You know the answer to that.' He tore off his coat and threw it aside. In seconds they were kissing and falling

against the door of the bedroom. Jim struggled with the buttons of her jacket. 'Bloody Norah, how do these undo?'

Pearl didn't care that her effort at a vegetable pie was wasted. It hadn't looked very appetizing anyway. And she wasn't bothered about the fire burning down. It was warmer in bed.

'Pearly-girl, I've missed you,' Jim growled passionately as she gripped his tough, strong shoulders and felt the muscles of his chest against her breasts.

'And I've missed you.'

She decided that this was one compensation for being apart. And taking full advantage of it, they made love into the early hours until they both fell asleep from exhaustion.

Jim pulled on his trousers and tiptoed to the kitchen. Pearl was fast asleep and she looked lovely, her blonde hair spread out over the pillow, her white skin gleaming in the moonlight. Although his mum's chop, roast potatoes and three veg had filled a very big hole, he was ravenous again. He might even find a beer in the larder. But though he searched, he found only Pearl's usual: half a loaf, a tin of Spam and a bowl of wilted veg. There was, however, a small wedge of cheese, an absolute luxury and he dived on it, eating it whole with an onion. He demolished the lot, then sank a mug of tea. In the barracks they had rations of sugar, but of course, Pearl wouldn't have thought of that. So he made do with a weak cup and powdered milk.

The fire had gone out in the living room, but the grey ashes still offered some warmth. He pulled his greatcoat round him and didn't bother with a light, moving aside the blackout to see what the weather was doing. Jack Frost was drawing frosty fingers on the windowpane. A bit different to the mildness of last year, he thought as he padded back to the armchair. Making himself a roll-up he rested his feet on the wicker stool and inhaled the smoke deep

into his lungs. Tomorrow was Saturday. Was Pearl at work? He hoped she'd got the morning off, but if not he'd busy himself with any jobs that needed doing.

Reaching out, he switched on the wireless. It was now positioned next to the armchair and he smiled. Pearl used to turn a deaf ear to the news. Now, however, it seemed as though she was cluing-up on world events.

A news bulletin began. The icy weather had helped the Soviet troops to push back the Germans in the Crimea. Manila had fallen to the Japanese and it looked like Borneo was next. The new head of Allied Forces in the south-west Pacific was Archibald Wavell, a Moniker sure to strike terror in the hearts of the enemy!

He sat up to listen, though, when a cut-glass accent talked of the newly reformed Eighth Army. A shiver went over him when he heard of a new Axis convoy of arms arriving at Tripoli. This could only mean one thing. The Desert Fox was preparing for El Alamein.

'Jim?'

Pearl's voice made him jump. 'Blimey, you gave me a fright.'

'I wondered where you'd gone.'

He switched off the wireless. 'Come and sit on me lap.'

She snuggled in close, wearing only her knickers. As he drew his coat around her, she kissed him and touched him and that was it. He had no control whatsoever when she was around and he found himself making love to her again.

They found time to eat, then made love again. Jim thought how lucky he was to have a wife who felt as eager as he did for sex. When they ended up on the floor in a heap, they began laughing.

'I prefer the bed.'

'So do I.'

He rolled over and scrambled to his feet. Wrapping his coat round her, he carried her back. Ten minutes later

they were lying side by side, staring up at the moon. Pearl twisted her dainty fingers through his.

'I feel greedy having you all to myself.'

'I like greedy girls.'

She giggled. 'You'd better only like one.'

'You know how I feel about you,' he murmured.

'When are you going back?'

'Sunday. I've got to report back by tea time.'

'You won't get posted straight away, will you?' she asked in alarm.

'It won't be long, I think.'

She threaded her arm around his waist. 'I'm not going to work in the morning. Let's stay in bed all day. I can pop down to Hemsley's for something to eat.'

'That'd be nice.'

'P'raps you can see your mum next time.'

'Don't worry, I called in today.' Jim knew instantly he'd said the wrong thing.

'You've seen her already?'

'On me way here. Thought I'd get it over quick.'

'How long was quick?'

'I just said hello.'

Pearl pushed him away. 'That's why you were late.'

'I thought it would be best.'

'I bet she told you I never go over.'

'She didn't at all.'

'I got off work especially early. And I made a bloody pie as well.'

He tried to take hold of her but she threw back the covers. He was on the point of bringing up Christmas and his old girl being left alone, but he thought better of it. It had upset him, though, to think of his mum wandering round an empty house on Christmas Day. He was surprised at Pearl. She could have put herself out a bit more to see that his mum had company.

Jim sighed as he lay alone. Why had even mentioned about going to Vale Road? Well, he had to, 'cos she'd have found out anyway from his mum. He'd leave her to cool off for a minute and have a fag. Climbing out of bed, he pulled the blackout curtains and switched on the light. Making a roll-up, he went into the other room to smoke it. Why did they always argue over his old girl? Granted, she was a bit difficult at times. But she wasn't a dragon, even though Pearl sometimes made her out to be.

On Sunday morning when it was time for Jim to go, Pearl wished they had spent more of their time making love rather than arguing. She sat at the kitchen table watching the husband she loved so much and wondered why Mrs Nesbitt felt such a thorn in her side. But Jim should have come home first. His mum only warranted an hour. Now they were to be separated again.

'Come on, love, buck up,' said Jim, speaking out of the side of his mouth. Carefully he used his cutthroat razor. 'It's a freezing cold day but look, the old currant bun is shining. We're alive and breathing, and we've got each other.'

'How can you be so cheerful?'

'It's easy when I look at you.'

'Oh, Jim, I don't want you to go.' It was all she kept saying. 'A weekend's not long enough.'

'Some of the blokes didn't even get that.'

'How will I know if you're in Africa?'

'I'll write to you.'

'But you can't say where in your letters!'

'Listen, we'll get a code going. If I tell you I miss me slippers, you'll know I'm in the desert. See? So keep up with the news and you'll have a fair idea of what's happening.'

'I only have to listen to Moira for that.'

He laughed, swirling the razor in the water and rinsing his chin by cupping his hands under the tap. He had

such a powerful body, Pearl thought longingly. He was all man, with long legs and lovely muscular thighs that had improved on the army diet. She knew every inch of his body and never wanted to let him out of her reach. Suddenly she jumped up and rushed to him. He turned, his eyes full of tenderness.

'I'm sorry I went on about your mum.'

'She ain't that bad.'

Pearl didn't say what she was really thinking, but stood on tiptoe and kissed him, pulling his head down with her hands so that their teeth met with a chink. She was wearing a soft blue slip and she deliberately let the straps slide down. She knew what she was doing and so did he. She didn't care if she made him late. He was her husband and the army had claimed him and she hated them for it. She didn't have the power to stop him going to war, but at least she could delay it.

Chapter 10

When would she hear from Jim, Pearl wondered as she walked home from work one cold Friday in February. Almost six weeks had passed since he'd gone back. Where was he? What was he doing and why hadn't he managed to send a letter? One page would do, a half, even.

Britain had experienced a freezing cold winter, one of the coldest in years. A snowstorm had been and gone. If he was in Africa, surely the censor would allow him to write about the weather? He'd told her all the blokes were always discussing it after reading letters from their wives and girl-friends. She would have thought he'd have something to

say on the subject, if not on anything else. Was the rest of the war always going to be like this – living on a knife edge until news came through?

Pearl knitted her brow in an attempt to concentrate on the food and fuel situation. The coalman didn't call as much these days. When he did, the sacks were half dust. Wood was scarce too, unless she paid a street kid to look for some. There were plenty of those about. Many had escaped evacuation and hung around street corners waiting for the nod from a housewife. It was so cold! On Saturday she was going to buy another eiderdown from the market. Without Jim beside her in bed, she couldn't get warm.

Hemsley's was packed out. Fitz's tall figure was head and shoulders above the others. When he saw her, he pushed the customers aside and hurried towards her.

Pearl saw the look on his face. 'What is it?' she asked, as he took hold of her arm and steered her away from the shop door.

'Pearl, we just got word a bomb's gone off,' he said, trying to sound calm.

'A bomb?'

'Yes, over Roper's Way. No need to panic. I'll come with you, if you want to go there. Hang on while I get me coat.'

'Oh God, no,' she gasped as Fitz ran back inside to pull on his jacket.

'Take care of yourselves,' shouted Gwen, but Pearl didn't hear. She had begun to run and didn't stop running till she got to Roper's Way.

The first figures she saw were the shiny suits and masks of the decontamination men. They were sweeping the road and moving slowly over the ground.

'It's our house and next door's,' whispered Pearl, staring at the two badly burned buildings. The windows were all blown out, leaving the tape hanging down like streamers. A

crack about a foot wide went from the top to the bottom of number twenty-four.

'Mum? Dad?' she screamed.

'Don't panic,' said Fitz. 'They might not have been in there.'

Pearl's gaze was on the walls of the front room, all covered in soot. But it was the crack that worried her most. The house looked as though it might collapse any moment.

She broke free and ran forward, but a warden grabbed her arm.

'Hold on, love, who are you?'

'Pearl Nesbitt,' she babbled. 'That's me mum and dad's house. They might be in there!'

'Hold your horses, love. No one goes near till the decontamination unit has finished.' He pulled her back. 'It's all right, your folks have been taken to a rest centre. They've had a shock, but they're all unharmed.'

Pearl felt her knees go weak. 'Oh, thank God. What about my sister?'

'A young woman was with them too.'

'Was it a raid? I didn't hear the siren go.'

'No. We think there was an explosion in the factory,' explained the warden. 'It went up with a bang and these house bought it too.'

'But that's where my dad works!'

'Yes, I know.'

'He ain't hurt?'

'No. It's Friday and the hooter went early. Most of the men had left before it happened. Your dad told me he'd gone off to get himself some baccy from the corner shop. He heard the bang from there. There was only one casualty, the caretaker, who we think's broke his leg as he was blown over. There wasn't any pedestrians as it was gone knocking-off time, and luckily your mum was shopping at the market and your sister walking home from work.'

'I can't believe it,' Pearl whispered to herself, and Fitz put his arm round her. 'What's going to happen to our house?'

'That I can't tell you.'

To Pearl it seemed impossible that something like this could happen when Roper's Way had survived nine months of the Blitz.

'What about number twenty-two?' she asked anxiously. 'It's an old couple, Mr and Mrs Sampson. I used to do their errands for them and Mum was always going in to see they were all right.'

'Not such good news there, I'm afraid. As you can see, it took a worse hammering than your place. The old boy was in bed with a cold and Mrs Sampson took a tumble down the stairs. They're both in hospital.'

Pearl closed her eyes. They were a lovely old couple, but very deaf. They'd lived in Roper's Way for years. So long in fact, Pearl couldn't remember anyone else living there.

'Once the gelly boys are finished we'll be able to start clearing,' said the warden gently. 'Meantime we'll have to find somewhere for your folks to live. Evacuation, no doubt.'

'Evacuation?' Pearl repeated. 'Mum and Dad would never leave the island.'

'They might have to.'

'They can live with me till our house is repaired.'

He frowned. 'Dunno if it will be, love.'

'But it's our home. They've got to mend it.'

'Yes, along with the rest of London. See that crack there? It's a bad sign. You won't be able to bodge that up, no.' He gave a sad smile. 'Well, come along and we'll get you off to be with your people. Your friend can be on his way.'

'I'd prefer to stay with her,' said Fitz. 'She's had a big shock.'

'Who are you?'

'A friend of the family.'

'Thanks, mate, but I'll see she's all right.'

'Don't worry about me, Fitz,' Pearl said shakily. She was still getting over what the warden had said. 'Go back to Gwen.'

'Are you sure?'

'Yes.' Pearl was led away by the warden. She didn't even have time to look back as a truck pulled up beside them. The driver climbed out and helped her in.

'Take this young lady to headquarters,' said the warden. 'She's related to the people in number twenty-four.'

There were two long benches facing each other under the big canvas roof. Pearl sat on one them, holding tight to the rail as the vehicle moved off. It had been a dreadful shock to see their home so black and battered. She had been rushed off quickly. But why? Were they going to break the news to her that something had happened to her family?

Pearl shielded her eyes from the big lights that shone down inside the building. Someone took her arm. 'This way, please.'

'Where are you taking me?' Pearl tried to hide the fear in her voice.

'You're going to see your family.'

'Are you sure they're all right?'

'Yes,' said the big woman in army uniform. 'You mustn't worry.'

'That's easy for you to say,' Pearl snapped, pulling away. 'You haven't just seen your home in pieces.'

'There's no use in creating a scene, my dear. Just calm down.'

Pearl was very angry. She had been robbed of her husband, now her old home had gone and they were telling her not to worry!

'Commander Knowles would like to speak to you. It's

called a debriefing, something that has to take place after a large, and in this case, unexplained event.'

She marched on and reluctantly Pearl followed. The female officer stopped and knocked hard on a door. It was opened by a tall man also in uniform.

'Ah, Mrs Nesbitt,' he smiled, reaching out to take Pearl's hand. 'I'm Commander Knowles. Please come in. That's all, thank you, Corporal.'

When they were alone, he gestured to a large leather chair. 'Do sit down and make yourself comfortable. Would you like some tea?'

'No. I just want to see my family.' Pearl sat on the edge of the chair.

'All in good time.' He took a seat behind his desk. 'This must seem rather cloak and dagger but we have to be on our toes. After an unexplained explosion, the Ministry of Defence has to investigate. Hence the decontamination unit.'

'But there wasn't a raid.'

'Exactly. So finding evidence is very important. It will tell us exactly why the factory blew up and unfortunately took several houses with it.'

Pearl shuddered. 'My parents and sister could have been killed.'

'Yes, this concerns us too.'

'How long will all these *investigations* take?'

He smiled and pleated his fingers. His steady eyes looked at her without blinking. 'A little while, I'm afraid. You see, one of our aims is not to cause panic amongst the general public. And in this case, as we don't know what actually happened, it's imperative that we be discreet about our work. It might take weeks, but more likely months.'

'Those men in shiny suits ain't very discreet.'

'No, but they are absolutely essential. When a major disturbance happens – and we are not under air attack

– then it's up to the special units to find out the cause. In cases such as this, we follow up every lead, yet try to keep a low profile. Gossip and panic soon spreads, and with them an undermining of the country's confidence.'

'But the factory only made things for ships. It was just an ordinary factory. Why should it blow up?'

'You are very astute, Mrs Nesbitt. The factory made steel, yes, and everything from bridges to blast furnaces. But also important parts for our warships and aircraft.'

'You mean someone might have done it deliberately?'

'What we have to remember,' he said evasively, 'is that the enemy know a great deal about us. Well-trained foreign saboteurs look exactly like you and me. They speak fluent English, mix freely with the public, sometimes marry and have families. If not detected, one insider can wreak havoc, disrupting the workforce or –' he paused – 'planting bombs.'

Pearl stared at him. 'You mean a spy could have blown Dad's factory up?'

'We investigate every possibility.'

'Do Mum and Dad know about this?'

'We have had the same conversation, yes.' Commander Knowles flattened his palms on the table. 'Now, our first concern is to get your family housed.'

'They can come and stay with me for the time being.'

'Have you enough space?'

'I've got two bedrooms. And there's only me there, now my husband, Jim, has been called up.'

'What's his name?'

'Jim Nesbitt. He's in the Engineers.'

The commander looked thoughtful. 'We shall have to talk about evacuation, if only for a short while.'

'But they've always lived on the island!' Pearl protested. 'Can't you get them somewhere here?'

'We shall have to see.'

Ten minutes later, Pearl was reunited with her parents

and Ruby. But not even her dad's big bear hug and her mum's whispered words of how lucky everyone had been to escape death, could comfort Pearl. They might still be alive but the war had taken everything else.

Two days later the back door opened and a hunched figure appeared. Unrecognizable in his woollen hat, Jim pulled down the collar of his greatcoat and grinned at his wife and sister-in-law.

'Jim!' screamed Pearl and Ruby together. They were standing at the sink, washing the breakfast dishes in cold water. Pearl dropped the cup on the drainer and rushed forward to be lifted off her feet.

He was laughing as she pulled off his hat. 'Hello, beautiful. Give us a kiss.'

She planted her lips on his and kissed him for all she was worth. Setting her gently down he scooped Ruby into an embrace.

'Oh, Jim, I thought you'd be in Africa.'

'Not yet.' The three of them hugged. Pearl forgot, like Ruby, that she was wearing her turban and dressing gown. 'I haven't even got me make-up on yet.'

'Nor me,' said Ruby, blushing.

'Why didn't you write to say you were coming?' asked Pearl breathlessly.

'Didn't know myself, did I? The CO got me a twenty-four-hours' leave pass after he heard from Commander Knowles. They told me all about Roper's Way.'

'I told him your name and that you was in the Engineers. I was in a bit of a state that night. But I didn't think he'd get you a pass.'

Jim grinned. 'Well, he did. Are Syd and Amy all right?'

The girls nodded. 'But Dad's out of work now,' Pearl explained. 'And we're managing here as Roper's Way don't look like it's going to be repaired very soon.'

'It must have been a shock.'

'The factory went up and took the houses with it.'

'What's going to happen?' asked Jim, taking off his coat.

'They want us to evacuate,' said Ruby.

'Blimey. Your mum and dad won't like that. Did they find out what caused it?' Jim rubbed his cold hands together.

'No, they're investigating,' said Pearl. 'They have to do that in case it's spies or something.'

'Did you manage to save anything?' Jim asked.

'We had our identity papers on us, and Mum had the ration books in her bag,' Ruby explained. 'We've got extra coupons for food and clothes. Pearl's given Dad one of your shirts and a pair of trousers. Mum and me are sharing Pearl's stuff.'

'Syd can have what he likes. I won't be needing civvies, will I?'

'We're going to the market to kit ourselves out,' said Ruby.

Jim put a hand on her shoulder. 'Must say, you're taking it very well.'

'Ain't no other way, is there?'

He hugged them again. 'Now, have you got something to eat for a hungry man?'

They both began to dash round the kitchen. Pearl was so excited to see Jim, she couldn't think what to do first.

'Look, sit down with Jim,' said Ruby, pushing them both in the other room. 'Make the most of the peace whilst Mum and Dad are at church. You won't get a word in edgeways when they're back. I'll make the tea.'

Jim's big hands pulled her against him when they were alone. 'Oh, Pearly-girl, I couldn't wait to see you. I was worried.'

'Why haven't you written?'

'You can blame the army for that. I've been on intensive training. Up at blooming four in the morning and on me

110

stop-and-goes till we're given the order to finish late at night. You remember that snow in January? We was out in it, running over the hills and down dales. Got right ballsed up when it started to thaw and we was swimming around in a load of mud. We were freezing, fed up, and I don't mind admitting I was ready to throw in the towel.'

'But you didn't, did you?' Pearl freed herself from his arms. Even the crackling fire her dad had built early that morning couldn't take the coldness from her words. 'You stuck it out.'

'I had to, love.'

'I would have pretended to run out of breath,' she said with a smile. 'And tried to get home to me wife.'

He clucked his tongue. 'Now don't start that, sunbeam.'

'I know, I know.'

He laughed and patted her hand. 'How are you all managing? Bit cramped, ain't it, with everyone?'

'They're lucky to be alive. The commander said it might be spies that blew up the factory.'

'Perhaps you can see why I've got to go to war.'

'S'pose so.'

'Every man is called on to do his duty. I was asked to do mine and I agreed. I could have walked away from it, but do you think I could live with meself afterwards?'

'You and your pride.'

He grinned, showing his strong white teeth. 'Now, Pearly-girl, what can I say that will make you happy?'

'Nothing, me broken heart will mend.'

Laughing softly, he slid his arms round her. 'Your heart's not broken, sweetheart, it's as sound as Big Ben. And now, for pete's sake, give us a kiss, a real one.'

She held his face between her hands and kissed him. It was a kiss of deep love and tenderness. She held all of her happiness in her hands, a man so precious to her that she couldn't bear to think of life without him. She felt

his strength and goodness, and she was beginning to see why he had done what he had. It had taken Roper's Way to make her realize that no one was safe in war, as he had warned her.

'Well, that was a surprise,' he croaked, looking into her eyes and searching her gaze. 'You ain't never kissed me like that before.'

'I've never felt like this before.'

'Blimey, I'll have to go away more often.'

'Just as long as you come back.' This time she spoke without bitterness. She was learning not to be selfish, but it was a very hard lesson.

'I'll always come back, remember that.'

'I'll try.'

'So we ain't gonna have our usual tiff?'

She smiled at the twinkle in his eye. 'No, I only want to make love.'

He jerked up an eyebrow. 'Bit difficult with your mum and dad and Ruby here.'

'Perhaps Dad will take Mum and Ruby to the pub tonight?'

'You reckon?'

'It's the only way we're going to cuddle.'

Jim pulled away as Ruby came in with the tea. They sat round the fire and discussed all that had happened. And when Syd and Amy arrived, there was yet another reunion.

All afternoon they drank tea and talked of the future. Pearl didn't want her parents or Ruby to evacuate. Even Jim said they were welcome to stay at Pride Place. But Pearl's mum and dad said they had come to a crossroads. With no home and no job to go to, her dad felt at a loss. Amy had heard of some nice places in the country that some of her evacuated friends had gone to. Places where Syd could have a real allotment, and perhaps chickens.

Pearl didn't want them to go. The commander had said he'd do his best, but what did that mean? He couldn't find another house on the island for them; all the empty ones were bombed and full of rats.

Pearl listened quietly to the conversation. Without Jim and her parents and Ruby she would be very lonely.

Later, Jim joked about square-bashing and life in the army. As usual, he was making fun of the mishaps. When at last he turned and looked at her, Pearl read the deep love for her in his eyes. Her thoughts would always be with him too, no matter where he went. But was her love strong enough to bring him safely home?

Chapter 11

'Gwen, I've got to sit down, my feet are killing me!' Pearl waddled into the shop and headed for the chair the Hemsleys kept by the counter. 'The warning went when I was on the bus. We had to get off and go to the shelter. It didn't last long and a good job too, as I desperately wanted a wee.'

'You never know what's going to happen after them raids in April and June.'

Pearl shuddered to think of the recent tit-for-tat bombing raids between April and June. The RAF had viciously bombed Lubeck and razed to the ground its ancient medieval buildings. In reprisal the Luftwaffe had used the Baedeker tourist guides to target similar towns and cities in Britain. As a result, everyone was nervous of what was going to happen next.

'Well, you're home now, so take the weight of your feet,'

said Gwen, pushing the chair under her. 'What did the doctor say?'

'I appear to be eating for two.'

Gwen laughed. 'All mothers do that. Not that I've had the experience meself.'

'Did you want kids, Gwen?'

'Yes and no. When you're young you do, but then the shop came along and filled the gap.'

Pearl wiped her sweating forehead with her hand. Placing her fingers on the bump under her cotton maternity dress she felt a small movement. She took a deep breath to find some air and the baby kicked again. 'Quick, come and have a feel. It's jumping all over the place.'

Gwen slipped her hand under Pearl's. 'It's a boy, got to be. Always on the go, and by the looks of you he's built like his dad. He'll be a whopper for sure.'

'I just hope he doesn't come out wearing overalls,' laughed Pearl as the kick came once more. 'Ouch, he just had a go at me ribs.'

'Are you putting your feet up? Your ankles are swollen.'

'Yes, Ruby sees to that. She fusses around like an old mother hen.'

'Good job she does. You've not got your mum to do it. How do they like the country?'

Pearl changed her position on the hard chair. 'Dad's got a job at the aerodrome and they've been allocated a council flat. It's on an estate, but Mum says it has two big bedrooms, a nice kitchen and living room, and a garden as well. All the houses are terraced and built in a square, so the backs meet in a sort of courtyard. It's very private, she said, and Dad has an allotment only five minutes away. You can smell the pig dung from the farm and buy eggs there too.'

'Eggs?' gasped Gwen, wide-eyed. 'What a treat!'

'They want Ruby to move down, but she don't fancy

114

leaving the island. And since I've left work, her bit towards the rent helps.'

'Me and Fitz were thinking about that. We could drop it till you get sorted.'

'The rent is low already.'

'We'd prefer you as lodgers rather than some noisy family who don't keep the place clean. And anyway, with Ruby staying with you, she can look after the baby. Give you a break.'

'Well, that would be helpful,' Pearl sighed. 'When I knew I was pregnant and had to give up work, I was really glad when Ruby said she'd stay with me.'

'Better having family than a lodger, love.'

'I don't think I'd like that much. Though I would if I was really down on me uppers.'

'I hope you've stopped your fire-watching duties?'

'The warden wouldn't let me do any more. Said I was a risk to life and limb, rolling about the place.'

Gwen laughed. 'You could always do a bit of knitting now.'

'I am, but the click–clack of the needles drives me barmy. I'm trying to knit all the baby's clothes from old jumpers and make some blankets for the first-aid parcels as well.'

'I've started on a few socks and hats for the baby,' Gwen admitted. 'White and lemon, just to be safe.'

Pearl giggled. 'Thanks. The last smock I did was red. As it's due near Christmas, I might call the baby Santa.'

They laughed and Pearl watched Gwen slice a thin rasher of bacon from a small joint. Her mouth watered.

'Have you seen your friends from work?' Gwen asked as she wrapped up the rashers.

'Em and Colin came over. They're still going strong.'

'Wedding bells, eh?'

'Might be.'

'Take this for a fry-up,' said Gwen, handing over the bag.

'And watch you take care. I don't like the look of those ankles.'

Pearl didn't like the sight of them either. Her ankles had always been slim, and it wasn't very nice seeing tree trunks in their place. Sometimes she thought of the miscarriage. She kept on asking Dr Cox if all was well and he'd said she was very healthy. It appeared that her 'quick canoodle' on the couch with Jim, when her parents had been staying there, had done the trick. A letter had gone off to Jim but she hadn't had a reply. The only letter she'd received had told her he was missing his slippers, his code for Africa.

'Well, I'd better go up. Thanks for the rashers.' Pearl trod heavily across the dusty floor. The bus ride to the doctor's had exhausted her on such a hot day.

'Oh, love, I nearly forgot,' Gwen shouted. 'You had a visitor today. A tall chap, good-looking and in uniform.'

Pearl froze. 'What sort of uniform?'

'Navy. And he wasn't no ordinary rating but an officer, by the look of his rings. Said he'd call back.'

Pearl's stomach dropped. Ruby hadn't said Ricky was due leave. She couldn't know. There was an hour to go before Ruby was home. Would he call again?

'See you later,' she mumbled, hurrying out.

When she got in, the baby kicked harder than ever before. A tight cramp went round her stomach. Full of dread, she sat on the chair. She didn't want to be alone when Ricky called. She prayed Ruby would be home very soon.

Jim had the trots and they were bad. Everything in the desert was magnified, if not by the sun, then the freezing cold nights when the boulders and silhouetted mountains of sand looked like a lunar landscape. He'd not thought for one minute that he'd be hiding behind a blooming great sand dune, clenching his buttocks and praying that his bowel movement wouldn't let him down. Rather, he'd

imagined himself on a camel like in the films, clad from head to toe in a sheik's outfit. But the reality was far different. There were no palm trees and belly dancers. Rations had been meagre: a daily helping of bread the size of his fist, a small tin of bully, a few hardtack biscuits and no tobacco. Some of the blokes had been surviving on this since before he joined the battalion in March. They were suffering the effects of diarrhoea and dysentery. He and Blackie had got a real dose.

As for the Boche, they were dead crafty. They'd shout out in English, trying to mislead them. But the boys of the Long Range Desert Group were no fools. And though Rommel's Afrika Korps had given a mauling to the Eighth Army, there was fresh hope. General Bernard Montgomery, the hero of Dunkirk, was their new commander.

A loud crack sounded suddenly. The unit's guns returned fire. The night lit up like a black-and-white picture show. All the blokes began to scurry here and there. They knew it soon could be hand-to-hand combat.

'You all right, Jim?' Blackie dropped beside him.

He nodded, relieved that he was with his old mate. Even though they hadn't recognized each other when their units had converged. Blackie had lost all his hair. He'd made Jim laugh when he admitted he was more likely to be called Baldy now. The sun had taken its toll on their skins. Blackie was the colour of coffee and Jim's own skin had been burned red. They were as thin as rakes.

Jim thought about yesterday. He had blown a man's head off and stared at the carnage. He'd told God that he was an engineer, not a bloody murderer. The next Boche bullet would have gone through his head if Blackie hadn't pulled him down. As he'd crouched low under the burning sun, he wished he'd listened to Pearl.

What was he doing here? He was no hero. He'd taken

a life. Probably more than one, but he'd not come face to face with the results before.

'Here, Jim, stick this in yer gob.' A dog end was pushed roughly into his mouth. 'Go on, chum, suck it in deep.'

Jim inhaled and Blackie slapped his back with a heavy hand. 'Listen, we gotta think of this as a game. Forget yesterday. It's them or us, ain't it?'

Jim nodded, coughing up phlegm. 'Just getting me bearings,' he managed to gasp. 'We've been cooped up in this desert for so long I'm losing me noddle.'

'It's that bloody helmet. It's too big for you.'

A runner scrambled over and drew his hand over his sweating face. 'New orders. We're reorganizing all the way up to Alam Halfa.'

Jim and Blackie exchanged glances. 'Where's that?'

'It's a bloody great ridge ten miles behind the front line.'

'Ten miles? You've got to be joking.'

The young soldier shrugged. 'Wish I was. We've been thrown in the deep end. Listen, tomorrow we're putting a road through a minefield. You'll be needed up front, Jim. They send the Engineers in first to clear the gaps. And, Blackie, you're with the first of the Churchills.'

Blackie groaned. A volley of gunfire cracked in the night.

'And another thing,' shouted the runner, 'it's almost impossible to tell us from them. So watch your arses.'

Jim crouched on his unsteady knees, his eyes alert for any movement. Blackie dug in beside him and for a while there was silence. Jim felt his stomach tighten. Christ help him if he was still throwing up by morning.

'What's that?' shouted Blackie in the darkness. 'Who goes there?'

Jim gave a low chuckle. 'It's me, you daft bugger. These trots are giving me wind.'

Blackie laughed aloud in the desert night.

*

118

The evening breeze blew in through the windows. Pearl had her feet up on the couch and was listening to the wireless. There had been heavy Allied losses at Dieppe. Lord Louis Mountbatten had denied that Allied forces had attempted a full-scale invasion of Europe. Rather it was a reconnaissance exercise against the enemy. But with so many casualties, people felt it was another cover-up.

She looked around the kitchen and wished Jim was here. If he was, Ricky wouldn't dare to call. Pearl wondered if it might have been better for Ruby to move to Abingley with their parents. Where would Ricky stay if he was on leave? How long was he going to be home?

Suddenly Pearl heard the sound of laughter. Her heart took a leap as she listened to the steps on the stairs.

'Pearl, look who's here!' Ruby called out as she burst in the door and hurried through. 'Ricky was waiting for me at the factory gates.'

Ricky slid off his officer's cap as he followed. 'Hello, Pearl.'

His dark eyes found hers and she looked away. 'I hope you don't mind me calling?'

'Course she don't!' Ruby exclaimed as she glanced at Pearl.

'I'm sorry to hear about Roper's Way.'

'Thanks,' Pearl replied coolly.

Ruby clung to his arm. 'We're all safe, and that's what matters.'

He smiled at Ruby. 'You echoed my thoughts. Bricks and mortar aren't important when lives are at stake.'

'Let's go and sit in the kitchen. We can catch up on the news.' Ruby pulled him after her.

Pearl thought miserably how happy they looked together. Did he really love her? Would Ruby carry out her desire to sleep with him?

After a while, Ruby appeared, straightening her blouse. She looked flushed and excited. 'Oh, Pearl, I'm so happy.'

'Yes, I can see.'

'I couldn't believe it when I saw him standing at the factory gates. All the girls nearly fell over themselves when I told them who it was. He looks so handsome in his uniform.'

'Where's he going to stay?'

'Don't know. Haven't had time to ask.' She giggled as she patted her hair. 'I took me turban off quick. I wished I could have looked more glam when he met me at work.'

'How long has he got?'

'Two weeks. He's been in sickbay for six, which is why he didn't write, as he didn't want to worry me. His ship got sunk and he was rescued.'

'Is he all right now?'

'He looks it to me.' She giggled again.

'Does he have any family to stay with?'

'No, don't think so. Pearl, can he stay to supper?'

'What, here?' Pearl lowered her feet to the floor.

'Of course here.' Ruby's chin stuck out as she frowned. 'After all, he has been away a year and got shipwrecked. But if you don't want him around, then we'll go out.'

'It's not that,' Pearl lied. 'I haven't got much in.'

'Gwen gave us some tinned fish. And there's spuds in the larder. I'll do something with the carrots and onions – you won't have to lift a finger.'

Pearl felt very selfish and didn't have the heart to refuse. Although she didn't want Ruby to think that she was encouraging a regular habit. But Ruby looked so crestfallen at her hesitation that she finally nodded. 'I'll cook the dinner,' she said standing up and wishing her ankles weren't so swollen. Her utility maternity dress looked like a tent above them. 'I'm sure you've both got lots to talk over.'

Ruby ran to hug her. 'Oh, thanks. I knew it would all be all right in the end.'

As she worked in the kitchen Pearl listened to the soft

murmur of voices in the living room, then a few muffled sounds; she knew how desperate Ruby would be for those kisses. But would Ruby fall straight into bed with him? And if so, where would they go?

She mashed the smelly sardines, trying not to think of what Jim would say if he knew Ricky was eating a meal under his roof. But Ruby was her only sister after all. And this was a one-off occasion.

Pearl jumped as the pan of potatoes sizzled loudly on the stove. 'Ouch!' She leaned against the draining board, as the baby kicked. Lowering the pan to the draining board, she took a deep breath. The midwife had told her to try to relax when this happened, breathe in and out slowly. Closing her eyes, she went through her routine as the tightness round her stomach wore off. When she opened them, she saw herself in Jim's shaving mirror. Sweat glistened on her brow. Her Veronica Lake hairstyle had turned into lank, uncombed waves on her shoulders. The bloom of motherhood had vanished under the tension brought on by Ricky's arrival.

To think, she used to be so particular about her appearance. Now she had huge ankles and a large belly. If only Jim were here. None of this would be happening. If he hadn't enlisted, Ruby would have gone to live in Abingley. Ricky would have gone to visit her there. Life in Pride Place would have been undisturbed. But that was not to be. Now she had to make the best of a bad situation.

During the meal, Ricky described his time at sea. The Arctic convoys were considered very dangerous, but he seemed to enjoy the excitement, his dark eyes shining as he told them of his adventures. Pearl listened to his smooth voice as he described the valiant merchant ships under threat from the many U-boats. For a moment she lost herself in the vivid picture he painted. As much as the British warships tried

to protect their little brothers and the supplies destined for England, there were many losses. Almost 100,000 tons of cargo had sunk to the bottom of the Arctic Ocean. Despite the Royal Navy's best efforts, only eleven of the thirty-seven merchant ships of his convoy had made it. He admitted that he had been remarkably lucky when his ship had been torpedoed by a U-boat. The light cruiser had been badly disabled and the crew had been rescued from the freezing sea as they huddled in a dinghy. Since then he had spent six weeks in sickbay.

'That was delicious, thank you,' Ricky said, leaving nothing on his plate.

'Yes, it was,' grinned Ruby. 'She's getting better.'

Pearl looked at the three empty dishes. 'I'm afraid there's no pudding.'

'Doesn't matter,' said Ruby.

'I couldn't eat a thing more,' agreed Ricky.

Pearl began to collect the plates but Ricky protested. 'You shouldn't be doing chores in your condition. It was enough that you cooked dinner. Leave the clearing away to us.'

Ruby nodded. 'Yes, go and sit down. You've been on your feet all day.'

Pearl didn't argue. She sat on the couch and lay back ...

It seemed much later when she heard Ruby's voice.

'Pearl?'

She sat up, blinking. 'I must have dropped off.'

Pearl looked at Ricky, who was sitting in the chair by the fire. Memories of the feelings she'd once had for him all came back in a rush.

'I waited to say goodbye,' he said quietly.

Pearl felt the baby move. She gave a little whimper.

'Are you all right?' Ricky and Ruby asked together.

'He don't like sharing his space with the sardines.'

Ricky laughed. 'You think it's a boy?'

122

'He's always on the go,' Ruby smiled as she sat beside Pearl. 'And November seems a long way off.'

'November?' Ricky repeated. 'Then this Christmas will be a very special one.'

'I hope Jim will be home,' Pearl said quickly. 'Perhaps he can get special leave.'

'Ruby said he's in the desert,' Ricky said as he adjusted his long legs under the sleek navy twill of his trousers and sat forward. 'Our boys in Africa are having it tough. I heard through the grapevine there was very little progress for some while, as Auchinleck fell out of favour with Churchill. But now they have a new leader, General Bernard Montgomery. The campaign should hot up.'

'We've read about Monty in the paper,' said Ruby, looking at Pearl. 'They say he has all the looks that Winnie hasn't, and the brains to go with it.'

Ricky nodded. 'I can vouch for the brains. He's already seized the initiative when Rommel tried to push into Egypt. The danger will be when Rommel regroups; the battle for El Alamein will be the most crucial of the desert war.'

Pearl felt alarmed. Would Jim be in this battle?

'I must go now.' Ricky rose to his feet. 'I've kept you late enough. Goodbye and thank you for the excellent meal,' he said quietly, sliding an arm round Ruby's waist.

After they'd left, Pearl sank back against the cushions. Ricky had frightened her with his talk of the battles in Africa. A year ago Jim hadn't known one end of a gun from the other. In wartime, it seemed men became machines in the blink of an eye.

When Ruby come back she was smiling. 'Oh, Pearl, he's my Mr Wonderful.'

'Where's Mr Wonderful staying?' Pearl asked, unable to keep the strain from her voice.

But Ruby didn't hear it. 'In a hostel, up Poplar. I wish I

could take time off work to be with him but I can't.' Ruby sighed as she sat down. 'If I did I'd lose me job. And Mr Brewer has been very good to me.'

'Yes, he has.'

'Although I was tempted,' Ruby added with a grin.

Pearl saw the look of love in her eyes. Her little sister was well and truly besotted.

All week Ruby didn't stop to gossip with the factory girls and stroll lazily back home in the evening. She also put aside her first-aid courses and could hardly eat for excitement. No sooner than she had gulped down her tea, than she went to prepare her clothes for the evening. Though nothing had been said, she hadn't invited Ricky in again. Each evening they met outside the shop. For a while, Pearl could hear their voices, then she would go to the window and watch them walk away. They were always hand in hand or had their arms round each other. Pearl ached for Jim.

She listened for every bit of news from the desert after Ricky had told them about El Alamein. But mostly it was Europe that took the headlines. The Germans had killed 50,000 Jews in Warsaw and the British air force had dropped 100,000 bombs on Dusseldorf. How could humanity be doing this, Pearl wondered, at exactly the same time as she was bringing a new life into the world? Would the war be over by November? She knew it couldn't be, but she still held out hope.

When a letter arrived from her parents, asking her to go to Abingley, she knew the tiring journey was beyond her.

On the Sunday of Ricky's last week, Ruby came home in the early hours. 'We've been to this little club in the Strand,' she told Pearl excitedly. 'Ricky bought us cocktails and oh, Pearl, it was so glamorous. Afterwards we walked all along the Embankment.'

'I hope you'll be able to get up in the morning.' Pearl hadn't been able to sleep as the baby was so restless.

'Don't spoil me fun.'

'I'm not. I only want what's best for you.'

'If you did, you would have made Ricky feel at home,' Ruby said resentfully.

Pearl shrugged. 'I haven't felt up to company.'

'Then you should have said,' Ruby answered in a high voice. 'There was me thinking it was to do with us.'

Pearl didn't want another argument over Ricky. 'You can bring him up for supper tomorrow night.'

But Ruby tossed her head. 'As it happens, I'm having the day off from work. Ricky is taking me up West to stay at a hotel.'

Pearl's jaw dropped.

'Don't look at me like that,' Ruby scowled. 'It's only one night.'

'Does Mr Brewer know?'

'Not yet. I'll just say I was sick.' Ruby waved her hands. 'Don't look so shocked, everyone does it once in a while. What difference is one little white lie going to make?'

'All right, all right.' Pearl gave up. 'You're old enough to know what you're doing.' Just then the baby moved.

'Pearl?' Ruby hurried beside her.

'I'm all right.'

'What shall I do?' Ruby grabbed her hand anxiously. 'Shall I go for the doctor?'

'No, don't fuss.'

'Is it a labour pain?'

Pearl felt the sweat trickle in between her breasts. 'Help me up, will you?'

Ruby took her arm. 'If you're trying to put me off babies, you're doing a good job.'

Pearl grinned. 'Now I've got to go to the lav.'

'I'll come with you. It's dark out there.'

'Don't worry, I've put a pail in me room. But come here and say good night.'

They hugged, both careful to avoid the bump. A faint whiff of soap from Ruby's skin took Pearl back to Roper's Way. As kids they would sit in the tin bath in front of the fire, spreading soap over each other's backs. It seemed such a long time ago now.

'You can borrow me blue frock tomorrow,' Pearl said, happy to see the smile back on Ruby's face. If only she could share Ruby's joy, but the man her sister loved was Ricky. And she could never tell Ruby of the heartache he had caused or warn her that it could happen again.

Chapter 12

When Ruby came home the day after next, she rushed into the kitchen. Her cheeks were flushed and her eyes were sparkling. 'Pearl! Pearl! I've got some wonderful news!'

Pearl looked up from the draining board where she was preparing the vegetables for dinner, a smile on her face. But it soon faded as Ruby threw down her bag and extended her hand. 'What do you think of this? It's a real sapphire and diamonds. Ricky told me to pick the ring I liked and not worry about the cost.'

Pearl gazed at the sparkling cluster. 'He bought you a ring?'

'Yes,' said Ruby excitedly, 'and now we're officially engaged.'

Pearl dropped the half-peeled potato and shook her head slowly. 'Engaged? You never said anything about being engaged.'

'That's because I hadn't been asked. Do you like it?'

Pearl wanted to pinch herself and wake up from this bad dream. 'Yes, course, but it's come as a bit of a shock.'

'It was to me, an' all,' nodded Ruby, turning the ring and pushing it under Pearl's nose. 'I nearly fainted when he asked. We was outside this jewellers in Oxford Street. He says, let's go in and have a look round. Well, I thought he was joking, but went in . . . and, oh, Pearl, all the customers all wore these posh clothes, even the salesgirl did.' Ruby took a quick breath. 'And then he asked to see the rings. Me heart nearly burst out of me chest – I couldn't believe it.'

'Neither can I,' Pearl croaked.

Ruby twisted her hand, gazing at the ring. 'It cost nine guineas, to be precise.'

'That's a lot of money.'

'I won't wear it at work, of course. I took it off today, but showed it to all the girls. You should have seen their faces.'

Pearl wiped her hands on her apron, trying to still the feeling of panic inside her. She wanted to say to Ruby that she had done a reckless thing. That she should have thought it over and not rushed into such a big step. But she knew it was too late. The sparkle in Ruby's eyes was as bright as the diamonds. Speaking her mind wouldn't achieve anything now. They would only argue again and the rift between them grow bigger.

'Did Mr Brewer say anything about you being off?' she asked cautiously.

'No. I said I ate something that upset me.'

Pearl sat down at the table. Her knees had gone weak. 'What was the hotel like?'

Ruby continued to stare at her ring. 'I wish you could have seen it. There was a bathroom next to it with hot and cold written on the taps. There was even soap and lovely white towels . . .'

Pearl felt more wretched than ever. She wanted to shake Ruby by the shoulders and tell her that what she had done could only bring unhappiness. But now all she could do was stand on the sidelines and watch as their affair gathered strength.

'You are happy for me, aren't you?' Ruby said, suddenly aware of the silence and Pearl sitting quietly at the table.

'It's all happened so quickly.'

'I know. I can shout that I'm engaged from the rooftops if I like.' Ruby twirled round and lifted her arms. 'Oh, Pearl, I'm the happiest girl in the world.'

Just like I was, thought Pearl desperately, when Ricky told me that I was the only girl he had ever loved.

'Listen, is that the siren?' Ruby said, suddenly standing still.

Pearl had so many troubled thoughts in her mind, even the siren seemed far away.

Ruby snatched up her bag. 'Let's go down to the storeroom. Gwen and Fitz shelter in there now. I can show them me ring. It will take our minds off the raid.'

Pearl put on her coat and followed Ruby down the stairs. When they were all seated on boxes in the storeroom, listening to the drone of the bombers, Ruby showed off her ring.

'Is it real diamonds?' Gwen asked, bringing the oil lamp close.

'Yes, and a sapphire.'

'You're very lucky,' nodded Fitz. 'These days a lot of girls don't get more than a trinket from Woolworths.'

'I know.' Ruby glanced at Pearl. 'I'll have to start me trousseau.'

'Yes,' Gwen nodded. 'You'll want to save up for your bottom drawer. Have you told your mum and dad?'

'No, but I will when I see them.'

'Don't a bloke ask the dad first?'

Ruby tossed back her head. 'Like going down on one knee, that's a thing of the past.'

'When do you plan to marry?' Fitz enquired as he chucked a mouldy cabbage in the leftovers' sack.

'Don't know. It's difficult in wartime.'

A succession of loud thuds stopped them from talking as dust came down from the ceiling. Pearl slipped her hand through Ruby's arm and Fitz sat close to Gwen until the all clear went.

'That wasn't long,' sighed Gwen as Fitz opened the door and daylight flooded in. 'Let's hope the Luftwaffe ain't coming back this way.'

'Could be flying up north to the ports,' said Fitz.

'You take care of that ting-a-ling, young lady,' called Gwen as Pearl and Ruby went upstairs. 'Take it off when you wash up. You don't want it going down the plughole.'

'No chance of that,' Ruby shouted as they let themselves in. 'It's going back in its box this minute.'

All the same, she wore it that evening. Pearl listened to Ruby dreaming her plans for the future. Just like Pearl, she wanted a white wedding, but she would rather wear a new dress and not their mother's. It would be satin, with a long veil, accompanied by matching shoes and gloves. Ricky had suggested they go to Scotland for their honeymoon. When he had joined his ship at Scapa Flow he had travelled through some beautiful countryside. One hotel in particular had caught his eye, on the edge of a loch, surrounded by mountains and forests.

But in all this fairy tale, Pearl noted, Ruby didn't refer to their stolen night of bliss. Had it been as perfect as she hoped? Pearl couldn't bring herself to ask about it.

A few days after Ricky had returned to his base, the leaves began to fall from the few trees that had survived the Blitz. September ended on a warm note but Pearl yearned for the

cooler weather. Her back ached, no matter what position she sat or laid in. It was better to keep moving, but if she did, her ankles swelled more. The stuffy heat exhausted her.

Walking up and down the stairs was a big effort. Other than a bus ride to the doctor's she rarely ventured far. The walk to Vale Road from the bus stop was too far and she'd had no word at all from Jim's mother.

After what Ricky had said about El Alamein, Pearl listened every day to the wireless. Bulletins about the desert campaign were now frequent. It was reported that Monty was achieving a slow but sure advance against Rommel, who was rumoured to be ill and his troops' morale at an all-time low. This had given the Allies fresh hope.

Then, in early October Pearl heard from Jim. The letter landed on the mat one Saturday morning. He had finally received the news of the baby and was overjoyed at becoming a father. It was all he wrote about, that and his slippers, their code for the desert. It wasn't a long letter, but it was full of love and hope.

'At last he got my letter about the baby,' Pearl said excitedly to Ruby one evening. 'He thinks it'll be a boy too.'

'Why does he think that?' Ruby asked distractedly.

'He was the only child and one of his grandmothers had only boys.'

'Does it run in families, then?'

'I don't know. It might do.'

Ruby sat down on a kitchen chair and dragged off her turban. 'Did you tell him about me and Ricky?'

Pearl thought of Jim's reaction when he knew. 'Not yet. Haven't had time.'

Ruby looked away, heaving a sigh. 'Don't say I told you so, but I was relieved to get my monthlies. It was only one night we was together, but even so, I've been worried.'

'Have you changed your mind then?' Pearl asked hopefully.

'What about?'

'Well, being engaged to Ricky whilst there's a war on.'

Ruby sat round. 'No, not that.' The colour rushed to her cheeks. 'It's something more personal. Can we go in and sit in the warm?'

With a sinking feeling Pearl accompanied Ruby to the living room. What was she going to say? As they sat down on the couch, Pearl thought how young and innocent her sister looked. Her working trousers and blouse were like a school uniform, and with her legs tucked under her, and wearing no make-up, she looked no more than fifteen. Pearl felt huge in her maternity smock from the second-hand stall. It was shapeless and dull. She wanted to fit into small sizes again, clothes that weren't utility or cast-offs.

'Pearl,' said Ruby slowly, turning to look at her, 'should making love hurt?'

Pearl could only swallow. This was a conversation she really didn't want. 'What do you ask that for?'

'Did it happen with you?'

Pearl felt guilty. Jim hadn't been her first lover but she couldn't tell Ruby that.

'I had to ask Ricky to stop,' Ruby said before Pearl could answer. 'It was painful and not like it is on the films. The girls always wake up in bed with smiles on their faces.'

'Don't forget, they're only acting.'

'Yes, but ain't it like that?'

'Didn't they tell you at the clinic?'

'No, they just gave me these things to put inside. But I was so nervous on the night, I couldn't.'

'No wonder you were worried about your monthlies.'

'I didn't think I would be.'

'So you kept saying.'

'It was romantic to start with,' Ruby went on. 'We undressed and he kissed me—'

131

Pearl drew a breath. 'Ruby, you shouldn't be telling me all this.'

Ruby looked surprised. 'Why not? What's changed between us? We've always told each other everything. And anyway, you're the only one I can ask.' She looked on the verge of tears. 'Especially as I don't know enough about sex.'

'Then why do it?' Pearl said before she could stop herself.

Ruby burst into tears. She buried her face in the pillow, her shoulders shaking.

Pearl felt a wave of deep regret and, putting her arms around her, she gently patted her shoulder. 'Don't cry, Ruby. What's done is done. At least the worst didn't happen.'

'I'm beginning to see there's a lot more to romance than having a ring on your finger,' stammered Ruby, her face wet as she got out her handkerchief and blew her nose. 'I feel such a dimwit.'

'You're not at all. But you've just had your first experience. You've become a woman.' Pearl knew from her own experience that Ricky, dressed in his naval uniform and being so handsome, cut a very dashing figure, and it was no wonder that Ruby had fallen for him. The same had happened to her six years ago, and she couldn't blame Ruby for falling for his charms. There was a glamour about him that most women wouldn't be able to ignore. But appearances weren't everything, as she had found to her cost, and she'd tried her hardest to make Ruby aware of this without being able to tell her the real truth.

'I've been thinking about going up to see Mum and Dad,' Ruby said, sniffing. 'Would you come with me?'

'Like this?' Pearl looked down at her stomach.

'Would it be very uncomfortable on the bus?'

'I couldn't sit still for that long. And I'd want to wee.'

'I just thought I'd ask.'

'I'd rather wait till after the baby.'

'I was thinking about going next Saturday,' Ruby murmured, twisting her damp hanky. 'I want to show them me ring.'

'It's up to you.' Pearl struggled to stand up. 'I've got to move, 'cos my back is murder.'

Ruby laughed as Pearl toppled back. 'You showed a nice bit of leg, then.'

'I don't recognize them.'

Ruby giggled.

'I'm glad you find that funny.' Pearl smiled at herself even though she felt she would never look feminine again. At least Jim didn't have to see her this way. Not that he would have cared. He would have made a joke and cuddled her as only Jim could. She missed him so much. Especially now, when the problem of Ruby and her love life was overshadowing everything.

Gwen, who was serving a customer, waved to Pearl from inside the shop. Pearl reached out for the lamppost. Her face was bathed in sweat. The pale sun had long ago disappeared as she had made her way home from her short walk to the park bench. The need for fresh air and exercise had driven her out. The pain was like the one she'd had before, starting from the back and making its way to the front. As the baby kicked she tried to signal Gwen. But by the time the customer had gone, Pearl was in trouble. The pain was turning to agony.

At last Gwen saw her and came hurrying out. 'Pearl, what's wrong?'

'I think it's me time.'

'What?'

'I know I'm early but it feels like it.'

'Oh Lordy, can you walk to the shop?'

'Don't know.' Pearl looked at the shop window. It went in and out of focus. Another pain came. She cried out.

'Oh!' Gwen pointed to the ground. 'Is that your waters that have broke?'

Pearl gazed down at the wet puddle. She felt very frightened. Was she going to give birth on the pavement?

'Wait there, ducks. I'll get Fitz to help us. He's in the storeroom.'

All Pearl could do was cling to the lamppost. 'Jim, where are you? I need you more than ever now. Why did you go off to that bloody desert?'

She was still talking to Jim when Fitz arrived. 'Come on, love, we'll get you inside.'

Between them they took her arms and helped her into the shop. 'I've got to push,' Pearl whimpered. 'Another pain's coming.'

She slumped to the floor by the counter. She knew she was going to have the baby. But it was too early. Was the baby going to die? Was she going to die? Would Jim ever see his son?

A man came in the door and stood still. 'Blimey, what's going on here?'

'She's going to have a baby,' cried Gwen, getting on her knees and holding Pearl's hand. 'Do you know Sally Crutcher, the midwife?'

The man nodded and dropped his straw shopping basket.

'She's number fourteen in the next road. Go and knock for her,' Gwen shouted. 'And tell her to hurry, there's a baby on the way.'

Fitz went down on his haunches. 'We'd better get you on a bed, love.'

'I want to push,' was all Pearl could say as she opened her legs.

'Oh Gawd!' Fitz jumped up, his face white.

Pearl knew she wouldn't be long in having the baby. She heard Gwen telling Fitz to close the shop and find some old sheets.

'Don't leave me,' Pearl gasped in between pains.

'I won't, love. But don't push yet,' Gwen said gently. 'Try to wait till Sally comes.'

Pain filled Pearl's entire body. Sweat and tears mingled on her cheeks. All she wanted to do was push.

'Good girl, it won't be long now.'

Pearl felt as though she was bursting with pain as Sally attempted to deliver the baby. It had seemed an eternity as she tried to persuade the baby's head into position. Thoughts went through Pearl's mind of the miscarriage. Was something stopping the baby from coming? Would he survive?

'Nearly there,' Sally said encouragingly. 'But only bear down when I tell you.'

'I want to now.'

'Breathe in and out instead. Wait for your next contraction.'

Pearl was in a world of her own. She could see Jim's face and hear his voice telling her he loved her. She was in the desert in the hot sun and there was only the heat, the flies and the dust. And bodies of the fallen. She couldn't have a baby here. If only Jim could understand . . .

An iron bar struck her stomach. She cried out, her nails sticking in to Gwen's hand. The makeshift bed of blankets and newspaper felt hard underneath her, but she didn't care about that. She didn't care about anything, except getting the baby out.

'Another contraction,' Sally promised, 'and we'll have the little darling with us.'

Pearl grunted, groaned and shrieked according to Sally's instructions.

'One last push now.'

With the last of her strength, she pushed. Then she heard a wonderful sound, a far-off cry that was like an echo. It was a sound she would remember all her life.

The faces around her were full of wonder. Fitz removed his spectacles and polished them on his overalls. Gwen brushed a tear from her eye as Sally wiped the tiny pink body clean.

Gwen clapped her hands together. 'Oh, Pearl, she's beautiful!'

'She?' Pearl was shocked. Not a son as expected, but a daughter. 'Are you sure?'

'Yes!' everyone said together. Sally wrapped the baby in a towel. Her eyes were squeezed tight in her tiny red face. Her knuckles were clenched as though she too, had fought a battle. Her bald head had a sprinkling of marmalade hairs.

Presenting her to Pearl, Sally smiled. 'Congratulations. She's early, but all seems well.'

Pearl held her baby in her arms. She was tiny, the smallest living body she had ever seen or touched. She was perfectly formed, with ten fingers and ten toes. Her mouth was a cupid's bow.

'She's a stunner,' said Fitz, a catch in his throat.

'The prettiest!' Gwen whispered.

Pearl nodded. 'I can't believe she's arrived on the floor.'

'Good job I swept it this morning,' said Fitz.

Pearl kissed the tiny head. 'I'm glad I did all me knitting in white. I only chanced one matinée coat in blue.'

'Now we can get cracking on pink,' said Gwen.

Sally gently pushed Pearl's legs apart. 'We aren't quite finished yet.'

'I've not got another one up there, have I?' Pearl gasped.

Sally laughed. 'No, but we have to clamp off the cord and there's the afterbirth to come.'

Pearl didn't mind about that now. She had her baby safely in her arms. Her and Jim's daughter, to make their family complete.

'I think I'll make tea,' said Fitz, getting up quickly. 'Don't know about everyone else, but I need it. All I can say is, I'm glad I'm not a woman.'

'I've always said that men have got it easy,' grinned Gwen as her husband lumbered away. 'Now perhaps you'll believe me.'

After he had gone, Pearl frowned. 'She's stopped crying. Is that normal?' She was still worried that things wouldn't be right.

'She'll be crying soon enough for her dinner,' said Sally with a chuckle. 'When I'm finished here, we'll get her on the breast.'

'I wish Jim could see her.' Pearl gazed at her daughter. 'When the pains were bad, I thought I was in the desert. I thought, I can't have me baby in all this sand. I reckon I know how Mary felt when she was in the stable with all that straw and cow dung.'

Sally and Gwen were still laughing when Ruby rushed in. She stopped dead at the sight of the afterbirth.

'What's that?' she screamed.

'Just the placenta.'

'Ruby, come and look, it's a girl!' called Pearl.

Ruby's face had drained of colour. She stepped closer and saw the baby. Then, gasping aloud she dropped on her knees. 'Did you say she?'

'Yes.'

'Oh, Pearl, I'm an aunty at last.'

'And I'm a mother,' Pearl whispered as she looked down at her beautiful new offspring.

Chapter 13

It was Sunday morning, two days after the birth, and Ruby was rocking the baby in her arms as she paced round the

living room. It had been a long night with the baby's continual crying.

Pearl stretched her back as she sat down on the chair. She was still in her dressing gown and slippers, though Ruby had dressed. There was no fire either, as everything had taken second place to the baby. 'Is she asleep yet?'

Ruby nodded. 'Nearly. With all that screaming she's done, no wonder.'

'I'm sorry she woke you. I didn't think you could hear.' Pearl had the cot beside her bed. She had bought it from Percy Flint, the rag-and-bone man, and had looked at it empty for so long that now it seemed strange that it was so full of life. The wooden bars were a bit scratched but it was clean.

'She's only two days old,' Ruby said as she gazed down at the tiny bundle. 'I expect babies cry at lot at first.'

'She's got a healthy pair of lungs.'

Ruby pulled down the blanket under the baby's chin. 'She's lovely when she's asleep.'

Pearl grinned. 'Has she put you off babies?'

Ruby sat slowly down. 'No, course not. But I realize I'm not ready to be a mother. I ain't even a wife yet.'

'At least you'll have some experience.'

'Do you want another one after what you went through?' asked Ruby.

'Mum told me women always forget the pain.'

'What will she say when she hears you gave birth in a shop?'

'I wish they was still living at Roper's Way.'

'You should see their new flat,' said Ruby. She had told Pearl that it was very big and had a garden. Pearl wished she could have gone with Ruby to see it.

'And Dad's got this lovely allotment. If you saw it all you'd understand why they like it there. There's hardly any raids either, only the planes having dogfights over the fields.'

Pearl knew that Ruby was impressed with Abingley. Although she'd only stayed there for one night, she had plenty of vivid descriptions to pass on.

'They was a bit surprised when they saw the ring.'

'So you said.'

'Dad said he would have liked to talk to Ricky first.'

'Dad wants the best for you.'

'Yes, but in wartime it's different and you have to take your chance when you can. Mum said all she wanted is that I'm happy. And if Ricky makes me happy, then they're happy too. She's got lots of ideas for the wedding. Whenever that might be!'

The baby's lips started to wrinkle. Ruby gasped. 'I can't believe it, she's waking up again.'

'Let me have her, then.'

'Are you going to take her to see Jim's mother?' Ruby asked.

'As soon as I get on me feet again.'

'At least the baby will drown out the complaints.'

They both smiled but Pearl wasn't looking forward to the visit. She'd had a good excuse not to go in the last months of her pregnancy. But sooner or later she would have to. Mrs Nesbitt had old-fashioned ideas about raising children. She'd voiced them loudly when Pearl had last spoken to her. According to her they should be seen and not heard. As for living in rooms without a garden and at the top of a dangerous flight of stairs, this was unthinkable.

Ruby hummed softly as Pearl rocked the baby. It was wonderful to have Ruby there. They were learning about babies together. Luckily they'd had the whole weekend to get used to the new addition but tomorrow Ruby must go to work.

'It was a shock seeing you on the floor in Hemsley's,' said Ruby when she stopped humming. 'At first I thought you'd had an accident. There was so much blood.'

'You came in at the right time,' Pearl smiled.

'There seems a lot to know about childbirth,' Ruby nodded. 'We didn't cover that in our first-aid courses.'

'Well, you missed the best part. I kept wanting to push and Sally was telling me not to.'

'Is it always like that?'

'Don't know. I'll tell you after the next one.'

Ruby giggled. 'That may be a long way off, with the war.'

Pearl sighed softly. 'I'm just grateful me and Jim have made a start. Fancy us thinking she was a boy. We were even going to call him James Junior.'

'What have you decided on now?'

'I've always fancied Cynthia. But I don't know what Jim will think.'

'We can't just keep saying "the baby".'

'All right then, we'll settle for Cynthia.'

'It will be shortened to Cynth, most likely.'

Pearl thought about this. But she didn't mind. Cynth seemed to suit the baby too.

'She's dropped off,' Ruby whispered as she looked over. 'Why don't you put her in her cot and have some kip?'

'That sounds like heaven.'

A few minutes later Pearl had tucked Cynthia under her blanket and was lying on the bed, her eyelids closing. It was exhausting having a baby. Would the crying lessen? Ruby would be at work so she, Pearl, would be in charge. Sally had arranged for the doctor to come and Pearl had many questions for him. Her right breast felt very sore. The baby had no teeth but felt as though she did. Why was that? And why did Cynthia seem so restless? A short while after her feeds she was crying again. Was that normal? Was Cynthia healthy? Pearl still thought about the miscarriage. She wanted to be a good mother but she didn't feel confident.

Pearl turned on her side to gaze at the cot. When

Cynthia got bigger she could take out the bars and make a small bed.

Closing her eyes she fell fast asleep. In her dream she was thinking up names for her daughter but she still liked Cynthia the best.

Pearl made her way down the stairs and Mrs Nesbitt's voice rang in her head. It was true that the stairs were a problem. Carrying a baby in one arm, a bag over the other and holding tight to the rail at the same time wasn't easy. She was always relieved when she got to the bottom. At least she had a pram, battered and old though it may be, and also from Percy, to take the baby out in. She made her way cautiously to the storeroom where Fitz was whistling.

'Here's me little darlings!' he exclaimed, stepping out from behind a large wooden crate. He brushed down his overall. 'Am I clean enough to give her a cuddle?'

'Course you are, but I don't guarantee silence.'

He laughed, stretching out his arms. 'Come to your old Uncle Fitzy.'

'She's been up since four this morning.'

Fitz gazed down and rocked the little bundle. 'Eight days old and up with the lark, eh?'

'She's louder than a lark.'

'Just wait till she's eating her meat and two veg.'

'That seems a long way off.'

'Yes, but drinking milk don't last for ever. She'll get fed up with it soon.'

Pearl laughed. 'I'm glad to hear that.'

'Go and catch Gwen now, ducks, the queue's gone. She'll be pleased to see you.'

'I thought I'd put Cynth in the pram first. Is it any trouble to get it out?'

'Course not. Look, I've pushed it over here. This afternoon, when I've cleared this lot, I'll put it by the door

along with the bike. Then all you'll have to do is come in and lay her in it. There might be a few carrot tops chucked in as well, but she won't mind that.' He bent and kissed the baby's head. 'Bless her little cotton socks.'

Returning her to Pearl, he pulled the pram out from under an old sack. It was quite serviceable but looked very old-fashioned, with its big wheels and half-moon chassis. Percy had called it a bassinet. Getting it up the stairs was impossible.

Fitz brushed the dust off the hood. 'I gave it a brush, but the spuds were by it.'

Pearl lay Cynthia under the blanket she had brought in her bag.

'A nice day for your walk,' Fitz said as they emerged into daylight. 'Does that wheel look a bit wonky?'

'It pushes all right.'

'Nice springs too.'

'And there's a big space underneath for me shopping.'

'Don't overdo it, now.'

Pearl grinned. 'Thanks, Fitz.'

Pearl pushed it through the alley and stood outside the shop. She kept rocking the pram, afraid that when she stopped Cynthia would wake up. Gwen left her customer and came out. 'Oh, doesn't she look an angel!'

'She does now,' Pearl nodded. 'But if you'd seen her at four this morning you wouldn't say that.'

'Bad night again, ducks?'

'She's always hungry. And Ruby had to go to work, so I tried to keep her quiet. Rocking her in my arms is the only way.'

'Has the midwife been?'

'Yes, she said to make the baby wait four hours in between each feed. Then she would be really hungry and drink her fill.'

'Hmm,' said Gwen doubtfully. 'All babies ain't the same, though.'

'I know.'

'You're looking a bit thin to me, girl. Are you eating?'

'Yes, course I am.'

Pearl knew she had lost weight and was getting too thin. Her clothes were hanging off her. She had shed the weight she had gained from pregnancy, but she knew there was still one big worry at the back of her mind. It was always her fear for Ruby. Could Ricky really be serious about her? What would happen if the same thing happened to Ruby as had happened to her? What would happen when Jim found out? She still hadn't had the courage to write to him about Ruby's engagement.

'Listen, I've a nice piece of halibut in me larder that the fishmonger brought round. Too much for me and Fitz. Call in on your way back and I'll cut you off a piece.'

'I'll pay you for it.'

'Don't be daft.' Gwen put a hand on her arm. 'Look, don't mind me saying, but I don't think you're taking enough care of yourself. A mother needs building up after a baby.'

'By the time Cynth's asleep and the nappies and clothes are washed, it's time for bed.'

'That's no excuse. Did you write to your mum?'

'Yes, she was thrilled about the baby. She might come up to see her.'

'That will be nice for you.'

'I'd better go.'

Gwen patted her shoulder and returned to her customer. Pearl smelled something unpleasant as she left the shop. Cynth had been sick on the collar of her coat. All her clothes and even her hair smelled of baby. As she walked up the road with the pram bouncing in front of her, she thought of how her life had changed. With Jim going to war and none of their savings left, it was only Ruby's wage that kept them afloat. Gwen and Fitz had lowered the

rent by two and six but there were bills too. The coalman wouldn't wait for ever.

Pearl stopped at the park. A strange sound came from the pram. She pulled back the covers. Cynthia opened her eyes. Her little nose wrinkled and the screams started.

Pearl picked her up, but she wouldn't stop. Then she caught sight of one of the pram's wheels. It had gone lopsided.

Pushing it back on was hard work. She was afraid of doing more damage but she couldn't leave it behind. When she stopped to rest, Cynthia began to cry. Was she hungry again?

As she turned into Pride Place she saw the coalman's cart. He was waiting to be paid. Last month's bill was outstanding. If she didn't pay him, he wouldn't leave any coal.

Suddenly tears were close. Cynthia began to cry again. 'Oh, Jim, what shall I do?' Pearl always asked for his help but of course there was never any answer. But this time an answer came. A small, neat figure was hurrying towards her, with arms outstretched.

'Pearl – Pearl love, it's me!'

Pearl quickly hid her tears as Amy hugged her. 'Mum, what are you doing here?'

'We got your letter yesterday.'

'Where's Dad?'

'He couldn't get time off. But he told me to stay as long as I'm needed. *If* I'm needed that is?'

'Oh, Mum, you don't know how much.'

'Well, that's a nice welcome! Now ...' She bent over the pram. 'Is this our little treasure?' She pulled back the blanket as Cynthia went red in the face. 'Oh, what a love!'

Pearl could only watch with a grateful heart. It was as if heaven had heard her desperate plea.

Amy lifted the baby from the pram. 'Now, now, sweetheart, what's wrong?'

'She's always hungry.'

Amy frowned at her daughter. 'Having trouble, are you, ducks?'

'The pram wheel's all crooked,' Pearl mumbled with a little sob. 'I thought I should feel different to this after having a baby.'

'It's quite natural,' Amy said as she rocked Cynthia in her arms. 'Sounds like a case of the baby blues.'

'What's that?'

'Your body's been through a big change. And a baby doesn't give you time for yourself. That's where another pair of hands comes in useful.'

'Mum, I'm so glad you've come.'

Just then the coalman came from the alley. 'I left yer enough sacks till after Christmas, missus. I'll call again in the New Year,' he shouted and jumped on the cart.

Amy chuckled. 'A little something from me and your dad.'

'Oh, Mum!' She hugged her close again.

'What are grandparents for?' Amy disentangled herself and placed the baby over her shoulder. 'Now, we'll soon have you sorted, cherub.'

Pearl pushed the lopsided pram into the storeroom. Now her mum was here she could see a light at the end of the tunnel.

'Show me how you usually feed her,' said Amy as Pearl put the baby to her breast.

Cynthia sucked greedily. But because she was so sore, Pearl flinched.

'Is the other side less sore?' asked Amy.

'Yes, but she likes this one best.'

'Let's give the other a try. And put this under her, love.' Amy pushed a cushion under the baby. 'Now, you can see what's going wrong. She's latched on to the tip, the sensitive

part. Slip your finger into the corner of her mouth and ease her off. If you pull, it will hurt.'

Amy cupped the tiny head and pushed it firmly against Pearl's nipple. 'Now keep her mouth over the pink.'

'I thought I'd suffocate her if I did that!' Pearl exclaimed.

'Babies ain't the best china, you know,' Amy smiled.

'I wish you was still round the corner.'

'I miss you girls too.'

'Ruby says you like the country.'

'Yes, we do.' Amy paused. 'Your dad and me were surprised when she showed us her ring.'

Pearl could tell by her mum's expression that they had been disappointed.

'Anyway, what's done is done. And what I remember of Ricky, he's a pleasant enough lad.' Amy stood up. 'Now, whilst you're feeding her I'll see what's in the larder.'

Pearl groaned. 'Not much, I'm afraid.'

Amy put her hands on her hips. 'Pearl Jenkins – sorry – Nesbitt, what am I going to do with you?'

By the time Cynthia was fed, a cup of tea stood at Pearl's side.

'I'm going to make a nice Woolton pie for tea,' said Amy, adjusting the straps of her pinny.

'We've not got much veg,' Pearl said doubtfully.

'I felt sorry for the mice when I looked in the larder,' laughed Amy as she took Cynthia in her arms. 'So I went downstairs and gave me list to Gwen. Fitz will run it up in a minute. Oh, yes, and he told me to tell you he's fixing the pram. You're very lucky to have such nice landlords.'

Pearl did up her blouse. 'I'm going to ask them to be Cynthia's godparents.'

'But you don't go to church.'

'No, but it's never too late.'

Amy giggled. 'I never thought I'd hear you say that.'

Pearl blushed. She had never liked Sunday school as a

girl and church services bored her. She'd soon stopped going when she got the chance.

'Now go and put the baby in her cot. Then we'll cook a pie.'

Pearl looked doubtful as she remembered all the failures Jim had suffered.

Amy chuckled. 'By the time I leave, you'll be able to make a decent meal.'

'Ruby will be pleased about that.'

They laughed and Pearl took Cynthia to the bedroom. Drawing the curtains, she gazed down at her daughter. For once Cynthia's eyes were shut. Was she really going to sleep? There was so much to learn about babies. Would she ever know enough?

In the kitchen Amy was busy at the sink.

'I miss Jim, Mum,' Pearl burst out. She wanted to cry.

'Course you do, love. Come on now, cheer up.'

'I don't know why I'm like this.'

'Remember? It's those baby blues again.' Amy patted her back. 'Sometimes it upsets your insides. And sometimes it upsets your head. Now, are you ready to make that pie?'

'I'll try.'

'By the time your sister comes home, we'll have dinner cooked. Go and check the baby. If she's sleeping, we'll start.'

Pearl went to the bedroom. Cynthia was fast asleep and Pearl sat on the bed. She couldn't share her worries about Ruby with her mother, and yet she longed to. She had to keep it all to herself. Just like she had when she'd first met Ricky. It was history repeating itself.

147

Chapter 14

A month passed and it was time for Amy to go home. Pearl felt a little better now as Cynthia was sleeping through the night. Everyone was thinking of Christmas. When the news came through that Monty had triumphed in the desert, the nation rejoiced. Bells of victory pealed the length and breadth of the country. Pearl wondered where Jim was now that the battle of El Alamein was over. Ricky had said it would be a deciding factor in the desert war and the newspapers seemed to agree with him.

It was a dull and drizzly Saturday when Amy left. 'We'll walk to the bus stop with you.' Pearl and Ruby had their coats on and the baby had just been fed. Thanks to her mum, Pearl had got into routine, as Sally too had advised.

'I'll miss you all, especially my little Cynth.' Amy, dressed in her headscarf and mac, with her travelling bag in hand, bent to kiss her granddaughter's head. 'I wish your mum would bring you to live in the country.'

'Don't know about that, Mum,' Pearl shrugged. 'Jim plans to go back to the council when the war's over.'

'What about you, Ruby?' Amy looked hopeful. 'From what you saw of Abingley, you seemed to like it.'

'Yes, I did.' Ruby glanced at Pearl. 'We shall have to see.'

Amy smiled. 'Will you visit us at Christmas?'

'Depends,' Ruby grinned, 'on our men.'

'Yes, course. I keep forgetting that you've both got responsibilities now. You still feel like my little chicks.' Amy sighed softly. 'Well, come on, girls, I mustn't be late for the bus. I've got to get home and see what chaos your father has caused.'

The rain had stopped by the time they got there. The hood of the pram and the apron was wet, but Cynthia

slept soundly inside. It was a tearful farewell as Amy waved through the bus window.

'I'll miss her,' said Pearl as they watched the bus turn into West Ferry Road.

'Me too,' nodded Ruby as they turned the pram back along the pavement. 'Would you ever think of moving?'

'Not if Jim gets his old job back.'

'As an engineer he'd get a good job in Abingley.'

'I know, but his mum's here too.'

Ruby giggled. 'All the more reason to move.'

Pearl hadn't visited Mrs Nesbitt yet. She'd enjoyed the company of her mum and each day had flown past. What would the reception be like when she called? Would the sight of Cynth mellow Jim's mother?

'Anyway, I like the Smoke, and Jim does too.'

'You haven't seen Abingley yet.'

'No, that's true.' They walked in thoughtful silence, until Pearl asked, 'If Ricky agreed, would you move there?'

Ruby frowned. 'I haven't seen enough of the place to know. I only spent a night there and an hour looking at Dad's allotment. But apparently there's a market and shops, and although I don't fancy going to church, Mum said she's made some good friends.'

'You sound tempted.'

'I wouldn't be if Mum and Dad still lived round the corner.'

On impulse Pearl turned the pram. 'I know, let's walk past Roper's Way and see if they're doing it up.'

But when they arrived they saw that number twenty-four was still standing, but only just.

'Oh, Pearl, how awful. There's just the walls of our house, and look at the Sampsons'. There's hardly anything left.'

'They've just let them crumble away,' sighed Pearl, rocking the pram back and forth. 'I'm only grateful Dad can't see it. He did so much to that house.'

'The tiles have gone from the roof. I thought the wardens were supposed to stop thieves.' Ruby looked up and down the street, but they were the only people there.

'They can't watch all the time.'

'S'pose not.'

'I can't see them coming to mend it.'

'Most of the other houses are boarded up too.'

Ruby sighed. 'Well, there goes our hope that Mum and Dad could come back.'

'Yes, looks like it.' So much had changed since the outbreak of war, Pearl acknowledged sadly. But when she really thought about it, the war was only a marker in time. Before Cynthia, the biggest questions in her life had been how to keep up with the fashion and what kind of hairstyle to wear. But having babies changed everything. It was easy to blame the war, especially the Germans, for spoiling everything. It was a national pastime. She had done it herself many times. But history was full of wars and people went on having them regardless. You just got on with your life and did the best you could. Now she had a child to think of. War or no war, Cynth was her priority, and without Jim, it was up to her to be both mum and dad.

'You're very quiet,' said Ruby as they turned away.

'I was thinking, we can't blame the war for everything.'

'Our house would still be standing if there wasn't one.'

'Yes, but it's given Mum and Dad a fresh start.'

'What about us?' Ruby said resentfully. 'It was our home too.'

'Yes, but we don't need it any more. I've got a home of my own and you have all your dreams. It's no use having regrets. We shouldn't look back, but go forward.'

'That's too deep for me.'

'I've just had a baby. I'm allowed to think deep.'

They laughed together and Ruby cast a quick look over her shoulder. 'Bye, old house.'

'Tell you what, let's go to the market and cheer ourselves up,' Pearl said suddenly, and Ruby nodded.

'That's a good idea. Mum left five pounds in the kitty.'

'And paid for all that coal.'

'And bought all the groceries.'

'It was like having Father Christmas early,' laughed Pearl, linking her arm through Ruby's.

'We'd better save it for a rainy day.'

The two girls looked at each other and smiled. They both knew that by the end of the day, that five pounds would be well and truly broken into.

Christmas was three weeks away and still a letter hadn't arrived from Jim. There hadn't been many raids, but rumours were circulating about spies. It was said a new invasion plan had been hatched by the Germans.

At Pearl's flat, the wet and foggy weather had caused the stairs to become slippery and the mould was back in the kitchen. 'I'll pop up and see what I can do,' promised Fitz although he never found time. He was always busy in the shop or storeroom.

Then just before Christmas, a buff-coloured envelope dropped on the mat, addressed in Jim's larger and familiar handwriting. Pearl opened it with trembling fingers.

My darling Pearly-girl,

I don't know when you'll get this, or even if the censor will allow it, but we've won El Alamein! I can't begin to tell you what the feeling is like. But sod the censor, I'm going to try. It all started just before dawn when the moon was full and blinding, like a whopping great cheese hanging in the sky. There was silence at first, as though we were waiting to hear our own breath. And then all hell let loose. Wave after wave of our artillery attacked on two fronts. Bloody brave blokes, real

heroes. Then it was our turn, the Engineers, clearing the minefields and making roads for our tanks to pass through. Funny to think the battered old Churchills were the very same ones I'd once seen rolling off the assembly line at Luton, bright as new pins. Anyway, by first light, we'd taken hold. Half of the enemy was Eyeties, poor buggers. See, it's a fact that Jerry despises them and chucks them right at the front like sitting ducks.

As for us, we was a mixture of British, Aussies, New Zealanders, Indians, Frenchies and Greeks. But, by God, we fought as one. Then there was the Americans, God love 'em, with their Shermans and self-propelled guns. So all together we hit the Afrika Korps and knocked 'em for six. We took Alamein from right under their noses.

Pearl put the letter down. Her imagination had come alive with Jim's powerful description. Her heart was beating so fast she had to catch her breath. He'd called the others heroes, yet he'd been there, in the minefields, for goodness' sake! For some time she just sat there, allowing the conflicting emotions to fill her: pride, fear, wonder, heartache and above all relief. Her husband and Cynthia's father, Jim Nesbitt, her hero of heroes, had come safely through a terrible battle.

It was some minutes before she read on. She wanted to savour every word. It was the first time the censor had allowed any real information to be distributed. She guessed that El Alamein was a long-awaited triumph and the Ministry of Information was eager to spread the good news. Jim ended with a flourish.

So Pearly-girl, we've cracked it. Can't say I wished you'd been here. But you and the baby was in my mind all

the time. My lucky mascots. How are you both? I'd like to say I'll be home for Christmas, but it's doubtful. Our time will come, I promise. One day we'll all be together again. Believe that, sweetheart, won't you? And PS. What are we going to call our girl?

Pearl put down the letter for the second time. It was a bitter disappointment, although she told herself she was lucky to have her man alive. He had spent the whole letter telling her what it had been like and in a very proud way. But why couldn't he be with her and Cynthia? He didn't even know her name.

She got up and went to the bedroom where Cynthia was lying awake, gurgling softly to herself. Lifting her into her arms, she kissed her soapy-smelling forehead. 'Daddy sends his love and says he'll see us soon. Your daddy is a hero and one day I'll tell you all about what he did. And you'll be as proud of him as I am.'

Cynthia gurgled contentedly. Pearl walked to the window to part the curtains. She wanted to see all the familiar landmarks: the rooftops and chimneys and houses, the shop below and the cobbles leading down to the corner. Jim's words had taken her to another world and it was nowhere as safe as this one.

But instead of a clear morning with a sky full of scudding clouds, an eerie mist spread along the gutters. It slithered over the windowsills and spread its tentacles across the glass.

'Look! It's a London fog, Cynthia!' She turned the baby towards the murky yellowness. 'We've got a real pea-souper whilst your dad is somewhere in the desert where there probably ain't even a nice cold glass of water to drink. But when he comes home ... *when* he comes home ... we'll have a bottle of beer in the larder and one of them Woolton pies in the oven, like your gran showed us how to make. It might not be Christmas, but one day, when he

walks up them stairs, it's going to be the happiest day of our lives. Remember that, sweetheart. We've got so much to look forward to. Nothing is going to stop us from being together again.'

Pearl smiled. She was going to keep telling herself and Cynthia that Jim would walk in the door one day. His blue eyes would be shining and he'd make them laugh as he always did.

He *would* come home to them one day. He would!

Part Two

Chapter 15

'Yer can't go pushing her around in that old tub, missus, she's bigger than the blooming pram!'

Pearl grinned up at the rag-and-bone man. Under his well-worn cloth cap Percy Flint smiled at her with big brown teeth. Cynthia wriggled excitedly when she saw the towering brown horse that pulled the cart. Pearl unclipped the reins attached to the side of the pram and lifted Cynthia out. She was a big girl for her age but, all the same, her red coat was two sizes too big. Pearl had learned the best way to dress her fast-growing daughter was to buy everything in larger sizes and sew back the cuffs and turn up hems. Even Cynthia's hand-knitted woollen hat was a size too large, but it pulled down over her sandy-blonde curls and kept them in place. Luckily the sun was shining this morning. Despite the early frost, the day had a warm glow.

Pearl knew Percy was right. Cynthia had outgrown the pram, with its wobbly wheel. On their monthly trips to Villa Road to see Mrs Nesbitt, it weighed heavier and heavier. Not that Mrs Nesbitt was eager to see them. Babies needed all the attention and didn't sit still or mind their manners. Still, it would be nice to have one of those new pushchairs to zip Cynthia around in.

Pearl lifted Cynthia into her arms to stroke the horse's mane. Cynthia, who loved all animals, threaded her fingers through the dirty brown mane.

'I got something on the cart might suit you.' Percy Flint dropped the reins and disappeared. He returned with a strange-looking article. 'What about this, then?'

'What is it?'

'It's a chair to push 'er in. Might be a bit old, but look at that lovely workmanship. Bone 'andle and a leather seat. Someone had it made special for a kid, someone with a few bob.'

'It looks more like one of them Bath chairs.'

'Not on your nelly. Take a good gander, missus. See, the wheels ain't bloomin' great big ones and they're all in good nick.'

'Where did it come from?' Pearl asked suspiciously.

'From a big house up Poplar. Seeing as I know yer, you can have first refusal.'

The old man took Cynthia in his arms and gave her a carrot. 'Come on, ducks, let old Barney 'ave a nibble while your mum has a gander.'

Pearl examined the chair and, to her surprise, it wheeled very well. 'I must admit it pushes better than the big one.'

'See, yer problem is solved,' the rag-and-bone dealer said over his shoulder. 'There's even a place to put yer stuff.'

Pearl noted the leather bag attached to the back. It was certainly an unusual piece.

'Let's put 'er in and give it a try.' He lowered Cynthia on the seat and pushed it back and forth. 'See, she likes it.'

Pearl pulled her collar round her ears as she considered the chair. She didn't have any money to spend as she'd just paid the rent. And although Cynthia seemed to like it, it was not what Pearl had had in mind.

'Tell yer what I'll do – you're a good customer, I'll do yer a swap.'

'What for?'

'The big pram, of course.'

Pearl guessed that Percy already had a customer lined up. But what use was it to her if Cynthia was too big to ride in it? 'I don't know ...' she hesitated.

'This won't 'ang about, gel.'

The chair was tempting. Perhaps she could disguise its ugliness with a blanket?

'I don't want any wheels going wonky like this one did,' Pearl warned him.

'Good as new, these are. Some posh kid's been sat in there. No stinky drawers 'ave graced that leather, no, sir.'

'All right then, I'll take it.'

'You won't be sorry, love.'

'I hope not.' Pearl watched him lift the big pram on his cart. With a wave and wink, he departed and Pearl started off home. She couldn't make up her mind if she liked the pushchair or not, but Cynthia seemed to like it. She could rest her feet on the footrest and look around.

Gwen and Fitz came out of the shop when they saw her. 'What have you got there?'

'It's a pushchair.'

'We can see that.'

'It's off Percy Flint's cart.' She was embarrassed as she helped Cynthia out and took off the blanket.

'What happened to the other one?'

'We did a swap.'

Gwen grinned. 'I hope that old scoundrel paid you to take it?'

Pearl blushed. 'It don't look much but it pushes well.'

'It ain't that bad,' said Fitz. 'And it won't take up no room.'

'Your sister came home a minute or two ago.' Gwen lowered her voice as she leaned close. 'I give her a tin of sardines and a small piece of cheese. It was no more than the size of me thumb, but I wouldn't let no one else have it. She looked a bit upset to me.'

'Upset?'

'Yes, you'd better run up and see.'

When Pearl and Cynthia walked in, Ruby rushed towards them. 'Pearl, I've got a letter!'

Pearl's heart sank. It always did when there was news

159

from Ricky. Pearl had hoped the novelty of being engaged had worn off for Ruby, but being parted from him had made Ruby's heart grow fonder.

'Ricky's home!' Ruby gabbled, shaking the piece of paper. 'This is from the matron of a hospital. She's writing for Ricky as he can't write himself.' Ruby pushed the letter into Pearl's hands. 'See, it's somewhere called Brawton Manor in Surrey and used for wounded officers.'

Pearl read the first few lines. The writing was neat and precise, written on white paper with a printed address.

'Is he wounded then?' Pearl asked hoarsely.

'She says his hands are bandaged, that's why she's writing for him. And she's given a telephone number. Told me to ring on Sunday morning when she's on duty.'

Pearl tried to think what this meant. But fear was freezing her thoughts. 'Will you phone?' she asked hesitantly.

'Yes, course. I wish Gwen and Fitz had one. I'll have to go to the box by the park.' Ruby clutched the letter to her. 'She doesn't say he's bad. She would, wouldn't she, if it was something serious?'

Pearl could only nod. What did this mean? Was Ricky seriously wounded? She knew Ruby was worried. What was going through her mind? The same things, probably, that would be going through hers if Jim was injured.

'I don't know if I'll be able to sleep tonight,' Ruby said unhappily. 'I wish she'd written what was wrong with him.'

'Try not to get upset.' But Pearl knew Ruby wouldn't rest until she found out the extent of Ricky's injuries.

When Pearl climbed out of bed the next morning, it was cloudy and grey. Had Ruby managed any sleep? Looking from the window, she saw a few people making their way to church. She liked to see everyone in their Sunday best clothes. She felt a twinge of guilt when she thought how she hadn't found time to have Cynthia baptized. Perhaps

she would have it done when Cynthia was older. Her mind flew to Ricky. Why couldn't he use his hands? Were they his only injuries? Maybe they were serious and that was why the matron hadn't said more. Would Ruby still want to be engaged?

Cynthia stirred in her cot, which, now she was sixteen months old, was a small bed as the bars on either side had been removed. Cynthia rubbed her eyes and grinned, showing her two white front teeth. Pearl loved her baby smell, though it was gradually fading. As she sat her on the little wooden chair incorporating a potty, Cynthia chuckled. 'Done wee-wee.'

'Good girl.'

Pearl was glad that Cynthia no longer needed nappies. The old towels cut into strips were becoming harder to find and took a long time to wash and dry. Now she needed only clean knickers.

'Let's wake Aunty Ruby.'

Hand in hand they went along the hall, but when they went into Ruby's room the camp bed was folded up. Pearl found a hastily scribbled note in the kitchen.

'Gone to telephone.'

Pearl sat Cynthia on the chair. 'Draw me a picture and I'll make porridge. We'll listen to the wireless, see if there's anything about where Daddy could be.'

'Daddy!' Cynthia shouted.

'Yes, your handsome Daddy,' Pearl smiled as she switched on the set. She had shown Cynthia Jim's picture on the dresser every day, so when he came home he wouldn't seem a stranger.

As she made breakfast, Pearl tried not to think about Ruby and the telephone call. Instead she concentrated on the news. Though Jim hadn't said where he was after El Alamein, he'd joked in a letter about throwing away his slippers. She took this to mean he'd left the desert and

might be with the British Army in Italy. Perhaps he'd be able to give her a hint in his next letter. When would he be home?

She longed to buy some clothes again. She had taken such a pride in her appearance once. Now she, too, had joined the ranks of utility wearers. Would Jim recognize her when he came home?

Cynthia blew bubbles and Pearl laughed. 'You're a card, you are, just like your dad. Look at the mess you're making!'

'Daddy 'ome soon,' gurgled Cynthia. She'd heard Pearl say this so often, she knew it by heart.

Just then the door burst open. Ruby came rushing in. She was wearing a jumper and slacks and breathlessly slid off her bicycle clip. 'I didn't sleep a wink and was up early.'

'Sit down, porridge is ready.'

'I can't eat. Me stomach's in a knot. Hello, Cynth, love.'

'Did you speak to the matron?' asked Pearl.

'Yes, she told me the hospital was once a country house owned by a very rich family.'

'Don't they live there now?'

'No, they've gone away.'

'Did you find out any more about Ricky?'

'Yes, his ship was torpedoed as it followed the German battleship *Tirpitz*.' Ruby pulled out a chair and sank down. 'Don't know much about it meself. But there was a fire on board and all the crew had to jump in the freezing water. It was somewhere near Norway and the sea is freezing. Ricky got dragged in a lifeboat, but he was burned by the burning oil that floated on the surface.'

'Was it just his hands?'

'No, his chest and shoulder is burned but she said he's in good spirits and is being treated by the doctors.'

'How long will he have to stay there?'

'I didn't ask.'

'Will he go back in the navy?'

'I don't know that either. She said I could visit and I'll find out everything then. The train stops at Brawton station and there's a bus I can catch to the Manor. She offered to make arrangements for me to stay overnight at the local pub.'

'Surrey is a long way to go.'

'I told her I'd have to ask me boss for a Saturday morning off.'

Pearl knew that Ruby was very upset and trying not to show it. 'This place might be a manor but it's still a hospital, after all. It won't be just coughs and sneezes,' she warned.

'I know that. I've done first aid, haven't I?'

'Yes, but you're not very good when it comes to the sight of blood,' Pearl pointed out.

Ruby smiled. 'If I faint they can put me in a bed next to Ricky.'

'Come on, eat your breakfast.' Pearl knew that Ruby was putting on a brave face but what was the real extent of Ricky's injuries?

Jim lay on his chest, his rifle beside him, as he peered through the green Italian grass at the foot of the hill. He was trying to take a breath but the air was full of dust. Not the desert dust that was dry and hot. But the dust that had rolled down the lush green hill, was full of the bitter taste of exploding shell.

His unit had been surveying a possible route up to the summit of the hill. A few hours ago a Benedictine monastery had been perched there. Now it was in ruins. For the past few days the noise of the assault had been deafening. Massed formations of American bombers had dropped bomb after bomb on the historic building. The Allied command had told them the monastery was occupied by the enemy. But Jim had his doubts. Even Jerry wouldn't desecrate a place so venerated, would they? And there had

been little or no return gunfire during the onslaught. The sky was a pall of smoke billowing over the once beautiful Italian landscape.

'It can't be right to do what we did to such a holy place!' exclaimed Reg, the young soldier beside him. Jim hadn't known him long, only since he'd been drafted out of Africa in the advance to the Italian capital. Like Jim, Reg had been at El Alamein. Instead of the leave they'd hoped to get they found themselves in the thick of it again. Now Monte Cassino seemed as much of a killing field as the desert, and Jim was sick of it. He agreed with Reg. It was a crime to have razed the old monastery to the ground.

'You reckon Jerry was in situ before we came?' asked Reg as he huddled close to Jim.

Jim merely shrugged. To demolish such a landmark was like wiping St Paul's off the map. And surely it was clear to the top brass that now there were ruins up there, the enemy had a better chance of holding the hill. Any attempt to drive through to Cassino would take longer.

A volley of gunfire shook the ground. Jim ducked, burying his face in the brittle woodland floor. Strafing whistled past his boots sending a spray of earth in the air. He dared to glance skyward. A plummeting silver bird, entrapped in a plume of smoke, was falling, falling. The whine of the plane's descent was heart-rending. The fuselage now a mass of flames, it was impossible to tell if it was enemy or Allied. But the pilot had bailed out. His parachute floated down like a dandelion. Did death or life await him?

'Was he one of ours?' Reg asked.

'Couldn't tell.'

'Poor bastard.' Reg wiped the dirt, sweat and filth from his thin face. 'Don't suppose anyone stopped to consider if there was monks and nuns inside that place.'

'Nuns don't live in monasteries,' Jim smiled grimly.

'No, but women and kids could've been sheltering there.

That's the place they'd go to, ain't it, thinking it would be safe? What heartless sod would give the order to shell it?'

'Some sod that ain't so holy, I expect.'

'It's been standing for hundreds of years. Until us and the Yanks come along.'

Jim felt sick at the thought of such a massacre. He had a wife and daughter at home. But if Jerry had landed in 'thirty-nine, his family might have died too.

'I reckon they got out before,' he decided.

'You gotta give the Yanks their due,' nodded Reg, adjusting his lying position as he scrambled closer. 'After Pearl Harbor, nothing was gonna stop them. Not even the bleedin' Pope.'

A barrage of artillery fire halted their conversation. Both men lay flat to the earth, as the woodland erupted. Jim hung on to his rifle, not moving an inch. This was going to be a hard push, but Reg was right. As bad for the Yanks as the bombing of Pearl Harbor was, it was a stroke of luck for the Allies.

For a few minutes the strafing came close again. Jim thought of his wife and his little daughter, Cynthia. Though he had never seen her or held her, she wasn't ever out of his mind. And if by chance he did survive this godforsaken war it would be the hope of going home again that saved him.

A gust of wind from the rubble swept into his throat. The cloud was filled with the scent of death. He coughed until his lungs hurt. Drawing up his legs, he dragged himself on his elbows to a bank of mossy stone and bushes. Daring a glance above, all he could see was a few feet in front.

'Looks like we're stuck here,' he growled, narrowing his eyes at the thick curtain of dust. 'Going nowhere fast and sitting ducks for snipers.'

'You don't need to tell me that, mate. I've taken one this time,' Reg answered.

Jim turned to look at his friend. He hadn't bargained for

the twist of his stomach as he saw the bloody chest wound.

Discarding his weapon, he took Reg in his arms. He could hardly bring himself to speak.

Reg arched and clutched him. 'Gotta fag, mate?'

Somehow he managed to light the dog end. Reg took a gulp, quivered and spat blood.

'Hang in there, chum. I'll run for help.'

'Bit bleedin' late for that.'

Jim held him tight as he groaned, but then his eyes became clear. They stared past him into the far-off distance. 'You've been a good mate, Jim. You'll have to look out for yourself, now. Keep that big ginger head of yours down.'

'You ain't going nowhere,' Jim answered roughly. 'Now let me take a look at this—'

Reg caught his wrist. 'You know, I've always wondered what it'd be like, but it ain't so bad after all . . .'

At these words, Jim felt a strange peace come over them. A sudden relief from the pain and fear as he slid the butt from his friend's lips and closed his sightless eyes. He wanted to stay in that place where Reg had walked ahead bravely, but he knew it was not his time. He was envious even, unwilling to be drawn back. And for that brief moment, he would have been willing to follow if offered the way. But as the body grew heavy – a weightless heaviness, almost – he came back with a bump to reality.

Ruby followed the matron along the corridor, her eyes going to each room as she searched for Ricky. It was a Saturday afternoon and the patients were in their beds or sitting in chairs beside them. All the first aid she had learned couldn't have prepared her for today. The hospital was full of the blind, deformed and limbless. Matron had told her to be prepared, but it was still a shock. She had also made it clear that Ricky was one of the lucky ones. The burns were across his shoulders and chest and could be hidden by his

clothes. He'd lost two fingers, one from each hand, but it wasn't the burning oil that had taken them. It had been the freezing cold of exposure to the elements.

As they walked on, the smell of disinfectant grew stronger. Ruby had had to wait a whole month to come here as Mr Brewer hadn't been able to let her go immediately. Though the Manor was imposing from the outside, with gardens all round and pillars in front, inside it was just the same as any hospital. The nurses all wore starched uniforms and the doctors stood discussing their patients at the ends of the beds. As it was the rest period, it was very quiet.

Finally the matron opened the door of a room and looked in. Ruby could see it was a small ward with only two beds. 'Ah, he's not here. I'll wait with you until he comes.'

Ruby's gaze went to the long window at the end of the room. The light reflected down onto a curtain pulled round the bed. Ruby could see a wooden frame sticking out at the bottom.

'Ah, here he is,' said the Matron, turning Ruby away.

Ricky strode down the passage towards them. Ruby's heart lifted, only to drop again when she saw his bandaged hands.

'Hello,' he said, smiling as he came closer.

The matron touched her arm. 'As soon as you're ready we'll serve you tea in the conservatory.'

'Thank you, Matron,' said Ricky and they watched her walk away.

'Oh, darling, how are you?' Ruby wanted to kiss him but knew she couldn't. The red marks of the burns showed under his collar and he held his bandaged hands at his side.

'Much better. And you?'

'I've missed you.'

'And I you. I'm afraid I can't use these yet.' He lifted his arms.

'It doesn't matter. Are they painful?'

'Not now.'

'Oh, Ricky,' was all she could say.

'How was your journey?' he asked politely.

'I took the train up and the bus brought me the rest of the way. Matron said someone called Arthur would have driven me, but this weekend he's away.'

'Yes, he's a nice old chap. Does a bit of running about for the hospital.'

'This is a very nice place. Well, outside it is.'

He smiled. 'Yes, it does have that effect on first-time visitors.'

Ruby felt very awkward. They were talking like strangers.

'Shall we go along to the conservatory?' he asked. 'It's much nicer in there. And my room is very small. Besides,' he nodded, 'Dick is not well.'

As they were leaving a young woman passed. She kept her head down as she walked to the bed with the frame.

'Fighter pilot. He's in trouble, I'm sad to say,' Ricky said softly as they walked along the corridor.

'You mean, he's—'

'I'm afraid so.'

'How awful.'

'Next on your right, through that door,' Ricky said in a matter-of-fact tone. 'Should be warm enough in there as the sun's been out all day.'

They walked into a large room over which there was a glass roof and below, wide open windows. The many kinds of potted plants, ferns and palms gave it an outside feel. Although it was warm Ruby was glad she had worn her new coat. Would Ricky notice it? She'd chosen the soft shade of green to go with her hat, gloves and black court shoes. Her black shoulder bag contained her train tickets, purse and make-up. Although Ricky didn't smoke she had brought cigarettes in case.

He led the way to two leather chairs with big cushions. They overlooked the view of the well-tended garden and stone-paved patio. In the centre of the patio was a waterless fountain decorated with cherubs. A wide set of steps led down to the lawns and in the distance was an imposing green hedge. Ruby wondered about the family that was wealthy enough to own a place like this and then had to leave it.

Soon more patients came in with their relatives and friends. The invalids shuffled on crutches and sticks, and some were pushed in wheelchairs. She hoped Ricky would tell her what happened on board ship so she could understand what he'd been through.

A young orderly brought the tea. Ricky sat down beside her. 'Apologies again.' He lifted his bandaged hands. 'Will you pour?'

Ruby was happy to be able to do something, however small.

'When you wrote to me about Roper's Way,' Ricky said as she stirred the pot, 'I was very surprised. Do you think it can be repaired?'

'Don't know,' she shrugged, wishing he would say how nice she looked. 'When we went to have a look it was just a shell.'

'Are your family happy in Abingley?'

'Yes, they've got a lovely flat, quite large, with a garden. Dad's at the aerodrome and grows veg on a small allotment. You know how mad he is about planting stuff.'

'Good for him.'

'There's a market and shops and lots of fields and green spaces,' she found herself saying. 'It's not at all like the Smoke. But they seem very happy all the same.'

'And what are you up to these days?'

'I'm still at the factory,' she said, wishing they could talk about something more intimate. She'd told him all this

in her letters. Why did he make her feel like a stranger? His thoughts seemed very far away. 'Ricky, I don't want to spend all our time talking about me. What happened to you? How did you get your injuries?'

'Perhaps we could discuss them some other time.'

'Don't you want to tell me?'

'There's enough sickness here. It's good to hear about the outside.'

Ruby nodded, but she didn't have much more to tell him. 'Would you like a cigarette?' she asked, opening her bag.

'Not with these, I'm afraid.' He lifted his bandaged hands.

'I could light one for you, if you like?'

'I've never been much of a smoker.'

There was a long silence.

'Ricky, I've missed you so much,' she burst out suddenly. 'Have you missed me?'

'Yes, of course.' He shifted and frowned. Was it pain on his face, she wondered. Why didn't he seem to be interested in anything?

'And how's Pearl?' he asked in the same polite tone.

'She's fine. Cynthia is full of beans.'

'The baby, you mean?'

'She's not such a baby any more. Jim will have a surprise when he comes home.'

'Ah, Jim. Where is he? Still in the desert?'

'Don't know,' Ruby shrugged.

'We were told Alamein was a brilliant show. Pearl must be very proud.'

Ruby frowned. 'Yes, she is.' She wondered what his thoughts were about Jim. Would the two men be friends when they met again?

'You know, I used to think you two girls were a cut above the others at the club,' he said with a sudden smile. 'Very single-minded and bright.'

Ruby blushed. 'Flattery will get you everywhere, though I didn't think you noticed me.'

'Oh, yes, the Jenkins sisters.'

Ruby smiled. 'I think Pearl had a crush on you,' she teased. 'Not that she said anything. But a sister can tell.'

Ricky stared at her. 'Now it's my turn to be flattered.'

She was disappointed as she'd only said that hoping he would say that he would have preferred her to have a crush on him.

'Well, we both did, actually,' she added lamely.

He nodded to his cup. 'I'm afraid I'll have to ask for help.'

Ruby lifted the cup to his mouth. It was such a wonderful mouth, set in a face that looked more handsome than ever. His black hair was turning grey at the temples and slender white creases sprang out from his eyes. She wished he would tell her how lovely she looked.

'Thanks.' He sat back, his eyes turning away. On her first-aid courses she had been told that some war veterans never talked about their experiences. Not for days or even years afterwards. She hoped that one day he would be able to confide in her.

Soon the visitors began leaving. Ricky leaned forward, saying quietly, 'I see you're still wearing your ring.'

Automatically she clasped it. 'Of course I am.'

'I'm surprised.'

'What do you mean?'

'It's just that I thought after this . . .' He looked down at his hands, 'you may want to change your mind. I've no idea how long I shall be here. I'm not at all certain the engagement was a good idea.'

'What? But I love you,' she cried.

'Before this happened I had a career with the navy, a job that I loved. Now I'm not certain that I'll be able to return to sea.'

'Does that matter?' she asked. 'Isn't it a good thing really?'

'How can it be good?' His face darkened.

'I don't mean it's good to have injuries,' she flustered. 'I just meant that you'll be out of the war.'

'The navy is my life,' he said gruffly.

'Yes, I know, but I hope I am too.'

'Ruby, what have I to offer you? At the moment, nothing.'

'Don't say that. When you're well, you'll find another job that you like as much as the navy.'

He turned cold eyes on her. 'You think so?'

'Ricky, I want to get married. I want to be your wife.' She was afraid she was losing him.

Once more he looked distant. 'Even if we did, we have nowhere to live.'

'We could stay at Pride Place,' she said eagerly. 'Just till we found somewhere.'

Once more he gazed down at his hands. 'How can I support a wife like this?'

'Oh, darling, it doesn't matter. As long as we have each other, something will turn up.' She leaned close and as the room was now empty, placed her lips on his. He didn't draw away and her heart leaped with joy. 'I know you love me, really. It's what's happened to you that's given you doubts. But I've enough love for both of us.'

When the bell rang, Ruby knew she must leave. 'I'll have to go.'

'Are you staying in the village?'

'Yes, at the Brown Bear. I wish we could be together.'

'That won't be possible for some time to come.' He looked very unhappy.

She wanted to throw her arms round him and make him well. She knew she had enough love to do it.

'I'll be here in the morning. Then I'll ask matron if we could be married here.'

'I don't think that's possible.'

'Anything's possible if you want it enough.' Once again

she leaned forward to kiss him. It was a very brief and he sat in silence as he watched her walk away.

Her eyes were full of tears as she waited for the bus. She wouldn't let their love die, she wouldn't. She was determined to enlist the matron's help tomorrow and marry Ricky before he changed his mind.

Chapter 16

Cynthia was dressed in her Sunday frock and sat on the high-backed carver, dwarfed by the big polished table in front of her. The ruby-red chenille tablecloth spilled over its edges and covered the four bulbous legs beneath. The furniture in the overcrowded front room was all depressingly dark wood. It reminded Pearl of a museum more than a home. It was no wonder that Jim, on leaving school, had found himself a job that took him away from home. He must have dreaded coming back to this atmosphere. Mrs Nesbitt, as usual, was eyeing Cynthia with disapproval as the crumbs scattered over the cloth and missed her plate.

'Look at your sticky fingers,' Mrs Nesbitt said sharply. 'Use your napkin, child, that's what it's for.'

Pearl caught her daughter's intake of breath as a wizened hand flew in front of her nose and snatched the napkin. 'Hasn't your mother taught you any manners?'

Cynthia's wide eyes went to Pearl and they shared a glance. Neither of them enjoyed their visits to Villa Road. Most of the time, Cynthia sat on Pearl's knee, sucking her thumb as she cowered away from her grandmother's scrutiny. Playing on the floor was forbidden. The china ornaments positioned strategically around the fireplace

were fragile. The lower shelves spilled with bric-a-brac, and books that were not to be read but dusted. Pearl often wondered if Jim got dusted as a child and told to sit in a corner and be quiet. No wonder he turned out to be noisy and talkative. All those years of living under this roof like an ornament must have driven him crazy.

She forced down the thin, tasteless food and the sugarless, watery tea. And when all that could be said about Jim was said, Pearl hoped they could make an escape.

But Cynthia wriggled round and caught her shoe in the tablecloth tassels. Before Pearl could prevent disaster, the plate and its contents went sailing through the air. Mrs Nesbitt's alarmed cry was followed by the splintering of china.

Pearl rushed to her daughter's aid. 'Don't cry, Cynth. It wasn't your fault.'

'My best china!' Mrs Nesbitt's hand clapped on her heart.

Pearl lifted her sobbing daughter, gently removing a slice of bread from her knee. Luckily she wasn't harmed, only terrified of the consequences as she clung to Pearl.

'It's all right, Cynth, it's only a plate. We'll buy Granny another one.' She held her tight, kissing the top of her head.

Mrs Nesbitt lifted accusing eyes. 'This china can't be replaced.'

'It was an accident,' Pearl repeated, unable to believe that her mother-in-law was more interested in her china than putting her granddaughter's mind to rest. 'She's only a baby yet.'

'Children should not leave the table until they're told.' Mrs Nesbitt shook her head as Pearl put Cynthia down and attempted to pick up the broken pieces. 'No, leave it alone. See to your daughter. You'd better take her outside.'

Pearl didn't need telling twice. She carried Cynthia out of the front door where the pushchair stood waiting. The backyard was off limits to Cynthia as once she had trodden

on the narrow flowerbed and crushed a flower. Pearl had never heard the last of it.

'I'm going to sit you here for a minute, love, all right?'

Cynthia hugged her teddy bear and nodded. Pearl wiped under her eyes. 'There, that's better.'

'Granny cross,' Cynthia sniffed, looking at the door.

Pearl made light of it. 'No, course not. Now, I'll just go in and say goodbye.'

Pearl thought that it was true, Cynthia was a bit clumsy but that was only because she was young. If Mrs Nesbitt couldn't see she was a delightful child by now, then perhaps she never would. When she went back inside, the front room was empty. The broken plate had disappeared and so had the remains of the tea. Pearl looked in the kitchen. Mrs Nesbitt was arranging the pieces on the draining board. 'I suppose this could be glued.'

'Can I do it for you?'

'No. It needs to be done properly.'

Pearl sighed. 'Well, we'd better be going.'

Mrs Nesbitt turned round. 'You'll let me know when you hear from Jim?'

'Doesn't he write?' Pearl asked as she put on her cardigan and slid her bag over her shoulder.

'I don't expect letters. Not with a wife to write to first. You're his first duty and I've no quarrel with that.'

Pearl knew that her mother-in-law had never forgiven her for taking away her son. And worse, that he had gone to war. No one wanted Jim to stay at home more than Pearl and she'd hoped that whilst Jim was away they could have become closer. But Mrs Nesbitt preferred to remain aloof. Pearl ached, not for herself but for her little girl, who sat silently outside in the pushchair with her thumb in her mouth.

As Pearl walked home she finally came to the conclusion that she had tried her best to make friends, but nothing had

worked. Jim's mother didn't really want her there. Should she finally give up on these awkward visits? As she looked at Cynthia in the pushchair, with her quick smile, lovely blonde curls and sunny nature, she couldn't understand why Mrs Nesbitt hadn't become a proud gran.

'Oh, Pearl, I've got so much to tell you.' Ruby sat down on the couch, her cheeks pink with excitement. She hadn't bothered to take off her coat as she talked about Brawton Manor. Even the cup of tea that Pearl had made was cold.

The evening was still light, but Cynthia was fast asleep. She was tired from the trip round the park after Mrs Nesbitt's. The swings were a distraction for her and gradually the unpleasant experience had faded. The other children playing there had included her in their games. Pearl had sat on the bench and watched them, relieved to see Cynthia's natural liveliness return. Then when they'd got home, they'd eaten the last of the stewed rabbit she'd cooked yesterday, a wholesome broth that warmed them through, and slowly Cynthia's eyes had closed in a contented sleep.

'Brawton Manor might have been nice once,' Ruby was saying as she sat on the edge of the couch, 'but now it's a hospital and very depressing. Some of the patients had legs and arms missing. I thought after all me first-aid training I'd have a strong stomach. But when you see that kind of thing in real life, it's different. In Ricky's room there was a young airman called Dick, who is very ill. A young girl came to visit.' Ruby's face went pale. 'I think he is going to die.'

Pearl had had a long and tiring day and although she felt very sad to hear this, she didn't really want to listen. It made her more frightened for Jim.

'He was a fighter pilot,' continued Ruby determinedly. 'Ricky's lucky to be alive. His hands were bandaged and I could see the burns on his neck. I tried to get him to talk to

me but he wouldn't. I was told on me first-aid courses that a lot of blokes find the memories too upsetting.'

'Will he go back to the services?' Pearl asked, slipping off her shoes and rubbing her sore feet.

'If he can't, then it doesn't matter. I'll just keep on at the factory.'

'Are you sure that's what you want?' Pearl said before she considered how this sounded.

Ruby's eyes flashed. 'You'd do it for Jim, wouldn't you? If he got injured and couldn't work, you'd be the one to earn a wage?'

'Yes, but we're married,' Pearl said quietly. She knew Ruby was not in a good mood after being at the hospital.

Ruby sat upright. 'Why are you so against us?'

'I'm not.'

Ruby reached for her bag and took out a hanky. She wiped her eyes. 'I thought I could tell you everything once. I thought we was best friends, not just sisters.'

'We are, Ruby.'

'Well, then, you'll understand when I say I want to get married as soon as possible.'

Pearl looked up. 'But he's in hospital!'

'We can get married there. The matron said so. All we have to do is get a special licence and the vicar will even give us his blessing, although it won't be a proper service.'

'But you want a white wedding, don't you?' Pearl couldn't keep the shock from her voice. What was Ruby thinking of?

'I want Ricky to know he's more important to me than anything. It's a sacrifice I'm willing to make.'

'But why do you have to make a sacrifice? What's brought all this on?' Pearl asked bewilderedly.

Ruby looked tearful. 'I'm afraid he'll change his mind.'

'Why would he do that?'

'He says he hasn't anything to offer now he's been injured.'

'Ruby, think carefully,' Pearl said anxiously. 'Ricky could be right. With his injuries, you don't know how long it will be before he's well again. You might regret rushing into marriage.'

'That's a horrid thing to say,' snapped Ruby.

They sat in silence and Ruby sniffed and wiped her eyes.

After a while Pearl said, 'What did the matron say about all this?'

'She told me that having someone he can lean on will be very important to his recovery.'

'But that's what nurses are for.'

'I can do it much better.'

Pearl sighed heavily. 'Have you thought about what Mum and Dad will say?'

'I'm not going to tell them till after we've done it.'

'Ruby, you can't!'

'Yes, I can. They'd only try to change my mind, just like you are.'

'They'll be very upset.'

'They'll get over it.' She leaned forward and clutched Pearl's hand. 'Please say you're happy for me.'

'Why do you want my blessing? You've always done what you want.'

Tears sprang from the corners of Ruby's eyes. 'Oh, Pearl, I've always thought that no matter what happens in life, you and me would stand together.' She sobbed softly as the tears trickled down her cheeks. 'I've never needed you more than I do now.'

'You're making this very hard for me.'

'I don't mean to.'

'There's nothing I can say to change your mind?'

'No.'

Pearl was silent again. This opportunity for Ruby to change her mind was what she had hoped and prayed for. That somehow fate would send along the chance to

escape Ricky. But Ruby was too infatuated to recognize it.

'Ruby, I don't know what to say.'

'Just give me a cuddle.'

Pearl took her into her arms. She brushed back Ruby's damp hair from her cheeks. 'Are you sure this is what you want?'

'Yes, I'm sure.'

'I hope you always will be.'

'There's just one thing more.' Ruby wiped her wet cheeks. 'Would you let me and Ricky stay here when he's discharged? We wouldn't be any trouble. It would only be for a week or two at the most.'

'Here?' Pearl gasped.

'Yes, we've got nowhere else to go. Just till we find our own place. It will give us chance to get a nice place.'

Pearl knew Jim would never allow Ricky to live here. It just wasn't an option. She must say no. But how could she turn her sister down? If it was only for a couple of weeks, perhaps Jim wouldn't have to know. And if it made their start to married life easier . . .

Ruby leaned forward and hugged her. 'Oh, what would I do without you?' she whispered into Pearl's ear, giving a deep sob, her voice husky with emotion.

By April the talk was of invasion and counter-invasion. It was a topic discussed on every street corner and in every home. By the small hints Jim wrote in his letters, Pearl guessed he was with the Allies as they drove up through Italy to Rome. It was hard to believe that she had not seen her husband in over two years. The only thing that could be said for separation was that she had learned to stand on her own feet. When Cynthia had arrived and her job ended, she'd learned how to manage on a shoestring. Running a household on next to nothing meant that she'd had to

acquire a few tricks. She'd even scavenged on the bomb sites for kindling when she couldn't afford a street kid to do it for her. Many a time she'd borrowed Fitz's screwdriver and hammer and done her own repairs. Jim would probably laugh when he saw them, but at least she had tried.

The knock on the door broke into her thoughts. Cynthia jumped down from the table as Pearl went to see who was there.

Em and Colin were full of smiles. 'My! Haven't you grown?' Colin bent to ruffle Cynthia's sandy curls.

'Can we come in?' Em asked as she caught hold of Cynthia's hand.

'Course you can. I'll put on the kettle.' Pearl thought Em looked very happy and attractive. Her pink blouse offset the dark grey utility suit and matched the flush of her cheeks. Her hair was tucked under a shell hat. Colin looked well dressed in a dark suit and brogues. Pearl hadn't seen them since before Christmas, when they'd brought presents for Cynthia.

'We was hoping you'd be in,' Em said as Pearl led them into the front room. They sat on the couch and Cynthia showed them her drawings.

'Now what's this?'

'Mummy, Daddy and Aunty Ruby.' Cynthia lifted the paper to kiss the squiggles.

'She always sends Jim a kiss,' Pearl told them.

'How is he?' asked Colin.

'All right, as far as I know.'

'Can you draw Aunty Em?' said Em, bringing Cynthia close. 'And don't forget me new hat. Make it nice and pretty whilst I help your mum with the tea.'

Cynthia was transferred to Colin's lap whilst the girls went into the kitchen.

'Where's Ruby?' Em asked as she set out the cups.

'She's gone to ring Ricky in hospital.'

'Oh dear! Is he ill?'

'No, he's been wounded.'

'Oh, the poor man!'

Pearl didn't want to talk about Ricky or the proposed wedding at Brawton. She had tried to convince herself it could never happen. 'I've a bit of cake if you'd like some?'

'Did you make it?'

'Never thought I'd hear meself say it, but yes.'

Em laughed. 'What's in it?'

'Mainly apple and carrot, but it tastes better than it looks.'

'You used to say you couldn't cook.'

'I couldn't. But the war has taught me a lot of things. When Jim gets home, he'll have the shock of his life. I'm gonna feed him up so well that he won't be able to see his feet.'

Em laughed. 'You must miss him.'

Pearl nodded. 'It's hard to remember what he looks like until I see his photograph.' She cut the cake and arranged it on the tray with the tea.

'Do you know where he is?' Em asked.

'Italy, I think, by the hints he gives and what I read in the papers.' She cleared her throat quickly. 'Now come on, let's hear all your news.'

'I've got something special to tell you.'

Pearl looked at her friend. There was definitely a sparkle in her eyes and colour in her cheeks.

Em laughed shyly. 'You've probably guessed already.'

'You're getting married!'

'Yes, we're making plans now.'

Pearl kissed Em's cheek. 'I'm very happy for you.'

Em blushed. 'Colin's a really nice person. I'm lucky to have found him. A white wedding, especially in wartime, is a big challenge. So we've made very careful arrange-ments, which we'd like you and Ruby to be part of too, as our good friends. We've set the date and the church

and, of course, we have the gowns to make. We'd like you and Ruby to be bridesmaids, or should I say, in your case, matron of honour?'

'It sounds very grand.'

'Do you think Ruby will agree?'

'You can ask her when she comes in.'

Suddenly the thought struck Pearl that this might be just the thing to bring Ruby to her senses. A white wedding like Em's was what Ruby had been dreaming of. Perhaps Em and Colin's visit had come just in time to remind her of what she was missing if she married Ricky in haste.

Ruby pedalled fast down West Ferry Road. It was a lovely April day and her hair flew out behind her. It was wonderful not to have her turban on, or her factory overall. Wearing utility slacks and shoes was a bit of a nightmare, but at least the restrictions weren't so bad. She even had her eye on a brand-new lilac costume. She'd saved all her coupons and was determined to buy it for the happy day. And after what Ricky had told her today, she might be wearing it sooner than she'd thought.

Ruby couldn't ride home quickly enough. She wanted to tell Pearl her news. There were several whistles along the way, even though it was Sunday. The Americans were all over the place. London was full of them, swanking about in their smooth uniforms that so outshone the rough English material. It was generally known that they were on nation-wide military exercises to keep the enemy guessing about when and where the next offensive might be. But for all their charm, thought Ruby wistfully, none of them could compare to her Ricky.

So eager was she to share her news that she just missed a Jeep coming from the docks. She jumped off the bike to regain her breath. The Jeep was full of American service-men, and once more she was treated to admiring glances.

'Can I teach you how to ride that thing properly?' called one handsome young soldier as the vehicle slowed. 'Sure as Jiminy Cricket I'd love the chance.'

Ruby blushed, tossing back her hair. 'No, thanks. Me fiancé will do that for me. As soon as he gets home, that is.'

There was a chorus of disappointed 'ah's and 'oh's, as the young men leaned out of the uncovered truck. 'You mean he's left a great-looking gal like you alone?'

Ruby laughed at the flattery. She was too proud to tell them he was in hospital. 'He's in the navy.'

'You don't say?' The soldier grinned. 'Then we wish him good luck. Reckon we'll all need it now Ike's given the thumbs up.'

Ruby sat back on the saddle. 'Thumbs up to what?'

'You don't know about the invasion, sweetheart?'

Ruby shrugged. 'We've all heard a lot of talk.'

'Well, ma'am, you better believe it. Uncle Sam is all set to win this war.'

Ruby stuck out her chin. 'We weren't doing a bad job of it before you came in.'

'The little lady is right!' another soldier nodded, knocking his companion's shoulder with his elbow. 'But remember, it was us that first gave you the real news! Hitler's Fortress is about to fall all the way down! It's goodbye to—'

Just then another Jeep sped up. All the soldiers sat down and were quiet. The officer looked across and spoke words that Ruby couldn't hear. Within seconds the first Jeep had moved on. The American officer saluted her, then drove away.

Ruby rode home slowly. She was thinking about what the Americans had said. She was glad Ricky wasn't returning to service. If they were right and this was the last push, once again Ricky would have been in the thick of it.

There were hugs and kisses all round when Ruby came in.

183

'Em has some wonderful news,' Pearl smiled as she poured tea.

'This is for you,' said Em as they all sat in the living room. She handed a white envelope to Ruby.

'What's in it?' Ruby opened the smooth paper. 'Pearl, do you know?'

'Yes.'

Cynthia sat on Ruby's lap. 'Come on, Cynth, you can help me open it. Oh, you're getting married!'

'As you can see, the wedding is in October,' Em explained as Ruby read it. 'We'd like you to be my bridesmaid and Pearl matron-of-honour.'

'How lovely,' said Ruby quietly.

'We've asked Gwen and Fitz too. So you'll be able to sit at the same table. Colin's sister, Hope, is a dressmaker and is designing and making the gowns. Hope will need your measurements to begin with, then perhaps you could come for a fitting? I think you will like the material we've chosen. Thanks to Hope's pre-war stock, I can wear white satin and you girls, pink. She lives in Poplar, off the High Street, and has her dressmaker's room there.'

'Pink is a good colour for us,' said Pearl, looking at Ruby, but her sister just sat quietly.

'I'm so glad. Now I have everything I want.' Em looked shyly at Colin.

'I want you to have the best,' Colin murmured. 'You deserve it after all you've been through.'

'Where will you live after you're married?' asked Pearl.

'We've bought our own house,' Colin said. 'But sadly it isn't on the island. Everything is in ruins here.'

'Yes, that's true,' agreed Pearl, thinking of Roper's Way.

'Colin's been given promotion,' said Em, 'to north London.'

'What about your dad?'

'He'll come with us. Though the kids don't take the mickey or throw stones as much as they used to because

Colin is around, he is better off with us. I don't think he could live on his own.'

Colin adjusted his spectacles. 'It will be a new start for us all.'

'Are you having a honeymoon?' Ruby asked softly.

'Yes, we're going to Cornwall, to spend a fortnight in a rather splendid hotel,' said Colin.

'We'll miss you when you move,' said Pearl.

But Em only smiled. 'You can come and visit. I'll have the house to show you. It does need a bit of redecoration, but we shall make it cosy.'

'I know you'll be very happy wherever you live.' Pearl glanced at Ruby, but her sister seemed far away.

'I've invited Moira and her husband too,' said Em. 'She left the office you know, Pearl.'

'No, I didn't. I've lost touch and didn't even know she was married.'

'Nor did I. But I sent an invitation to an address that Mr Hedley gave me. She wrote back asking if it was all right to bring her husband.'

'Is it Arnie, that fellow we met at the dance?'

'I don't know. But it will be interesting to see if he turned out to be her Prince Charming.'

Ruby sat on the edge of her chair. Her eyes were very wide as she suddenly said in a very high voice, 'With all this talk of weddings, I'd better tell you my own news.'

Everyone turned to look at her. Even Cynthia, who was playing on the floor.

'Me and Ricky are getting married too.'

'Oh, Ruby, congratulations!' cried Em. 'But Pearl said he's in hospital. Is he well enough to leave?'

'It's not really a hospital,' Ruby said waving her hand. 'Brawton Manor is an old country house and is the country seat of Lord and Lady Brawton. We've decided it will make the perfect setting for our wedding.'

'It sounds delightful,' said Colin.

'However, it's in Surrey so I'm afraid we can't invite many guests.'

Everyone was silent. Ruby looked at Pearl. 'Except you, of course.'

'Me?' Pearl asked in surprise. 'But I can't come all that way. I've got Cynth.'

'Won't Gwen look after her?'

'They've got the shop.'

'We'll take care of her,' said Em hesitantly, looking from Ruby to Pearl. 'It will give us a bit of practice.' She blushed again as she glanced at Colin.

'Oh, that's wonderful!' exclaimed Ruby.

'But I've never left her before,' protested Pearl.

'You can count on us,' said Colin. 'We look after Hope's two youngsters and there's been no complaints.'

'And your honeymoon?' Em asked.

'We're considering Switzerland after the war,' said Ruby airily. 'Ricky has so many wonderful ideas that it's hard to choose between them. It was Scotland to begin with, but we'd rather wait until we can go somewhere special. In the meantime we'll look for our house. Like you, we will move off the island to a nicer area. We want a house with at least three bedrooms, so we can have guests to stay.'

'Well, again, congratulations,' nodded Colin. 'Your plans sound very exciting.'

Pearl sat in bewildered silence. It was the first she'd heard Ruby speak of a honeymoon in Switzerland, or that a lord and lady owned Brawton. It was also the first she had heard of a house with three bedrooms.

'What was all that about?' asked Pearl when they'd gone.

'What?' asked Ruby, her cheeks flushed as she looked through her bag.

'You've never said you wanted to go to Switzerland.'

'You've never asked. You never seem interested, so why should I say?'

'I am. It was just a shock to hear you talking like that.'

'I'm getting married too, you know.'

Pearl looked away. 'I don't know about leaving Cynth.'

'It seems you're still hoping I won't get married.' Ruby closed her bag with a snap. 'If you come or not, I don't care now as the plans are made. Ricky and me are tying the knot on Saturday the twenty-ninth of April.' Swinging her bag over her shoulder she flounced off.

Pearl sat down on the chair and hugged Cynthia. So the date had been set. It looked like nothing could stop Ruby now.

Chapter 17

Pearl sat on the comfortable seat of the train and though she'd had reservations about leaving Cynthia, she was enjoying the countryside. The fields were emerald green, full of cows and sheep. Except for her honeymoon in Margate, the last time she had been to the country was when she was twelve and had gone on holiday with the club. The Country Holiday Fund, as it was known, had sponsored her and Ruby's stay in Gloucestershire. It had been a wonderful seven days for children who only knew the Smoke. None of them knew what the country looked like. Now it came back to Pearl's mind as the train sped along.

Two horses galloped in a field, their thick manes flying behind them as though they were trying to keep up with the train. Even the people waiting at stations looked well dressed. There were no crying kids with dirty faces or East

End accents. Some English servicemen had sat with them for a while and had been very flirtatious. Pearl wondered if Jim acted in the same way when he saw pretty girls. He couldn't be fighting the enemy all the time. And she'd seen pictures in the paper of the Allies being given a warm welcome as they liberated the towns and villages of Italy. If only she knew more about his whereabouts …

'Penny for your thoughts,' said Ruby, nudging her arm.

'I was only thinking about Jim.'

' 'Spect he's thinking about you too.'

'I hope so.'

'I wish he could be at the wedding.' Ruby sounded upset. Had she forgotten Jim's feelings towards Ricky?

'You know Ricky and Jim didn't get along at the wedding,' Pearl said hesitantly.

'It will be different,' shrugged Ruby dismissively. 'When Jim knows the price Ricky has paid for serving his country, he'll change his mind. They've got a lot in common now.'

'I don't know about that.'

Ruby turned quickly. 'Pearl, I'm pleased that you finally agreed to be with me today, so don't go and spoil it.'

Pearl sighed and turned back to the window. She had been undecided about coming to Brawton, but, as usual, Ruby had won her round. There wasn't anything she could do about Jim's feelings, however. Ruby had convinced herself that Ricky and Jim would be friends in the future. And although she was right in saying that Ricky had paid a big price for serving his country, was that enough to make Jim change his mind?

'How do I look?' asked Ruby, poking Pearl's arm.

'Beautiful.' Pearl ran her gaze over the new lilac costume her sister had bought. It fitted her slender waist and hips perfectly. A cloche-style hat in the same colour covered her blonde hair and moulded to the shape of her head. Her eyes were shining. She looked very much in love.

'I hope Ricky thinks I look beautiful too.'

'Course he will. Any one of those soldiers or sailors would have married you on the spot.'

'It was nice to hear their flattery,' Ruby smiled dreamily. 'The tall officer was staring at you.'

Pearl blushed and Ruby laughed. Pearl had been surprised the officer had smiled at her. She felt dull in comparison to her sister as the suit she was wearing harked back to the days when Jim was on leave from Luton. She hadn't worn it since and had lost so much weight it hung on her. She glanced down at the freshly ironed skirt and remembered the hole in the hem that she'd mended. It hadn't taken Jim long to take it off her. She shivered at the thought of his hands caressing her. What would it be like when they made love again? Would they still be mad for each other? Two years was a long time. It would be even longer by the time he next got leave – *if* he got leave.

'What was that?' Ruby frowned.

'Didn't think I'd said anything.'

'You mumbled about the war.'

Ruby waved her hands. 'Some Yanks I met said President Eisenhower has given the thumbs up.'

'Where did you meet them?' asked Pearl curiously.

'It was the day Em and Colin visited. I nearly ran into this Jeep on me bike. They said Hitler's Fortress was about to come down. Well, that means France, doesn't it?'

Pearl didn't want to get up her hopes. Was this just another rumour? And even if the Allies landed in France, it would mean yet another battle. Where would Jim be in all this?

They sat quietly as the train sped on. Pearl's thoughts turned to Cynthia, whose happy laughter she was missing. She hoped there wouldn't be any raids whilst she was away. Em and Colin were going to stay the night at Pride Place as everyone thought it would be better for Cynthia to be

in her own home. But when she woke tomorrow morning, her mum wouldn't be there.

'Mum and Dad should've got my letter by now,' Ruby said suddenly.

'I hope they'll forgive you.'

'It was the only way.'

'So you keep saying.'

'They would have tried to talk me out of it.'

Pearl knew they would be shocked and hurt. And even though Amy liked Ricky, Ruby was her baby. She'd had great plans for the day when Ruby got married.

'I tried to explain that the reason is because of Ricky's condition,' Ruby said insistently.

'Not because you're worried he'll change his mind?' Pearl pointed out.

But Ruby shook her head. 'They wouldn't have understood.'

'They might have.'

'Don't be a wet blanket now. Remember, this is my wedding day.'

How could she ever forget it, Pearl thought as she returned her gaze to the countryside. From the very start, Ruby hadn't wanted any opposition to her plans and had told Pearl many times nothing was going to spoil them. Their parents would have advised delaying the wedding until Ricky was well again, and Ruby knew that.

'Surrey is such a romantic setting for a wedding,' said Ruby, unable to keep still. 'And I don't suppose there's many who can say they got married in a manor house owned by a lord and lady. I feel very lucky to have the opportunity for such a special affair.'

A village church and a small cemetery flashed by, then a row of cottages. Ruby had certainly talked herself into this special affair, Pearl reflected as she admired the thatched roofs and tiny windows of the half-hidden cottages. Could

she imagine herself and Jim living here? But the Smoke was where they came from, where they'd always be. There was always the hustle and bustle of the docklands, and friends and neighbours to speak to. Perhaps living in the wilds would have its advantages. Especially if you knew a lord and lady to have afternoon tea with!

When they got off the train an elderly man wearing a brown cap and tweeds was waiting on the station platform.

'Miss Jenkins and Mrs Nesbitt?'

They both nodded.

'I'm Arthur Forsythe. I live in the village and though I'm retired now, I've offered my driving services to the hospital. I understand this is rather a special occasion?'

Ruby blushed. 'Yes, I'm getting married today.'

Arthur smiled under his walrus moustache. 'Indeed. Matron has asked me to act as your driver.'

Ruby looked surprised. 'We thought we'd have to get the bus like I did last time.'

'Can't have the bride using public transport on her wedding day,' Arthur said in a cultured voice as he patted the big pockets of his smart country jacket. 'Matron tells me you're staying at the Brown Bear. Have you any bags to leave *en route*?'

'Only this.' Ruby lifted the attaché case containing their few personal effects.

'I can stow it in the boot,' Arthur nodded. 'We'll drive straight to the Manor.'

Arthur took the attaché case and led the way from the platform. Outside an old and battered, but sturdy-looking motor car awaited them. Arthur opened the door and Pearl and Ruby climbed in. 'Welcome to Brawton,' he said with a grin. 'Sit back and enjoy the view.'

Once more the trees and fields flashed past and it was not long before they entered an imposing drive. The bushes on either side were glossy and thick. The trees overhead rippled

like a green sea. Pearl gasped as the red-brick Manor, its dozens of windows reflecting the sun, came into sight. The roof had many tall chimneys, and two white pillars stood at the big front door.

'Told you, didn't I?' whispered Ruby as Arthur brought the car to a halt. 'Don't get your hopes up, though. I went on about it to Em and Colin, but it's a bit of a shock when you get inside.'

Pearl had never seen anything so grand in her life. Brawton Manor was like something out of the films. Perhaps Ruby hadn't been so foolish; this did seem like a very special place to be married after all.

But when they stepped inside the first thing that Pearl noticed was the strong, sickly odour of disinfectant. Even the cup of tea the matron offered them in the small refectory seemed to taste of it.

'I don't want to hurry you,' the matron said to Ruby as they put down their cups, 'but your fiancé is waiting. If you'd like to come this way ...?'

Looking very official in her dark uniform and white cap, she led Pearl and Ruby briskly over the highly polished wooden floors, their steps echoing loudly. Pearl braced herself for the sight of the ailing patients as Ruby had described, but they saw none.

'She's taking us another way,' Ruby whispered, and Pearl nodded silently.

Ruby seemed very relieved at this and Pearl was left to imagine that, before requisitioning, the Manor had been very splendid indeed. However, most of the carpets, wall hangings and antique furniture had been removed.

Finally the sisters were led into a room where an extended dining table had been covered by a white table-cloth. A wooden crucifix stood in the centre, between two big vases filled with fresh flowers. The long windows

were open to the scents of the spring fields. Under the windows were several rows of wooden dining chairs. Pearl sat beside Matron whilst Ruby took her place with Ricky and another uniformed man in front of the makeshift altar.

Pearl felt her heart lurch when she saw Ricky. Was it because he looked thinner and older? He turned briefly to nod. His dark eyes were just the same, black and intense, an expression that haunted her.

'The man in the next seat is Captain Lockwood,' Matron leaned close to say. 'He's performing the registration ceremony.'

Pearl noted the distinguished-looking older man, who had discreetly put his papers to one side. The vicar then joined them to give his blessing. Ricky, bandaged and burned, showed no emotion but Ruby gazed lovingly into his eyes.

It came as a shock to Pearl to see Ricky for once looking less than immaculately turned out. He wore his naval trousers and a white shirt, but no jacket because of his burns and bandaging.

Pearl's eyes filled with tears. She couldn't help it. Ruby looked so much in love. There was no exchange of rings as it had been deemed that only Ricky could put a ring on Ruby's finger, and he couldn't manage that with the bandages. Captain Lockwood had suggested it was done at a later date.

Pearl wished that Jim was beside her. His heart would surely soften at the poignant sight. As for herself, what did she feel? Did she still regard Ricky in the same way as she once had? Could she forgive him for what he had done in the past? If he was a changed person and truly loved her sister then the answer was yes.

When the ceremony was over, Pearl hugged her sister as they stood in the dining room where a small buffet had been prepared. 'Congratulations, Mrs Winters.'

Ruby looked radiant. 'I'll have to pinch myself when I wake up.'

Pearl raised her eyes to Ricky. She tried hard to think of him as her brother-in-law and not the man she once knew. It would be a big effort to put the past behind her but she was going to try.

Pearl left everyone to talk and went to the buffet table. A few of the nurses came in to wish the happy couple good luck. Several men, with sticks or on crutches, shuffled around the rather uninteresting-looking food. They didn't eat but smiled and talked quietly between themselves. What did the future hold for the survivors of this war? How would their disabilities affect their wives and children? Ricky might not entirely recover from his wounds. What kind of work could he do? What was in store for Ruby? She had started her married life by giving up her dreams, even though she insisted she and Ricky had others. If Ricky couldn't find work, then she would have to stay at the factory. So far, Mr Brewer had been very good about time off, but what if Ricky was ill and Ruby had to be with him?

Pearl saw her sister look up at her husband. Her green eyes filled with love and pride. Would Ricky prove a better husband than the lover Pearl had known? As for their affair, Pearl prayed it would always remain a secret. Jim and Ruby were everything to her and always would be.

Pearl waited in the car with Arthur Forsythe. Ruby was saying good night to Ricky. The sun was setting through the trees of Brawton Manor. The day had ended with a sky of burnished gold. Even with such beauty, Pearl was eager to get home. She was missing Cynthia. This was about the time she would tuck her into bed. Em and Colin had assured her they would follow instructions to the letter. But was Cynthia missing her? Pearl couldn't help but wish her

little girl was in her arms. She wanted to breathe her in, to feel Cynthia's plump little body tucked warmly under the bedclothes. Absence was certainly making her heart grow fonder. And that was true of Jim too.

Again, the question came to mind: what would he say when he knew Ruby had married Ricky? One day she would have to tell him. She must break the news gently ...

The car door opened. Ruby was clutching a hanky. Her hat was askew and her eyes very bright.

'It all went very well,' Pearl said as Ruby sat beside her.

''Spose so.' Ruby glanced at the back of Arthur's head. 'Thanks for waiting.'

'Congratulations, Mrs Winters.'

Ruby smiled.

As the car went along, she was quiet. Pearl knew she was missing Ricky. But he couldn't come out of the hospital. Leaving her husband at the end of the day was the price Ruby had paid for instant marriage.

'Cheer up.' Pearl took her hand.

Ruby stuck out her chin. 'It just feels strange.'

'It's bound to be.'

'I'm leaving me husband behind on my wedding night. Not many brides do that.'

'It's what you wanted.'

'Yes, I know and I don't regret it. I just want him home with me.'

Pearl thought to say, yes, but you haven't got a home to go to. But she couldn't be unkind.

'Did Matron tell you when he might leave?'

'No. I'll ask tomorrow.'

The Brown Bear came into sight, an old pub with a thatched roof and swinging sign, under which stood wooden seats. The street was bathed in dusk and a few stars had already begun to twinkle.

Arthur stopped the car and helped them out. 'I hope

you'll be comfortable here. It's not a bad place to stay, but it can be a little noisy sometimes. There are a lot of Americans still around.'

'We don't mind that. We was lucky that Matron managed to get us a room,' Ruby said gratefully as Arthur handed her the attaché case.

'Ten in the morning, shall we say?'

'Yes. I'll be waiting.' Ruby glanced at Pearl. 'Do you want to come too?'

'No. I'll walk to the station and meet you there.'

They watched Arthur drive off and stood for a moment in the still, spring evening. The smell of newly mown grass filled the air. Sounds of loud laughter came from inside the pub.

'That's the Yanks Arthur told us about,' said Ruby.

'We'll give the bar a wide berth,' nodded Pearl. 'They don't mean any harm.'

'I hope our room's at the back,' grinned Ruby.

'Look, isn't it pretty?' The narrow street was filled with tiny cottages and lattice windows. Thick, flowery vines grew up to the eaves, and most of the gardens had white picket fences. 'Don't half look like Gloucestershire,' said Pearl on a nostalgic sigh.

'Yes, it does. I could quite get used to this.'

'You mean you could live in the country?'

'I don't see why not.'

'This does take me back to Gloucester. We used to play in fields like those ones, remember? There was always real birds in the bushes and trees, not gulls, but little ones with red chests and pretty whistles. And the farmer's wife let us collect the eggs from the barn. Real lovely eggs they were, all warm and brown. I used to feel a bit sorry for the chickens.'

'Why was that?'

'Well, it was their babies.'

196

Ruby giggled. 'You daft thing.'

Pearl was glad she'd brought a smile to her sister's face. 'Come on then, let's go inside.'

Ruby opened the heavy, creaking pub door. They could see American uniforms through the window of the public bar as they went up to the tiny desk and said who they were. A large, red-faced woman wearing a white blouse and black skirt handed them their key. 'Congratulations, Mrs Winters.'

Ruby smiled. 'Thank you.'

'The matron is a friend of mine. When she telephoned to make the booking she said she wanted a special room for a new bride and her sister. It's a shame your husband couldn't be with you but I've given you the best room we have. I hope you two don't mind sharing a double bed.'

'As long as it's a big one,' grinned Pearl.

'The matron even found us a driver,' said Ruby. 'I should have offered to pay for the petrol.'

'Oh, don't worry about that,' dismissed the woman. 'Arthur has a petrol allowance from the authorities for driving for the hospital. It does him a good turn as well.' She nodded to the big wall clock. 'Are you hungry?'

Pearl looked at Ruby. Neither of them had eaten much of the hospital food as it, too, seemed to taste of disinfectant.

'I can find you some beef pie if you like?' said their host.

'Beef pie?' they both exclaimed at once.

'Real beef, you mean?' asked Pearl.

'Yes, of course.'

Ruby rolled her eyes. 'We haven't eaten beef in years, since before the war.'

'This is the country, don't forget. We raise our own animals. Come down in an hour. I'll put you in the snug, away from all the noise. Now, up the stairs and last on the left.'

'Did I hear right?' Ruby whispered as they went upstairs. 'Did she really say beef?'

'I hope it ain't one of them lovely brown cows we saw on the way,' said Pearl, which drew a chuckle from Ruby.

'Well, wherever it comes from, we'll eat it.'

When they opened the wooden door of their room, Pearl gasped. 'Oh, Ruby this is lovely. Look, the bed's huge.'

Ruby threw herself on it. She laid back and closed her eyes. 'So this is what a real bed feels like. I've been sleeping on that old camp bed of yours for so long I reckon me back has warped.'

Pearl smiled as she lay beside Ruby. It felt so soft and warm on the patchwork quilt cover.

'Look at them black beams above us,' said Ruby.

'And the panes in the window. They're like little diamonds.'

'I wish I was looking at them with Ricky.'

Pearl laughed softly.

'What are you laughing at?' demanded Ruby sitting up.

'Don't suppose many brides have slept with their sister.'

Suddenly they were both laughing and soon the tears rolled down their cheeks.

'How much did this room cost?' Pearl asked, bringing them back to reality.

'Don't know. Ricky's seeing to it. I only had to pay for the train.'

The room was growing dark. 'Let's look out of the window before the blackout,' said Pearl jumping up. 'Oh, just look at that!'

The blackout was still in force, but not to such a degree as in London. Little lights could be seen along the backs of the houses. It was quiet as the room overlooked the big yard. The trees made shadows everywhere, something not seen on the island.

'I wonder if the warden still comes round and tells them to put them out?' Ruby drew the curtains. She yawned

and stretched, then fell back again on the bed. 'Oh, this is heaven.'

Pearl sat on the dressing table stool and gazed in the mirror. 'Is the matron married? She seems very dedicated to her work.'

'Ricky told me her husband died in 'forty-two. He was in the air force, like that poor man that was in Ricky's room. He also died, I'm sad to say.'

'Don't let's think about the war,' said Pearl, turning round on the stool. 'This is your wedding night. Although it's not me you want to be with, I'd like to see you enjoy it.'

'You're not bad for a sister.' Ruby kept a straight face. 'Though I dare say there's better.'

Pearl threw a cushion as Ruby collapsed with laughter and so began a pillow fight as they'd done so many times as kids.

It wasn't until later, when they had washed and renewed their make-up, that Pearl reminded Ruby that downstairs in the snug, a delicious beef pie awaited them.

That night, Pearl and Ruby lay in the big double bed, well fed and content. Pearl had never eaten such a big, crusty pie, full of delicious brown meat. The vegetables had been cooked very lightly and tasted more like sweet nuts than the tough ones she bought from Hemsley's. There was a lot of difference between city and country food.

'I've been thinking,' said Ruby in the darkness. 'I really would like to live in the country. The food is lovely and all the people seem very friendly.'

'Yes, it's nice for a change, and very green. But I don't know about living in it.'

Ruby pulled the eiderdown up. 'Anyway, Ricky's got to get well first. I know that when he leaves hospital it will all be different. I'll prove to him that it doesn't matter about his injuries. A kiss and a cuddle go a long way.'

Pearl still didn't like to think about that, but now Ruby and Ricky were married, she had to make a special effort to accept the idea.

Ruby giggled. 'Like I said, you're not bad for a sister.'

'Nor are you.'

'Good night, then.'

'Good night, and sweet dreams.'

Pearl was awake long after Ruby had fallen asleep. The day she had been hoping might never come had been a surprise. Other than the lingering smell of disinfectant, there had been a charm to the service. Love shone from Ruby's eyes. But did Ricky feel the same about Ruby?

When at last her eyes closed, Pearl's last thoughts went to Cynthia and Jim. Drifting slowly asleep, she surrounded them with her thoughts of love and gratitude.

Chapter 18

On the morning of Tuesday 6 June, five weeks after Ruby's wedding, Pearl switched on the wireless to hear a broadcast made from the Home Service of the BBC. Shortly after midnight, three airborne divisions, the US 82nd and 101st and the British 6th, had flown over the English Channel to secure the beaches of Normandy for the D–Day landings. No longer was the invasion of Europe a rumour, it was a reality.

Pearl stopped what she was doing and, with Cynthia, rushed down to the shop. The whole street were talking about the news. Little by little the information was coming through that everyone had waited so long for.

'This is it then,' Fitz said as Pearl pushed her way through the shop. 'God bless all our lads and bring them home safely.'

Gwen was twiddling the knobs of the old wireless in the shop. 'Makes you proud, don't it?' she called, and Pearl nodded, experiencing the feeling of national pride as more news crackled out of the set. John Snagge, the BBC commentator, had revealed that at six thirty in the morning, when Britain was just waking up, the first landing craft had begun the assault on the French beaches. So far, the country was told, everything was going according to the Allied plan for the liberation of Europe.

Once again Pearl wondered where Jim was. Two days ago, the newspapers had reported that Rome had been liberated by the Allies. It was said that the city had fallen easily after the harsh and bloody battles of Anzio and Monte Cassino. Women had thrown flowers to the troops, and even given bottles of wine. The pictures in the papers had shown English and American soldiers being embraced and kissed. Had Jim enjoyed such a welcome? The young Italian women were beautiful. It would be easy for any man to fall into temptation. Especially after two years away from home.

It was Fitz who, as usual, gave a word of warning to his assembled customers. 'If we're successful and they pull it off, Hitler won't take it lying down. We have to be prepared for reprisals.'

'Like what, you old Jonah?' a woman in a headscarf demanded.

'The secret weapon he has up his sleeve,' declared Fitz. 'I don't want to be a killjoy, but we must be vigilant.'

'How can we be vigilant against something we don't know?' shouted another woman, looking annoyed. 'And you are a bloody killjoy, Fitz. Can't you wish our boys success?'

A man in a cap next to Pearl rolled his eyes. 'That's been the story of this war. There's always something invisible round the corner to be frightened of. You can't even celebrate a small victory.'

Fitz heard the comment. 'Well, it's only my opinion.'

'And you know what you can do with it,' chuckled the woman in the headscarf. 'Now sort me out some of them spuds, ducks, and I can get home and turn me own wireless on without all these interruptions.'

'And hurry yourself up, Fitz!' called Gwen, hands on hips as she stood at the counter. 'Just because we're winning the war at last don't mean we ain't got a business to run.'

Fitz grinned at Pearl from behind his spectacles and turned his attention to the potatoes. Pearl hurried back up the stairs. The air of excitement and expectancy was palpable. In the kitchen, she sat at the table with Cynth and the wireless.

'Throughout the night, British aircraft have pounded the German batteries along the French coast. Our paratroopers and marines have landed at the beachheads, whilst the US Air Force have continued the attack. Our ships have set sail, from large and small ports alike, converging on Normandy for the operation called Overload. The big question is, can the Allies supply reinforcements from the sea faster than the Germans can by land?'

Pearl couldn't wait for Ruby to come home. Her Factory would have heard the news by now. Tonight they would be glued to the set as they ate their dinner. Would we be successful in the most daring and closely guarded secret of the war? It was a question on everyone's mind. The outcome would affect every family in the United Kingdom.

Exactly a week later, Pearl was listening to another announcement. A pilotless plane carrying one ton of high explosives dropped its deadly cargo in Grove Road, Hackney, killing six people outright. Fitz was right: the secret weapon had arrived. People were hanging their heads in disappointment and blaming the government for spreading the good news too early.

As London braced itself for a repeat of the Blitz, a brief and uncensored letter from Jim gave Pearl the news she had been waiting for. He was in Italy. But that was all he said. It was a very short letter and he said he would write more at a later date.

Meanwhile, Hitler's doodlebugs or buzz bombs, as they were called, flew on automatic pilot at low altitude over Britain. When their tanks ran out of fuel, they would simply drop from the sky. The curious engine whine they made was soon feared by everyone. People would stop and look above them, praying the bombs would continue over.

It was as Pearl was walking home from the market two days later that she too heard the eerie sound begin. She stopped the pushchair, her heart racing as she looked at the sky. Was it right that as long as you could hear it you were safe? Unlike during the raids in the Blitz, there was no time to find shelter. The rockets were a law unto themselves.

Lifting Cynthia into her arms, she looked for cover. The other people in the street were leaning against brick walls or running away. Doors opened all along the road to let people in. It was a frequent sight now, though everyone knew that when a buzz bomb dropped there was no chance of survival directly beneath. The blast wave was lethal.

'Come in, ducks, come in,' said a woman in an overall and turban as she opened her front door. The whine of the doodlebug was growing closer. Pearl hurried in, leaving the pushchair outside.

'The first this morning but it won't be the last,' said the woman, as they stood in her dark passage. Pearl could smell cabbage and mothballs, and as she held Cynthia close, she knew she would forever associate this smell with doodlebugs. She closed her eyes. The whine was overhead now. The woman pressed up against her and Cynthia.

The whine continued overhead and onwards. Pearl

breathed a deep sigh of relief, but felt guilty for doing so. 'It's gone,' she whispered, and the woman nodded.

'Some poor sod has bought it,' the woman sighed.

'Thanks for letting me in,' Pearl said as she opened the door. 'It's frightening to be in the street. But you can't stay in all the time.'

'Course not. Have you got someone in the forces?'

'Yes, my husband. He's an engineer in the army.'

'Was he at Normandy?'

'No, he's in Italy.'

'Well, be careful, ducks. I heard on the wireless that over seventy of these new bombs have landed since Tuesday. Who knows what will happen in the next few weeks?'

Pearl stepped out cautiously. 'Goodbye, and thanks again.'

It was the first of many occasions that Pearl sought cover. The anti-aircraft guns were no help as they only made the situation worse over built-up areas. Even the news that the French landings had been a success couldn't cheer people up. Whole rows of houses were being demolished by a single V1. Why hadn't our armies stopped them?

'Be careful; go inside someone's house as soon as you hear it,' Pearl warned Ruby as she set out each morning.

Ruby was terrified of them. She wouldn't have gone to work if she wasn't now the breadwinner.

Pearl knew as well as her sister that it was pot luck when it came to the buzz bombs. Life had to go on, but the skies always held a threat.

On Sunday afternoon Pearl was washing up the dinner things when Ruby rushed into the kitchen. 'Turn on the wireless, Pearl. I was looking out the front window when Gwen shouted up from the street. The Guards Chapel, St James's, has been hit in the middle of morning service.'

The news was unbelievable. 'Over a hundred killed,' Ruby gasped at the end of the announcement. 'More possibly.'

'It can't be true,' Pearl whispered, but it was. The eventual death toll was one hundred and forty-one, and the nation was shocked.

The following morning, Ruby took the bus to work. 'I don't feel like riding me bike,' she said as she left. 'It's not so easy to hear them coming if you sit up the front with the driver, with the noise of the engine.'

Pearl didn't want to go out shopping either. But she knew she must, even though news of the terrible death toll spread an intense gloom. The newspapers announced that ack-ack guns and barrage balloons were now established in a line along the North Downs in Kent. These were meant as a trap for the pilotless planes. But confidence in deterents was waning, and people dreaded the ominous whine in the sky.

By the end of the month it was recorded that over one hundred and twenty-five doodlebugs had left their mark on the city. And the following week Ruby brought home even worse news.

'A V1 went into a dive outside the Air Ministry in the Aldwych,' she breathlessly told Pearl when she arrived home.

'What happened?' Pearl asked as she poured a cup of tea for Ruby, who was shaking.

'The Aldwych was packed 'cos it was the lunch hour. The wall outside the Ministry stopped a lot of the blast but even so, the wave went down the street and killed people. The girls sunbathing on the roof of the Ministry were killed, and even the passengers in the buses. Some were sucked out of their office windows.'

Pearl shook her head. 'Don't tell me any more.'

Ruby sank down on the chair in a daze. 'That bloody Hitler.'

'If this goes on, what will happen?'

'Someone's got to do something.'

A noise in the street made them jump up. They listened, attuning their eyes to the sky above. But there was no whine.

Cynthia banged her fists on the table and blew bubbles. She laughed, showing her baby teeth. Pearl gave her a smile, then looked at Ruby. 'It's just a plane. We'll become nervous wrecks if we let these things get the better of us.'

'Yes, that's true.'

'And anyway, if one fell on us, we wouldn't know a thing about it.'

Ruby nodded slowly. 'I don't think I want anything to eat. I wish Ricky was here. But at least there are no buzz bombs at Brawton.'

Pearl went to the drawer and took out the cutlery. She placed it on the table in front of Ruby. She had waited in a queue at the market for an hour this morning for a piece of fish the size of a finger. She'd spent a further two hours trying to make it look tasty. She felt desperately sorry for the Aldwych victims, but life had to go on. Since D-Day everyone had been in a state of tension. Most families had someone in France as the Allies moved forward towards Paris. There had been hundreds of thousands of casualties and letters weren't getting through. They had to believe what the newspapers and BBC said. As for the pilotless planes, well, they were a fact of life and had to be dealt with.

In no uncertain terms Pearl told Ruby she was going to eat her dinner come what may. They weren't going to waste a forkful, despite what was going on overhead.

Jim opened the letter with eager fingers, his eyes flying over the greeting. 'My darling Jim'. No doubt she'd be over the moon about the Normandy landings. Someone had managed to get hold of a newspaper yesterday that showed the King and Monty on the French beachhead, with the Tricolour fluttering over Cherbourg. It wouldn't be long

now before we broke through to Caen and the open road to Paris. Britain must be waiting with baited breath for every new development . . .

Jim wanted to linger on each sentence but his brain was so desperate for news that he was on to the second page before he realized what he was reading. This was not about the invasion, but Ruby and, God forbid, Ricky Winters. She had only gone and married the man! What in the world had made her do that? And how could Pearl condone such a thing? She knew very well his views on the bastard. Now he'd wormed his way into his sister-in-law's life and put a ring on her finger.

He read the next paragraph and his bottom jaw dropped. His own wife had been at the wedding! At some high-falutin country house, turned into a hospital, according to Pearl. Ricky bloody Winters wasn't any ordinary mortal. He even had to do getting wounded in style. An icy sensation crept over Jim, though it was stinking hot in the fields of the Italian countryside. What had been going on in his absence? He knew Pearl well enough to guess that she wasn't writing everything. She could write pages on Cynthia, and although he loved his daughter, there was only so much you could say about teething and nappies and breast-feeding. But Pearl had found a dozen different ways to describe the stages of her growth and what she said and did, and what a lovely kid she'd turned out. And give Pearl her due, she was a true homemaker, telling him every detail about Pride Place and the Hemsleys and their friends, and Amy and Syd in Abingley. But she'd not said much about Ruby, though he hadn't noticed before. Some of the letters went missing anyway, so he'd not thought much about it. Now, out of the blue, it turns out Ricky Winters had his feet under the table and there wasn't a thing he could do about it.

In frustration, he screwed up the letter. He'd never done

that before. He treasured his letters from home. He swatted away the midges that taunted him as they circled his sweating and dirty skin. In the ruins of the old barn, where once a tractor had stood along with the cows in the byres, there were now just burned-out relics. The landscape was grilled to charcoal during the fighting where once there had been a thriving farmyard.

They were still on the alert for snipers, but Jerry was long gone from here. The dawn had spilled a rosy light into the spines of the bombed building. A battered but intact Jerry helmet acted as a makeshift pee pot. At night it was too dangerous to stumble outside.

Fury swelled inside Jim and he strode over and booted the helmet. The contents flew into the dust. A lone chicken, a miraculous survivor from the battle, scuttled out with singed wings.

With all the force of his right fist he aimed a blow at the charred beam. It splintered noisily, coming down at his feet.

What in God's name was Pearl thinking of? What wasn't she telling him?

'Jim?' A tall, sunburned soldier strode across the barn floor, a frayed leather bag on his hip. 'Another one for you. Missed it first time round.'

Jim barely heard, but found the envelope in his hands. He was not even conscious of opening it, not until he saw the name 'Blackwood' and his mind made the connection.

Dear James or Jim,

I'm very sorry to have to tell you that our son, Albert, known to his friends as Blackie, died of his wounds at the Mareth Line, North Africa on 29 March of this year. A letter was written on his behalf by one of the nurses who tended to him. He said he wished to be remembered to you and to wish you good luck. We wish you the same and hope that this letter gets through. If you

ever feel like looking us up when you're home, the address is as above.

Regards, Dolly and Albert Blackwood (Senior)

Jim sank to his haunches, dropping his head to the ground. He wanted to weep for Blackie – do something, react in some way – but war had robbed him of emotion. He wasn't equipped to express his grief now; he'd seen too much death and dying.

He wanted to shout 'Stop!' To reclaim his old life and start where he'd left off. But he'd chosen his path and left his family behind in the process.

He put his hands over his lice-riddled head and rocked, listening to the sound of his breath.

In the middle of July the Prime Minister announced that well over one hundred flying bombs were being launched against Britain every day. This figure was followed by the number of deaths they had caused, which equalled the number of individual bombs: over two thousand seven hundred so far.

Pearl had reluctantly agreed to Fitz's proposal of setting up a Morrison shelter in the kitchen. The Andersons were no use with these types of bombs. Fitz had just finished building a Morrison for Gwen and himself, and was eager to make another.

'I can't see a wire box is much protection,' said Pearl one Saturday morning, as Fitz showed her the pieces of welded mesh. 'If one of them flying bombs lands on us, a cage ain't going to save us.'

'The government says they're very successful, Pearl. And this one will be big enough for the three of you. I don't feel happy having one meself and there's you up here, undefended.' He went on his knees and with his glasses on the end of his nose, studied the sheet of directions.

Pearl put her hands on her hips. 'I don't know where it's going to go.'

'You can use it as a table.' He indicated the flat parts and horizontal struts that were to be screwed together to make the oblong box. 'It's six foot six long and four foot wide. Put a nice clean cloth over it and Bob's your uncle, you've got a table.'

'But I like the table I've got. It's just right for Cynth. She draws on it all the time.'

'She'll be able to draw on this too. And play inside it.'

At that moment Cynthia appeared. She was holding a rag doll Amy had sent her. She saw Fitz and sped across the kitchen floor, seating herself beside him. She was all smiles and both Fitz and Pearl began to chuckle.

'Your mother doesn't approve of this, young lady, but I'll bet you do.' He showed her the picture of the Morrison. 'See, you can crawl inside and play. Or you can eat off it. Or draw pretty pictures in your book.' He lowered his voice as he handed Cynthia the instructions. 'Now, just tell me what nut and bolt goes where.' Their laughter almost drowned the knock at the door.

When Pearl opened it at first she didn't recognize the visitor. He wore a trilby hat and a dark coat with the collar turned up. His gloves seemed far too dressy for such a warm day. It was then the penny dropped.

'Ricky?'

He smiled, slowly raising his arms to carefully take off his hat. 'I'm sorry, I've given you a shock.'

'No ... well, yes,' she admitted. 'You ... are the last person I expected to see this morning.'

'I've left Brawton.'

'Have you had the all clear?'

'In a manner of speaking.'

Pearl felt a tug at her skirt and looked down. Cynthia was staring up with her blue eyes. A lock of sandy-blonde hair dangled in front of her nose.

Ricky stepped in. 'So you must be Cynthia?' He bent down, smiling. 'I've heard all about you and am very glad to meet you.'

Pearl watched her daughter as she slid her thumb in her mouth. Swaying back and forth on her heels, she was quick to return the smile.

'A lovely child,' Ricky said in a quiet voice. He touched his upturned collar self-consciously. Then looking into Pearl's eyes, he added, 'As lovely as her mother.'

Ruby stepped off the bus and searched the sky before hurrying along West Ferry Road. There had been several alerts this morning, but the noise at the factory had drowned out the stomach-churning sound. She couldn't pretend she wasn't scared, because she was and it showed. She hadn't been herself since the Aldwych tragedy. She just wanted to be with people. Not that it would make any difference if the bomb dropped on the bus or in the street or on the house. But at least if you were in company you could share the danger. Some East Enders even made a joke of it, like the bus conductor when he shouted over his shoulder that his bus, the number fifty-seven, was faster than any V1.

As Ruby approached Pride Place, she breathed a sigh of relief. Her ten-minute walk home had been uneventful. The first thing she was going to do was wash her hair. The heat of the factory and smell of machinery was ingrained in it under her scarf. Then she'd change from her working slacks into a skirt and perhaps she and Pearl could chance a walk to the market. It was too nice to stay in. And why should the fear of the doodlebugs prevent them from going out? She was still giving herself a pep talk as she waved to Gwen in the shop and turned into the alley. Fitz wasn't in the storeroom, so perhaps he was carrying out his promise to build the Morrison shelter. The thought gave Ruby a shudder as neither she nor Pearl fancied one of the ugly

contraptions. Dad had refused to have one at Roper's Way, preferring the Anderson. But then, of course, there had been no V1s.

As she ascended the stairs, a low whine could be heard in the distance. Ruby froze, her ears pricked for the direction. A V1 was in flight, but where was it? She grabbed the handle of the door and with a sweat breaking out over her skin, rushed inside.

'Pearl! Pearl! One's coming over!' she screamed, and almost fell over Fitz.

'Steady there, gel.' He stood up as the noise grew louder. Then two figures appeared from the living room. As the buzz bomb travelled closer, Ruby's face crumpled.

'Ricky? Oh, Ricky! Is it you?'

He opened his arms and she fell into them. The sound of the high-pitched whine was so loud that everyone ducked. She buried her face in his chest and closed her eyes. For a moment she didn't care about dying. If she died it would be in the arms of the man she loved. Then, as the noise faded and continued into the distance, she could hear only the beat of her heart.

'Ruby, it's gone,' he told her. 'You're safe now.'

She looked up at him as if waking from a dream. Then she saw Pearl with Cynthia in her arms. They all stood still, waiting for the inevitable crash. It came as the bomb found a target.

'With a bit of luck, it might have gone in the drink,' said Fitz, even though they all knew it hadn't.

Ruby looked up at her husband. 'Why didn't you write to tell me you were coming home?'

'I didn't know myself.'

'Why was that?'

'I've decided they can do nothing more.'

'But what about your hands?'

'I shall keep my gloves on. I don't want to upset you.'

212

Ruby put her arms around him. 'You'd never do that. Oh, Pearl, isn't it wonderful he's home?'

'Yes, it is.'

Just then there was another knock on the door. Fitz hurried to open it.

'Fitz, you daft 'aporth,' shouted his wife, her hands on her hips, 'I tried to get in the Morrison, but you've nailed the bloody thing together.'

Fitz frowned. 'Oh dear.'

'And by the time the bomb had gone over I'd broke the bread knife trying to get it open. As far as I'm concerned you can move the perishing thing to the yard and put a couple of rabbits in it.'

'But, Gwenny—'

'Don't Gwenny me, Fitz Hemsley. I want it out of me way right this moment.' She stopped, out of breath, her annoyed expression fading as she saw Ruby in Ricky's arms. 'Oh, sorry, I didn't know you had company.'

Ricky nodded. 'It's good to see you again.'

Gwen smiled uncertainly. 'You too, love.'

'Well, we'll be off,' said Fitz, taking his wife's arm. 'I'll come back to fix that later.'

Ruby felt like laughing. Was it the relief that the bomb had missed them or was it because Ricky was home and everything was going to be wonderful again?

'You can have my room,' Pearl said after Cynthia was in bed and they were discussing the sleeping arrangements. 'The camp bed won't take two.'

'I won't hear of you giving up your room,' said Ricky as he sat beside Ruby, her arm linked over his. 'I shall be quite comfortable on the couch.'

'For tonight you can sleep on it,' said Pearl, already having made the decision. 'And tomorrow we'll change over.'

Ruby smiled. 'I can't believe you're home.'

'You won't have to put up with us for long,' Ricky said as he smoothed the cloth of his gloves.

Ruby glanced at her husband. 'Pearl doesn't mind.'

'I'm going to the Labour Exchange on Monday. They are sure to offer me something. I can write now, albeit slowly. And although I can't do manual work I have a good head for figures.'

Pearl wondered how successful he would be. Even healthy men were finding it hard to get jobs. Though Ricky had eaten his meal wearing the special cotton gloves that the hospital had provided him with, was that acceptable in the real world? The burns on his neck had turned a pale pink and weren't so noticeable. But he'd told Ruby he had discharged himself from Brawton. Had that been wise?

'Have you any clothes?' Pearl asked.

'Only these.' He glanced down at his thick navy twill trousers, jumper and service shoes. 'But I've coupons to spend at a gents' outfitters.'

'You'll soon be looking your old self,' Ruby said eagerly.

'Yes, I hope so.'

Pearl thought how, if that was Jim, he'd not give a hoot as to how he looked. He'd be off down the market for something cheap and cheerful. But that was not the case with Ricky. He was still very particular about his appearance.

'There's a jug and basin in the bedroom,' Pearl said. 'I'll put Jim's clothes away for now. If you want to shave in the kitchen, Jim's mirror is on the shelf.'

'I'm obliged to you,' Ricky nodded. 'And I don't expect charity as I'm still receiving my officer's pay.'

'That doesn't mean you can go back to the navy?' Ruby asked in alarm.

'No, more is the pity.'

'Well, I'm delighted,' said Ruby laying her arm lightly across his chest. 'I'll have you all to myself.'

214

'I don't regret a day in the navy,' Ricky said tightly. 'I would do it all over again for my country.'

Pearl saw Ruby's eyes fill with pride. 'You are so brave, darling. But now you don't have to be. You can get well slowly without any rush. After all, I have my job at the factory.'

'That isn't the point, Ruby. We can't live on such a meagre wage.'

'Eventually it will be different,' Ruby smiled. 'I'm just so happy to have you home.' She snuggled against him.

Pearl stood up. 'I'll fetch the bedclothes.'

'I don't want to be any trouble.' Ricky stared at her. 'I owe you and Jim my thanks.'

Pearl could imagine Jim's reply: that no amount of thanks was going to square Ricky Winters sleeping under his roof.

When Pearl undressed that night, she gazed at the bed. It was very dear to her, full of memories. She and Jim had nearly worn it out. Lovemaking was a big part of their lives. She might have been put off it for ever if it had been left up to Ricky. But Jim had turned sex into love. She hoped that would happen for Ruby too. With the right man, marriage was wonderful. Pearl smiled as she thought of the time Jim had come home and it had been so cold they'd jumped into bed right away. She also remembered the time when Jim had tried to tell her they couldn't solve all their problems in bed. But to Pearl, that was the perfect place. As she climbed between the sheets she hoped that it wouldn't be long before she was back here, and Ricky and Ruby had begun the new life that Ruby was dreaming of.

Over the next few weeks, Pearl's worst fear was not of the doodlebugs, but what Jim would write back after reading the letter she'd sent, telling him Ruby was married.

Amy and Syd hadn't taken the news well. There had been several letters back and forth between Ruby and Amy.

Each time one came, Ruby just said the same thing to Pearl: that it was done and done with, and eventually they would accept it. But Pearl had her doubts. When at last she found the courage to write to her parents herself, she only referred to the wedding briefly. The rest of the letter she filled with her news of Jim, Cynthia and the raids. She told them not to worry, that everyone was getting used to the bombs. But she knew her mother had been hurt by the snub of the wedding and was worried about the doodlebugs.

Each evening followed the same pattern. Pearl and Ruby cooked dinner, and Cynthia sat at the Morrison with her chalks. Ricky would sit by the fire and scour the newspaper for any news of prospective work. Ruby would talk about her day, telling Pearl that Ricky was determined to find a job.

'He goes to the Labour Exchange and waits every morning. Then he walks round, asking if there are any vacancies. I'm so proud of him as he doesn't just mope around but goes to help at the Disabled Servicemen's Centre.'

Pearl was beginning to think that Ricky really had changed. He did what he could to help around the house and, despite his hands, made an effort to play with Cynthia and had even taken her for walks. Pearl could see he was trying to be a good husband and slowly her feelings towards him were changing.

One evening after work, Pearl had a letter addressed to Ruby. 'It's from Mum and Dad, by the looks of the handwriting.'

Ruby tore it open.

Pearl paused as she peeled the potatoes. 'What do they have to say?'

'Mum wants to know if Ricky's got a job.'

Pearl could see that their mother's constant enquiries made Ruby irritable. 'They're bound to be concerned.'

'Why does she keep on, though?' Ruby said crossly.

'She wants to see you settled.'

Ruby dropped the letter. 'You want to get rid of us, is that it?'

'No, course not.'

'Ricky tries everything to get a job. But I don't think they appreciate how difficult it is, even for someone who's well.'

Pearl wiped her hands on her apron. She didn't want to get into an argument, especially as Ricky seemed to be doing his best.

'Ruby, it will all work out in the end.'

'I hope so.'

'Now go in with your husband. You've had a long day at work and I don't expect you to help with the chores.'

Ruby sniffed and slid the turban from her head. 'I had a bad day. The bombs are driving me mad. One of the girls in the machine shop was killed in the Co-op over Dulwich last Saturday. I only knew her vaguely but it's very upsetting.'

'Yes, but you and Ricky still have each other.'

Pearl watched her walk slowly away. She wasn't coping with the doodlebugs. When Lewisham market had been bombed and sixty people had died, she had brooded over it for days. Even now she refused to shop at the market. She never used to have bad days at work. She always enjoyed the factory. But could there be something more?

'Mummy, look!'

Pearl turned to her daughter, who was waving her drawing in the air. 'What's this, sweetheart?'

Pearl gazed at the drawing of the group of stick figures with happy faces and big smiles. How wonderful it was to see life through a child's eyes. Why couldn't it be like that in real life?

A thought that Pearl quickly forgot as a familiar whine began in the distance and Ruby ran, ashen-faced, from the living room.

Chapter 19

Pearl was trying to make space in the little bedroom that she and Cynthia were now squeezed into when she heard shouting. Going into the living room she lifted the sash to look down. Gwen rushed out of the shop and her customers followed. Percy Flint was sitting on his cart and waving his arms. Then he slapped the reins and moved off. Pearl took Cynthia downstairs.

'Pearl! Pearl!' Gwen took her arm and squeezed it. Her eyes were wide in her long, thin face.

'What's up?'

'Paris is liberated!'

'Are you sure?'

'Yes, Percy said so. Eisenhower's troops surrounded the city and the French Resistance helped them. The Nazis were forced to surrender.'

'They just gave up?'

'They knew when they were beaten. Trust the Yanks.'

Pearl heard an old woman singing 'La Marseillaise'. Although she didn't seem to know the words, it was good enough for the others to join in. Gwen and Pearl smiled as they watched the comical scene. The crowd linked arms and swung their shopping baskets, as the tune soon turned into the British national anthem.

'Just think what it'll be like when we win the war,' said Gwen as they strolled back to the shop. She waved at Fitz inside, who was surrounded by customers. He stuck up his thumb and Gwen made the Victory sign.

'I suppose this means we're in with a chance,' said Pearl hopefully.

'I should say we are,' nodded Gwen.

'I wonder if Jim's in Paris? The last I heard he was in

Italy.' She didn't know whether to be pleased or not. The French women were supposed to be even more alluring than the Italians.

'You'll get a letter soon, love. There will be lots to write about if he is.'

Pearl lowered Cynthia to the cobbles. She was getting heavy now. 'Go and see Fitz, love,' Gwen said, patting her golden curls. 'See if he's got a little sweetie for you.' Gwen looked at Pearl. 'August the twenty-fifth is a day the world is going to remember. But when the Allies put Hitler in handcuffs, I reckon the world will go crazy.'

'I hope Jim will be home by then. If he was back by October, he'd be here in time for Cynth's birthday. And then there's Em's wedding the week after.'

'Oh, I forgot to tell you, your friend sent me and Fitz an invitation. Now ain't that nice of her? But it will only be me, I'm afraid, as we can't afford to close the shop.'

'Will Fitz manage on his own?'

'He will for one day. It will give me a chance to put me glad rags on.'

Pearl smiled. 'We're going for our fittings tomorrow. Colin's sister is a dressmaker and has got a place up Poplar.'

'Do you want me to have Cynth for you?'

'But you'll be in the shop.'

'She can help me sort out the shelves.'

'Well, that would be nice—' Pearl stopped abruptly as she heard a stomach-sinking noise in the distance. The street went from dancing and laughing to complete silence. Then the whine fizzled out and there was a plopping sound.

One man threw back his head and laughed. 'That ain't no doodlebug, it's a bloody bilge pump!'

But the threat was enough to end the celebration and everyone began to disperse.

'Bloody bombs,' said Gwen, and opened her arms to Cynthia, whose mouth was full. 'What's old Fitzy given you?'

Cynthia chuckled and swallowed at the same time. 'Sweetie,' she said, wiping her sticky mouth with the back of her hand.

'Lucky girl. He don't give Gwenny sweeties. You must be his favourite. Now how is your uncle Ricky these days?' She addressed the question to Cynthia but Pearl knew it was meant for her.

'He's much better thanks.'

'Still wearing them gloves, I see. No job in the offing?'

'No.' Pearl looked along the alley. 'But he's trying his best. I know he thinks so much of Ruby that he wants to make her proud.'

'Let's hope he can, then.' Gwen smiled hesitantly. 'Don't forget to leave Cynth with me tomorrow,' she called as Pearl took her leave.

Once upstairs, she turned on the wireless. The news was all about the liberation of Paris. Not only were our troops there, but some of the launching sites of the V1s had been found and destroyed by the Allies. Pearl couldn't wait to tell Ruby some good news for once. All they needed now was Ricky to find himself a job and life would seem perfect again.

The following day, Saturday, after Ruby returned from work, she and Pearl caught the bus to Poplar. With the news about the doodlebugs not coming over so much, Ruby was in a good mood. Gwen was minding Cynthia and Ricky had offered to cook supper. Pearl had left vegetables on the drainer and opened a tin of sardines for fish pie, to make it easy. Although he still wore his gloves he said his hands were much better. Each night Ruby washed the gloves out and hung them on the line to dry, making Pearl smile as she tugged at them like cow's udders.

'Ricky wants to show he's still useful,' said Ruby as they sat on the back seat of the bus. It was hot and the sun shone

through the windows onto their bare arms. 'It's just that he don't like showing his missing fingers.'

'What about his burns?' Pearl paused. 'Don't answer if it upsets you.'

'It's not that,' Ruby shrugged. 'It's just that he don't say much about what happened. The scars are still red across his chest and he don't take his vest off.'

'The pain must have been awful.'

'He said he was lucky. Some of his mates didn't make it, although they tried to hold on to the lifeboats.'

'Didn't the rescue ships come along?'

'No, they didn't want to be torpedoed themselves. If your ship goes down, you don't stand much chance in the sea. And sometimes the merchant ships only have four escorts and the German wolf packs are huge.'

'Wolf packs?'

'That's what they call the subs when they hunt in packs.'

Pearl sighed softly. 'Little did we know what was going to happen at the beginning of the war when the *City of Benares* was torpedoed.'

'Yes, all them poor kids on a harmless refugee ship sailing to Canada! It was said that even the Germans were sorry to have killed so many youngsters.'

Pearl nodded. 'But our side has done bad things too, only we ain't told about them.'

'You sound like a right rebel.'

'I don't believe everything I hear on the wireless.'

Ruby shuddered visibly. 'For myself, it wasn't the Blitz that terrified me, it's these doodlebugs. It's that noise they make. It's worse than the Luftwaffe. God, I'll remember it all me life.'

They were silent for a moment, considering this, until finally Ruby said slowly, 'Pearl, me and Ricky feel it's not fair to put on you much longer. I mean, you're sleeping on a camp bed and there's us in the lap of luxury.'

221

'I don't mind.'

'If this war does come to an end, Jim will be home.' Pearl glanced at her sister. What kind of reply should she give? But Ruby was quick to continue. 'If Jim is demobbed, he'll want his bed back.'

'It's not happened yet.'

Ruby held up her hand to shield her face from the sunshine. 'Actually, Mum and Dad want us to go and visit.'

'I didn't read that in her letter.'

'Mum gave me her neighbour's telephone number to ring. A girl called Patty.'

'You kept that one quiet.'

'I wanted to talk to Ricky before I said anything, as I didn't know if he'd want to go there until he's well enough.'

'And does he?'

Ruby looked down. 'No, he don't, not yet.' Once again they were silent until Ruby said, 'I can't wait to see our dresses.'

'What will we do for shoes?'

'Don't know. We'll have to see the colour first.'

'I can't afford new ones but I've still got me wedding shoes, so perhaps they'd be all right.'

'The ones that looked as if the person who had them before had bunions?' asked Ruby.

Pearl turned to see a big smile on her face and they didn't stop laughing until the bus stopped in Poplar.

'The measurements Emily gave me were perfect,' said Hope Haskins in a quiet voice, pushing her spectacles along the bridge of her nose with the tip of her little finger. 'The dresses fit perfectly. Look in the mirror.'

Pearl and Ruby stood side by side in front of the long mirror hanging on the wall. They had been surprised at how nice Hope's house was inside, even though outside it was over the High Street tobacconist's. The building

was three floors high and the attic room was for Hope's dressmaking business. It was a long climb up the narrow flights of stairs but was worth it. Amidst the rolls of materials, overflowing shelves and drawers was a long worktop stretching from wall to wall. Beside it stood a full-sized headless mannequin. In the corner was a treadle sewing machine and another counter hidden under a mountain of cotton, scissors, threads and boxes of pins.

'Oh, this is lovely!' exclaimed Ruby as she twirled around and the skirt of the plum-coloured dress opened in full.

'And look at this embroidery on the waistbands,' Pearl said as she smoothed her hands over her dress. 'It's so well finished.'

'I'm glad you like them. The shade is enhanced by your colouring.'

Pearl thought how nicely Hope spoke. She used long words like 'enhanced'. She had been very clever to make such stunning gowns. With a few nip and tucks, the dresses seemed complete.

'Now, to the hems,' said Hope, sitting back on her heels. 'An inch higher, don't you think, Ruby?'

Ruby, who was shorter than Pearl, nodded. 'Yes, to keep up with the fashion.'

Hope made the change, then looked at Pearl's slightly large bodice. 'If you'll raise your arms . . .?'

Once again she made the adjustments, taking pins from a sponge tied on her wrist.

'That will do.' She frowned, causing Pearl to smile as she looked so much like Colin. Not as skinny as Colin, but she had that same studious expression under her spectacles.

After the fitting, Pearl didn't want to take off her dress. It reminded her of the feminine clothes she used to like to wear before the war. How could she have let herself go like this? All her attempts to resist utility wear had failed. And now there was little choice on the market stalls either.

Ruby slid the dress over her arms. Pearl tried hiding her grey underwear. Her petticoat and bras had had so many washes they were thin and discoloured. Her brown skirt and fawn blouse looked old and tired in comparison.

'Do you need us again?' Ruby asked, buttoning up her blouse.

'I'll let Emily know if I do.'

'Can we see Em's dress?' Pearl asked.

'I don't see why not.' Hope led them out of the room and down the stairs to the living quarters. Two small children were sitting with an older woman on the couch. 'My mother and my children,' Hope introduced. The boy was about six or seven, the girl a little younger. They looked up from the floor where they had been playing and said hello. The older lady, dressed in a smart suit with her hair coiled stylishly at the back of her head, merely nodded.

Hope took them into a bedroom. Pearl noted how well furnished it was, with an art deco suite of furniture and big double bed with a silk cover. Inside the shiny wardrobe was Em's wedding dress.

'I keep my finished pieces in here,' explained Hope, carefully bringing out the gown and laying it on the bed. It was stunning, long and slender, with lace sleeves and a ruffled neckline.

'Oh, it's a dream,' said Ruby, the envy clear in her voice. 'Has it got a veil?'

'Yes, I'm working on that at the moment.'

'You're so clever,' said Pearl, noting the tiny, embroidered stitches around the cuffs. 'Em's a lucky girl.'

'I would say that Colin is luckier,' said Hope with a smile. 'He has very high standards and Mother and I had almost given up hope that he'd find the right girl. Have you known Emily for long?'

Pearl nodded. 'I used to work with her in the Borough Surveyor's department.'

'She speaks very highly of you.'

'Does she?' Pearl blushed.

'And Cynthia, of course. Which reminds me, would you like me to make a dress for your daughter with the remnants of the material? She's two, isn't she?'

Pearl was delighted. 'She will be, a week before Em and Colin get married.'

'I'll style it as a smock to allow for growth so she can wear it to parties afterwards. All the measurement I will need is her height.'

'That's good of you,' said Pearl. Not that Cynthia had any parties to go to.

On their way out the two children both said goodbye politely, as did Hope's mother.

Sitting on the bus, Ruby was the first to comment. 'Ain't they posh, Pearl? Did you hear the way Hope called her mum "Mother"? And those two kids – it was definitely the King's English they spoke, not cockney like us.'

'I'm not surprised, as Colin speaks well.'

'Has Em ever mentioned her in-laws-to-be?'

'No. But once Colin did. Don't you remember? It was when they looked after Cynth that weekend. He said that him and Em sometimes looked after his sister's children.'

Ruby was pensive. 'I'd like my kids to grow up some-where nice like North London. I should start watching me p's and q's. Ricky speaks nice and I don't want to let him down.'

'Where was he born?' Pearl said, trying to recall what she knew of Ricky's background.

'Blackheath. On the other side of the river.'

'How did he come to the island?'

'His parents were well off, but they died and Ricky had to make his own way in the world. I suppose he just landed up here. But he's always wanted to better himself. It's just unlucky that the navy put paid to his dreams.'

Pearl glanced at her sister. 'But you'll make other ones between you.'

'I don't seem to be getting pregnant.'

Pearl smiled. 'You will when you don't try.'

Ruby turned away again. Pearl wondered if this was what was worrying her. She wished she could tell her sister that once she too had thought that, after a miscarriage, another child might not come along. Yet Cynth had been born, a healthy bouncing baby, conceived the night that she and Jim had slept on the couch together. Pearl sighed to herself. The secret of her affair with Ricky and miscarriage could never be shared. It was a memory that she alone had to bear.

'What about a wedding present?' asked Pearl, looking out of the window at the shops.

'Dunno,' said Ruby disinterestedly. 'It will have to be cheap.'

'What about linen?' said Pearl. 'If we started saving now, we'd have enough coupons between us. You could give sheets and me pillowslips. We could embroider E and C on the corners to make them personal.'

Ruby shrugged. 'If you like.'

Pearl knew that whatever they gave would be appreciated by Em, even if it was only sheets and slips. But she knew that Ruby was ashamed because they couldn't buy something that would befit Em's grand new lifestyle in North London.

On 7 September, the Chairman of the War Cabinet Committee for defence against German bombs, Duncan Sandys, made an announcement. 'Except for possibly a few last shots of V1s,' he confidently told the nation, 'the attacks on London are over.'

'No more doodlebugs, thank God!' Ruby exclaimed that night as she sat on the stool in the bedroom, brushing her hair. 'Won't it be wonderful?' She glanced over her bare shoulder to the bed where her husband lay.

He was reading a newspaper and she knew he didn't want to be disturbed. What was going through his mind? Why couldn't she penetrate the wall he'd built round him since leaving hospital? Was he like this because of his injuries? If only they had made love and could enjoy each other physically. But lately his desire for her seemed to have cooled. If she looked at him, as she wanted to, with desire, he turned away. If she looked elsewhere and talked instead, that irritated him too.

Returning the brush to the drawer, she stood up. Her deep blue nightdress was the one she had worn for their hotel rendezvous. He had wanted her so much then. Was it her fault that the physical side of their marriage wasn't working out? She would give anything to make him want her like that again.

She shivered in the cold room and folded back the eiderdown. 'Ricky?' she whispered as she slipped in beside him.

He didn't reply and Ruby slid her arm around his waist. He gave her a brief glance, but his eyes showed no expression.

'Can we talk?'

'What about?' he murmured, still reading the paper.

'Well,' she began a little resentfully, 'can you put that down. Or is what you're reading more important than us?' She touched the buttons of his long-sleeved vest lightly, knowing how self-conscious he was of the scars underneath.

He folded the paper away. 'So, what is it you want us to talk about?'

'Everything,' she answered, relieved to have caught his attention. 'Like what we're going to do with our lives. Where we'll live. How many children we'll have—'

'I've not had the sniff of a job,' he interrupted her angrily, 'and we haven't got a bean to our name, no savings and very little to cover the costs of daily expenses. How can you expect me to comment on a future?'

'But we should make plans.'

'There are none to make.'

'Don't say that.' She ran her hand down to his thigh. 'I thought after we were married—'

'You thought,' he snapped, pushing her away, 'that marriage would somehow cure this unsightly body of mine and solve all the problems that now seem to be ten times worse than they were before.'

'That's not a nice thing to say.' Ruby felt her lips tremble.

'Oh, don't start that.'

'I'm not.'

Whenever she tried to get close to him, he would say something hurtful. Did he do it deliberately, or did he not understand just how much he drove a wedge between them?

'Ricky, I love you.'

'You don't know what love is.'

'Ricky!' She sat up. 'You say some rotten things.'

He threw the covers off. Getting out of bed, he snatched up his dressing gown, then stopped at the door. 'You have no idea what it's like to walk the streets day after day with no work in sight, no challenge, no aim. The navy was all I had and now it's gone. I'm adrift.'

Ruby stared up at him. 'Why haven't you told me this before?'

'We have no privacy.'

'Come back to bed, Ricky. I'll listen.' She wanted to put her arms round him, but instead he went out of the room.

She sat in bed alone, the tears very close. What was going wrong with their marriage? Wasn't she attractive to him any more? Or was it like the matron had once warned her? Some men never got over their experiences of war. Perhaps he needed a doctor's help to recover and he'd left Brawton too early.

She laid down and tried to sleep. The minutes crawled

by as she stared into the darkness. Then she heard the door open. Ricky climbed back into bed and said gruffly, 'Go to sleep.'

She put her arm out. 'Oh, darling, I wish we could move away, make a really new start.'

'It would be no better anywhere else. In fact, it would be worse. At least there are the docks here, and factory offices. Something must turn up one day, even if it's only sweeping floors.'

Ruby felt very alone and unhappy as he turned away from her and fell asleep. She lay awake in the darkness, feeling more bewildered than ever.

The next day, Friday 8 September, there was an explosion in South-West London and another one at Epping. No one was certain what they were. Over the next two days there was speculation as to whether it was the gas mains that were responsible. But on Monday Pearl went down to the shop where Gwen and Fitz were convinced it was not the gas, but Hitler's next and most terrifying secret weapon.

'A customer who was south of the river,' said Fitz, 'heard this roar and then a kind of echoing boom. It wasn't a bit like a gas mains as she knew what a gas explosion was like from the Blitz.'

'There's been talk of rockets,' nodded Gwen from the other counter where she was attending to a customer.

'Big ones,' said one of the customers. 'All the way from Germany.'

'Could a rocket fly that far?' asked Pearl.

'Oh, yes, they could do a lot of damage, according to the newsreels. I saw it on the flicks yesterday. They are big buggers and twice as lethal as the V1s.'

Fitz closed the till noisily. 'The government should keep us informed. It's diabolical that we aren't put in the picture.'

'Ruby has only just got over the V1s.' Pearl turned

Cynthia's pushchair round. 'I don't know what she'd be like if anything worse started.'

'Poor love,' sympathized Gwen, taking out her pocket knife and slicing a carrot in two. She gave one half to Cynthia. 'Enjoy that, ducks. You'll never need specs like old Fitzy over there, if you eat yer carrots.'

Pearl smiled as Fitz made a funny face.

'Maybe it's just another rumour,' Gwen shrugged, and everyone nodded half-heartedly. But by the next day the truth was out. The V2s, as they were named, came flying over thick and fast.

That night Ricky read from the newspaper. 'The V2 rockets make a sound like a train followed by a boom after they've exploded.'

'That's what a customer said in Hemsley's,' Pearl agreed as she cleared away the dishes from the top of the Morrison.

Ruby left her Spam and cold potatoes. 'I'm not hungry.'

'You must eat something,' Pearl told her.

'I thought it had all ended,' whispered Ruby folding her arms over her chest and shuddering. 'That Sandys told us the battle for London had ended.'

'On many fronts we are winning,' said Ricky, closing the newspaper and standing up. 'It does no good to get despondent or complain.' He left the room, taking the paper with him.

Pearl went to her sister. 'Ruby, you look awful. Where's your make-up?'

'I can't be bothered.'

'But you're always so particular about your appearance.'

'I'm fed up with trying. Me nerves can't take much more.' She looked down at her working slacks and a tear fell on her hand, to be swept quickly away.

Pearl sat down at the Morrison. 'Listen, why don't you and Ricky go to Mum and Dad's for a week or two? After all, they haven't seen you since your wedding. Mr Brewer

would let you take your holiday. You haven't had a break in ages, not since Brawton. And you did say you had it in mind.'

Ruby shook her head. 'I wouldn't leave you. Not with these rockets flying over.'

'Ruby, I'm more concerned about you than them.'

'Ricky wouldn't come with me.'

'Why not?'

'He still doesn't feel well enough.' Ruby shrugged. 'And anyway, there's Cynth's birthday coming up and Em's wedding after that. We might need another fitting and there's presents to buy.'

'I can do that. And the fitting can be postponed.'

Ruby shrugged. 'I'll give it some thought.'

'Well, don't wait too long.'

Ruby nodded, but Pearl wondered if the real reason she didn't want to go away was because married life wasn't turning out to be easy. And their mum could read Ruby like a book.

Chapter 20

Cynthia's birthday arrived with a small celebration at Gwen's after the shop had closed. They were treated to a real cake that Fitz had managed to get from a baker in Poplar. It had no icing, but two candles were found in the shop drawer. Everyone played hide-and-seek in and out of the yard, and Cynthia unwrapped her presents by the fire. By the time the week was over, Pearl and Ruby had had their final fittings for the wedding.

October had been a cold and wet month but Saturday

the 28th there was a brief show of sun as Pearl and Ruby stood at the church door. The organist at St Bart's played Em's chosen hymns and the guests sat waiting inside the draughty church. Em was being given away by one of Colin's uncles as her father, reluctant to appear in public, felt unable to attend. On Em's side of the church there was Mr and Mrs Hedley, Moira and Arnie, who had turned out to be Moira's Prince Charming, and Gwen and Cynthia. Ricky had declined the invitation.

Colin's side was full of his family and friends. His mother wore a tailored lemon suit with a Gainsborough-style hat. His father looked just like Colin and wore a smart grey suit, as did the best man, Colin's brother-in-law, on his left. Hope and the children sat next to them. Hope was wearing a long oyster-coloured coat with wide shoulders, whilst the two children looked like royalty in deep blue velvet.

The church usher gave the signal and the bride, in her long white dress with lace sleeves and ruffled neck-line, walked down the aisle on Colin's uncle's arm. Ruby and Pearl followed, carrying their small posies of pink and white chrysanthemums. Hope had rather elaborately finished their dresses with leg of mutton sleeves, and still had had enough material over to make Cynthia's dress. All in all, it was a lovely spectacle, Pearl thought, as she glanced at Ruby, who for once had a smile on her face.

At the altar, Colin stepped forward. He was dressed in dark grey and looked very handsome. Pearl glanced to where Gwen was sitting with Cynthia. She was very proud of how her daughter looked in a fawn-coloured coat with a brown velvet collar that she'd had on her birthday last week. It was only cheap from the market, but underneath she wore her new pink smock that Em had made.

Soon the strains of 'Ave Maria' filled the church, sung by a young girl standing in the organ loft. It was very touching. Pearl wondered how Ruby was feeling. She was wearing

her wedding ring, though Ricky couldn't wear his yet. Was she thinking that if only she'd waited, her own wedding day could have been like this?

When the vicar smiled, 'I now pronounce you man and wife,' Colin took Em in his arms. They seemed to be a perfect couple. Pearl wished Jim was home, sitting in the pew with Cynthia. They had had such a lovely wedding. If he was here they could remember it together.

The wedding march boomed out and Em and Colin walked slowly down the aisle. Pearl and Ruby followed and the guests were all smiles. Cynthia called out, 'Mummy!' and clapped her hands. Pearl blew her a kiss and she blew one back. She was so proud of her little girl! And she knew Jim would be too.

After the photographs, the guests filed into the church hall. It was decorated with fresh flowers and the tables were covered in white tablecloths and napkins. Like Pearl's own wedding breakfast, the buffet was on a luxurious scale for wartime. There was a two-tier wedding cake, which wasn't cardboard. The sandwiches were white, not grey, and had no crusts. There was no trace of Spam or carrots, and gleaming cutlery had been placed on every table. There were even fluted glasses for the champagne. Em had told them that Colin's aunt, the wife of the uncle who gave her away, worked at Lyons and had arranged everything.

After the meal and the speeches, Em and Colin got up to take the floor. The violin, flute and harp sounded wonderful to Pearl's ears, if very far removed from the kind of knees-up they were used to. Cynthia sat on Pearl's lap, entranced at the sight of the bride and groom and the musicians dressed in tail coats.

'Lucky, ain't she?' said Moira, who sat beside Pearl, looking plump and matronly in a dark green suit and fur collar. 'Who'd have thought Miss Prim-and-Proper would turn

up a bloke like Colin. Got a few bob in the family, I hear. Still, I ain't got no complaints with Arnie, though he's a bit partial to his wallop. Least I know where he is on a Friday night.'

'Didn't even know you'd got married,' said Pearl.

'Yes, in 'forty-two. He's in a reserved job now, security, you know.' Moira lifted her chin. 'So what happened to Jim? Did he go to Africa after all?'

'Yes.'

Moira narrowed her eyes. 'Bit of a shock for you, no doubt.' She nodded at Cynthia. ''Specially with a kid to bring up.'

Pearl looked round for Ruby, who seemed to have disappeared. 'I'm going to wish the happy couple good luck.'

'Suit yourself,' muttered Moira.

Glad to have found an excuse to leave, Pearl took Cynthia's hand and joined Hope and Ruby at the big table. The conversation was all about how Hope had refused to evacuate her children and taught them at home. 'We had a private teacher to help us.'

Pearl saw Ruby's jaw drop. Private teaching was unheard of on the island.

'That must have cost a lot,' said Ruby.

'Not really,' Hope explained. 'As a lot of the schools were shut down, some teachers were grateful for the work.'

Suddenly Cynthia's laughter rang out noisily. They turned to see the three children running around the next table. Hope told them stop, but Cynthia carried on running.

Pearl caught hold of her hand. 'Come here, scallywag.' She glanced over at their own table, which now, thankfully, was empty. 'We'd better go back and finish our drinks.'

'Yes, me too,' nodded Ruby.

'Have you ever heard such a thing?' Ruby said as they returned to their seats. 'Private teachers!'

'All right if you can afford it. I just hope that when Cynth starts school, the war will be well and truly over.'

'There's bound to be a lot of good schools in North London,' Ruby said thoughtfully.

'There are on the island too,' Pearl said.

'But the kids have all got cockney accents.'

'There's nothing wrong with that.'

Ruby didn't answer. Pearl knew that today, they'd had a glimpse of life on the other side of the tracks. In a way Moira was right: money did make a difference. You could buy a lot if you had it. But as Pearl looked down at Cynthia, who had made herself comfortable under the table with a sticky mouth full of jam tart, she had to smile. Hope's children were made to sit still beside their parents, looking like angels in their blue velvet outfits. But you only had to take one glance at their faces to see they were bored.

'What's so funny?' asked Ruby with a frown.

'Nothing, I'm just happy to be free.'

'Of what?'

'Needing money to be happy.'

Once more Ruby said nothing. Pearl knew by the look on Ruby's face that she was envious of Em. But Ruby could have had all this if only she'd waited.

Two weeks after Em's wedding, Churchill admitted that Britain was under attack again. Each day there were more casualties. The V2s left craters ten feet deep and caused an earthquake effect that rippled across the city. Tens of thousands of people were robbed of their roofs, windows, running water and gas supplies.

One Monday morning, in between showers, Pearl was about to take Cynthia out in the pushchair when a car pulled up by the shop. Pearl and Gwen went to the window to see who it was. Cars were rarely seen in the vicinity now that petrol was so scarce. A tall gentleman got out and went

to the passenger's side. He was middle-aged and dressed in a smart business suit.

Gwen leaned forward to get a closer look. 'Looks like an office wallah to me.'

When he helped a young woman from the car, Pearl gasped. 'That's our Ruby!'

'It is, an' all.'

They rushed out. 'What's the matter? What's happened?' cried Pearl in alarm.

'I was ill at work,' Ruby mumbled. 'This is Mr Brewer.'

'I brought Mrs Winters home as she is too distressed to catch the bus,' he explained.

'Thank you.' Pearl had never met him before, but he seemed very pleasant and, in Ruby's case, very considerate.

'I'll help you in—'

'No, we'll manage,' said Pearl as Gwen took hold of Ruby's arm.

Mr Brewer looked concerned as Gwen led her away. 'You must be Mrs Nesbitt?' He held out his hand and she shook it. 'I hope you don't mind me saying, but she hasn't been at all her old self lately.'

Pearl nodded. 'No, she hasn't.'

'She is a highly regarded employee. I'm very grateful she has stayed on at the factory through thick and thin. I know she has to look after her husband. Perhaps you could persuade her to take some time off?'

'I was trying the other day,' Pearl sighed.

'Please tell her I shan't expect her back until she is fully recovered. And she'll have her wage packet at the end of it.'

'Are you sure?'

'Yes, I think a holiday might do her good. And she must want to be with her husband.'

'I'll tell her,' Pearl promised as he climbed back in the car.

Pearl found Gwen and Ruby in the kitchen. 'Cynthia's

in her room with her toys,' said Gwen, frowning down at Ruby. 'Do you think Ruby should go to the doctor?'

'No,' said Ruby quickly.

Gwen shrugged. 'Well, give me a shout if you need me.'

When she had gone Pearl frowned. 'You look very pale.'

'What did Mr Brewer say?'

'He wants you to have a holiday.'

'He's a very nice man.'

Pearl nodded thoughtfully. 'Is he married?'

'He's a widower. Everyone says he's married to the factory.'

'Well, as long as he's good to you. Now, tell me what happened?'

Ruby pushed back her hair and sighed. 'I was sick in the ladies. The girls gave me some smelling salts.'

'Have you felt sick before?'

'Yes, in the mornings.'

'You could be expecting.'

'Expecting!' Ruby struggled to sit up. 'Come to think of it, I'm late. But I didn't give that a thought.'

'You've been married six months.'

'But what's Ricky gonna say?'

Just then a figure dressed in an overcoat walked in. 'What's all this?' He snatched off his hat, frowning.

'I was sick at work and Mr Brewer drove me home. Darling, I think I might be pregnant.'

Pearl saw Ricky's face drain of colour. 'What?'

'I hope you're pleased.'

'Couldn't it be the flu or something?'

'It might be, I suppose. But I haven't had my monthly.'

Ricky stared at his wife and a silence followed. Pearl went to join Cynthia in the bedroom, leaving her sister and brother-in-law alone to discuss the unexpected turn of events.

That evening after their meal, Pearl and Ruby sat alone.

'I'm sorry to waste it,' said Ruby, frowning at her half-eaten Spam and mash fritters.

'I'll keep them to heat up tomorrow.'

'If I am pregnant,' said Ruby uncertainly, 'I'll have to tell Mr Brewer.'

'He was very worried about you today.'

'He's very considerate to his employees. That's why I stay at the factory even though the work can be boring.' She frowned. 'In the morning I'll go to the doctors.'

'I'll come with you if you like.'

'Thanks.' Ruby got up and stood by the sink. She looked quickly over her shoulder and whispered, 'I think Ricky is upset that I might be expecting.'

At these words, Pearl felt icy cold, as the memories began to tumble back. Ricky had been very angry when, on that snowy night at the club all those years ago, she had told him she'd missed her monthlies. They'd quarrelled bitterly and she would never forget the moment she had fallen down the slippery stairs, with no sympathy at all from Ricky. He'd seen the blood under her coat that left a stain in the snow. He had callously ignored the possibility of what might have happened and when Dr Cox confirmed her fears, Ricky had told her that it was the best thing to have happened. Once again she had to bear the hurt alone.

'Pearl?'

'Sorry, what did you say?' Pearl felt very upset. She thought Ricky had changed but now she wondered.

Ruby carried her plate to the sink. 'Whatever Ricky thinks, I'm glad I'm having a baby. I know it will bring us closer together.' She yawned, rubbing her eyes. 'It's been a long day. Do you mind if I go and sit down?'

'Course not. Would you like a cup of cocoa?'

Ruby made a face. 'Even the smell makes me sick. I hope I don't get swollen ankles as well.'

'All the more reason for you to rest and have a holiday.'

'Don't go on about that.' Ruby opened the door and yawned again. 'Sorry about leaving you with the dishes.'

Pearl piled the rest of the dishes by the sink and, taking the kettle of warm water from the stove, she filled the bowl. As there was no soap, she used a teaspoon of washing flakes, just enough to soften the water. Piling in the dirty crocs, she tried not to let her mind wander. It wasn't fair to judge Ricky by his past actions. She had promised herself she would give him a fair chance.

'I'll dry those.' Ricky's voice made her jump.

'Where's Ruby?'

'Gone to bed.' He lifted the cloth and began to wipe a wet dish.

'You might wet your gloves,' she warned, feeling uncomfortable at being alone with him. Yet, why should she? Was she letting her fears get the better of her again?

'I like to help with the chores.' He moved closer.

Hurriedly washing the dishes, she clattered them on to the draining board.

'What's the rush?' he asked as he slowly took a plate from her hand.

'I want to write to Jim.'

'Ah, the loving wife.'

She didn't like the sarcasm but said nothing.

'How long have you known about the baby?' he asked as she continued to wash the dishes.

'Only as long as you.'

'It was a shock,' he said, his manner abrupt. 'And who is this Brewer?' Ricky stared at her. 'Why should he take an interest in Ruby?'

'He's a considerate employer,' Pearl shrugged, aware of the suspicion in his voice. 'He cares about all his staff.'

'Ruby is only a factory worker. Why should he care?'

Pearl put down the wet rag. 'There's nothing to be jealous of.'

'I'm not, of him.'

'Under the circumstances I would have thought you'd be grateful he did care enough to drive Ruby home.'

'Under the circumstances,' he mocked, 'I wouldn't describe what I feel as gratitude. I'm having to rely on my wife's wage to exist. Not a very satisfactory state of affairs for a naval officer.'

Pearl disliked his arrogance. 'Everyone is hard up in wartime, Ricky. You're no different from thousands of others. We all get through somehow.'

'I don't want *just* to "get through",' he replied angrily. 'I risked my life at sea, and not for the reward of a cold shoulder from the government, or marrying in haste.'

Pearl swung round. 'That's a terrible thing to say.'

'Terrible but true,' he shrugged. 'I was crazy to agree to Ruby's idea.'

'Are you saying you don't want to be married?'

'There's only one woman who interests me.' He raised his dark eyebrows as he looked towards her. 'And you know who that is. Perhaps you didn't catch what I said just then, but I'm not jealous of Ruby. It's someone else altogether who is constantly on my mind.'

Pearl looked at him in dismay. What was he saying?

'Is it the sight of these gloves that upsets you?' He put down the cloth and one by one tugged at the fingers of the gloves. Pearl stared at his scarred, red hands and the gap of a missing finger on each one.

She lifted her eyes to his. 'I don't care about them.'

'I'm glad to hear it. Ruby politely turns away when I take them off.' He walked closer. 'You used to like my hands once. You couldn't get enough of them running over you and doing all the things we did together. You and I are two of a kind, Pearl; we like the same dangers and excitement.'

A cold fear swept through her. 'You and I are nothing alike,' she whispered, backing away.

240

A smile played on his lips. 'You know, don't you, that I've hardly been able to keep my eyes off you all these months. I've had to pretend that nothing ever happened between us, and all the while I've wanted you with more passion than I ever felt for your sister.'

Pearl was trembling. 'I won't hear you talk about Ruby like that.'

'The loyal sister, eh?'

'Stop saying those things.'

'Why should I? They're true. Ruby has no imagination, whereas you, Pearl, you were born to satisfy a man.'

Pearl felt her back against the wall. For a moment she couldn't breathe. It was as though her lungs had lost their power. He reached out and took her arms. She couldn't believe he had such strength in his deformed hands as they gripped her.

'You see, you haven't forgotten,' he said softly, running them over her shoulders and into her hair. 'You're beautiful, Pearl.'

'Let go of me.' She turned her head to one side, afraid to scream as Ruby might hear. What would happen if she walked in? Was he mad? Or did he want Ruby to see this?

He took hold of her chin and made her look at him. 'Everything about you is so womanly.'

'You didn't think that once,' she said, trying to push him away, but he was too strong.

'I've always thought it,' he growled angrily. 'In time you'll see that you're wasting yourself on a man who doesn't appreciate you. And I have only so much patience, Pearl. Six months of hell has been a big price to pay for my mistake of being sweet-talked into marriage.' He laughed when he saw her shocked expression. 'Oh, take that silly look off your face, Pearl. It's a bit too late to play the innocent, about eight years too late. But don't worry, your secret is safe with me – for *now*.' He kissed her then, his hands going down to

her breasts, trying to open her blouse. It made her feel sick to have his touch on her and she knew that she couldn't fight him without waking Ruby.

But even as she opened her mouth to scream, he shook her violently. 'Shut up, you silly girl!'

'I'll scream if you do that again,' she half sobbed, the tears running down her cheeks.

'You know what I'll say if Ruby comes out?' he breathed hoarsely into her ear. 'I'll tell her it was you who threw yourself at me.'

'R-Ruby would never believe you,' she stammered as he squeezed her against wall.

'Is that a risk you're prepared to take?'

Pearl felt the hot tears stream down her cheeks. 'I ... I hate you, Ricky. For what you've done to me and what you're doing to Ruby.'

'This is nothing to what I would like to do,' he whispered, his hands fumbling for the buttons on her blouse.

It was as he released her a little to slide his hand inside that she managed to break away. As she fell against the draining board, the dishes clattered into the sink.

He grabbed her roughly and spun her across the room. Pearl was dazed by the blow he landed on her head and she crumpled down, shielding her face with her arm.

As he approached, Ruby's voice rang out from the bedroom. Pearl's heart was beating too loudly to hear his shouted reply. But the next moment he turned, opening the door of the kitchen, and banging it closed behind him.

Shakily Pearl climbed to her feet. Her right side felt bruised where he'd thrown her against the wall and her head was throbbing. She had been so wrong to think that he had changed. He was still the bully he'd always been and always would be. She was afraid for herself, but more, she was afraid for Ruby.

Jim had been right. A leopard can't change its spots.

Realizing she had only a short time to escape, she opened the kitchen door. The front room was empty. She hurried quickly through the hall, terrified he would appear again.

In her bedroom, Cynthia lay fast asleep. With trembling hands she pushed the back of the chair under the door handle and waited. All was silent. She didn't take off her clothes but sat on the bed fully dressed with the light on. She knew she wouldn't fall asleep that night.

'Oh God,' she whispered as she tried to wipe away his touch on her lips, 'this can't be happening to me.'

But it was.

Pearl woke with a start. She had fallen asleep after all, slumped over the bed. Ricky's cruel words and actions went through her mind. She wondered if he meant what he'd said about marriage to Ruby. She rubbed her head and shoulder as she moved. He had tried to rape her. She had been very lucky that Ruby had called. But had he vented his frustration on his wife?

There was a tap at the door and Ruby called out, 'Pearl, you awake yet?'

Pearl jumped up and pulled away the chair, opening the door to her sister.

'You look awful.'

'I . . . I didn't sleep very well. Cynth was a bit restless,' she lied as she glanced at the little body tucked well under the bedclothes in the small bed.

Ruby tiptoed over to the camp bed where Pearl was sleeping. Pulling her dressing gown round her, she sat on the small stool.

'Ricky's gone early,' she whispered. 'He came to bed late last night. He must have been worrying about work as he didn't say much. And this morning we didn't even say goodbye as I was being sick in the lav.'

Pearl was relieved that Ricky had left her alone.

'I still feel sick,' Ruby complained.

'If you eat it will help.'

'I don't know about that.' Ruby stood up. 'Just talking about food makes me queasy. I've got to go again.' She ran to the door.

Pearl closed her eyes, glad to be alone. Her head felt as though she'd run into a brick wall and her right shoulder ached. But when she thought of what might have happened, she had got off lightly.

Pearl left Cynthia to sleep and went out to the kitchen. The first things she saw were Ricky's soap and razor on the draining board. She quickly placed them out of sight on the shelf behind the curtains. Why had she ever agreed to him coming here?

'It's foggy out,' said Ruby when she came in and shivered as she sat down at the Morrison. 'I've just brought up half me stomach. If I ain't pregnant then this upset is lasting a long time.'

'We'll see the doctor later.' Pearl rubbed her shoulder whilst Ruby wasn't looking. What was she to do? As much as she tried to gather her thoughts, they were in turmoil. What *could* she do? Ricky had said their secret was safe for now. What did he mean by that? Was he planning to tell Ruby if Pearl didn't let him have his way? Had he been planning this all along? How foolish she had been to trust him.

She wished she could get away. Then, as she made up the fire and the orange flames leaped up and warmed her, an idea came to mind. But it was a wild idea and one she would have to persuade Ruby of before she could attempt it.

'Come in by the fire,' she called to Ruby, plumping up the cushions on the couch, her hands shaking as she thought of what she was going to suggest.

'Me teeth are chattering it's so cold,' Ruby said as

she came into the warmth and sat down on the couch. 'Does feeling as rotten as this always happen when you're pregnant?'

'I didn't have much sickness, but the ankles made up for it.' Pearl poked the fire distractedly. 'Ruby, if the doctor says you're pregnant why don't you, me and Cynth go to Abingley?'

'What!' Ruby looked startled.

'It will make up for not telling Mum and Dad about your wedding.'

'But I can't just go.'

'Why not? Mum will be over the moon when she hears she's going to be a grandmother again.'

Ruby frowned. 'I wouldn't like to without Ricky.'

'But he doesn't want to go, does he?'

'No, I suppose not.'

'It would be nice if you could talk to Mum about babies and everything. It's what I really missed when I was having Cynth. When Mum came down for that month and helped me with the breast-feeding, I never looked back.'

Ruby nodded slowly, then she looked puzzled. 'But Ricky's hands are still bad. How would he manage on his own?'

'He seems to do all right.'

'I wish he'd come with us. I'll ask him again.'

Pearl's stomach dropped. She had thought Abingley would be the one place Ricky wouldn't go. 'Have you ever thought that he might like a little time on his own? We're always around.'

Pearl was surprised to see Ruby look happier. 'Yes, that's true. He did once hint at that.'

'Well, then, let's go and see what the doctor says.'

As she made breakfast, Pearl wondered if her plan would work. Maybe Ricky would think of something to stop them from going. If he persuaded Ruby not to go, then Pearl couldn't go without her. What would happen then?

Pearl held her hurting head. Why hadn't she listened to Jim? She wouldn't be in this mess now if she had.

That night as Pearl sat by the fire in the front room she listened to the raised voices in the kitchen. The quarrel had started when, after supper, Ruby had told Ricky that the doctor had confirmed she was having a baby. Instead of welcoming the news as Ruby had hoped, Ricky had taken it badly.

'If we are struggling now, how will we manage with a child?' Ricky was shouting.

'We'll manage,' Ruby replied in a resentful tone.

'You'll lose your job and there's little hope of me finding one.'

'It's not my fault,' Ruby began to protest. 'It does take two to make a baby.'

'Don't you know anything?' Ricky shouted, making Pearl jump. 'There are ways and means of stopping them. It's not too late, even now.'

There was a brief silence before Ruby sobbed, 'You can't mean that.'

'I most certainly do.'

'You'd want to get rid of our child?'

Ricky laughed coldly. 'I never wanted it in the first place.'

Pearl heard Ruby burst into tears. She wanted to go in there, but knew that she mustn't. It would only inflame Ricky's anger.

'For God's sake, stop it,' she heard him yell. 'Crying is about the only thing you can do these days.'

'Why can't you be happy about the baby?' Ruby screamed. 'It should be a wonderful thing for two people.'

Pearl held her breath as Ricky's reply was lost in the noise of a chair scraping on the boards. Pearl jumped. She was afraid of what he might do to Ruby. She rushed to the kitchen in time to see the back door bang.

Ruby was sitting at the Morrison alone, her head in her hands.

'Ruby?' She sat down beside her.

'Did you hear what he said?' Ruby sobbed, revealing her anguished face.

'Yes. I couldn't help overhearing.'

'I can't believe he wants to kill our child.'

Pearl couldn't say that she had no doubt as to what Ricky was capable of. Jim had once said he was a bad penny and that was true.

Pearl reached out for Ruby's hand. 'You wouldn't do something like that, would you?'

'Course not.' Ruby looked down at her stomach. 'Not after wanting a baby so much.'

Pearl sat forward. 'Ruby, let's go away as I suggested. It will give Ricky time alone and perhaps he'll realize what he's missing.'

Ruby wiped her eyes. 'Perhaps that isn't such a bad idea. He might miss me enough to change his mind.'

'Let's catch the bus tomorrow.'

Pearl wasn't certain if Ruby would feel the same in the morning but she hoped and prayed she would.

'What if Ricky doesn't like the idea?'

Pearl thought quickly. 'You could say you're going away to think over what he said.'

'But I won't be. I'd never get rid of it!'

'I know that. But if you start another quarrel, it won't help the situation.'

'You could be right.'

'So go and put some clothes in a bag.'

Ruby nodded slowly, the tears running down her cheeks. Pearl wanted to comfort her, but what could she say in Ricky's favour? There was nothing. He was a violent and dangerous man and, although he had disguised his true character from them both, his real colours were now showing.

On Wednesday they sat on the crowded bus filled with

247

women and children eager to escape the V2s. Pearl sat by the window as Cynthia slept on her lap and Ruby dozed in the next seat.

'Are we nearly there?' Ruby mumbled as she woke.

'Not far now.'

'Me stomach is turning over again.'

'Shall I ask the driver to stop?'

'I'll try to hold on.'

Pearl smiled. 'After this, you can sit still and let Mum spoil you rotten.'

Ruby sank back, looking white. 'I wonder why Ricky didn't come home last night. I feel guilty when I think of not saying goodbye.'

Pearl knew her sister was already weakening. Ricky had so much power over her, just as he had had over Pearl. It was a stroke of luck that he stayed away all night, although Pearl was exhausted from staying up again as she had the night before. The cat naps she had taken hadn't lasted long. She had listened for every sound and had been so relieved to see dawn break.

'It was probably sour grapes on his part,' Pearl said with a shrug. 'The note you left him will let him know where you are.'

'It's all right for you to say that,' Ruby muttered. 'Jim never told you to get rid of Cynth.'

Pearl knew Jim would never be capable of such a thing. He was the kindest man she had ever met, without a bad bone in his body. Why hadn't she taken more notice of the fact that he had got so upset over Ricky on their wedding day? She should have seen that Ricky had got under his skin like no one else ever had. Jim was trying to protect his nearest and dearest. If only she had been able somehow to prevent Ruby from marrying Ricky!

Syd Jenkins was digging on his allotment, not that there

was much left to save from the summer. Perhaps a few old, spotty potatoes and shrivelled-up carrots that somehow had survived the first frost. But he had found himself a nice barrow of pig manure from the farm. Enough to fill his fallow patch, a good start for the winter ahead. He smiled at the sight of the rich brown earth he had just turned over with his fork. This Oxfordshire soil was a real treat, compared to what he'd been used to on the island. All the veg he could grow for Amy, and some left over for the market! Life had been very good to them since they'd moved. He'd never dreamed that he'd enjoy his job on the gate at the aerodrome either. Not at nearly sixty, when a lot of blokes were staring old age in the face. He had his own little guard box to sit in and a pigeon hole for his flask and sandwiches. And at Christmas he'd got tips as well.

Amy was happy in their little flat although she missed the girls and little Cynth. Syd couldn't wait to pick his granddaughter up in his arms for the first time and give her a hug. But as for Ruby, the bitter disappointment of her actions still hurt. She was their golden girl and Amy had so many plans for the future. The day Ruby's letter had come saying that by the time they received it, she would be married, had been a bitter pill to swallow. Amy had cried buckets. Where had they gone wrong? Was it the moving away that had caused Ruby to cut them out of her life? She had been very dependent once. Perhaps they had left her too early.

He stuck his fork in the ground and sighed. He'd been over it again and again in his mind. If only the pair of them would visit. He'd met the lad only once or twice. Ruby was all full of him in her letters, but all that was needed was a handshake and a hug for Amy.

Syd looked up at the glowing horizon. It was getting late. Perhaps he should stop whilst the going was good. Amy

would have the supper on and about now she'd be ironing a fresh shirt for tomorrow. He liked to look smart in his navy-blue uniform and tie.

Even so, he was reluctant to leave. The fine November evening gathered softly around him and the sunset refused to fade. You never got this in the Smoke, the clean, biting air and the big sky, unblemished by fogs. Last week there had been a few showers too, good for the earth and the remainder of his veg.

He rolled a cigarette and stuck it between his lips. It was colder now, but his old donkey jacket and gardening trousers kept him warm. He looked down at his boots covered in mud. What a lovely sight! People didn't appreciate just how lucky they were in the country.

Over his wiry grey hair he pulled on his woolly hat. Ten minutes more and he'd really have to get cracking.

Then he saw a figure coming down the lane. It was a woman and at first he thought it was Amy. But then his eyes widened in surprise.

'Dad! It's me, Pearl!'

'Strike me,' he muttered, dropping the dog end and opening his arms. His daughter, clad in a winter coat and Amy's old boots, rushed into them. He hugged her tight. 'Pearl! What are you doing here?'

'Oh, Dad, it's good to see you.'

'You can say that again. I thought it was your mother.' He looked over her shoulder. 'Where's the little one?'

'She's with Mum. The three of us came down on the bus. I said I'd bring you back for dinner.'

'You mean Ruby's here too?'

'Yes,' she laughed. 'Me and Ruby decided it was about time we paid a visit.'

'You're not wrong about that. What about Ruby's other half?'

'He's busy looking for work.'

Syd frowned. 'That was a rum do, those two getting hitched like that. Your mother was very upset.'

His daughter nodded. 'I knew she would be. But it's not been easy for Ruby.'

'Even so, she might have wrote.'

'Ricky being in hospital changed everything, Dad.'

He sighed, reflecting that he might have done more where Ruby was concerned. 'We blame ourselves for not being around. Ruby was always a bit on the wild side.'

'It wasn't your fault,' Pearl assured him. 'Ruby made her decision and didn't mean no harm by it.'

He grinned. 'Trust you to stick up for your sister.'

She held her nose. 'What's that stink?'

He laughed. 'Pig shit, love. Horse dung don't hold a candle to it. Come and see me shed.'

Syd wasn't inclined to ask more about Ruby. If he knew his wife, she would now be giving their youngest daughter the third degree. Not that an explanation wasn't justified. When a dearly loved daughter just ups and marries a bloke you barely know, it leaves a nasty taste. But he and Amy had come to accept the deed was done. And Amy, God bless her, even whilst hurt and bewildered, would be in seventh heaven at this very moment.

'Come inside and have a sit-down.'

'It's better than the Anderson,' she smiled as she looked round at the forks, spades and rakes hanging from the beams. 'And a lot tidier than our yard used to be.'

'I'm a reformed character, love. Help yourself to that stool.'

'Is this what they use for milking? You ain't got a cow here, have you?'

They laughed and Syd nodded. 'The thought has crossed my mind.'

'Dad, would you ever come back to the island?'

Syd rolled himself another cigarette. 'Would you leave all this, love, if you was us?'

'No, don't think I would – if I was you.'

'What's it like up there with all them V2s?'

'We thought it was over with the V1s.'

'Your mother worries, you know. Thinks you'd all be safer with us.'

'Mum says you like your job,' his daughter said, changing the subject.

Syd knew that Jim wanted to go back to the council after the war. And they had a nice little home at Pride Place. No, he couldn't see Pearl and Jim moving here, but what about Ruby?

'Been there over two years now,' he nodded.

'I thought you was a dyed-in-the-wool boilermaker.'

'You ain't never too old to change, ducks.' He patted her hand. 'Come on now, tell me about Jim.'

She smiled and her green eyes shined. 'Last time he wrote he said he was still in Italy.'

'The poor sod is probably exhausted after the desert.'

'I can't wait till he sees Cynth. Must get fed up with me saying how much we miss him.'

'That's all a man needs to hear.'

'Do you think the war will be over soon?'

'Next year, I reckon. It's my belief the V2s are Hitler's last gasp.'

She shivered. 'Oh, Dad, I hope you're right.'

He took one last gulp of smoke. 'It's getting parky. Let's go home.' He put away the stool and slid the bolt on the shed, then rested his arm on his daughter's slim shoulders.

She was still his Pearl, a bit older and wiser, but she'd always be that lippy little mare who he admired for standing up for herself and her sister. She had spirit, did Pearl. It was a bloody good job she had, after all that happened since

252

'thirty-nine. He wished he could be there for his daughters at Roper's Way, but it wasn't meant to be.

'You are a little darling,' said Amy as she lifted her grand-daughter from the bath that night. 'Look at you, all arms and skinny legs, like a little deer.'

Pearl laughed as she wrapped a fluffy white towel round her daughter. 'Mum, she ain't never seen a deer.'

'Oh, if she was here long enough, she'd see plenty. They come over from the woods, eating up all Dad's allotment.'

Pearl laughed. 'Come to that, Cynth's never seen a white bath before. Or had hot water come from the taps and a real basin to wash in.'

'If you and Jim was to move here,' replied Amy, 'you'd get a place with a bathroom. That's what I keep telling your sister. Move down here, out of the way of them V2s. Your father could put a word in for her husband at the aerodrome.'

'Mum, the V2s won't last for ever.'

'No, but I worry about Ruby. She was saying how fright-ened she is of them. And I can't help feeling it was our fault she got married in haste.'

'It was nothing to do with you.'

'So she says. But leaving you both like that—'

'Mum, you didn't have a choice,' Pearl told her again after enduring the same conversation several times since arriving. 'Now, can we just enjoy being with you?'

'Course,' Amy smiled repentantly. 'And who knows, one day I might persuade you both to live down here.' She turned to Cynthia. 'Now let's get you dressed and snug under the sheets. Granny has made up a snug bed for you next to your mum and Aunty Ruby. Pearl, go and get a few extra blankets from the glory hole in the hall in case it's very cold.'

Pearl went to fetch the bedding from the spacious

cupboard under the stairs. When she returned Syd was reading to Cynth.

She sat on the bed, transported back to their bedroom at Roper's Way. It had been half the size of this, with only a small window to let in the light. But it hadn't mattered to two happy little girls who'd watched their dad hold the book so carefully in his big, workmanlike hands.

When Cynth was asleep they all sat round the fire and Pearl could see that Ruby had put aside her quarrel with Ricky as she told their parents about his search for work. When Ruby suddenly revealed she was expecting, Amy jumped up from her chair.

'A baby!' she cried hugging her daughter. 'So this is why you came.'

'I wanted you to be the first to know,' said Ruby glancing at Pearl, 'to make up for not saying about the wedding.'

'Of course it has,' said Amy, delighted.

But Syd only nodded. 'Congratulations, love.'

'I wish Ricky could be here too.'

Pearl knew that her sister was already regretting her quick escape. She wanted the fairy tale to be true; that Ricky would be the man she imagined him to be.

Amy looked eagerly at her daughter. 'I'm sure it wouldn't take Ricky long to see that Abingley is a lovely place to live.'

'Yes, but he needs a job. There can't be many going round here.'

'Your father might be able to help.'

'If I put in a good word at the aerodrome, would you and Ricky consider it?' asked Syd.

'I'm sure we would,' Ruby nodded, to Pearl's concern. Once again, Ruby was only thinking of what she wanted.

'I'm sure he only wants the best for his wife and child,' said their father quietly.

Pearl saw Ruby's expression change as they both remembered how Ricky felt about the baby.

'This calls for a celebration,' said Syd, going to the sideboard. 'Let's wet the baby's head.'

At this Ruby looked pale. 'I don't feel like a drink.'

'Are you all right, ducks?' asked Amy.

'I've got to go to the lav.'

When she'd gone, Pearl enjoyed a sherry with her father and mother.

'To the baby,' he said, grinning.

'So Ruby's happy, is she, love?' Amy asked Pearl uncertainly.

'Yes, course,' Pearl nodded.

'Do you really think she'd move here?'

'Don't know, Mum.' Pearl didn't want to give them false hope. She didn't know what would happen when she and Ruby got back to the Smoke. Ruby was already forgetting how cruel Ricky had been. Pearl shuddered at the thought of seeing him again. At least she had a few days to think what to do for the best.

Her mother's cheeks were red with the sherry. 'They might move, if you and Jim did, Pearl. We could all be one happy family.'

Pearl looked away. She knew that could never be.

'Amy, don't let's forget what's been said today,' Syd interrupted before Pearl could reply. 'Our girls have got their own lives to lead and their husbands to think of.'

But Pearl knew by the look in her mother's eye that this wasn't the end of the matter.

Chapter 21

When Pearl woke the next morning, Ruby brought her a cup of tea. She was wearing their mother's dressing gown and slippers.

'What time is it?' Pearl sat up.

'Half-past seven.' Ruby glanced across at Cynthia, asleep on the Put-u-up and whispered, 'I didn't sleep very well. I was thinking of Ricky and wondering if he was all right.'

Pearl felt her stomach drop. 'Have you forgotten what he wanted you to do?'

'Course not.' Ruby sat on the bed. 'Perhaps he didn't mean it.'

'You told me he did.'

'Yes, but anyone can change their mind.'

'Does that mean you've made up your mind to go back?'

'No.' Ruby looked away. 'I'm still feeling sick. I know that upsets him. And I'd like him to miss me, as we said.'

Pearl knew that Ricky wasn't capable of any decent feelings. She was more frightened than ever for Ruby. 'Do you like it here?' she asked as she sipped her tea.

'Yes, it seems very nice.'

'Can you see yourself living in the country?'

Ruby smiled and nodded. 'Perhaps, if Ricky liked it too.' She sat on the edge of the bed. 'I've decided to phone him as I've got the number of the Disabled Servicemen's Centre. I'm going to ask him to come down and see Abingley for himself; tell him that Dad might be able to get him a job. I'm sure that will make a difference.'

Pearl nearly dropped her cup. 'Ruby—'

'Anyway,' sniffed Ruby, tossing her head, 'it's about time we got dressed. Mum said we can borrow Patty's pushchair and walk into town.'

Pearl was left with a feeling of desperation. Ruby had chosen to ignore all the warning signs with Ricky. She had conveniently forgotten his violent behaviour and threats, and was now imagining a life of peace and tranquillity in the country.

Later that day, as they walked round the market, they saw many well-dressed people shopping at the stalls. The farmers looked prosperous, with their cloth caps and corduroy trousers, and Ruby became excited when she saw a notice hung on one of the empty animal stalls.

'See what it says? A stockman is wanted to help the auctioneer on market day.'

'You're not thinking of Ricky, are you?' Pearl couldn't see Ricky in boots and an overall.

'Well, it's a job,' Ruby pouted.

'You're right, love,' said Amy eagerly. 'It would be a start.'

'I'll tell Ricky when I phone him.'

'There's a telephone box on the way home,' said Amy, 'but before we go, let's see the rest of the town.'

Although Pearl was filled with misgivings, she couldn't voice an opinion. She tried to enjoy their walk meanwhile, as the air was fresh and clean, and a river, which wasn't dirty like the Thames, ran under a grey stone bridge. Narrow brooks ran off it and ducks and swans bobbed on its surface. All the houses looked quaint and were well-tended, which reminded her of Brawton. Even the pub, called the Crossed Keys, was like the Brown Bear. The thought brought back bittersweet memories.

'Good morning, Amy.' A woman in a smart check coat and hat with a feather in its rim, stopped them.

'Morning, Frances.' Amy gave a big smile. 'I'd like you to meet my two daughters, Pearl and Ruby, and my granddaughter, Cynthia.'

'I'm pleased to meet you. What a lovely little girl.'

Pearl smiled. 'Thank you.'

When she'd gone, Amy whispered, 'Frances Butterworth is the secretary of the Churchwomen's Guild. She's a very well-to-do lady and has taken me under her wing.'

'She seems very friendly,' said Pearl, as Amy pulled back her shoulders and touched her hair into place.

'Come along, girls, I'm going to take you for a treat.'

Amy led them to the rows of shops in the market square. Some of them sold souvenirs and paintings of the town and the animals that were kept in pens on market day. At the end of the row was a tea shop.

Inside, they sat at a window table. Amy ordered real cream cakes with cream from one of the farms. Pearl noticed that Ruby couldn't take her eyes off the white tablecloth with roses embroidered on it and the dainty china and leaded light windows.

'Mum, this is really quaint,' said Ruby, all eyes.

'Yes, it is, love.' Amy poured the tea. 'I meet my friends from church here once in a while. It's better than a draughty old church hall that we had to put up with on the island.'

Pearl was helping Cynthia to eat her sponge when she heard this. It didn't sound like her mum. All her life Amy had been an islander. But was she trying to impress Ruby?

'And they've got very good schools,' continued Amy, nodding at a little girl dressed in a blue uniform, white socks and beret. She was sitting at the next table with her mother. 'Talks properly too,' whispered Amy, nudging Ruby's arm. 'All her pleases and thank yous and not gulping her food down.'

Ruby stared at the little girl.

'There's a school in this road called St Boniface,' said their mother. 'It's run by the nuns, but they take non-Catholic children, if you allow your child to learn the catechism. It's to get more Catholics, you see, but you wouldn't mind that in exchange for a good education.'

'No, I wouldn't at all,' agreed Ruby eagerly as her attention strayed back to the little girl.

Amy went on to describe the new flats and houses being allocated to evacuees. 'If your name was to go down now,' said Amy as they finished their tea, 'you'd have a place by next year. Frances had friends who fell on hard times and she put a word for them. She would do that for me if I asked.'

Pearl glanced at her sister. Ruby was nodding her head.

Ruby was in the telephone box and looking agitated.

'What's wrong, do you think?' Amy asked Pearl as she frowned at her daughter through the small panes of glass. 'Could Ricky have something against them moving here?'

'Mum, they've been married only six months.' She rocked Cynthia back and forth in the pushchair. She knew that Ruby and Ricky were arguing again. If only Ruby had left him alone.

'All the more reason to move before the baby. I wish you would encourage your sister.'

'She's a big girl now.'

Amy sighed impatiently. 'You're the last person I thought would be against them moving. After all, Jim will be home after the war. What will they do then?'

'I know you want the best for Ruby—'

'And why shouldn't I?' Amy demanded. 'After all, it's almost two years since I last saw Cynthia, my only grandchild. I expect it'll be another two years before I see her again.' Amy put her hand on Pearl's. 'I'm sorry, I don't mean to sound selfish, but I can't help it.'

'Ruby has her own mind.'

'Yes, but if they were to move here, your dad and me could keep an eye on them.' Amy looked at the telephone box again. 'Ruby's not as bright as you, Pearl. You're level-headed, always knew where you were going and what you

wanted. But your sister's always been a bit on the impulsive side.'

Pearl continued to rock Cynthia, who had fallen asleep under the blanket. It was at times like these that Pearl wished she could hide her head under the blanket too. Coming to Abingley had seemed a good idea at the time, but now it was causing more problems.

Ruby burst out of the telephone box, weeping.

Amy folded her daughter in her arms. 'There, there, what's wrong, ducks?'

'Nothing,' sobbed Ruby.

'There must be something.'

'I'm all right.' Ruby pushed herself away.

'So what did Ricky say?'

'I told him about the job in the market and he said how could he do it with two fingers missing? S'pose he's got a point, but it won't be that easy in an office, either.' Ruby blew her nose.

'Did you tell him your dad was willing to help?'

Ruby nodded. 'He just shouted at me.'

Amy slid her hand through her daughter's arm. 'Give him time to think it over. You can phone again at Patty's. She won't mind.'

They walked on. Pearl had a heavy heart. Because of Ricky, they were all in a big mess. Ruby couldn't tell Amy what Ricky had said about the baby, and Pearl guessed that his opinion hadn't changed.

After a while, Amy pointed to a block of houses all built in the same clean, neat style. 'See them? They're all new, with young families going in them from the Smoke.'

Ruby dried her tears. 'They're very nice. And there are trees in the back gardens. It must be wonderful to look out of the window and see all green.'

Pearl strolled on with the pushchair. She knew her mother and sister wanted to be near one another. But she

also knew that Ricky, a bully and a coward, would never tolerate an outside influence.

The next day was cold and rainy. Patty from next door sent her little girl, Elizabeth, to play with Cynthia after school. She was five and had just started her first term at St Boniface.

Pearl was sitting with them, when Ruby appeared. She sat down with a big sigh. 'I phoned Ricky from Patty's.'

'What did he say?'

'He's going to see a firm of hauliers at Aldgate. They need a clerk in their office and he won't change his mind about the market job and so we'll have to stay in the Smoke.' Ruby looked sorry for herself as she stared out of the window at what their mother called 'the green', a large expanse of mowed grass that was bordered by a thick hedge. The top deck of the buses was just visible as they passed by. Unlike London, there were trees all along the road.

'The Smoke's not so bad,' said Pearl with a shrug.

'But Abingley's better for a child,' said Ruby determinedly. 'When I met Hope and her children, I thought, that's what I want. I suddenly realized it wasn't enough to have a pretty face and big smile. They don't get you what money can buy. I used to be happy at Brewer's, but it's just a factory, as Ricky keeps telling me. I'm only a worker on an assembly line.'

'There's nothing wrong that.'

'No, but it's not for me.'

'Do you really want to move to Abingley?'

'Yes, I do. I've made up my mind that's what I want. There's the baby to consider, and its future. Although Ricky is against it at the moment, I'm sure he'll come round.'

Elizabeth looked up and they smiled at the pretty child with silky brown hair, neatly clipped back with a slide. She had large, intelligent brown eyes and a clean face, as opposed to Cynthia's grubby one.

'The children are so well behaved in the country,' said Ruby thoughtfully. 'There's no swearing or putting out their tongues and making faces like the little horrors around where we live.'

'They're not all like that,' said Pearl, wishing she'd taken time to run a flannel round Cynthia's mouth. 'They haven't got fields and woods to play in and have to make do with the bombed sites.'

'That's why I'd like to live here. It will take years to clean up the East End. But if we were here we could have that house I've always dreamed of, and you and Jim could come to stay. And our children will all speak properly and be well mannered, like Elizabeth.'

Cynthia laughed loudly. Even at her tender age, her broad cockney accent set her apart. But that was the way islanders were, Pearl reflected. You had to shout louder than the next ten kids to be heard.

'I'm sure if Ricky came to visit,' Ruby mused as she rested her chin on her hands, 'he'd change his mind and see that we could have a good standard of living here.'

'You've only just got married,' Pearl replied cautiously. 'There's plenty of time to build a new life.'

'I've given him time,' Ruby insisted. 'He's just being stubborn. This is the chance of a lifetime. We would be classed as evacuees if we moved now and given priority. Like Mum says, when the war ends it will be every man for himself, and all the nice places will be taken.'

Pearl didn't have the answers to Ruby's problems. She was struggling with her own. If Ricky was determined to turn all their lives upside down, he would. But only she knew it.

The next day was Saturday and, after being very sick, Ruby clearly wasn't well enough to go out.

'Sit down and put your feet up,' said Amy as Ruby appeared with a white face.

'I thought I was getting better.'

'You should eat something,' Pearl said as she had so many times before.

'Even a biscuit would help.'

'I've got some plain arrowroot from the aerodrome canteen.' Amy hurried off.

Ruby was sick again before she returned and Amy persuaded her to go back to bed. It was much later when Pearl heard a shout. She rushed into the bedroom and found Ruby doubled up. A red stain was on the sheet. She knew that she had to get help quickly. Opening the window she waved at Amy and Cynthia in the garden. 'Mum! Come in quick!'

Memories were flooding back of her miscarriage. Could this be happening to Ruby?

Pearl was staring from the window across the green to the path where the ambulance had been. She was wondering if she should walk up to the aerodrome with Cynthia and tell their dad what had happened. Amy's last words as she'd thrown on her coat and snatched up her bag before accompanying Ruby to hospital were that she'd phone Patty as soon as there was news.

'Aunty Ruby gone.' Cynthia wriggled in Pearl's arms. She had watched wide-eyed as the two ambulance men had carefully wrapped Ruby in a blanket and laid her on a stretcher. Patty had offered to have Cynthia, so that Pearl could also go in the ambulance, but Amy was worried about Syd.

'Granny will let us know how she is,' Pearl said as she led Cynthia to the kitchen. 'Let's make a sandwich for Granddad.'

'You all right, Pearl?' It was Patty, ten minutes later,

poking her head round the back door. She was a slim, dark-haired woman in her mid-thirties, who had lived all her life in Abingley. Amy had said that Patty's husband, Dennis, was manager of the local cinema and his job entitled him to have a telephone. This, from Amy's point of view, had been a real boon.

'Yes, have you heard from Mum?' Pearl asked hopefully.

'No. Is there's anything I can do?'

'Don't think so.'

'Does her husband know?'

Pearl shook her head. 'No.'

'Do you want to phone him?'

'Not yet.' Pearl had no intention of speaking to Ricky, but she couldn't say that to Patty.

'Try not to worry.' Patty closed the door but opened it again. 'Send Cynthia in this afternoon, if you like, to play with Elizabeth.'

'Yes, I will.'

With a brief smile she left, and Pearl set out the cold meat and pickles for her father's lunch. No sooner than she'd finished, he walked in the door.

'Hello, love.' He took off his navy-blue greatcoat and bicycle clip. 'That's a big hug,' he grinned as Cynthia ran into his arms.

'Aunty Ruby gone.'

'What's that?'

'Dad, Ruby wasn't well this morning. She had to go to hospital.'

His face went grey. 'What's wrong with her?'

'It might be to do with the baby.'

Syd looked bewildered. 'She won't lose it, will she?'

Pearl shrugged. 'Mum will ring us from the hospital.'

He sank down on the chair. 'Soon as I get me breath back I'll cycle over there.'

'Have something to eat first.' She put his meal in front of

him. It wasn't any use telling him to stay home. Ruby and the baby meant the world to him, much more than they did to Ricky.

That afternoon, when Syd had left, Cynthia went to play with Elizabeth. Pearl washed out Ruby's sheets and hung them on the line to dry. Was she losing the baby? She had been in pain but luckily the ambulance had come quickly after Patty had made the 999 call.

Pearl busied herself with housework and, after putting Cynthia to bed, she peeled the vegetables for supper. She would make a hot meal, though she didn't know if anyone would want to eat it. What had happened at the hospital?

Pulling the blackout curtains together she thought of home. Of the dirty roofs and smoking chimney pots, the sounds of the river that she always took for granted. The hoots and horns and whistles and the smells of the oil and tar and wood, and the flotsam that washed up with the tide and dried out on the mossy stone wharfs. And as always she thought of Jim and their little love nest. When would it be their own again? Would they ever be free of Ricky?

The sound of the back door opening made her jump. She rushed into the kitchen and saw her mother.

'Hello, love,' Amy said tiredly. 'Sorry we're late. Your dad had his bike and we walked back from the hospital.'

'How's Ruby?' Pearl asked as Syd came in.

'They think the baby's all right. Ruby could be short of iron and will have to stay in hospital for a while. She don't like it much, but it's for the best.'

'They'll look after her,' said her father, hanging their coats up in the porch cupboard outside the door.

'It was a fright this morning,' said Amy fretfully as they all sat by the fire. 'The doctor said she won't be fit to travel for some while so your dad phoned Ricky from

the hospital. Ruby gave us the telephone number of the Disabled Servicemen's Centre.'

Her father's expression gave nothing away. 'He'll be here tomorrow.'

Pearl felt quite sick. Ricky was coming here. It was the worst thing that could happen.

'We'll put him up for a few days,' said her mother cheerfully. 'I'll have a nice roast in the oven. Your dad brought home a chicken from the farm and some veg from the allotment. And although I wish Ruby was with us, it will be lovely to see our son-in-law at last.'

Pearl stood up and went quickly to the kitchen to make the tea. She couldn't let her parents see how distressed she was. She couldn't escape Ricky and had no choice but to face him.

That night Pearl lay awake, staring at Ruby's bed. The sound of Cynthia's breathing was a comfort, but the thought of seeing Ricky made Pearl feel distraught.

She hadn't drawn the blackout as the moon was a round silver ball shining in the sky. It reminded her of her honeymoon in Margate. If only she had listened to Jim. If only she hadn't agreed to go to Brawton Manor.

So many 'if onlys' . . .

Pearl wondered what would happen tomorrow. Were Ricky's feelings towards Ruby and the baby still the same?

She closed her eyes and said a prayer. She knew she was being selfish when she prayed that Ricky wouldn't come.

But she knew he would. And she dreaded tomorrow.

Chapter 22

Amy washed the last dinner plate and carefully set it on the draining board. She had used her best china, hoping to impress their son-in-law, along with the roast chicken that had turned out a real treat.

The soft hum of voices came from the front room as she turned to meet her elder daughter's gaze. 'You all right, ducks?'

'Yes, thanks.'

'Why don't you go in and join the men?'

'No, I'll help you.'

Amy paused, her frown deepening. 'I hope you're not sickening for something.'

'No, I'm fine.'

'You haven't said boo to a goose all morning. Why don't you go and get ready to visit your sister?'

Amy was concerned. She would have thought Pearl, being so close to Ruby, would be pleased that Ricky had finally come to visit. Not under the best circumstances perhaps, but now that he was here, perhaps they could all get closer after a difficult start. Pearl, however, was very quiet. She hadn't said much to Ricky at all, although it may be that she was worried about her sister. From little girls they'd been inseparable. They'd shared everything and, unlike many others, had rarely argued. The bond between them was special, as both she and Syd knew, sometimes to their cost. They'd always back each other up, like two peas in a pod they were. She smiled as she remembered two little girls, blonde and green-eyed, playing dressing-up in the back yard at Roper's Way, amongst all Syd's clutter. Unlike a lot of the neighbourhood kids, they'd been content with each other's company. She'd never had a minute's trouble

from either of them, but it was true, Pearl looked out for Ruby like an old mother hen.

'Yes, all right,' nodded Pearl in an absent-minded way. 'I'll put me slacks on and a warm jumper.'

'I'm going to doll up a bit,' Amy grinned. 'Can't let the side down, can I?'

'You always look nice, Mum.'

'Yes, but I'm making a special effort. Ricky is a very nice young man, don't you think?'

'Ruby thinks so.'

Amy took her hands from the water and dried them. 'Abingley is perfect for a young family. And if Ricky doesn't fancy the market job, he could get work at the aerodrome, if Syd put a word in for him.'

'Have you and Dad talked it over?'

'Yes, and he's more than willing to vouch for Ricky if he should get an interview. Once he's got the offer of a job, it speeds the application they would make to the council for housing. Frances told me.'

'Has Dad talked to Ricky about this?'

'No, but he will.'

Amy frowned as she saw her daughter's expression. 'We're not interfering, you know. But I know what Ruby needs. Your father, God bless him, is the best husband in the world but he's spoiled Ruby in the past and now she has to grow up. You've always been so independent, love, whilst Ruby is a daydreamer. Perhaps that's why me and your dad took it so hard when they did what they did. I had high hopes of a good start for Ruby, just like we did for you.' She sighed gently as she looked into her daughter's face. 'Life's funny sometimes. Things just didn't work out the way you thought. Take Roper's Way – whoever would have thought we'd leave it, or should I say, that it would leave us? Whoever would have thought your dad would leave his job as a boilermaker and start work at an aerodrome? I

mean, we've done very nicely thank you, as a result, but at the bottom of our hearts we've been wondering if we left Ruby too early – not that she didn't have you, but she does need that extra bit of guidance.'

Pearl made no reply and Amy couldn't understand why. Ruby was a wife now, and soon-to-be mother. But it didn't stop her from being, in their eyes, their baby. Was Pearl feeling left out?

'That's not to say we don't think a lot of you and Jim. Of course we do. And I do wish you'd put on a bit of weight. You're skinny, my girl, not like you used to be, well rounded. Are you worried about something?'

'No.'

Amy tried again. 'You must be missing Jim.'

'Yes, I am.'

'He'll soon be home safe and sound,' Amy smiled, patting her daughter's hand. 'Now we must get ready for the hospital. The nurse said they don't like everyone round the bed at the same time. So we can go in in twos. Me and your dad and you and Ricky. You youngsters don't want old duffers around anyway.'

'Mum, perhaps I shouldn't go.'

'Don't be daft.'

'She'll want to see only Ricky.'

Amy shook her head. 'What's come over you? Where's that lovely smile? Now cheer up and ask the men if they'd like a cup of tea.'

Amy watched her daughter reluctantly leave the kitchen. It must be Ruby's condition that was putting Pearl out. She certainly wasn't the same light-hearted and easy-going girl as she used to be. And her weight loss was dramatic. But Jim had been away for such a long time. He'd been lucky to get through the desert campaign, luckier still not to be wounded. But if the war ended soon, then they could start life over again.

269

Amy washed down the drainer, squeezing the cloth and draping it round the tap. She had her family around her at last. Not that she wished Ruby in hospital, but it had brought Ricky into the fold. He would see what a decent place Abingley was. A perfect setting for his future. From the bus, she could show him the market and shops. Then there were the new houses behind the pub. She'd mention them casually and they were sure to catch his eye. Perhaps if Ruby and Ricky did evacuate, then Jim and Pearl would be tempted to follow ...

Amy looked in the small square mirror nailed to the pantry door and tidied her hair. Removing her apron, she tucked her new blouse into her skirt and turned down the collar. Taking out her lipstick from the purse on the larder shelf, she smoothed on a fresh coat of red. Then, after applying a liberal dusting of powder to her nose, she felt ready for the men. Though she wasn't one to put on airs and graces, she wanted to be at her best. After all, their son-in-law had served his country bravely. Would his hands be permanently covered by those ugly gloves, she wondered as she turned to put on the kettle. Had the burns on his body healed properly? It was understandable that they had wanted a low-key wedding service. Perhaps she would have done the same in Ruby's position.

Pearl returned as Amy was closing the larder door. She was looking paler and more tense than ever.

'Dad said they'll give tea a miss.'

'Yes, we don't want to be late. The bus goes in half an hour.' She turned off the kettle.

'I'll get changed.'

'You can borrow my best coat if you like?'

'Mum, we're not going to the Ritz.'

Amy shook her head in concern. Pearl was definitely out of sorts. But then she reminded herself these were no ordinary times. Her girls had lived through the Blitz of London

and were now in fear of the V2s. They had been forced to look after themselves without their men. Little Cynth had grown up without a father. And Ricky, a dis-abled veteran, was just becoming one. No, these were not ordinary times at all.

Pearl sat in the waiting room outside Ruby's ward. They had taken turns in seeing Ruby, and now Ricky was in with her. Pearl was listening to her mother, who hadn't stopped talking since they'd sat down.

'It was lovely to find Ruby looking so well. And did you see her face when Ricky walked in? Oh, Syd, they make a lovely couple.'

Her father nodded and Pearl wondered what had been said between the two men earlier that day.

'So, we'll sleep Ricky and Syd in your room, Pearl, and you and I can share the double, and Cynth can go beside us. Now, when we get home there's cold chicken for supper and I can fry up some bubble and squeak—'

'Amy,' Syd stopped her, shifting his position uneasily on the hard hospital chair, 'it might be best to give the lad a bit of a breather. I'll walk him across the green to the Badgers for a pint.'

'Just remember you've got work tomorrow.'

'I said a pint, love, not a skinful.'

'Yes, a man-to-man chat might be a good idea,' agreed Amy thoughtfully, 'whilst me and Pearl get the beds ready.' She tapped her husband's arm. 'You can take your time, love, and show him them nice houses at the back of the pub. That little estate by the fields.'

'Showing him the inside of the Badgers will be as far as I get this evening, Amy. Me feet are killing me in these shoes. I should have left me boots on.'

'You're getting old before your time,' sighed Amy. 'Getting you to dress up is like prizing a winkle out of its shell.'

Pearl glanced across at her father and he gave her a wink. At least Ricky would be occupied for the best part of the evening. But what was going to happen next week? How long was he going to stay? Nothing had yet been said.

When the bell rang for the end of visiting, Ricky walked out.

'All right, lad?' said Syd.

Ricky nodded abruptly as he did up the buttons on his jacket.

'We're just in time for the bus,' said Amy, urging them all along the corridor. 'It leaves in ten minutes.'

Outside the last of the sun was shining over the green hedges and through the tall, leafless chestnut trees. The leaves that were left in the gutters were crumpled and orange, the only reminder of summer.

Pearl was careful to keep beside her mother as the two men walked ahead. She had managed to avoid Ricky's gaze, but she was living on her nerves.

That evening, after Cynthia was asleep and supper was over, Ricky, who had said very little, turned to Amy. 'Thank you, Mrs Jenkins, it was a most enjoyable meal.'

'Well, you need building up,' said Amy, patting his arm but taking care to keep well away from his gloved hand. 'You must have missed Ruby's cooking. She can turn out a very nice dish.'

Ricky nodded. 'Yes. Both your daughters can cook very well.'

'What, our Pearl, an' all?' said Amy, surprised.

'Yes, indeed.' Ricky looked at Pearl, his gaze dark and enquiring. She turned quickly away.

'Jim will be pleased with that verdict,' said Amy with a chuckle.

'Ah, talking of Jim . . .' Ricky stood up, 'I have a letter for you, Pearl.' He left the table and went out to the hall where

the coats were hung. 'I'm sorry, I should have given it to you when I arrived,' he said when he returned, passing her an envelope. 'I'm afraid that with all that went with Ruby, it slipped my mind.'

When she read her name, written in Jim's sprawling handwriting on the front of the Blue Triangle air-mail letter, her heart gave a leap.

'We'll give Pearl a minute or two on her own,' said her father, signalling to Ricky. 'I fancy a smoke outside. You coming, son?'

Ricky accompanied her father outside and Pearl opened the letter.

'I'll get on with the washing-up,' said Amy, collecting the plates and leaving her alone.

In the silence she began to read Jim's words. The tears were very close as they always were when she heard from him. But this evening, his words felt even more special.

Syd wasn't a man to be judgemental, but he was in two minds about his son-in-law. Not that he'd share his concerns with his wife, because he could see that Amy had been well and truly won over. She'd forgotten just how upset she'd been when they'd received Ruby's letter in April, telling them she'd be married by the time they received it. Ruby had said it was Ricky who'd been her first concern, that because of his disfigurement he didn't want any photos taken. She'd also admitted that it was she who'd taken the decision to marry in hospital. But to Syd's mind, it was marrying in haste for no reason. The lad would have recovered sooner or later, and if it was later, then Ruby should have had the good sense to wait. But that was Ruby all over. She'd act before she thought, and Syd knew the real reason she'd not asked them was because she knew he would have talked her out of it.

Enjoying the quiet evening, Syd looked up at the sky

273

as he smoked. He'd asked Ricky if he could roll one for him, but was refused. He was certainly a different kettle of fish from his other son-in-law, Jim. Were the two men now friends? After that little shindig at the wedding, neither Pearl nor Jim had elaborated. But Syd liked Jim. He was a solid sort. And a man who wouldn't take umbrage without good reason.

Syd stamped his chilled feet into life. It was a cold November night and the weather turning to frost. What sort of things was this young man interested in? What aspirations did he have? And those gloves of his, did he really have to wear them?

'So, did you lose your ship, son?' Syd asked as his breath curled whitely into the air.

'Yes, twice, I'm sorry to say.'

'How do you account for that?' Syd asked curiously.

'We have radar-equipped aircraft now. They attack the U-boats on the surface and it was bad luck that we were holed, just when things were getting better.'

Syd didn't miss the passion of this reply. 'Read a bit about the Atlantic campaigns; bloody cold and dangerous waters those. About time we sent that Dönitz packing.'

'Indeed. But as a commander, Dönitz is a hero to his submariners. It's widely known that if the Führer had listened to him earlier and made more U-boats, our navy would have been in dire trouble.'

Once again Syd was struck by such enthusiasm. 'You miss the navy, do you?'

'It is – *was* – my life.'

So that was it, Syd thought with a glimmer of under-standing. He was missing life on the waves. Some men would be glad to be out of it, but not this one. 'Any chance of a desk job along those lines?' he asked matter-of-factly.

'If there was, half of those now demobbed would want it.'

274

'So what is it you're after?'

The tall silhouette turned slowly. 'To be honest, I don't quite know.'

It was a fair enough reply and Syd didn't press the point. Just as he was about to bring the job at the aerodrome into the conversation, Amy opened the back door. 'Put out the light, love!' shouted Syd, dropping his roll-up and squashing it firmly under his slipper.

'Syd! Come in! Quick!'

Turning, he hurried after her. The first thing he saw was Pearl's wide, frightened eyes as she held the letter in her hand. 'What's up? What's wrong, love?'

'Jim's been wounded.'

'Christ.' Syd went to his daughter and took her arm. 'Come and sit down.' He led her to the couch. 'Now, is it bad? Where is he?'

She handed him the letter. Syd found his glasses and, taking a seat on the couch, read aloud: '"Not much to write home about this time, Pearl, as I've got meself a leg wound. I'm writing from the field hospital, can't say where and nothing else neither, but I can tell you, I'm kitted out to move tomorrow and am likely to be shipped home very soon."'

'Blimey, he's on his way,' Syd breathed heavily.

'Dad, a leg wound,' said his daughter. 'Why don't he say more about it?'

'The censor is tough in instances like this,' interrupted Ricky. 'I was unable to let Ruby know before Brawton.'

'Jim says he's being shipped out,' Syd nodded. 'That means they'll bring him across the Channel. Well, ducks, looks like you'll have your old man back quicker than a shake of the dog's tail.'

'I can't believe it, Dad.'

Syd grinned. 'Better get your things packed.'

'What?' Amy burst out. 'She ain't been here five minutes. And our Ruby's still in hospital!'

Syd shrugged. 'Her husband comes first, no doubt about that.'

Amy's eyes filled with tears. 'Just when I had my family around me. This bloody war don't give anyone a chance to be together.' She took out her hanky and hurried from the room.

Syd squeezed his daughter's shoulder. 'She don't mean nothing by that. Under normal circumstances, she'd be putting out the flags for Jim.'

'I know, Dad.'

'This bit of news changes the lookout for you too, son.' Syd looked up at his son-in-law. 'With Jim needing his bed back, you'd best be resigned to staying with us. Not for ever mind, just till Ruby's on her feet and we can work out what's best to be done.'

Syd waited for a reply and found none forthcoming. But like it or not, the lad would have to see sense.

'So, Pearl, you'd best be saying cheerio to your sister.'

'Yes,' Pearl replied quietly.

Syd glanced down at the thin blue sheet, hiding his concern that Jim had said so little about his injury. Would it make a difference to his job prospects when he was demobbed? Would he be able to get his old job back? He sighed softly to himself, wishing that he could be of more help to his first-born. But Pearl was a strong girl, in mind and body, and she'd take it on the chin whatever it was. Ruby needed him more right now, and perhaps when all was settled he could take the bus up and shake Jim's hand in person.

Syd caught his daughter's glance. 'He's out of danger now,' he said cheerfully. 'Your Jim has come through and, whatever the injury, he's pointed in the right direction. You've been a brave lass and I'm proud of you.'

There was nothing he could add, but one thing he knew

for certain: Jim Nesbitt was leaving behind him a living hell and it wasn't a moment too soon.

On Tuesday, Amy's eyes were full of tears. 'I've packed a nice big sandwich and an apple for Cynthia,' she said as she bent to kiss her granddaughter. 'Now, Cynth, remember your gran loves you and tell your dad we'll be thinking of him.'

'Better go, love,' said Syd, picking up Pearl's bag and patting Cynthia's head.

'Bye, Mum.' Pearl stepped outside but Ricky followed, drawing her into his arms. 'This isn't the end,' he whispered as he kissed her cheek, 'not by a long chalk.'

Pearl took Cynthia's hand, walking quickly to join her father. She was trembling, but she didn't want Ricky to see.

'Don't forget to write,' called Amy, 'and watch out for them V2s.'

They set off across the green to the bus stop, Cynthia skipping on the grass. Pearl glanced back when they turned the corner. Ricky was standing beside her mother, his tall figure looming over her. What had he meant, 'This isn't the end'?

'You all right, love?' Syd asked.

'Yes, thanks.'

'Don't fret about your mum. She knows you have to go back to Jim.' He caught hold of Cynthia's hand as they crossed the road.

They stood at the bus stop in the cold morning air and Pearl turned to her father. 'I'm going to miss you, Dad.'

'Me too, ducks. Keep in touch.'

'Patty said I could ring her.'

'You do that, but don't forget your skin and blister ain't your responsibility now. She's got her husband at her side, and whether by luck or judgement the lad found himself here, to my mind the timing of Jim's return is a blessing. Now, here's a fiver, put something in the larder when you get home.' He pushed a rolled-up note into her pocket.

'Dad, you shouldn't.'

'Give us a kiss, the bus is coming. I'll have a word with the driver about Ruby and Ricky's things, slip him a few bob to pick them up from your end and drop them off at the depot. You got someone to give you a hand with them?'

'Yes,' Pearl agreed quickly. 'Fitz will.'

'Good, that's settled then.' Syd gave her a last hug.

Pearl seated herself and Cynthia at the back of the bus as Syd made arrangements with the driver.

'We're going to see Daddy,' Pearl whispered to Cynthia, relief filling every part of her body. Despite her concern over Ruby, she knew that her parents would see no harm came to her sister. Ricky couldn't put up any opposition to the baby now.

'See Daddy?' Cynthia asked, and Pearl nodded as the bus started up. They were on their way home.

Pearl fell into Gwen's open arms, dropping her bag on the pavement. 'Oh, Gwen, it's good to be back.'

'We've missed you! It's not a week but it seems you've been gone years.' She smiled as Cynthia was thrown into the air by Fitz, her giggles echoing through the street.

'Is everything all right? Have any V2s dropped over here?' Pearl asked.

'South of the river is getting it worst. Last week a rocket came down on Lewisham and killed thirty-six. The poor buggers didn't stand a chance. What's it like in the country?'

'You don't get as many,' Pearl said.

'Good to see you back, gel.' Fitz lowered Cynthia to the ground. 'What's been going on down in the sticks?'

'Give the girl a chance, Fitzy. Now take her bag up. Is the key on the back of the door?'

Pearl nodded. 'Yes, where I always leave it.'

'Good, come on young Cynth, come into old Gwen's and see what I've saved for you.'

Pearl gazed around the shop. It smelled just the same – of vegetables, strong bacon and paraffin. She was glad to be home.

'Here you are, ducks.' Gwen gave Cynthia a brown paper bag. 'There's a few sweeties specially for you.'

Pearl smiled at the sight of her daughter making short work of the sweets as Gwen sat her on the counter.

'My, you've got heavy. Your granny been feeding you up on all those farm eggs.' Gwen pulled the chair from the corner and told Pearl to sit down. 'Now, what's been happening? We seen 'is nibs shooting off on Sunday. Walks by us without so much as a good morning. Had a face on him like a week-old batter pudding.'

'Gwen, Ruby's in hospital.'

'What?'

'She's expecting and lost some blood. The doctors won't let her home just yet.'

The bell tinkled and Fitz appeared. 'What have I missed?'

'Ruby's in the family way,' Gwen burst out before Pearl could answer, 'and was taken to hospital as she was so poorly.'

'Is she all right now?'

Pearl nodded, but felt very tearful.

'Come on, love.' Fitz patted her back. 'She's in good hands, I'm sure.'

'You must start looking after yourself,' said Gwen, knitting her brow. 'I've watched the weight fall off you. You don't look as though you've been sleeping well, either, not with them bags under your eyes. Don't mind me saying, but how are you going to manage upstairs with another little 'un on the way?'

Pearl smiled hesitantly. 'Jim's coming home.'

Gwen's eyes went wide. 'On leave, you mean?'

'I had a letter to say he's been wounded. He could be home any time.'

'Oh, blimey, gel,' said Fitz, 'you'll have a full house.'

'Mum and Dad said Ruby and Ricky can stay with them.'

''Spect your mum's pleased about that,' nodded Gwen. 'And it's only fair, after all. You've had to shoulder the lion's share so far.'

'Now, you won't have anything decent in the larder,' said Fitz. 'How are you off for coupons?'

'I didn't use any at Mum's.'

'In that case, we'll sort you out a few things. I'll bring 'em up later.'

Pearl found herself in Gwen's arms, a big kiss planted on her cheek and one for Cynthia. She had wonderful friends in the Hemsleys. It was good to be back. She couldn't wait for Jim to see Cynthia. She was so proud of their little daughter.

They had so much to look forward to. No matter what Jim's wounds were, like Ruby, she would find a way to help her husband recover.

Was it possible that in time, they could all be happy again?

Chapter 23

That evening, whilst Cynthia drew with her chalks on the Morrison, Pearl lit a roaring fire. The kitchen smelled damp, and Ricky had left dirty dishes in the sink and newspapers scattered round. Pearl felt his presence in her little home. She wanted to scrub it all out, to make the place her own again.

When Fitz delivered the groceries, Pearl asked him if he would help her with the bags.

'It'll be me pleasure,' Fitz nodded. 'We'll load them on

the barra. Have you got enough suitcases to put everything in?'

'No, don't think so.'

'I've got an old leather one at the back of the storeroom. Don't shut properly but you can tie string round it.'

'That would do nicely.'

'I'll bring it up.'

After Pearl had made tea and put Cynthia to bed, she began packing the battered and lockless case that Fitz had given her. Ruby's clothes and Ricky's two suits, shoes and uniform fitted perfectly. The things that were left over she folded into his naval duffel bag. It was when she found the small attaché case behind the curtain of the dressing table that she was suddenly filled with sadness. Ruby had been happy before Ricky. Would she ever be as happy again?

Quickly Pearl filled the attaché with Ruby's personal items. Snapping the locks tight, she placed it carefully with the suitcase tied with string and the duffel bag.

When all was done, she kicked off her shoes and sat on the bed. Tomorrow she would wash the sheets and pillow-cases, and drag Cynth's bed back to her bedroom.

But no, she couldn't do that. Cynth now had a room to herself. Goose bumps spread over Pearl's skin as she thought about Jim's strong body, his arms wrapped round her, his lips kissing her neck and his breath in her hair. Making love was what she had missed so much.

What would it be like to be with him again? They could never get enough of each other once. Would it still be the same? Pearl smiled as she sat there, her fingers stroking the eiderdown. She bounced once or twice and laughed aloud. She hadn't laughed in such a long while. But now she had good reason. Jim would soon be home.

By Friday, every room had been swept and cleaned. Pearl had sewn curtains for the boxroom from a length of red

and white gingham, and stored Cynthia's clothes, toys and chalks in a chest of drawers that she'd bought from Percy Flint. Cynthia liked her room. The camp bed was folded up and there was space to play.

That afternoon Pearl left Cynthia with Gwen whilst she went to the telephone box. First she spoke to Mr Brewer and told him the news. He sent Ruby his best wishes, promising to send on her wages if Pearl could provide an address. Next she telephoned Patty.

'Ruby's still in hospital,' Patty told her. 'Your mum's gone to visit.'

'What's wrong with her?' Pearl asked quickly.

'Nothing for you to worry about,' Patty assured her. 'Your mum told me she's much happier now her husband's here.'

As Pearl walked home, she remembered what her dad said. Ruby wasn't her responsibility now. She had Ricky to lean on, or so they all hoped.

In the early hours of Saturday morning, Pearl woke with a start. It was two weeks from the day Jim's letter was written. Her bedside clock said half-past four, but she couldn't sleep.

Climbing out of bed, she put on her dressing gown. Everything was in place; all Jim's clothes returned to the wardrobe, his shoes arranged neatly beneath. The dressing table and mirror was under the window and on its shiny surface were the pretty pink jars that Jim had bought her.

When would he be home? Going to the wardrobe she took out her honeymoon suit. Yesterday she'd ironed it and sprinkled lavender water on the collar. But perhaps a skirt and jumper would be best? She couldn't decide.

The living room was freezing. She put a match to the fire she had prepared last night and soon the coals began to glow red. Thanks to her dad's five pounds, there was enough coal to see them through Christmas.

She stared into the flames. This year Christmas would be their first family Christmas. She had enough put by for a chicken or rabbit, plenty of gravy and roast potatoes. She would cook them until they were brown and crusty, just how he liked them. This caused her to think of Mrs Nesbitt, who she hadn't seen lately. But now Jim was home perhaps things could be different and they could visit as a family.

Through a chink in the blackout curtains she saw it was still dark. Her mind was full of Jim as she returned to the kitchen and sat at the Morrison. Would he be able to climb up the stairs? How bad were his wounds? And when would Ruby come out of hospital? She hoped her mum would write and tell her all the news.

Restless again, she sat by the fire. Closing her eyes, she began to dream of the future and how it was going to be ...

With a start, Pearl opened her eyes. The warmth of the fire had made her doze off. She rubbed her cheeks and blinked and thought she was dreaming as she looked up at the tall man in the army greatcoat leaning heavily on a wooden crutch. 'J-Jim?' she stammered, lifting her head from the cushion.

'Don't move. I want to look at you.'

Pearl felt a lump in her throat so big she couldn't swallow. In the firelight she saw a stranger standing there, his face hollowed and gaunt, his body twisted at an unfamiliar angle. But then she looked into his eyes and at their deep colour, which hadn't been tarnished by war. It was her Jim. It was!

They kissed long and hard, hungry kisses that drove everything from his mind – the war, the death, the suffering, the pain and the fear of more pain. Jim wasn't even aware of his crutch slipping to the floor with a clatter, and the slight tremble running through his wife's body as she gripped

him, her lips burning on his and not a breath taken between them. For years he had imagined this moment; in the dust and filth and cries of the dying, he had imagined Pearl and her body and the feel of her skin beneath his fingers. He swayed slightly as his head throbbed, his muscles arched and contracted in need, and his gut turned over and seemed to sail from one side of his body to another. If he let her go, if she slipped out of his arms, if he woke up from this dream ...

'Jim, Jim ... let me breathe! I ain't gonna run away.' She was half laughing and he groaned softly, embarrassed at his tight hold.

'Sorry ... sorry ...'

'Don't be. Oh, Jim, I can't believe it's you.'

'It's me, all right.' His laughter was awkward as he damped down the desire, the animal need of a man on the brink.

'Come and sit down.'

He let himself be helped, but he was grateful to clutch the back of the couch and steady himself.

This wasn't how he'd imagined it, not the return of the victorious hero, straight-backed and gung ho, as the films had portrayed before the war. Now he was having to grit his teeth, torn by the want inside him and the knowledge that half of him was no man, a leg he dragged, that caused him to cuss and blind, and then be ashamed of himself when he saw others who were worse. He'd seen plenty of those – the crippled and maimed that still filled his thoughts – and, if given half a chance, he'd chisel out the part of his brain that threw up the unwelcome reminders.

He leaned painfully and eased himself down as he'd been taught by the nurses, an old man's action that he hated with all his heart. When seated he stretched out the stiff limb, tore his eyes back to his wife.

'Blimey, gel, so this is what the old place looks like.' He glanced around the darkened room, lit only by the shadows

of fire. 'Christ knows there've been times I never thought I'd clock it again.'

'I ain't even put the light on. Or dressed. Or brushed me teeth.'

He took her in his arms, hiding the grimace that shadowed the pain. 'Your pearlies are sparkling, sweetheart. And in the dark you ain't gonna get a shock looking at your old man.'

'Jim, what happened to your leg?'

'Put it like this. I won't be going for no long runs just yet.' He nodded to the wooden crutch on the floor. Its top was covered by dirty old cloth that eased the discomfort as he leaned. 'I gotta use that thing to get me along.'

'Will it get better?'

'Dunno. Gotta see the doc about that.'

'Does it hurt?'

'Too bloody right it does. Got stiff in the van that brought me home. There was two other blokes, all of us was in hospital together.'

'Hospital? Where?'

'Southampton. But they ran short of beds, so the VADs were brought in. Suited me, though. Didn't matter what time of night it was when we left, as long as I got home. But listen, I'll tell you me morbid 'istory later. Right now, I want to see our nipper.'

Pearl threw her arms round him. 'Jim, she's lovely! We've got a beautiful daughter!' He smelled her hair, her body, her breath, and he kissed her again, so hard that it didn't seem to matter for a moment that he wasn't the man he used to be. Slowly he held her away. 'I want you bad, Pearl, but let me see her first.'

This time, he accepted her assistance as she linked his arm round her shoulder. He kicked his crutch dismissively from their path as he hobbled to the hall, attempting to carry his weight on his good leg.

'I'm a right old hop-along,' he joked, inwardly squirming at his disability. 'You'll need to give me a good kick up the arse to get me going.'

She looked up at him and laughed. 'Jim, you ain't changed.'

He wanted to tell her he had. Oh God, he'd changed in a thousand ways on the battlefield. He'd killed rather than be killed. He'd slaughtered in anger and passion, and he'd ended the lives of men that he hadn't even known. Men who were no more than boys, and others with wives and kids, just like he had Pearl and little Cynth. But instead, he took her face in his hands.

'I love you, Pearly-girl.'

'And I love you, Jim.'

'Come on then, push open that door.'

He remembered it was the boxroom where they stored all the junk. But in the weak light that trickled down from the living-room fire, he saw a small bed sheltering a child's shape, curled and still under the covers.

'Is that her?' His voice trembled.

'It's our Cynth.'

'I must be dreaming,' he rasped, too full of emotion to let himself cry. Though he wanted to. He wanted to shed the tears that for once were of joy and came from a life-giving source. 'Can we go a bit closer?'

They shuffled in and his heart beat a tattoo on his ribs. He saw her in the dark, a tiny head, a hand outstretched, heard the soft, regular breathing and he swallowed the sob in his throat.

'Do you want to sit on the chair, love?'

'No, she's asleep, ain't she?'

'I could wake her . . . slowly, like.'

'That wouldn't be fair.' Jim stared in fascination, bitter-sweet joy and a deep knowing that he'd missed the best thing that God ever created: the birth of his first-born and her first two years of growing up.

★

Pearl lay in bed, her body bathed in a golden glow. She knew this feeling only came as a result of being truly loved. Before Jim had gone away, the physical side of their marriage had been passionate, with all their tiffs ending between the sheets. But now their lovemaking was something different. Despite Jim's hip and thigh being covered by bandages – or, perhaps, because of it – and the fact that he'd been self-conscious of the way he'd had to get into bed, holding on to the headboard and dropping slowly down with his leg outstretched, they had laughed at their awkwardness.

But after the laughter, she'd seen the pain on his face as he tried to make love to her as he once had. But it wasn't until she'd told him it didn't matter, that she just wanted to be held, that his kisses had grown tender. Finally they had found a way and at last he'd wrapped her in his arms and exhaustion had taken them both.

Now he was in a deep sleep beside her. The dawn was showing through the chink in the blackout and she longed to see him. Slowly, she slipped from the bed, glancing back as he groaned in his sleep. She paused, waiting for him to settle, then reached the window and separated the curtains.

One muscled arm lay over his chest. A chest that she had kissed and caressed and that was now streaked with scars. She shivered at the thought of what had caused them and bent to lift her nightdress, abandoned so carelessly on the floor.

Her body tingled as she went to the jug and poured water into the bowl. Quietly she washed, not wanting to wake him. Taking her dressing gown, she left the room, closing the door gently behind her.

In the kitchen she looked out on the grey Saturday morning. The roofs of the houses were just the same as they always were: smoke-strewn and battered, with tiles missing and gutters blackened above the Anderson shelters.

Not a green shoot existed, except on the piles of rubble and debris. There were no birds, only gulls, swooping and diving.

How was it possible to love this place so much? It was just as the old saying went: home is where the heart is. How true that was.

'Blimey, it ain't, is it?' Gwen dropped the potatoes she was about to weigh on the scales and opened her arms to the man standing in the shop door. 'Jim Nesbitt! You're home!'

She ran round the counter and hugged him. 'Oh, love, when did you get back?'

'In the early hours,' Jim told her, with the same grin on his face that she remembered. But his grin was about the only thing that was the same. One shoulder was higher than the other under his duffel coat. He was thin as a rake, and leaned on a crutch, the bags under his eyes so big they looked like bruises. His sandy hair had turned grey at the sides and was cut short, almost to his scalp. He'd been such a fine fellow of a man, with hair a woman would give her eyeteeth for. Gwen did her utmost to disguise her shock.

Fitz came in from the back of the shop. 'Jim, you old son of a gun!'

'Hello, mate.'

Gwen watched her husband take hold, grasping first the crutch, then seeing his mistake, hugging Jim with apologies.

'Don't take no notice of this,' Jim joked. 'It's me new cricket bat.'

'How are you?' Gwen knew this was a daft question but it had to be asked.

'I done all right, Gwen, compared to some.'

'How you gonna manage them stairs?'

Jim chuckled. 'On me bum, I reckon.' He shuffled over to the counter. 'No, it's good practice. Strengthens me leg muscles. Now quick, before Pearl and Cynth come down,

288

can you give me an ounce of liquorice or something? I want to surprise me daughter.'

Gwen nodded. 'I'll sort you out something. Jim, what do you think of your little girl?'

'She's a cracker. And didn't mind this.' He pointed to the crutch. 'Thought she might be afraid when she first saw it. But Pearl's been telling her all about her daddy; showed her me ugly mug enough times. She sat on me lap to eat her porridge, good as gold. Drew me a picture on the Morrison and gave me a blooming great kiss that brought tears to my eyes.'

'Tell you what, Jim, she's a bright kid,' said Fitz, as Gwen tipped a few cough candies into a bag. They were pre-war, kept for emergencies, and this seemed to be one of them.

'Don't take after her old man, then,' grinned Jim, and Gwen noticed he leaned heavily on the counter.

'Go on with you.' She gave him the bag. 'Look out, they're coming.'

Gwen watched as little Cynth ran in and caught hold of her daddy's hand. If Jim still had his hair and his good looks, they'd be the spit of each other. There were smiles all round and a neighbour came in and slapped Jim on the back. Gwen saw the sparkle in Pearl's eyes that had been missing for so long.

To her mind, it was a bloody good job that Ruby and her old man were out of the picture. Pearl fretted far too much over Ruby. And Gwen didn't care at all for her stuck-up other half. He didn't seem like Jim's type, so with a bit of luck, this little family would have time to themselves. Though by the look of that leg it was going to be slow going. Still, they were young. And if anyone could laugh at himself and at life, it was Jim Nesbitt.

Pearl couldn't have felt happier. They had all walked up to the corner of West Ferry Road, very slowly for Jim's

benefit. Stopping at the park, he'd given Cynth a push on the swings, then found a bench where he could sit and watch. He'd cheered his daughter on and even managed to grab her as she fell on the grass. His disability hadn't affected his sense of humour. He was the same Jim, wisecracking and making his wife and daughter laugh. Cynthia loved her dad, sitting astride his crutch as though it was a hobbyhorse. Jim's eyes had creased in laughter. And when they'd come home, Pearl had made pie and mash, and drowned it in gravy. Jim's had stared in disbelief at the meal before him.

Now they were sitting in front of the fire, Cynth fast asleep and Jim's arm around her shoulders. There was so much to be said, yet neither of them wanted to begin.

Pearl laid a gentle hand on her husband's thigh. 'Does it hurt when I touch there?'

'I wouldn't complain if it did,' he grinned.

She snuggled up. 'Can you tell me about it?'

'What, me leg?'

'Yes, I want to know everything.'

'Might bore you stiff.'

'It won't,' she whispered, looking up at him. 'I couldn't be with you to share things, so at least we can share them now.'

'Some of it ain't very nice, gel.'

'I still want to know.'

He drew his hand through her hair. 'It was in Italy, this happened,' he told her slowly, stroking her hair as he spoke. 'Just after I'd heard Blackie had bought it, poor sod.'

'Oh no, Jim!'

''Fraid so. His old girl wrote to me, saying he'd died of his wounds in March at the Mareth Line.'

'Where's that?'

'North Africa. It was a place used by the Eyeties and Jerry to stand against us.'

'Dying of his wounds,' murmured Pearl. 'That must have been awful.'

'I just hope it was quick. 'Cos, believe you me, no bloke wants to hang around in a bad state.'

'I'm so sorry, Jim.' Pearl snuggled closer.

'I was too. But I was even sorrier when Jerry landed one of their surprise packages on me.' Pearl waited, listening to his heart as it beat faster. She knew it must be terrible to remember. 'Their trick was to fire half a dozen bombs one after another, make a bloody great racket, putting the fear of God in the enemy. Didn't know what hit me, just blacked out and came to as the stretcher-bearers picked me up. Well, I wished I hadn't come round, as the first thing I saw was half of me leg hanging out.'

'Oh, Jim!' Pearl closed her eyes.

'Sorry, gel, don't mean to upset you.'

'Go on, I want to hear it all.'

He took a deep breath and sighed. 'You sure?'

'Course I am.'

He bent and kissed the top of her head. In a husky voice he went on, 'The shells were still raining down. But they got me to the casualty clearing station. The MO shoved a needle in me and that was it, thank God. I was out like a light. The bugger of it was, our unit came under fire again, and they had to move us to a tent hospital. We ended up near Rome, but by then I'd lost too much blood for 'em to operate. Took them time to bung it back in me. Eventually they got me on the table. Surgeon done a good job putting the leg back together, but after, it got infected.'

Pearl sniffed. 'Why didn't you write about all this?'

'What, like, "Hello, Pearl, me leg's smashed up, but the weather's nice over here"?'

'You could have said you was injured and in hospital. I worried because you never said much. Your last letters was so brief.'

'You had your own worries, gel. You never went on

291

about the bombing here. But I knew from some of the others that London was on the hit list again.'

Pearl wanted to say something about Ruby, to break the ice. But she knew this wasn't the right time. 'What happened when you got the infection?'

Jim cleared his throat noisily. 'I thought I would lose the leg.'

Pearl hugged him tighter. She felt very tearful. She hadn't been with him to comfort him. He'd been in a foreign land, amongst strangers and was very sick. She couldn't imagine how lonely and frightening that must have been.

He gave a sudden laugh. 'They was about to put me under again and I remember telling the doc that if they couldn't save it, he was to put his saw away and let me kick the bucket. But somehow I woke up with it still on.'

'Jim, it ain't no laughing matter. You could have died.'

'Yeah, but I didn't, did I? I just kept thinking of you and Cynth. And in October they transferred me to the hospital ship. The Red Cross took us to Southampton. They done another op there, dug out some more mortar. Dunno if it's all gone. We'll have to wait and see.'

'You mean it could be bad again?'

'Didn't ask no more. Ignorance is bliss, don't they say?'

'Jim, we've got to know what to do for the best.'

He chuckled, squeezing her hand. 'I'm just out of the sympathy vote, that's all.'

'Sympathy is something you've never wanted, Jim Nesbitt. You're too proud.'

He turned, easing himself slowly to look into her eyes. 'Listen, gel, the only thought I had in my mind when I was in hospital, was, I'm going to get home, shit or bust. I told the nurses every day, that nothing and no one was going to stop me from seeing you and Cynth. The poor cows didn't understand English, let alone cockney, but God love them, they looked after me. And I made it, didn't I?'

'Yes, Jim, you did.'

'Now there's just us, no bloody Hitler to fight, and the war will soon be over. So come on, give us a kiss, let's leave the talking till later. We've got plenty of time for that. I want you so much. And I want to tell you how much I love you and shut the rest of the world out.'

Pearl threaded her arms around his neck and kissed him. She had so much to tell him, and she'd have to break all the news about Ruby and Ricky living here. But he had just said that he wanted to shut out the world. And she was more than prepared to do that.

They were sitting at the Morrison the next morning when news came over the wireless that a V2 had landed on Woolworths at New Cross. Pearl turned up the volume as Jim sat with Cynthia on his knee, his porridge untouched. They listened in silence to the description of the huge explosion where, so far, the death toll was over one hundred and fifty people and as many wounded.

Pearl sat down heavily. 'And we thought the war was over.'

Jim stroked his daughter's fair curls. 'It's got to be, Pearl. This killing can't go on.'

'But it is. All those poor people out doing their shopping. Innocent people who had kids, fathers and mothers . . .'

Jim looked at her. 'We have to be thankful it's not us.'

'I feel guilty at being alive sometimes.'

'The only thing we can do is go on.'

She reached for his hand. 'I know. It's just every time I hear something like this, my legs go to jelly.' She smiled. 'But now I've got you, it's not as bad.'

'Turn the damn thing off, Pearl. We'll hear enough about it in the days to come.' He frowned down at Cynthia. 'Come on, petal, let's do some drawing together.'

Despite the tragedy that was unfolding, after switching

off the wireless, Pearl turned her mind to the letter she must write to her parents and Ruby. What would she say about Jim's homecoming? Jim hadn't asked about Ruby and Ricky. They hadn't discussed the outside world and Pearl knew that neither of them wanted to.

She listened in contentment to her daughter's laughter as she sat with her daddy. Jim adored his little girl. The time spent apart was only bringing them all closer. What more could she ask for?

Chapter 24

On Tuesday morning, as Pearl was helping Jim to get dressed, there was a knock at the door. Jim rolled his eyes and grinned. 'Caught with me trousers down again.'

'It's probably Gwen.' Pearl pushed her hair from her face as she helped him pull up the leg of his trousers. She knew he didn't want to be dependent on her so she always made light of whatever help she gave. Even Cynthia joined in as she sat on the bed, waving Jim's braces.

'Go on, love, answer it. Cynth and me will finish the job.'

Pearl hurried to the kitchen. When she opened the door, her jaw dropped in surprise. 'Em! What are you doing here?' Pearl stared at the slim figure in a smart silver-grey suit with a fur collar.

'I've come to thank you for our wedding present. We moved as soon as we came home from Cornwall, and before I start the decorating with Colin, I decided to come and thank you.' She paused as Cynthia's laughter rang out and then Jim's deep chuckle. 'But if you're busy . . . ?'

'No, course I'm not.'

Em stepped through and Pearl closed the door. ''Scuse the mess.' She nodded to the unwashed breakfast dishes. 'Jim came home on Friday.'

'Oh, Pearl, that's wonderful news. Is he on leave?'

'No, he was wounded.'

'Oh dear. Is it bad?'

'No, we're managing.' Pearl pulled out a chair. 'Sit down and I'll put the kettle on.'

'I've called at an inconvenient time.'

'No, it's lovely to see you.' Pearl glanced in Jim's shaving mirror as she filled the kettle. She hadn't even had time to brush her hair. Jim was priority in the mornings. Getting him washed, shaved and dressed came even before making a fire.

'So what's your new house like?' Pearl asked as she set out the cups. It was very cold in the kitchen but Em didn't seem to notice.

'Very nice. But there's a lot to do.'

'Is Colin any good at decorating?'

'He doesn't have much time. But Dad can paint walls just as long as he only does one at a time.'

Pearl had forgotten about Em's dad. 'How is he settling in?'

'Very well. It's a quiet street.' Em blushed. 'He still doesn't go out much, though.'

'I expect he will in time.'

Just then they heard the scrape of the crutch on the lino and Jim appeared. Cynthia came rushing in and Em caught her in her arms. 'My, haven't you grown in only a few weeks?' She looked up and smiled. 'Hello, Jim. You might not remember me. I'm Emily Harris, or was when I last saw you at the firm's Christmas dance.'

'That was a few years ago,' Jim smiled as he limped forward and held out his hand. 'Nice to see you again.'

'Perhaps you remember Colin, who is now my husband?'

Jim nodded. 'Yes, o' course I do. And congratulations. When did you tie the knot?'

Em glanced quickly at Pearl. 'Don't you know? It was at the end of October.'

'Ruby and me was Em's bridesmaids,' Pearl explained quickly. 'I was going to tell you in me next letter, but there wasn't time.'

There was an awkward silence before Jim smiled. 'Oh, well, plenty of time now to catch up.'

'Are Ruby and Ricky at home?' Em asked, looking through to the front room. 'I'd like to thank them for the sheets.'

Pearl looked at Jim. She said quickly, 'Ricky and Ruby are in Abingley with Mum and Dad. Ruby had to go in hospital.'

'Oh, is it serious?'

'No, she's expecting and the hospital want to keep an eye on her.'

'Expecting?' Em repeated. 'How marvellous for them both. But won't it be a bit crowded here for you all?'

Pearl didn't dare look at Jim as she explained that Ruby and Ricky would be staying in Abingley. 'So what was Cornwall like?' she asked hurriedly as she placed the cups on the top of the Morrison.

'Beautiful,' Em smiled. 'We felt very lucky to be able to have a honeymoon at all under the circumstances.'

'I'll say cheerio,' Jim muttered in a tight, low voice. 'Give me best to Colin.' He hobbled to the back door on his crutch. Snatching his coat from the peg, he slung it over his shoulder.

'Where are you going?' Pearl called after him.

His face was full of anger as he looked at her. The door slammed loudly after him.

Pearl felt sick with anxiety. She turned back slowly, embarrassed as she looked at Em.

'Sorry about that.'

'It was me, going on about my wedding. How tactless of me, when Jim's been away fighting for all our lives.'

'Doesn't matter.'

'Daddy gone,' Cynthia called as she slipped from Em's lap and ran to the door.

'He'll be back soon.' Pearl smiled at her daughter.

'Look what I brought, Cynthia.' Em opened her bag and took out a small bag. 'It's traditional shortbread, from Cornwall. I hope you like it.'

There was soon a big smile on Cynthia's face as she began to open the packet. 'Take it in your bedroom, Cynth, and don't eat them all once,' Pearl said quietly.

'I must go.' Em stood up after she'd kissed Cynthia's cheek. 'And thank you again for the lovely pillowcases, Pearl. Please thank Ruby for me when you see her.'

'Thanks for calling, Em.'

'Here is our address.' She gave Pearl a slip of paper. 'If you and Jim are over our way, please call in. I'm not working now, just looking after Dad. So please keep in touch.'

'Yes, I will.'

'And I hope Jim will forgive me for being so thoughtless.'

'Don't be daft, Em. It was nice of you to come all this way.'

When she was alone, Pearl went to the window. She looked up and down the street, but Jim wasn't in sight. Where had he gone? He couldn't go far with his crutch, and it was cold. If only she had told him about Ricky and Ruby living here.

The evening drew on but there was still no sign of Jim. Where was he? She'd spoken to Gwen and Fitz, and neither of them had seen him. Later, she'd taken Cynthia to the park and walked to the corner of West Ferry Road. It was a cold November day, with a mist creeping up from

297

the docks. Where could he have gone to keep warm? He couldn't have gone far. Had he gone to his mother's? But how would he get there?

Pearl sat down on the couch and read Cynthia a story. When the clock struck seven, she closed the book. 'Time for bed now.'

'Daddy 'ome?' Cynthia asked as Pearl put on her pyjamas.

'Soon, love. He'll come in to say good night.'

But time passed and Jim didn't come home. Finally Cynthia fell asleep and Pearl went to the window and stared out on the mists. 'Where are you, Jim?'

She paced the floor. What was she to do next? Tears sprang to her eyes. If only she had opened her heart to him. They might have resolved their differences if she had.

It was nine o'clock before Pearl heard the clop of hoofs in the street. She looked into a swirling fog and saw the pale light of a Tilley lamp, but the fog soon swallowed it up.

When the back door opened she rushed into the kitchen. 'Oh, Jim, thank God you're home.'

He didn't look at her. 'Is the nipper asleep?'

'Course she is. It's gone nine. We waited but you didn't come.'

He leaned his crutch against the wall. Slowly he took off his coat and hung it on the peg. Pearl thought how tired he looked. She wanted to hold him in her arms, to comfort him, but his manner told her he didn't want that.

'Where have you been all day?'

'At Mum's.'

'How did you get there?'

'Percy Flint gave me a lift.'

Pearl frowned. 'Why didn't you say where you was going? I wouldn't have worried.'

Without replying he limped past her.

'Jim?' she called as she followed him into the front room. 'I'm sorry about what happened this morning.'

He sat in the fireside chair and the crutch clattered noisily beside him.

'Let me explain.'

He looked up. 'When were you going to tell me about them living here?'

'I was going to, only I didn't want a row.'

He looked at her in surprise. 'A *row*?' he repeated incredulously. 'Christ Almighty, Pearl, what did you expect? A pat on the back?'

'I said in me letter they was married.'

'Yes, thanks very much for that,' he nodded, curling his fists on the arms of the chair. 'I was in a barn at the time, with snipers ready to blow my head off. My wife announcing she was Ricky Winters' sister-in-law was just the bit of encouragement I needed.' His eyes were full of reproach. 'What in heaven's name was you doing going along with it all?'

Pearl choked back a sob. 'I didn't, but when Ruby asked me I couldn't say no.'

'Couldn't or wouldn't?' He pointed his finger at her. 'Still fancy him, do you? 'Cos you did once, didn't you?'

Pearl felt her knees go weak. 'I ... I don't know what you mean.'

'I ain't a half-wit, Pearl. Did you think I never knew what was going on at the club? You got rid of me so you could give him the nod.' He tilted his head. 'Surprised, are you, that I sussed it out? Well, you shouldn't be. Fact is, I was mad about you. There was this lovely little thing, with her big green eyes and angel face. She always laughed at all me jokes and made me feel like her big brother. But I didn't want brotherly love. I wanted her to look at me the way she looked at him. And, by God, when war broke out and I saw you in the council offices, I didn't hesitate. It was my moment of glory, I told meself. You'd forgotten him and it was goodbye and good riddance to that smarmy bastard.

But blow me down, he turns up again, at me own flamin' wedding! And there was me wife with that look in her eyes – that look I'd have given my eyeteeth for—'

'Jim, you're wrong!' Pearl broke in. 'Marrying you was the best thing I ever did.'

One eyebrow rose questioningly. 'Shouldn't that be, the next best thing to having lover boy – here – whilst your old man is away?' He pushed himself up from the chair, steadying himself on the mantel, his blue gaze piercing as he stared at her. 'The simple fact is, Pearl, you knew the state of play between me and him. You knew it, yet you let him stay here, in my gaff, and enjoy a good laugh at my expense.'

Pearl shook her head. 'It wasn't like that.'

'Then what was wrong with them finding their own bloody place to stay?'

'I know, I should have refused,' she agreed. 'I wish I could turn the clock back and make it different. I was daft, I was weak. But they've gone now and that's all that matters. Just you and me and Cynth.'

Searching her eyes, he whispered, 'Can you swear to me, Pearl, that you ain't never had feelings for the bloke? Can you do that? If you can, this stops here. We put the whole damn thing behind us.'

Pearl moved her trembling lips. All she had to do was tell one small lie. If push came to shove, it would always be Ricky's word against hers. Jim was certain to believe her. It was a way to make all their troubles disappear ... to start afresh.

Just then, a noise made them turn. A small figure in pyjamas stood at the door. Jim dragged himself over and scooped up his daughter. 'Hello, little princess, I was just on me way to say good night.'

Cynthia hugged him. 'Daddy 'ome?'

'Yes, love, your dad's home.'

Pearl listened to her husband's gentle words, sentiments

300

that she had dreamed of hearing for so long during the years he'd been away. Words that now made her realize how impossible it would be to give him an untruthful answer. It would only be continuing in the same old way, hiding the same old secret.

'Jim—' she began, but he was already carrying Cynthia back to her room, his crutch dragging on the lino.

That night, he refused her offer to help him undress. They lay in bed in silence until she put her arm across him, but he turned away. Why was this happening? She loved him so much, but he wouldn't believe that Ricky meant nothing to her.

In the morning he was up before she woke. She heard him laughing with Cynthia and quickly she went along the hall to join them.

'Mummy, Daddy 'ome,' Cynthia shouted from the floor where she was playing underneath the blanket that Jim had draped over his crutch like a tent.

She bent down and kissed her forehead. 'You two are up early,' she said, smiling. 'I'll go and make the breakfast.'

'Don't bother for me,' he told her as he rose from the chair. 'I'm going now.'

'Going where?' Pearl asked in astonishment.

'I've got meself work at Percy's yard.'

'Work?' she repeated as he gave Cynthia's curly hair a ruffle. 'But your leg isn't—'

'He don't mind,' he cut in sharply. 'Just as long as I can move on it.'

'You're only just out of hospital.'

'I ain't no cripple, Pearl. And I'm lucky to be offered a job.'

She clutched his arm. 'But you need to see the doctor first.'

'The doctor don't put bread on the table, does he? Now,

301

come on, Cynth, give your daddy a smacker. I'll be home to play with you before bedtime.'

Cynthia crawled out from under the blanket. He drew her close and kissed her. 'You be a good girl for your mum, all right?'

Pearl followed him to the back door. 'Jim?' She tried to kiss him but the door closed. Her eyes filled with tears. She ran to the front room and looked out of the window. Percy's cart was waiting in the street below. Jim threw his crutch on the back and heaved himself up. She knew every movement must be painful. When the cart moved off, he didn't look back.

'Oh, Jim,' Pearl whispered as she sank down on the couch. Could he ever forgive her?

Jim pushed the broom with one hand and propped himself on the crutch with the other. He'd swept Percy's yard and mucked out Barney's stable. It was slow and laborious work, and his leg was tender after the morning's work. But he was grateful that Percy had offered him a lift to Vale Road. He hadn't had much to do with the old codger before the war, but they had a lot in common. Percy had been in the Buffs in 1915 and got a bayonet in his back. It had missed his heart and his lung and he'd survived to carry on in his father's rag-and-bone trade. Jim had a feeling that it was because of his leg that Percy had offered him work.

He couldn't have stayed at home, even if Percy hadn't offered him a job. He couldn't even look at Pearl without thinking of Winters. Bad thoughts had been tormenting him like the mosquitoes in Africa, always flying around and biting him where it hurt most. Winters, living at Pride Place, seeing Pearl every day, smiling smugly as if to say, you lose again, Jim Nesbitt.

Jim shook his head, trying to silence the taunts. He was jealous, he didn't mind admitting that. It was a pain worse

than his leg. But why had Pearl gone and done what she did, when she knew his opinion of that bastard? Why hadn't she been able to answer that question? Had he touched her, kissed her? The fact that he'd got hitched to Ruby, made no difference. He knew Winters' kind and he knew they never changed. That bloody letter Pearl had sent about Ruby and him getting married! It had given him sleepless nights, more than all the snipers, the shelling, the cries of the wounded and the scurrying of the rats over his body. How could she have encouraged it? The only reason he could come up with, was that she wanted to. And then the way it all came out, from Em. When was she planning to tell him?

'You all right, son?'

Jim turned to find Percy at his side. He hadn't heard the cart come rolling into the yard. 'Yes,' Jim said quickly. 'What do you want doing with them crates over there?'

'Leave 'em be, lad, you've done enough for the morning.'

'It ain't much.'

'When you gonna see the doc?'

'Dunno.'

Percy rubbed his bristled chin with rough hands. 'Look, I'll take yer down Millwall this afternoon. It's on me rounds. I can drop you off at the quack's.'

'Don't want to put you to trouble.'

'And I don't want that wife of yours after me for doing her old man in,' Percy chuckled. 'Good girl you got there. Sold her a few bits now and then and she's looked out for your little 'un while you've been away. She's stuck with you, which is more than I can say for some others.'

Jim watched the old man lead Barney to the stable. Percy was right and that was the bugger of it. He did have a good wife – once. Before Winters had come along. But then Winters had been there in the old days, though Pearl had never said nothing about that. But he just *knew*. God help

him, Africa and Italy had been bad enough, but now he had returned to something he couldn't shoot at. An enemy he couldn't see.

He began sweeping again, silently wrestling with his emotions as Percy fed the old horse.

The days passed and Pearl had a letter from Amy. Ruby was home from hospital and, with Syd's help, Ricky had got a job at the aerodrome, as a clerk in the offices. Pearl wanted to know more about Ruby but Amy was full of her son-in-law.

Pearl wanted to share the letter with Jim, but it was as though he had locked her out of his feelings. Percy called for him in the mornings and dropped him off at night. After supper, he played with Cynthia, but after she'd gone to sleep, he had taken to going to the pub. It wasn't far to walk to the Nelson. She felt more lonely now than she had in the war. Then, she had known he wanted her. Now, she didn't know if he did.

On the first two Saturdays of December, Pearl took Cynthia to the market. She wanted to send her mum and Ruby something in the post for Christmas. But money was short.

The week before Christmas, a parcel arrived from Abingley. Once again the letter was about Ruby and Ricky. Cynthia's Christmas present, a large stuffed bear from the sale at the church, was wrapped up carefully in paper and tied with string.

Pearl kept it aside, to put in the big red woollen stocking she had knitted to hang by the fireplace. With Fitz and Gwen's gifts, and a set of coloured chalks from her and Jim, the stocking would be full on Christmas morning.

When Sunday 24 December arrived, Jim returned in the evening without his crutch. Instead he leaned on a walking stick.

'Your dad can walk with this now,' he told Cynthia as they all sat in front of the fire.

'Did you get it from the yard?' Pearl asked.

'Percy was given it on his rounds. This means I'll be able to drive the cart soon.'

'Are you going to stay on at the yard, then?' Pearl was surprised.

He shrugged. 'Don't know.'

'What about your old job with the council?'

'Can't see meself marching over the rubble just yet.'

Pearl felt excited. They were talking again. Tonight she had a small present to give him, a pocket knife for work. She had dressed in her best skirt and blouse and washed her hair. She'd waved it between her fingers over one eye like she used to.

The front room looked very festive. All the walls were decorated with paper chains that she and Cynthia had made, and Fitz had given her a cardboard cut-out tree from the storeroom. Cynthia had coloured in green branches and white blobs of snow. And the best surprise of all was the chicken she had saved all her coupons for. It was under the gauze in the larder, waiting to be cooked tomorrow, with carrots and peas and a batter pudding.

She gave him his present. 'Happy Christmas,' she said softly.

He unwrapped it and slipped it in his pocket. 'Thanks.'

'I've got a nice roast chicken for tomorrow.'

'Don't trouble for me. Thought I'd take Cynth to Mum's.'

'But it's Christmas Day.'

'We'll be back later.'

'What about the chicken?'

'Do as you please,' he shrugged as he stood up. 'I'm off to the Nelson for a quick one.'

Pearl's eyes stung. He hadn't asked her to go with them to Mrs Nesbitt's tomorrow.

'Jim, don't go out tonight,' she pleaded. 'Let's spend Christmas Eve together.'

He reached for his stick and took Cynthia to her bedroom. Tears slipped down her cheeks. He hadn't forgiven her after all. Now she was to spend Christmas alone.

Later that evening, she filled Cynthia's stocking, but without Jim, it was so lonely. She had dreamed of him being with her on his first Christmas home and what they would do. But now she knew he couldn't forgive her. Gazing sadly into the fire, she thought of her hopes for 1945. But none of them could come true if Jim couldn't forgive and forget.

Part Three

Part Three

Chapter 25

Tuesday 8 May 1945

Pearl pushed her way through the crowd in Hemsley's towards the wireless set that was the focus of attention. VE day had arrived and the long line of tables outside were decorated with bunting, Union Jacks and red, white and blue rosettes. The announcement everyone had been waiting for was imminent. Millions of wireless receivers were tuned to the Home Service.

Pearl found a place by the counter where the wireless stood and lifted Cynthia on the top of the big sack of potatoes. All was silent as Fitz made another attempt to tune the set.

Gwen waved her hand and pulled him away. 'Leave it now, Fitzy, Winnie is about to speak.'

Pearl leaned forward, as did everyone else, to listen to the commentator's voice as he introduced the momentous occasion.

'This is London. The Prime Minister, Right Honourable Winston Churchill.'

Pearl held her breath, as this was followed by the most famous voice of the war years. A voice full of courage and strength, a voice that had urged Britain on to victory through its darkest hours. 'Hostilities will end officially,' declared the Prime Minister, 'at one minute after midnight tonight.'

There was a volley of cheers inside and outside the shop. Pearl found herself being hugged and kissed as caps and hats decorated with red, white and blue were thrown into the air.

'Quiet,' hissed Gwen as she disentangled herself from Fitz's embrace. 'He ain't finished yet.'

'We may,' the leader continued, 'allow ourselves a brief period of rejoicing.'

'Brief?' a man yelled. 'You've got to be kidding, old son. It's been five years of blue murder and we ain't gonna stop celebrating till the cows come home.'

'Too right,' agreed a woman next to him, 'come on, we're missing the fun.'

Pearl stood back as everyone hurried out to the parties that were just beginning to get into their stride. They had been going on since yesterday when crowds had filled the city centre, waiting for the official proclamation of peace in Europe. The houses were strung with flags and bunting, and women wore Union Jack aprons. The men sported waistcoats and caps in patriotic colours. Since early that morning Pearl had been helping to prepare the tables in the street for the children. Now the plates of jam tarts, cakes, Spam sandwiches, bread and butter, buns, and bowls of jellies and blancmanges were being uncovered for the youngsters, who for so long had been deprived of such luxuries.

A little girl with dark brown hair and dressed in a red, white and blue striped tunic came running in. Dillys lived across the road and was friends with Cynthia. Now that the nights were lighter, Pearl allowed Cynthia to play in the street, provided she was accompanied by seven-year-old Dillys and her older brother, Robbie.

Cynthia slid down from the sack and ran to meet Dillys. 'I'll be out soon,' Pearl called after them as they ran to the festive tables placed end to end along the length of Pride Place. Each child had been given a flag to wave and most children were already singing the national anthem as loud as they could before eating.

'Well, that's it then,' said Gwen, turning off the wireless, which was being drowned out by the noise outside. 'Peace is official.'

'It's hard to believe we ain't at war.'

'Yes, but thousands of our boys are still on active duty,' Fitz pointed out.

'I wonder what peace is like for the German people,' Pearl hesitated. 'They're like us, bombed out from their homes and hungry. The women have to feed their kids somehow. Many of them are widows too, their men lost in action. It wasn't them who caused all the trouble; it was Hitler and his Nazis.'

'And good riddance to him,' said Gwen fiercely. 'Though it would have been better for the world if he hadn't hid like a coward under the Chancellery in Berlin and blown his brains out. We could have brought him to book and he knew it.'

'He had too much to answer for,' agreed Fitz. 'Suicide was the easy way out. All those concentration camps, for instance. The Nazis trying to destroy a whole race — by God, he would have had had no escape from that.'

Pearl wound a stray lock of silky blonde into the pins that kept her hair in place. She didn't want to talk about the atrocities reported in the papers. Or the starving and deprived and war-torn nations that had suffered in the six years of conflict, which was still going on in the Far East. Like everyone, she wanted to celebrate, to forget all the unhappiness, even if it was only for a few days.

'Think we should go out to the kids now.' Pearl straightened the belt on her one good frock, a util- ity dress of dark blue decorated on the skirt with tiny Union Jacks that had been given away free for VE day. The warmer, more thundery weather had caused most people to leave off their coats. Pearl had dressed Cynthia in the plum-coloured dress that Hope had made for Em's wedding. It was too small now, but she'd turned down the hem and pinned red, blue and white rosettes to the bodice.

311

'Your Jim coming to the party?' Gwen asked as she lifted the tray of sliced carrots and apples on sticks.

'Depends on what Percy wants done.' She tried not to let Gwen see how upset she was that Jim was absent again. She knew that if he wasn't at the yard, he'd be at the Nelson.

'Well, at least it's work, ducks.' Gwen narrowed her eyes at her husband. 'And talking of work, I'll leave you to get the storeroom sorted, Fitzy. Don't want it smelling like a dosshouse.'

'It's all right for some,' he grumbled with a wink at Pearl. 'Leave all the hard graft to the old man and go off and enjoy yourself.'

'Too bloody right I will,' chuckled Gwen as they left the shop. 'With a couple of days partying ahead of us and no trade, the veg will go rotten and stink.' She laughed, nudging Pearl's arm as they mingled with the noisy crowd. 'Remember when Jim's mum first saw this place and wanted to know if the smell would drift upstairs to your place?'

Pearl managed to smile, but she felt sad that Jim had never asked her to go with him and Cynthia to Vale Road. Not that they stayed long, and Cynthia always came back subdued. But she had always hoped they could visit as a family.

Pearl knew that Gwen must have noticed that Jim stayed away from home. Once he had been eager to talk, now he did his best to avoid them. Fitz had seen him when he was worse for wear and Pearl had always made light of it. But now she was running out of excuses.

As the day wore on, news came in of thousands of revellers outside Buckingham Palace. They were all waiting excitedly to cheer the King and Queen. The feeling of freedom was everywhere. No more V2s, and the men and boys were coming home. The requisitioned factories, like Mr Brewer's, could now return to their former trades.

But what would happen to the women who had filled the men's shoes, Pearl wondered. They had worked as hard and as long as men, and had defended the country with their lives.

As Pearl watched all the merrymaking, she thought about Jim. If only they could be as they were. VE day could be one of the happiest of their lives. Instead, she was coping alone once again. Like many other women she had learned to be independent. She had always paid the rent and kept the wolf from the door. When Cynthia went to school she could find a job. She wouldn't be needed at home if there were no more babies to care for.

Pearl sighed. Jim hadn't made love to her in weeks. Even when he had, he'd turned away afterwards and left her feeling more lonely than ever. It had brought back all the old memories of Ricky and her feelings of shame.

Pearl scooped one more spoonful of jelly onto Cynthia's plate. Britain was victorious, just as Churchill had assured the people they would be. The bombing was over, the Home Guard had been disbanded and the French President, De Gaulle, and Stalin had agreed a treaty of alliance. But in the hearts and homes of many East Enders after all the excitement was over, it was back to the day-to-day running of their lives. The food at this party would be a distant memory. Rationing was still in place and showed no sign of ending. As Cynthia ate all she could, along with the other children, Pearl wondered if Ruby was happy. She hadn't had a letter since January, when Ruby had said that the doctor had told her the baby was fine. Had they celebrated VE day?

Pearl found out sooner than expected. The letter from Abingley came three days later. A letter that made Pearl's heart sink as she read it. Ruby had been taken into hospital. Amy suggested that Pearl came down as soon as possible as

the situation was critical. Syd would meet her at the depot, where they could take a bus straight to the hospital. Jim was also welcome, but Amy said they understood it might be difficult to take time off work.

It was as Jim was finishing his breakfast that Pearl joined him at the table. Cynthia was playing with her toys and the May sunshine was spilling through the window. The Morrison was covered by a red and white cloth from VE day.

'Jim, this came this morning.' She placed the letter in front of him.

'Who's it from?'

'Mum.'

He looked at her, his hand shaking slightly as he held the spoon. She was worried about him. He had lost weight and never regained it. The dark shadows had never left his eyes. Though his hair had grown longer, it had lost its rich colour. He was wearing overalls for his work at the yard, and though she tried her best to clean and sew them, they were old and frayed. Even when he had worked as an engineer, he'd managed to look half decent. But he had let himself go and she wanted to put her arms round him and tell him she loved him. But she knew he wouldn't welcome that.

He picked up the letter, the frown on his forehead deepening as he read the first few lines.

'Jim, Ruby might lose this baby,' she said quietly.

He was silent as he put the letter down. 'I'm sorry to hear that, but there's nothing we can do. She's in hospital and they'll take care of her.'

'But we're family, Jim. I'm her sister.'

'You're also my wife and I can tell you this: I will never be family to him.'

Pearl sat down wearily. 'Jim, how can you hold such a grudge?'

He turned on her angrily. 'Listen, Pearl, haven't you learned your lesson yet? I'm not holding a grudge against Ruby, as daft as she may be for marrying like she did. And I'm sorry she's got herself in trouble with the kid. But I won't have you anywhere near that bastard. So you can put going down there, as your mum said, right out of your mind.'

Pearl took the letter and folded it. Her heart was thumping as she came to a decision. 'Jim, she's my sister. I have to see her.'

She jumped as he banged his spoon on the table. 'No you don't, Pearl. She has your mum and dad and him. For God's sake, isn't that enough?'

'You don't understand,' she insisted. Why wouldn't he listen to her?

In silence he rose to his feet. 'As a matter of fact, I do understand, Pearl. It's you that don't. I asked you once if he'd ever touched you and I never had a reply. I've waited and hoped that I'd get the truth, because not knowing has done me head in. Don't you see how I've needed you to tell me, to be up front about the one thing that's driven us apart? But no, you carry on as normal – as *if* we was normal. And as soon as your family crooks a finger, that's it, you're off to be with them – and him. How do you think that makes me feel?'

Pearl shook her head. 'I'm sorry . . .'

'No, it's not enough to say sorry. It's either him or me. I want to know that my wife is my wife.'

'I am your wife, Jim.'

'Then prove it.'

Pearl fought back the tears. 'Jim, please . . .' she whispered, reaching out in desperation. 'Ricky meant nothing to me. I swear to you that whatever happened in the past—'

Before she could finish a loud sound filled the kitchen. It came from Jim, as his eyes seemed to bulge from their

dark sockets. 'This is the last time you'll ever make a fool of Jim Nesbitt,' he rasped. 'If you go, you won't find me here when you get back.'

She ran after him as he snatched open the back door and went down the stairs.

The sobs caught in her throat. She hadn't meant it to come out like that.

'Mummy?' Cynthia stood behind her.

Pearl hugged her close.

'Mummy cryin'?'

'No, love, I'm blowing me nose.' She took her hanky from her sleeve. 'See, Mummy's all right now.'

They went back in and Pearl sat Cynthia at the table. Would Jim carry out his threat to leave if she went? But her mum had said the situation was critical. What if the baby's life was in danger, or worse, Ruby's? Her mind was in turmoil. If only she knew what to do.

On the bus the next day, Pearl felt very low. Jim hadn't come home last night. She knew he would have been to the pub and slept the drink off at the yard. On VE day there had seemed to be hope for the future, but all that had changed. Jim had threatened to leave her if she came away. Yet, she didn't have any choice. If Ruby fell very ill, she had to be by her side. She would never forgive herself if she wasn't. And would Jim really consider leaving Cynthia? They were so close. She was certain that no matter how angry he was with her, he would put Cynthia's welfare first.

Pearl looked down at their daughter as she gazed from the window. She was growing more and more like Jim, with her sandy hair and quick smile. Even the way she laughed was the same.

Pearl sighed, dragging her mind back to the moment. She had telephoned Patty yesterday from the public call

box to say they were coming. This morning she had waited for Jim, but when he'd not come, she had written a note. Again she told him that she loved him and hoped he would understand that she had to see Ruby. She also wrote that there were things she wanted to tell him on her return. Now, as the bus sped through the countryside, she wondered if he would give her the chance to do so.

When the journey came to an end and the bus pulled into the depot, Pearl's heart sank. It wasn't her father who waited to meet them, it was Ricky.

'Hello, Pearl.' He took her bag as she stepped down.

'What are you doing here?'

'Your parents have gone to the hospital. I offered to meet you as I thought they deserved time alone with Ruby. We'll catch the bus there straight away.'

'How is Ruby?' she asked anxiously as she took Cynthia's hand in hers.

'She's been very unwell. The baby is in distress.' His hand gripped her arm and steered her forward. 'I'll tell you as we wait across there.'

Pearl was frightened. Why had he come to meet her? He looked as though he was back to the same old Ricky, dressed immaculately in a navy-blue belted mackintosh, white collar and tie and brogue shoes. Pearl thought that his job at the aerodrome must be paying well, although she'd never seen her father dressed as well as this.

'Here we are. Let's all sit down on the bench over there, away from the crowds.'

'I'd rather stand.' She wanted to be with other people waiting in the queue. But Ricky insisted. 'Sit down, Pearl.'

She did as she was told, keeping Cynthia close beside her.

He settled himself beside her. Sliding his gloved hand along the top of the bench, he murmured, 'Relax, Pearl. You seem very nervous.'

317

'I'm worried about Ruby.'

'She's being attended to.'

'Aren't you concerned that she might lose the baby?' she asked in dismay.

'I never wanted it in the first place.' He took off one of his gloves. 'As you can see, my hands are healing.'

Pearl looked quickly away. The badly scarred and deformed hand looked horrible.

'And you'll be pleased to hear the burns on my chest have healed. It won't be long before I'm back to the way I used to look. The way you used to like me, Pearl.' He took hold of her wrist. 'Don't move away. You've your daughter to think of. We don't want her upset. Now listen carefully. The doctors think Ruby is going to have a dead baby.'

'Dead!' Pearl gasped.

'Yes, it's probably dead already.'

She saw the cold expression in his eyes and heard his emotionless voice. Was there something wrong with him? 'When it's over, I'm going to leave her,' he said calmly.

Pearl felt her head spin. She clutched Cynthia tighter as he smiled a strange smile. 'I despise it here,' he said bitterly. 'I hate the aerodrome and being confined to an office. I yearn for the sea, the adventure, the thrill of battle. And you are the only one who understands me.'

Pearl closed her eyes as he gripped her. 'Ruby will find someone else. A man who can offer her what she wants. An upstanding member of the Church perhaps? She seems to like going there enough. But you and me, Pearl, we're two of a kind. We've always had something special, the love of excitement, of the unknown. I'm never going to let anyone take that away from us again.'

'R-Ricky,' she stammered, 'don't say those things.'

'Why not? You and I now have the chance to be together.'

'Ricky, I'm married.'

His eyes flickered as though he barely remembered. 'Your husband is a fool, always has been. He doesn't deserve you.'

'Ricky—'

'I've thought about leaving Ruby for a long time,' he continued in a composed voice. 'When your mother told me she'd written to you, I realized the time had arrived.' He glanced at Cynthia. 'I do understand, however, that you have a daughter and I know you wouldn't be happy to leave her.' He smiled. 'You see how considerate I can be?'

Pearl didn't know what he was talking about. What plans did he mean?

'We are going to start a new life, Pearl. The war is over and I've got plenty of money. All we need are papers to get out of the country. The black market trade is flourishing, if you know the right people to approach. With cash you can buy anything. That's what the war has done for Britain. It's opened doors that were previously closed to people like us.'

Pearl swallowed nervously. 'Ricky, you're frightening me.'

He looked slowly back at her. Passing his hand across his forehead, he nodded. 'I'm sorry. But it has to be done like this. Now here is the bus. And when we arrive at the hospital, I want you to behave as normal for everyone's sake, especially Ruby, who has to be kept calm. Cynthia will be left at the sister's office as children aren't allowed in.' He held her arm tightly as they boarded.

He tried to take her hand, but she pulled it away. Why hadn't she listened to Jim? If only she could put back time.

Syd walked away from the nurse, who had broken the news they had all been dreading. The long, half-tiled corridor with its Victorian embellishments reminded him of the gaslight era. He braced himself for telling his family. It wouldn't be easy, as Amy had convinced herself that she was

about to be a grandmother for the second time. Rounding the corner, he saw Pearl and his son-in-law sitting on the hard wooden chairs next to Amy. They all stood up when they saw him coming. Even before he got there, he could tell they guessed what he had to say.

'I'm sorry, son,' he said to Ricky. 'She lost the baby.'

His son-in-law frowned. 'And Ruby?'

'She'll be all right.' Syd looked into the dark eyes that in all these months had never really regarded him with warmth. He didn't know what to make of the lad. He was a closed book, no doubt about that. But he was Ruby's choice of husband and that was the end of the matter.

He opened his arms to his daughter and wife.

'Can we see her?' asked a tearful Amy.

'In a minute. They're giving her something to calm her down.'

'What was the baby?'

'A boy.'

'A boy,' whispered Pearl, brushing the tears from her eyes. 'Oh, Dad, poor Ruby.'

Amy began to cry and he tried to console her. 'Come on, love, let's walk up the corridor.' He glanced again at his son-in-law. 'Me and Amy will wait till you've seen Ruby. The nurse said she'd come and take you in.' He guided Amy away, passing her his handkerchief.

'Poor Ricky,' Amy sobbed as they walked, 'he must be devastated.'

'Yes, reckon he must.'

Amy blew her nose and sniffed as they rounded the corner. 'Still, they're young, they can always try again.'

'Course they can.'

'A boy. Was something wrong with him? Did they say?'

'No, wouldn't tell me nothing.'

'Syd?' Amy lowered her voice. 'Do you think they'll stay in Abingley now? I don't think I could bear it if they went

back to the island. Oh, why did your bloody factory have to blow up? It was the start of all our troubles.'

He held her against him as she wept. 'No use going on about the past, Amy. It ain't the factory to blame, or moving down here. In fact, we got a new lease of life when I lost my job. We're happy, ain't we? You've got the Church and all its good folk and I've got me allotment. Now, look on the bright side. Ricky's got a good job and is earning decent money. They've only got to wait a couple more months before they're in a council place. They'd be silly to up sticks because of this.'

But the honest truth was he didn't have the foggiest what was going to happen. Ricky wasn't a man to share his thoughts or his plans for the future. In fact Syd found him a bit of a cold fish. There had never been a real bond between them. Not after the way he'd gone about marriage to Ruby. In Syd's opinion, it wouldn't have hurt to have waited till he'd come out of that hospital to ask them for the hand of Ruby in marriage. Not all formal, like, but just do them the courtesy of respecting Ruby. Still, that was water under the bridge.

Syd patted his wife's back and, as he always did, talked his wife into reason. 'Listen, ducks, our Ruby will have other little 'uns and you'll be a granny again. I'm willing to bet me bottom dollar that Mr and Mrs Winters will be living just round the corner in them nice new houses behind the pub, by Christmas.'

Amy pushed herself away. 'Do you really think so?'

'Course I do.'

She nodded, blowing her red nose again. 'You're right, I must pull myself together. We've been through a lot, what with the Blitz and Roper's Way going. But Ruby, bless her heart, has her whole life before her and a good man to make her happy.'

'That's more like it, love. Now let's get back and see

how they're doing.' Syd was proud of his Amy. She just needed encouragement. She'd been a darned good wife all these years, as Ruby would make, if her bloke thawed out. They'd make a fair marriage, given time.

As for Pearl and Jim, they were salt of the earth. They had no worries with them.

Chapter 26

'Wake up now, son. Go home and get yourself a wash and shave and a decent meal.'

Jim struggled to open his eyes. 'Is it morning?'

'I'm going out on me rounds.'

'I'll come with you.'

'No, you won't. You'll do as you're told.' The rag-and-bone man extended his arm.

Jim was pulled to his feet. His coat was filthy and so were his overalls. He knew he stank, worse than Percy probably, as he hadn't bathed for over a week.

'Look, Jim, it's no business of mine. You work bloody hard in this yard and now I've got used to your ugly mug, I'd miss your company if you wasn't here. But you sleep with the 'orse more than you do with your wife.'

'You're right, Percy. It ain't your business.'

'Please yerself.' Percy climbed down the ladder that led up to the hay loft.

Jim followed a few minutes later, only to find the old man climbing aboard the cart and leaving the yard. He pushed his hands deep in his pockets and felt a few coins. Enough to satisfy his thirst at the Nelson. He'd asked Pearl point-blank if Winters had ever touched her. She hadn't

denied it, couldn't. He'd looked into her eyes and seen her guilt. And he'd known without doubt there was something between them. Well, Jim Nesbitt had been a walkover for too long.

He rubbed his unshaven jaw as he entered the pub, the thirst building inside him. He threw back the first pint and felt the ale swim down to his legs. He swallowed another and the pain was eased. He'd have one more and then go back to Pride Place. Was she there or had she gone to Abingley? Was it Winters or him she'd chosen? Jim stared into his empty glass. If she'd decided to stay, there might be some hope . . . just a little, for a desperate man.

'Ruby? It's me.' Pearl bent down to her sister. She was ashen, her damp blonde hair spread over the white pillow.

'Oh, Pearl, my baby is dead.'

'I know, Ruby. I'm so sorry.'

'What did I do wrong?'

Pearl took her sister's small hand. 'It wasn't you. It happens sometimes.'

'But why?'

'The doctors will be able to tell you that.'

Tears rolled down her cheeks. 'I'm so unhappy.'

'You'll get over it in time.'

Ruby looked up at her. 'It's all right for you to say. You don't know what it's like to lose a baby.'

Pearl wanted to say that she did. That she understood what Ruby was going through. Her child hadn't been formed like Ruby's, but she had mourned it just the same. One day her grief would end, but how could she tell Ruby that?

Ricky stepped beside her. Pearl shivered at the touch of his arm against hers.

'I want my baby, Ricky. Why did they take him away so quickly?' Ruby's voice was a whimper.

'Come along,' Ricky said coldly. 'These things happen sometimes.'

'Please take me home.'

'You must wait until they say you can leave.'

Ruby began to sob.

'Is there anything you need?' Pearl asked quietly.

'No. Ricky, please ask the doctor if we can see our son to say goodbye.'

'I don't think that's a good idea, Ruby. You'll only upset yourself.' Ricky returned her hand to the bed. 'Now, you really should buck up, for your parents' sake. They're very worried about you. Pearl and I will visit again tomorrow.'

Ruby's eyes filled with fear. 'Promise me you will?'

'Of course.'

After Pearl had kissed Ruby goodbye, and Amy and Syd had gone in to say a final farewell, Ricky took Pearl aside. 'Tomorrow we'll see Ruby for the last time. So you'd better be ready to say your goodbyes.'

'Goodbyes?' Pearl repeated in alarm.

'I told you, we're leaving. And don't make a fuss. Not if you don't want me to tell Ruby all about us.'

'You wouldn't, not with Ruby in this condition.'

'Are you willing to take that chance?'

'But she's just lost her baby!'

'Then you'll do as I say, won't you? Believe me, once we're away you'll thank me for what I'm doing.'

'A-away where?' Pearl stammered.

'We're going up to the north of England to someone who can get us papers to slip quietly out of Britain.'

Pearl could only stare at him. Was he serious? Did he mean to force her to go? How could he?

'It's in your best interests to do as I say. Don't forget, apart from Ruby, your father is an old man. He has enough to contend with and I'm sure you wouldn't want to add

to his burden. And then of course there is Cynthia. You wouldn't want anything to happen to her, would you?'

Pearl felt sick. She looked up and down the corridor for help. But who could she tell? Who would believe her?

'Pearl, be sensible,' Ricky whispered in her ear. 'If you cause a scene, it will upset your parents. And, of course, if I'm put in a position, then I will have to explain how their daughter so willing threw herself into my arms and deliberately deceived them.'

She said nothing, as the feeling of shame spread over her.

He put his arm around her. 'Now, tomorrow, have your bag ready for the hospital. You can tell your mother you have some clothes for Ruby. I've arranged that we'll make the afternoon visit and your parents will go in the evening. I said that after our visit we shall be taking Cynthia for a tea somewhere as she will have been cooped up here. That will give us plenty of time to be on our way.'

Pearl couldn't believe that he had planned this.

'I've also told Amy that I'm happy to sleep on the Put-u-up tonight whilst you and Cynthia have our room. I sleep lightly, so if you have any questions about the future, you can come and talk to me. In fact, I would welcome that. I've missed you, Pearl. And I know when you've given this some thought—'

Just then Syd and Amy came out of Ruby's room. 'I'm afraid Pearl is upset,' Ricky told them, drawing his arm away.

Amy nodded, wiping her eyes. 'We all are.'

'I'm going to collect Cynthia,' Pearl said as she stepped away from the little group. If this was her only chance to escape, she had to take it.

'I'll come with you,' Ricky said, quickly following her.

'See you all at the bus stop,' called her father.

Pearl's heart plummeted. She knew Ricky wasn't going to let her out of his sight. What was she to do?

Fitz Hemsley woke with a start. It was just past eleven by the clock. He'd only been asleep half an hour. Why had he woken? He could hear loud thumping and crashing, and even though VE day had come and gone, for a split second he thought it was a V2 landing. It was difficult to get out of the old habits. After he had found his spectacles and put on his dressing gown, he looked down at Gwen and pulled the tangled bedclothes up over her shoulder. He was thankful that when she slept, it was for England. If there was a punch-up outside he would switch on the shop lights and knock on the window. No sense in disturbing his wife. Pushing open the door that led into the living room, he paused, tilting his head. The banging had stopped, but there was an isolated crash. It didn't sound like the street, but he hurried along the passage to the door that opened to the shop. All was quiet. He went to the window, feeling his way along the counter. For the first time he looked out without the hindrance of the blackout. Not that it made much difference. The street was as black as Newgate's knocker. Pressing his face up to the glass, he frowned. Nothing. Not a squeak.

Perhaps it had come from across the road? They had a new set of noisy neighbours, a big family with three strapping great sons and a loud-mouthed father who drank like the proverbial fish.

Just as Fitz was making his way back, a crash sent his heart racing. He turned on the passage light and stepped outside. There was light coming from Pearl's kitchen. But she'd gone away this morning. Who was there?

A tap on his shoulder made him jump. He turned to the figure beside him. 'Christ Almighty, Gwen, you gave me a fright.'

'What's going on?'

'You tell me. Someone's up there.'

Gwen pushed an escaping clip under her turban. Although it was a warm, starlit night, she pulled up the woollen collar of her dressing gown.

'Well, it ain't Pearl. Not making that racket. And anyway, she only went off this morning.'

'I'd better go up and see.'

'Fitz, be careful. It could be a looter.'

'Fetch my bat then.'

Gwen was gone for a few seconds, then returned with the cricket bat that dated back to the Ark. But it was a solid piece of wood and kept under the counter in case of emergencies.

Fitz crept slowly up the stairs. He could hear more smashes, which sounded like china breaking. Who would be doing such a thing? He stood on the landing, listening, the bat clenched firmly in his hand. He hoped there weren't two of them. But looters wouldn't make a racket like that.

As he waited, he heard talking from inside. Not exactly talking, but mumbling, and when he heard Pearl's name he knew instantly who it was. Opening the door, he peered into the kitchen.

'Struth, Jim, what are you doing?'

A figure stood in the kitchen. Around him there was chaos. Fitz could smell the booze from where he stood. The table and chairs were on their sides, the china on the floor. Even the yellow gingham curtains had been torn down. Jim stared at him, blinking and muttering. Then he leaped forward. Fitz raised the bat and it collided with Jim's head.

'Fitz, you've knocked him out,' Gwen gasped as Jim lay on the floor.

'I never touched him.'

'Well, the bat did.'

'What shall we do? We can't leave him up here.'

'S'pose we'll have to get him downstairs.'

'Just look at the mess!'

'We can't do nothing about that tonight.' Gwen bent down. 'I'll take his feet.'

Fitz put aside the bat and helped Gwen. They slid Jim down the stairs and dragged him into the back room.

'He's no lightweight,' said Gwen, puffing loudly as they heaved him onto the couch.

'And I'm not getting any younger.'

'Out of the way, love, I'll take a look at his head.'

'I thought he was coming at me. It was self-defence.'

His wife examined the bump. 'He'll live. Now go and fetch the brandy and smelling salts.'

'He's had enough to drink already.'

'The brandy is for you, daft 'aporth.'

Fitz took himself off to the kitchen. He found the smelling salts and had a whiff himself. He was shaking after the shock of hitting Jim like that. The fine and dandy was in the shop. They'd last had a drop after the birth of Cynthia. Fitz went to the counter, poured a small measure into the mug and downed it.

'Should we get the doctor?' Fitz asked when he returned.

'No. He opened his eyes just now.'

'Did he say anything?'

'Nothing a lady can repeat.'

Fitz sat down on the painted wooden chair and leaned his arm on the table. 'I didn't mean to hit you, old son,' he murmured as he watched Gwen apply the iodine.

'Give us them salts.' Gwen took the brown bottle, undid the top and passed it under Jim's nose. The effect was to have Jim's arm come up and knock Gwen flying.

'Take it easy, chum,' Fitz warned, as he helped his wife up. 'You've caused enough 'avoc in one night.'

'Christ, what happened?' He held his head.

Fitz gently pushed him back. 'You've had one over the eight, chum.'

'I told her it was him or me,' Jim mumbled looking up with difficulty. 'I didn't think she'd go. I thought ... I thought ... when it came to it ...' His eyes closed and he slumped back.

'Best put them salts away,' Fitz advised. 'We'll leave him to sleep it off.'

'Did you hear what he said?'

'Yes, and I didn't like it.'

Gwen sighed. 'We've done all we can. I'll put a blanket over him and leave on the light.'

'What about upstairs?'

His wife shrugged. 'We'll see about that in the morning.' She went off to bed and Fitz unlaced Jim's boots. He was breathing regular and the bump on his head was no bigger. The poor sod hadn't been right since he'd come home from Italy. But Pearl had never complained. Is that why she'd gone away? Because of the drinking? Or was it what Jim had muttered?

I told her, it was him or me. I didn't think she'd go.

What did that mean? Pearl wasn't the type to play away. But when Fitz was climbing into bed again and trying to sleep, he couldn't forget what Jim had said. Had she found someone else? Was this the reason for Jim's drinking?

Pearl was awake and listening to Cynthia's soft breathing. She hadn't slept all night, worried about the door with no lock on it. Now, it was dawn. How could she escape him?

Ricky had told her to pack her bag and say it was clothes for Ruby. Pearl looked at the window. Could they climb out of it? She would have to wake Cynthia. But what could she tell her? What would her parents think? Was Ricky just trying to frighten her? Tears filled her eyes.

'Oh, Jim, I've been a fool,' she whispered. 'I should have listened to you.'

Pearl brushed her wet cheeks with trembling fingers. She had lived in fear of the past for so long. Was it the end of all the pretending? Her tears dripped on the eiderdown.

Just then the bedroom door opened. Pearl was filled with fear as the tall figure crept in. Ricky closed the door without a sound and, glancing briefly at Cynthia, came softly towards her.

Chapter 27

Jim woke with a headache and found a lump the size of a hen's egg. What had happened? Where had he been? Where was he? Easing himself up, he closed his eyes at the pain that stretched from his temples and over the bump on his head. He lowered his feet carefully and stared at the floorboards. They weren't any that he recognized. He certainly wasn't with Barney in the stable. Raising his head carefully, he looked around him. It took him a while to recognize Gwen and Fitz's back room.

Just then Fitz walked in, a mug in his hands. He wasn't wearing his brown overall, but a pair of dark trousers and a sweater with a V neck.

'The top of the morning to you, sunshine.' He placed the mug of steaming tea in Jim's hands. 'And before you ask what happened last night, you had a fight with me cricket bat.'

Jim tried to steady his hands. 'I don't remember.'

'Not anything?'

'I was at the pub.'

'You don't say.'

Jim looked up. It was too painful even to smile. His stomach felt as though it was about to come up. He couldn't even look at the tea, let alone drink it.

'You must have a blinder.'

'How did I get here?'

Fitz sat beside him. 'Gwen and me brought you down from your gaff. You was smashing it up. The devil was in you last night, old son.'

Jim lowered the mug to the floor and put his head in his hands. What had he done?

'Sorry, mate.'

'Sorry I clobbered you.'

'You should have finished the job.'

Fitz jabbed his arm. 'What kind of talk is that? Look, whatever your problem is, it can't be as bad as you being blown up and your leg nearly torn off. Just look at you now, no crutch and you don't need your stick half the time. You can get around most anywhere. You've come out of that blood bath, whilst millions of others have perished. Life should taste good to you.'

Jim sighed heavily. 'It would, if it was like it was before I joined up.'

Just then Gwen came in. She stood in her paisley pinafore with her hands on her hips. He met her kind eyes. 'Sorry about last night, Gwen.'

'What happened, Jim?'

'I had one too many at the Nelson.'

'Your place is a bomb site.'

'I'll clear it up.'

'Don't know what Pearl's going to say.'

Jim was beginning to have flashes of memory, slowly, like pulling a tooth: his journey back from the pub, his hopes that Pearl would be home. Then he'd found that

note saying she'd gone to Abingley. Her words of love had sent him crazy. If she loved him, she would be there.

'You'd better nip the booze in the bud,' said Fitz in a softer tone. 'It's doing you no favours. Nor Pearl.'

Jim rose to his feet. The room swam, his head felt as though it was about to explode. 'Got to go,' he mumbled, falling against the couch and staggering into the passage. He burst through the back door and sprinted for the lav. As he retched, he could hear Sunday bells tolling. The war had ended, churches all over the land were allowed to ring their bells. But Jim knew that for him, another war had begun. Last night, as he'd looked into his empty home, he knew he had already lost it.

'Don't make a noise or Cynthia will hear. And if she wakes up, I will have to take certain measures.' Ricky's voice was a whisper as he sat on Pearl's bed.

'Wh-what do you mean?' Pearl stammered, holding the sheet tight against her.

'I know how much she means to you. Now, you have a choice to co-operate, or you might find yourself saying goodbye to your precious daughter.'

Pearl could barely speak. 'You . . . wouldn't . . . couldn't . . .'

He leaned closer. 'I most certainly would.'

Was he in his right mind, she wondered, to threaten such a thing. Was he really prepared to take Cynthia from her if she didn't do as he asked? In the dim light she could see he was wearing a white shirt, open at the neck, where his scars were visible. She felt like screaming as he touched her, but she knew she couldn't for Cynthia's sake.

'Pearl, I want you.' His hands were on her shoulders, sliding down her nightdress. 'You're so beautiful and I've wanted you for so long.'

'No, no!' She tried to wriggle out of his grasp.

'Those other women meant nothing to me,' he

continued, catching hold of her again. 'It was only you I ever cared for.'

Pearl shrank back. 'Please, Ricky, leave me alone.'

'Kiss me, Pearl, kiss me like you used to.' She let out a cry as he pulled away the bedclothes. 'You haven't changed, you were made for me. I must have been crazy to let you go.'

Pearl smothered her sobs as he began to touch her. When would this nightmare end? Was he going to rape her?

'You make me want you all the more,' he gasped as she sobbed. 'You haven't forgotten how I need sex to be exciting.' He fondled her breasts, his hands then moving down to her hips. 'You always were a free spirit. I'm going to enjoy taming you all over again.'

'Mummy?'

Cynthia's small voice came in the darkness. Ricky stiffened, his grip loosening and Pearl pushed away with all her strength. Once out of bed she stumbled across the room. 'It's all right, Cynth, Uncle Ricky's just leaving.' She hugged her daughter tightly.

Ricky stood up slowly, a dark outline in the centre of the room. Pearl was terrified. Would he try to take Cynthia from her? All she could hear was the loud beat of her heart. If he took a step closer, what would she do?

'Remember what I told you,' he whispered, his voice low and menacing. 'If you know what's good for you and your daughter, you'll do as I say.'

Pearl stared up at him. What was this man capable of?

Then suddenly he turned and Pearl heard the door close. Taking Cynthia in her arms she rocked back and forth. She was trembling from head to foot and trying not to show her tears.

'Brought you in a nice cuppa, love.' Syd looked down at his daughter and realized there was two heads in one bed.

He smiled at the sight of his granddaughter's blonde crown snuggled against her mum.

Pearl sat up slowly.

'She's soundo, ain't she?'

'Yes, she woke up in the night.'

'Probably upset about having to stay in that nurse's cubbyhole while we were with Ruby. Kids don't like hospitals; it's the smell, ain't it?' He placed the cup and saucer on the bedside table. 'Your mother's cooking fried eggs and bacon from the farm. Bet you ain't tasted good food since you was last down here. Pity Jim can't be here to enjoy it too.'

'How's Mum?'

'Not bad, considering.'

He watched his daughter drink her tea. She hadn't said much about Jim, but then, with all that had happened with Ruby it wasn't surprising. 'Anyway, I'll give you a shout when breakfast's ready. Ricky's just gone for a paper. Think he wanted a bit of a breather. He was up and dressed this morning before I was.'

'Are you all right, Dad?'

'Better than yesterday.' Syd didn't miss the swift change in subject. He'd noticed that Ricky and Pearl seemed a bit distant. Not surprising really, as everyone's nerves were on edge. 'We've all got to pull together for Ruby.'

'Yes, I know.'

'See you in a minute.'

When he left the room he came face to face with his son-in-law. 'Blimey, lad, didn't expect you back so soon—' But Ricky pushed past him, almost bowling Syd over. No sooner had he found his bag in the glory hole, than he was off.

Syd stared after him. What was up with the lad? Where was the newspaper? And what did he want his travelling bag for at this time of the morning? Before he could ask, the front door knocker went.

'Yes? Can I help you?' Syd asked the two men who stood on the step.

'Does a Richard Winters live here?' asked the taller man.

Syd didn't much care for his tone of voice, or the look of the long belted raincoats and trilby hats. They were the Law or he was a monkey's uncle. 'Why, what's it to do with you?' he demanded gruffly.

'I'm Detective Inspector Chalmers and this is Detective Constable Price from the local constabulary. We should like to talk to Mr Winters. It's a matter of some urgency.'

Syd felt his stomach drop. 'Is it about the hospital?'

'No. Is he here?'

'Syd, what's going on?' Amy appeared in her crossover pinny, a lock of hair falling from her turban. She grabbed Syd's arm and squeezed it. 'Is it to do with Ruby?'

'Don't think so.' His wife was pinching his arm so tight he was forced to draw it away. 'They was asking about Ricky.'

'He's not here,' said Amy quickly in a cold tone of voice he rarely heard her use. And what was she saying? Ricky had been under his nose only a minute ago.

'But he does live here?' said one of the men suspiciously.

'He went out for a paper,' said Amy defiantly.

'How long ago?'

She folded her arms across her chest. 'What's this, the third degree?'

'They're the Law, love,' Syd explained. 'Look,' he said reasonably as he pushed Amy back gently, 'you ain't called at a good time as Ricky's wife, our daughter Ruby, is in hospital. She's just lost her baby.'

The two men glanced at one another. 'I'm sorry to have disturbed you,' said the first man. 'We'll wait in the car until he returns.'

Amy leaped forward and called after them, 'You might

335

have a long wait. He could have gone for a walk or anything. It *is* Sunday, you know.'

The policemen stopped and glanced back. Syd dragged Amy in and closed the door. 'What the Dickens has got into you, love?'

'Nothing.' Amy stuck out her chin.

'You told them he wasn't here.'

'Well, he's not now.'

Pearl came out of the bedroom. 'What was that all about, Dad?' she asked as she tied the belt of her dressing gown.

'I don't know, ducks,' said Syd. He looked at his wife. 'But you obviously do, Amy.'

'Ricky's gone out the back way.' Amy looked guilty.

'Gone?' said Pearl. 'Gone where?'

'I don't know, do I?' Amy snapped. 'He just grabbed his coat then went through the gardens at the back.'

'So what did he say?' said Syd, thinking that, unusually, this conversation with Amy was like drawing blood.

Amy pouted again. 'He just told me that a bloke at the aerodrome had got into trouble. The police are making nuisances of themselves, going round people's houses, trying to get them to say something against him. Ricky didn't want to be bothered with all that whilst Ruby's ill. So he asked me to tell them he hadn't come back from buying the paper.'

Syd stood trying to work it all out. 'Has he gone to the hospital?' he asked bewilderedly.

Amy's eyes filled with tears. 'How should I know? I was frying the bloody bacon at the time. Stop having a go at me.'

Pearl put her arms around her mother. 'It's all right, Mum. Don't get upset.'

'Look, love, I'm not having a go,' said Syd gently. 'I'm only trying to get at what happened. You was squeezing me arm so tight when those coppers came you nearly stopped me blood from circulating.'

'I was afraid you'd say he was here,' said Amy tearfully.

'And why shouldn't I?' replied Syd defensively. 'He shot past me not two minutes before they knocked on the door.'

'It's not fair of the police to pester him at a time like this,' Amy sniffed. 'And I cooked such a nice breakfast an' all. You'll have to eat it, Syd, as it can't go to waste.'

Syd could smell the fry-up and usually his mouth watered at the aroma. But today he'd lost his appetite. As his wife and daughter went into the front room, he tried to puzzle out what had gone on. Ricky had taken a bit of a liberty in persuading Amy to lie on his behalf. What was all the rush? Spending ten minutes with the local bobbies wasn't going to eat much into his day. Syd scratched his head as he walked into the front room and sat down at the dining table.

Pearl served him his breakfast; the plate was overflowing with crispy brown bacon, eggs and fried bread cooked just how he liked it. But it was a sight that seemed criminal during rationing. 'Blimey, your mother's gone a bit over the top, ain't she?'

'It's better than giving it to the pigs.'

He saw her hand was shaking. 'You all right, Pearl?'

'Yes. Why?'

'You look a bit off colour this morning.'

'I'd better go and wake Cynth.'

When on his own, Syd pushed away his plate. What was going on with these women? His daughter couldn't string two words together this morning and his wife had just told a whopper to the Law. As for Ricky, he'd disappeared in the space of two minutes and with no real explanation as to why. Syd got up and went to the bay window, looking across the green to the road.

That flaming police car was still there!

Jim was sitting in the Nelson, staring into his glass. One half

of him wanted another drink, the other half wasn't drunk enough to forget his bad behaviour. All Pearl's china in pieces, the pots and pans scattered across the floor and he'd made mincemeat of the old Morrison in an effort to get his revenge. He'd even smashed the wind-up gramophone under the maple bookcase. In the bedroom, he'd stepped on tiny fragments of pink glass. The jars had been Pearl's favourites. The only room he hadn't touched was Cynth's. The thought of his daughter seeing what he'd done was too much for him. He'd walked out again, but not before taking the few pennies on the kitchen shelf.

The door of the pub opened and Percy appeared. Walking over to where Jim sat, he pulled out a chair.

'I just spoke to the 'emsleys. They said you'd gone off like a dog with a boot up its arse. What you done to your old loaf of bread?'

'Walked into a lamppost.' Jim shrugged, trying not to slur his words. 'You gonna have one with me?'

'I took the oath years ago, son, after the first war. As I was lying on that 'ospital bed, I thought about the way I conducted meself and I didn't much like what I came up with. Promised me maker I'd turn over a new leaf if I lived to see a better day. The rest is 'istory.'

Jim looked down. 'The sad truth is, Percy, I need what's in this glass.' He gulped back the ale. Why didn't everyone just leave him alone?

'Come on, lad, you've had enough. Sleep it off down the yard.'

'I ain't had me quota yet.'

'You've had more than that.'

'If I drank the Thames dry,' Jim muttered as he wiped his mouth with his sleeve, 'it would never be enough.'

The old man stared at him through narrowed eyes. 'I'm sorry to see you chuckin' your life away.'

'Yeah, well, it's a life of me own making.'

'You're a good man, with an honest heart and you've a good wife too.'

'You reckon?'

'What's that suppose to mean?'

'Nothing.' Jim grabbed his glass. 'Well, if you won't drink with me, I'll just have to drink on me own.'

'Jim, I'll ask one last time. Come back to the yard with me.'

'I don't work Sundays, remember?' Jim stood up and felt the room sway. Percy gave him one last look as he went to the bar and threw down his coppers. He wanted to be left on his own with his throbbing head and bitter heart.

'Look at this!' Gwen gasped.

Fitz put down his broom and swiped his forehead with his handkerchief. He was puffing and blowing after all the clearing-up. 'What is it?'

'A china ashtray.' Gwen turned over the broken pieces. 'It says "Margate" on this side. Do you think you could glue it back together?'

'I'll have a go.'

'It was from their honeymoon.'

Gwen sat down with a sigh on Pearl's couch. Fitz joined her, hoping that soon they could go home for some elevenses. They had cleared Pearl's kitchen and bedroom, and left the front room till last. It was going to be a long day, as they still had to have the shop ready for tomorrow. But after Jim had done a bunk, they couldn't just leave the place as it was. It would break Pearl's heart if she saw it.

Fitz examined the two pieces, turning them over and frowning. 'It ain't been used for fags and it's a clean break luckily.'

'It was only a souvenir,' Gwen nodded. 'Pearl don't smoke and Jim didn't before the war.'

'All her glass bits in the bedroom went the same way. He must have been on a bender to do what he did.'

'Where's he gone, do you think?'

Fitz scratched his head. 'Beats me. Wasn't going to clear this up, was he?'

'What did Percy Flint have to say?'

'Nothing much. Just that he'd nip in the Nelson to see if he was there.'

'I only hope Jim don't keel over after that bash on his head.'

Fitz groaned. 'Don't make me feel worse.'

'It was his fault, not yours.' Gwen stood the two small pieces of china on the arm of the couch. 'Just think, when they bought that, they was madly in love. Here, Fitzy, you don't think there's any truth in what Jim said? That she's left him for another bloke.'

Fitz shook his head firmly. 'He was three sheets to the wind and talking rubbish.'

'Yes, but when he'd sobered up he said he didn't know if she was coming back. So what's that supposed to mean?'

'Could mean he didn't know. Like she didn't know herself, till she found out how her sister is.'

'Or it could mean a lot different. What do you think?'

Fitz felt uncomfortable talking about his friends like this. He pushed himself up from the couch. 'Blimey, Gwen, I'm not the oracle.'

'You know what I think?' Gwen said as she also rose to her feet. 'I think this is to do with 'is nibs.'

'Who, that Ricky?'

'Who else? We know there was a bit of a ruckus at the wedding. Jim and him never got on. Pearl's never breathed a word, but I don't reckon Jim gave the nod for him to be here.'

'She never said as much,' Fitz protested. 'Nor did he.'

'No, but he was all eyes for Pearl. Creepy, I call it.'

'That's guesswork,' said Fitz quickly picking up his broom. He didn't like this. It was murky waters, women's stuff.

'The old green eye is the devil's tool,' replied his wife. 'Because I'd stake me life Pearl has never looked at another bloke. In fact, I'd say she went out of her way to avoid Ruby's old man.'

'And you would know, would you?'

'They live right under our noses, duck. I can't help seeing all their comings and goings.'

Fitz began to whistle his way into the kitchen again. He had the most disturbing feeling that Gwen had taken enough interest in the little family upstairs to know what she was talking about. He'd always discouraged gossip in the shop. Turning a deaf ear to some of the women when they came in was second nature. But the Nesbitts were a different kettle of fish. Nice people, part of the family. Especially little Cynth. And he supposed that was what worried him most. Would the kid be dragged into all this? He hadn't hesitated when Gwen suggested they go up and clear the mess. If it was just the two of them, the adults, he would have let them sort it out. But if Cynth was to see her home in that state, it didn't bear thinking about.

'I've got a funny feeling this ain't the end of it,' said Gwen.

'Course not,' said Fitz, relieved to hear a bit of sense at last. 'They're sensible people. Jim will snap out of it and they'll pick up the threads again.'

'Oh, I didn't mean them two,' said Gwen indignantly. 'I was talking about their ex-lodger. He's the loose cannon in all this.'

Fitz rolled his eyes to the ceiling. It was no business of theirs. Let sleeping dogs lie, he wanted to say. But of course, that would be no use to Gwen.

Chapter 28

It was Sunday afternoon and visiting time at the hospital. Pearl had helped Ruby to dress and sit in the chair beside her bed. She looked thin and pale as she listened to Syd, who had been pacing nervously around the room.

'He told your mother that someone at the aerodrome is in trouble,' Syd said with a frown, rubbing his square chin. 'Said he didn't want to get involved with the police.'

'So why didn't he come here?' Ruby asked.

'It's only four o'clock,' replied Syd, glancing at his watch. 'He could show up any moment.'

'I don't understand,' said Ruby bewilderedly. 'He's not said anything to me about trouble at work.'

'Try not to worry.' Syd patted her shoulder and Pearl saw the desperate look in her father's eyes. 'Ricky will explain when he shows up.'

Ruby's pale hands gripped the arm of the chair. Pearl wanted to say something to ease her mind, but what was there to say? Ricky had vanished.

'Keep your pecker up,' continued Syd as the bell was rung for the end of visiting time. 'Now, has the doctor told you when you can leave?'

'I'll find out tomorrow.'

'Good. You'll be home soon.' Syd beamed a big smile as he stood up.

'I miss Ricky,' Ruby whispered as Pearl bent to kiss her.

'I know you do.'

Outside in the corridor, Syd was angry. 'Whatever is going on? I can't forgive him for treating Ruby like this.'

Pearl could only remain silent. She knew some unguarded word might arouse suspicion.

'He had better have a bloody good reason for treating

her this way. My gut is telling me something is wrong, even though I told your sister he's bound to show up. If I'd stayed any longer she might have read me mind.'

Pearl kept turning the past few hours over in her mind. Ricky had tried to rape her and had threatened to kidnap Cynthia. He was a violent and heartless man and Ruby was better off without him. He had said there were people up north who would sell him papers. Is that where he'd gone? Had he run away from the police and intended to escape the law by leaving the country? But the question that was worrying Pearl the most was, would he come back and do something terrible before he left for good?

There was no sight of Ricky that night, nor the following day. Pearl was too afraid to leave Cynthia alone and kept her in sight all the time. She was worried that Ricky could appear or carry out his mad threat. On Wednesday morning, it was arranged by Amy and her friend Frances Butterworth that Frances would drive Ruby home.

'Here they are now,' Amy called as the big grey Austin pulled up at the green.

Pearl took Cynthia's hand and all three rushed to greet them.

Frances helped a very white-looking Ruby up the step. 'She still hasn't got her sea legs back,' Frances smiled at Pearl. 'It's nice to see you again. Hello, Cynthia. You've grown tall.'

Cynthia hid shyly behind her grandmother.

'Will you come in, Frances?' asked Amy.

'No, I have some errands to run.'

'Thank you for bringing Ruby home.'

'I'm glad to be of assistance. Now here are Ruby's things.' She passed the brown paper bag to Amy. 'I think this young lady needs a good tonic to buck her up. Well, I must be hurrying along. See you at church, Amy.'

343

'Goodbye, Frances.'

When she had gone, they all went to the front room. Ruby looked round dejectedly.

'How do you feel, love?' asked Amy.

'Don't know. Is Ricky here?'

Pearl glanced at her mother, who was looking very strained.

'No, love, he's not.' Amy plumped up the cushions. 'Come along, sit yourself down and let me spoil you. I'll put the kettle on.'

Pearl sat beside her sister as Cynthia played on the floor. Ruby stared into space. The cardigan she was wearing looked too big, as did her dress. She wore no make-up and had tied her hair in a knot. 'I don't suppose Dad's found out anything at work?'

'No, he hasn't. But you must try not to worry.'

Ruby looked into the distance again. 'I've lost a child and my husband's disappeared. I can't help but worry.'

Pearl sat quietly. She couldn't help Ruby in her distress. She knew so much that Ruby didn't know. Ricky wasn't worth a minute's concern, but she couldn't say that.

Amy came in with the tea. 'It's lovely to have you home, ducks.'

'Mum, have you seen Ricky?'

Amy looked away. 'I'd tell you if I had.'

'You were the last one to speak to him.'

'Yes . . . but it was only quickly,' Amy faltered, sitting down on the edge of the chair.

'Didn't he say something – *anything* – about me? Something you might have forgotten?'

'Oh, love, I've gone over that moment a thousand times in my mind,' said Amy, 'but he was in a rush and I was cooking—'

Ruby burst into tears.

As Pearl tried to hold her, there was a knock at the door. Ruby looked up expectantly. 'It might be Ricky.'

Amy hurried to answer it but it was only one of the policemen who had been there on Sunday. 'This is my daughter Ruby,' said Amy stiffly as she showed him into the room. 'Ruby, this is Detective Inspector Chalmers.'

He took off his hat when he saw Ruby. 'Good morning, Mrs Winters.'

'Have you seen my husband?' Ruby asked.

'No. I'm sorry to say I haven't.'

Ruby slumped back in her seat.

'Is there any reason why your husband would go missing?' DI Chalmers asked as he sat down.

'Course not,' Ruby mumbled. 'We've just lost our baby.'

'My condolences to you,' said the detective gently.

Ruby lifted her tear-filled eyes. 'What else do you want to know?'

'Would you know of anyone – a friend or someone at work, perhaps – that he might have gone to stay with?'

'He hasn't made many friends,' Ruby shrugged. 'There's only Dad at work that he really knows.'

The policeman hesitated. 'I have to ask this, and please don't take offence. Had you and Mr Winters argued recently?'

Ruby blinked. 'What do you mean?'

'They've only been married a year,' Amy protested, putting her arm round her daughter's shoulders. 'What a thing to ask!'

'I'm afraid it's standard procedure.'

'It's all right, Mum, he's only doing his job.' Ruby lifted her chin. 'Ricky and me are very happy, Inspector. I love my husband and he loves me. I don't know why he's gone missing. I wish I did. It's as much of a mystery to me as it is to you.'

The detective looked down at his hat and turned it slowly in his hands. 'I think it only fair to tell you, Mrs Winters, that we are investigating a theft at the aerodrome.'

Ruby sat with a shocked face. 'A theft?'

Detective Inspector Chalmers nodded. 'Quite a substantial sum of money from the offices.'

Amy put down her cup. The tea splashed into the saucer. 'What's a theft got to do with my son-in-law?' she demanded.

'We would like to eliminate him from our inquiries,' said the policeman.

For a few moments they were all silent until Pearl spoke. 'When did this happen?'

'Certain irregularities came to light quite recently.'

'Ricky would never steal anything,' said Ruby, jumping up and placing her hand over her mouth. 'He's a very honest and conscientious man.' She ran from the room.

Amy's face was red with anger. 'I don't believe a word of it. My son-in-law is absolutely trustworthy. In fact he's a war hero and was blown up on his ship twice. He's fought for his country and nearly died. How can you upset my daughter by telling lies like that?'

'Mrs Jenkins, you must understand—'

'No, *you* must,' shouted Amy, wagging her finger at the policeman. 'How dare you come into this house and make such an accusation when Ricky isn't here to defend himself?' Before he could reply she jumped up and hurried after Ruby.

Pearl thought about what the detective had just said. She was the only person here who really knew what Ricky was like. He was a liar, cheat and womanizer, but could he be a thief too?

'So you've no idea why he's disappeared?' the detective asked her.

'No.'

'I'll see myself out, then,' said the policeman, rising to his feet.

She watched him walk out and heard the front door close. From behind the lace curtain, she saw his tall figure

346

walk to the police car. A cold chill went through her. Was Ricky guilty of theft? Is that why he'd run away? Ruby's heart was breaking over her lost baby. It would certainly break again if this turned out to be true.

Throughout the next day, Pearl tried to lift Ruby's spirits. As the newspapers refused to stop reminding the nation that fifty thousand people in Whitehall and the Mall had gone wild with joy at the Prime Minister's broadcast, it was plain to see that everyone wanted the celebrations to continue. From the moment the Royal Family had appeared on Buckingham Palace balcony, scenes of unrestrained joy had erupted throughout the country. Even Abingley had had its fair share. People still cycled over the green with Union Jacks on their handlebars. The bunting flew from the windows and roofs, and the children still waved their flags. Even though the weather was warm and spring-like Ruby refused to go out. But when Friday came, at last she gave in.

Patty loaned them the pushchair and Amy took them down to the river. Pearl was careful to keep Cynthia with her at all times. Even though Ricky was now a wanted man, she knew how dangerous he was. Would he try to snatch Cynthia in broad daylight? It was unlikely, but all the same, she held tightly to the pram and searched the faces in the crowds.

All along the tow path to the market square, people were still in party mood. Union Jacks and bunting were draped over the boats and cow pens alike. In the little café where they had eaten before, the red, white and blue tablecloths were still visible. A big picture of Winnie smoking his cigar was placed by the counter. But Ruby grew tired so they made their way home. Pearl was anxious to get back to the safety of four walls. She could only relax when the door was closed and locked.

★

'Ruby, I'll have to go home next week,' Pearl said as they sat together that night after supper. Syd was still at the allotment and Amy was next door with Patty.

'I expect you'll be pleased to leave.'

'What do you mean?'

'It can't be much fun here.'

'Don't be daft. But I do have Jim to look after.' She felt very guilty about leaving him. Had he found her note? Would he be there when they arrived back? She didn't want to leave Ruby, but it was true, she did have a husband to consider.

'Pearl, I wish we'd never moved here.'

'But you like Abingley.'

'I didn't tell that detective, but Ricky hates it. I think he blames me for making him leave the island. And I think that's why he's gone.' She stopped and looked at Pearl with wide, sad eyes. 'I don't believe he stole any money, of course. But what I do believe is that all this is my fault.'

'You mustn't blame yourself.'

'But I do.'

Pearl took her sister's drooping shoulders. 'What matters is that you get well. Worry won't make Ricky appear.' Pearl was praying that Ricky would never, ever appear again. If he'd fled the country, it would be the best outcome possible for Ruby, although she couldn't know it now.

A tear trickled down Ruby's cheek. 'I'll miss you.'

'And I'll miss you. But you've got Mum and Dad.'

'And you've got Cynth and Jim.'

They smiled. 'Then aren't we lucky?' Pearl nodded.

For the first time since the death of the baby, Ruby seemed more like her old self. They talked about Roper's Way and their outings to the market on Saturday afternoons. They recalled the first-aid lessons Ruby had taken that had never cured her of feeling sick at the sight of blood. And they smiled when remembering Cynthia's

arrival on the Hemsleys' shop floor. Ruby even admitted she missed the factory.

But when Ruby began to talk about Ricky, the man she still loved and missed and hoped would return one day, Pearl knew that it would be a long time before Ruby came to accept the truth.

Pearl stayed until Saturday, and it was a tearful goodbye. Syd carried her bag to the depot as Cynthia ran ahead, her sandy plaits bouncing on her shoulders.

'You'll remind Mum to write?' said Pearl as they made their way slowly to the stop.

'She won't need no reminding.'

'Look after Ruby, Dad.'

'You can be sure of that,' her father said angrily. 'She married a wrong 'un, that's clear. But it will take her a while to accept it.'

'Do you think he stole the money?'

'Wouldn't put it past him.'

'They can't prove it without finding him first, I suppose?'

'You know, that's right,' Syd nodded. 'But I'd like to get hold of him personally and do him a mischief after what he's done to Ruby. If I had my way . . .' He gave a loud grunt. 'You know, I always had me suspicions. I never could joke with him, not like I can with Jim. But I gave him the benefit of the doubt for Ruby's sake. What excuse could he offer if he came back now? He turned tail and fled when those coppers came. And he got your mother to lie for him. There's nothing, *nothing*, that could account for that.'

At the depot Pearl shivered when she saw the bench that Ricky had forced her to sit on. She looked round, thinking he might appear. Was he really gone from their lives? She shivered.

'You cold, love?'

'No.' She shivered again. 'Someone just walked over my grave, don't they say?'

Her dad smiled. 'You give Jim our best, won't you? Tell him that we're looking forward to seeing him as soon as he can take time off from work,' he shouted as the bus pulled in. 'And tell him we're proud of him for all his graft and for looking after you and our granddaughter. Believe me, ducks, after this little lot, you should consider yourself a lucky young woman.'

'I do, Dad.' Pearl felt her eyes sting. She had made such a mess of things. She loved Jim dearly and would do anything now that he wished. But was it too late? Could she ever find a way back to the happiness they once shared?

'Look, here's a few quid.'

'No, Dad, you gave me five pounds last time.'

'So here's another. I doubt we'll be seeing you for a while. And don't worry about your sister – she's a Jenkins, after all. You just take care of yourself and your family.'

Syd helped them to board and they waved from the window. As usual Cynthia stuck her nose on the glass. The bus pulled out and Syd's figure disappeared.

As the bus travelled past the market, Pearl sighed with deep relief. She was going home to safety, coming out of the nightmare. She wanted to remember the good times with her family and hoped they would come again for the three people she loved so dearly; that Ricky would stay out of their lives for ever.

The fields and billowing trees flashed past. Spring had brought the countryside to life. But never more had Pearl longed for the sight of the smoky roofs and blackened chimneypots of the island, lost in the river mists. She missed home. And most of all she missed Jim.

Chapter 29

Gwen was weighing out potatoes on the big brass scales when the bell on the door tinkled.

A tiny figure sped across the floor. 'Gwenny, Gwenny!'

'Oh, Cynth, my love, you're home!' Gwen dropped the potatoes in the scales and opened her arms as Cynthia flew into them. 'You lovely little scamp, I've missed you so much. And so has old Fitzy. Run inside and see what he's got for you.'

Gwen let go of the little bundle, pulling her plaits gently as she sped off to the hall where Fitz was working. All Gwen could hear was laughter. She knew Fitz had missed the little girl even more than she had.

'Hello, Gwen.'

'Pearl, my love, it's good to see you.' Gwen spread her arms once more. 'Let me have a look at you! Well, you ain't put on any weight, that's for sure. I thought you'd be twice the size on your mother's cooking.'

Pearl smiled tiredly. She pushed her untidy hair from her eyes and dropped her bag on the floor. 'You all right, Gwen?'

'Better now you're back. The place don't seem the same without you. How's Ruby?'

'She lost the baby.'

'Oh, no. The poor kid.'

'It was a boy.'

Just then Fitz came through with Cynthia in his arms. Her cheeks were bulging as she chewed on a sweet from the brown packet she held in her hands. 'Don't mind, do you love?' he asked Pearl. 'I saved a few lemon drops for her.'

'Hello, Fitz.' Pearl went on her toes to kiss his cheek.

'You've had a long journey. Like a cuppa?'

'I think I'll go upstairs.' She looked at them both. 'Is Jim in?'

Gwen's heart sank. 'Not now, he's not.' She lifted the bag and glanced at her husband. 'I was weighing up the spuds for the old gent next door. But I'll leave you and Cynth to do that whilst I go upstairs with Pearl.'

He nodded. 'Good to have you back, Pearl. Really glad, as we—'

'Hurry up with them spuds,' Gwen interrupted, giving him a stern look. It wasn't the right time to go over what Jim had said. The poor girl looked all in.

Gwen led the way through to the alley. A soft breeze blew around them as they climbed the stairs. They'd cleaned Pearl's place, but she would soon discover that home wasn't what it used to be.

Pearl drew the key from the letter box and Gwen put a hand on her arm. 'Before you go in, love, there's something I should tell you. A few bits and pieces got broken while you was away.'

Pearl stood upright, the key dangling from her fingers. 'Did you say broken?'

'Thought I'd mention it to soften the shock.'

Pearl unlocked the door and a musty smell came out. Gwen wrinkled her nose. She'd left the sash open a few inches in the kitchen but being shut up hadn't done the place any favours.

Gwen put the bag on the kitchen table.

'Where's the Morrison?' Pearl asked. 'Did Jim put this one back?'

'Not exactly, ducks. Me and Fitz did it.'

'You did? But why?'

As Gwen was thinking how to put Jim's actions in a kinder way, Pearl went to the window.

'And where's me yellow curtains gone?' She looked

352

round, walking slowly to the blue cupboard, running her hands along the empty shelves. 'And my china, the cups and saucers and plates ...' She turned and rushed into the front room.

Gwen waited, knowing she would be staring at the bare mantel. There was a big chip missing in the two halves of the ash tray that Fitz had stuck together. The wind-up gramophone was stacked in pieces in the hearth. Then there was the maple bookcase, which wouldn't hold any more books until Fitz could mend the shelves. And what about all those little pink jars that had gone from the dressing table?

Gwen sighed as she heard the soft movement from room to room. Sitting down heavily in one of the two kitchen chairs, she continued to wait.

After a while, Pearl came in. Under her thin, worn coat, her shoulders drooped. 'What happened?' She sank down on the other chair, leaning her elbows on the table.

'It was the night you went away,' said Gwen carefully. 'Fitz heard a commotion, thought it was the family across the road or even a V2. Then he saw your light on and thought it was burglars. So he took his bat and went up, but it was Jim. He'd had one bevy too many and caused a right old stink.'

'He broke it all?'

'Yes, 'fraid so.'

'But why would he do that?'

'You'll know the answer to that, my love.'

Pearl sat in silence.

'Accidentally, Fitz caught him with the bat,' Gwen continued as Pearl stared around the kitchen. 'So we carried him down to our place. I mean, we couldn't leave him here, out stone-cold on the floor. He slept the night on the couch but in the morning ...' Gwen lifted her shoulders, 'he went.'

'Where to?'

'Percy's yard, no doubt.' Gwen patted her hand. 'I 'spect it's just a bit of a tiff, ain't it?'

Pearl shook her head slowly. 'He didn't want me to go to Abingley.'

'Why was that?'

Pearl put her head in her hands. 'Because of Ricky.'

Gwen folded her arms. 'It ain't my place to say, but I just couldn't warm to that man.'

'I shouldn't have let him come here. I didn't have the courage to refuse. I wish I had, as he's left her now.'

'What, after losing the baby?'

'Yes.'

'Oh, the bugger!'

Just then Fitz came in with Cynthia.

'At least Jim left her room,' said Gwen as she tickled Cynthia's chin and made her giggle. 'Me and Fitz had a good clear-up. It ain't half as bad as it was. I can let you have a few bits of china, and the saucepans are only dented. Fitz tried to mend the ashtray but he ain't done a very good job.'

'It was only cheap, but thanks all the same.' Pearl gave Cynthia a pat on the bottom. 'Run along and see all your toys.'

Cynthia scampered off and Pearl sighed. 'Oh, Gwen, I wish I'd never gone to Abingley. Jim was right. My place was here.'

'I'm sorry for your sister's loss,' said Gwen stiffly, 'but you have a family of your own.'

'Percy says your Jim is kipping at the yard,' Fitz said quietly.

'I'll go to him, then.'

'Do you think that's wise?' asked Gwen hesitantly.

'I've got to see him.'

'You know best, ducks.'

354

Fitz handed Pearl his handkerchief and Gwen got up and kissed the top of her head. Pearl was like a daughter to her. The daughter she'd never had. If that silly sod Jim didn't appreciate her worth, then he was a fool. He of all people should know that no jealousies should be allowed to cause such heartache. Wasn't that what he had been away fighting for – a new life, free of tyranny, with the chance to make a fresh start?

It was an overcast day in the middle of May, with thunder rolling in the distance and Jim was working in the stable. He'd got himself a rough bed rigged up over the old horse's quarters, in the hay loft above. As soon as he finished work in the yard he'd be off down to the Nelson. Last night he'd stumbled home early, out of readies and still with a thirst on him. His leg ached and he'd used his stick to alleviate the pain. And climbing the ladder up to his bed, he'd missed a rung and fallen. By the time he'd finally hauled himself up, he was stone-cold sober.

He'd lain awake for hours and then came the dreams. The dry, barren desert and the dust in his throat. The Italian hill and the ravaged monastery. Reg's face, as clear as if it was happening all over again. That moment when he stuck a roll-up between his lips and he'd said his last goodbye. Then he was running towards his outfit, waving his arms, trying to warn them the footbridge was mined. He couldn't run fast enough, his pack and rifle were slowing him down. And then the mortar tore into his hip, just as it had on the battlefield. His mates sailing high in the sky, limbs falling like bloody confetti.

Jim wiped the sweat from his face and neck with a dirty rag. A clap of thunder broke overhead. It had been stormy all week and Barney shuffled uneasily, as a bright flash lit the stable. Jim gave him a gentle pat. The slow munching calmed him, as did the smell of the dung and old straw

littered with flies. Another clap of thunder rumbled. Jim turned round to close the stable doors and found his wife standing there.

'Christ, you made me jump!'

'Hello, Jim.' She looked smaller, somehow, and the pain of separation filled him.

'Where's Cynth?' he barked.

'With Gwen. Jim, I'm sorry I went away.'

He felt the anger in his chest. 'It was a big comfort seeing a bit of paper there in me wife and daughter's place,' he snarled before he could stop himself. This was what he was afraid of: his emotions spilling over, more than he could control.

She walked slowly towards him and he turned his back to lift the bridle from the peg.

Her voice was very small behind him. 'Ruby's lost her baby and Ricky's left her. You were right, Jim. All along you were right.'

His fingers tightened around the leather. He spun round to stare at her. 'Bit late to be saying that, ain't it?'

'I thought I should be with Ruby. She could have died.'

'And what about us? We've had to go through a war.' He held out his hands. 'I asked you a question and you never answered me. Don't you think you owed me the truth?'

'Jim, I did nothing to deceive you. I swear it. I never meant to hurt you.'

'And you think you haven't?' He angrily threw aside the bridle. 'I'd rather go back to the front than go through the torture of thinking what went on between you and him.'

'Nothing went on, Jim, honest to God, not since we've been married. It was years ago at the club, and over in a few months. I should have known better but I was young.' She held her hands over her face. 'Oh, Jim, I'm so sorry.'

He shook his disbelieving head. 'Why didn't you tell me?'

'I was ashamed.'

'But, Christ, Pearl, I'm your husband.'

'Yes, but I was scared of losing you.'

He gritted his teeth so hard he couldn't swallow. 'I was crazy about you at the club. Was you seeing him then?'

She nodded, hanging her head. 'He didn't want me to tell anyone and I didn't.'

'Just like Gladys.'

She raised her eyes, full of tears. 'More like Gladys than you think.'

It was a few seconds before the penny dropped. His mouth fell open. 'You didn't . . . you weren't—'

The tears ran down her cheeks. 'I lost it.'

He couldn't believe the things he was hearing. 'I don't understand,' he mumbled, shaking his head. 'I told you all about Danny and Gladys, I warned you of Winters, but you must have known all along after what he did to you. But the next minute you let him come and live in my gaff? What in heaven's name possessed you?'

She moved forward, clutching his arm. 'Ruby said they had nowhere to go—'

'And as usual, you did as she wanted.' He pushed her away. 'And you think by telling me now, it makes us all right?'

'Give me another chance, Jim.'

But all he could feel was emptiness. As he stared down into the face that he had once loved so much, he didn't recognize her. 'I've been going half barmy thinking about you and him together. I cared for you more than any other person on God's earth. Yet when you married me, you never said a dickybird. Do you expect me to believe it was all innocence while I was away?'

'It was, I swear it.'

Jim felt a hand on his shoulder. 'Leave her be now, lad.' Percy pulled him back. 'Calm down.'

He stood, dazed, in Percy's firm grip. He felt nothing but hate and anger. Without a word, he pushed past the old man and made his way to the Nelson, shuddering with rage.

'He'll cool off, love.' Percy scratched his head. Females, especially of the weeping variety, weren't his line of country. His old mum had never shed a tear, had been like a bloke, a real East End tough nut. She could muck out a stable as good as any feller and knew all the ins and outs of the rag-and-bone trade, same as his dad did. He'd once seen her lay out a six-foot drunk with a kick to his balls that even old Barney couldn't equal. Now, if there'd been another like her along his life's path, he'd have put a ring on her finger. But he'd not had the luck and he was quite content to be a loner. However, he liked this little lass. She was half tidy compared to some of the floozies he'd seen on his rounds throughout the war. Some poor buggers didn't know the half of what they got up to when they came back from service.

'Give him a day or two to kick his heels,' he said as he wrapped his arms around her. 'He's a proud man, is our Jim.'

'There's no excuse for what I did,' she whispered.

'We all make mistakes.'

'Yes, but we don't keep on making the same one.'

'If I was you, I'd go home to your nipper.'

'It's not home without Jim.'

Percy waved his hand dismissively. 'Listen, whatever it is you've done, it ain't half as bad as what yer think. Take it from me, gel. I've lived all me life round these parts. I've heard stories from dock dollies with tongues like Irish navvies that would turn your hair white. I've watched blokes sell their wives for a pint of ale and I've been offered the comfort of a nice warm bed in exchange for the rags

358

orf me cart. But you, love, whatever you think you've done, you're an angel compared.'

She clenched her hands. 'Jim don't think so.'

'You and I know he'll not solve his grieving with the drink,' Percy reasoned gently. 'Grieving is what the man is really doing. The war took a lot away from 'im, like it did a lot of blokes. They come home not knowing who they really are. They've seen killin' and 'ave killed. Those memories don't leave much of a soft spot in a man's soul. He needs a good missus to bring him through. And in his heart he knows that.'

'Do you really think so?'

'No doubt about it. And when Jim comes to his senses he'll be big enough to come home. Now you better hop off afore them clouds open up.'

He watched her walk out, a slip of a girl. Jim had a devil inside him to behave as he did. Should he go after him and try to talk reason? But no one ever spoke louder than the demon drink. Whatever it was that ailed him, he wasn't to be reasoned with.

Percy, feeling his age with vengeance, rose to his feet and went to feed Barney instead.

Pearl tried to go on as normal. She wrote to her parents and enclosed a note for Ruby, though she only got a short one back from Amy, saying she was still very worried about Ruby. The detective had called, but with no further news to share.

Gwen brought up some china and Fitz distempered the damp patch in the kitchen. Percy arrived with an old radiogram, a relic of the Blitz, but it had a wireless and turntable that operated. Everyone made a fuss of Cynthia. She missed her daddy.

Despite her troubles, Pearl listened with sympathy to the plight of the German people. They were said to be hungry

and crushed, and many of their leaders were expected to stand trial for war crimes. Meanwhile politicians world-wide were competing for recognition in the new world order. It was only Japan who was determined to continue the war, refusing to make peace with the Allies.

Three weeks after Pearl's visit to the yard, Jim arrived one Sunday morning. For a moment Pearl's heart leaped as she saw him standing on the landing. Had Percy been right when he said Jim would finally come home? But in a few words he crushed all her hope. 'Thought I'd take Cynth over to Mum's,' he said as Cynthia ran into his arms.

Pearl looked into his thin face. Though he looked clean and was dressed in a white shirt, the shadows under his eyes were dark.

'Don't know when we'll be back.'

'Take her coat as it might get chilly.'

As she gave him the coat, their fingers touched. Pearl felt a deep sense of longing. They had once been so close. She kissed Cynthia goodbye and watched them leave. Cynthia was all smiles at seeing her daddy.

Pearl got out her duster and broom and tied on her pinny. She pushed the broom round and round the kitchen, her tears falling onto the handle as she went.

It was late when Jim brought Cynthia home.

Pearl stood on the landing as Jim refused to come in.

'Will you come next Sunday?' she asked, and he nodded.

'Cheerio,' he said, and winked at Cynthia.

They watched him go down the stairs. He was limping again and Pearl knew he was in pain.

'Did you have a nice time at Granny's?' she asked her little girl. But Cynthia couldn't wait to see her toys. Pearl knew by her response that her granny's opinion of children being seen and not heard hadn't changed.

*

Jim was true to his word. He called again the next week, but this time he left his wages on the table. As the rent, gas and electric had to be paid, Pearl took it without comment. The next Sunday arrived and the next, and Cynthia was happier now she could spend the day with Jim.

At the beginning of August, a letter came from Abingley. Pearl was disappointed to see it was only a page. Amy said that she had found Ruby one morning with an aspirin bottle. Syd had been very angry and Amy distraught. Ruby had confessed she had thought about doing something silly.

Pearl felt sick when she read this, wondering if Ruby really had tried to end her life. Was she capable of doing what Gladys had done?

Syd had made Ruby promise not to cause herself harm. It had been very distressing for them all. Her mother wrote a postscript telling Pearl not to worry, and that Ruby had asked them not to tell Pearl.

Pearl felt the tears threaten in her eyes. Jim had warned her this might happen. If only she had listened to him that first day of their honeymoon. If only she'd had the courage to tell him the truth. Jim might have forgiven her, and Ruby might never have fallen in love with a monster.

A few days later, Mr Clement Attlee, England's new Labour prime minister, released a statement to the country. By executive order of President Truman, two atomic bombs had been dropped on the Japanese cities of Hiroshima and Nagasaki. This devastating weapon had killed thousands and thousands of people, injuring and maiming many others. Pearl was shocked to hear that it was both British and American scientists who had created this weapon of destruction. It was said there was a huge mushroom cloud in the sky full of radiation. The victims who had survived were so badly burned they couldn't be recognized.

'Japan has surrendered, the last of our enemies has been laid low,' said Attlee triumphantly.

'God help them poor people,' Gwen murmured as Pearl and Cynthia stood in the packed shop. It was Tuesday morning, the day before VJ day. King George had announced that the return of peace was to be honoured by a two-day holiday.

'Don't much feel like a party,' admitted Gwen.

'Them Japs have been like animals to our blokes, worse than the Jerries,' retorted a small woman filling her shopping basket. 'They deserve their punishment.'

'But two whole cities were destroyed,' said Pearl.

'My cousin's boy was out east. He got tortured in a POW camp and he's half barmy. Won't never be the same again.'

'I'm sorry,' said Pearl, 'but I don't feel like waving flags for the deaths of innocent women and children.'

'Winnie said the Germans had the atom bomb as well and it was by God's mercy that we let it off first,' another commented.

As the argument grew more heated, Pearl placed the small slice of cheese that Gwen had saved for Cynth, in her basket. Cheese was Cynth's favourite but it was even harder to obtain now than at the beginning of the war. When she returned to the conversation the topic was politics.

'Winnie's gone now,' said a man. 'Attlee's top dog. That is, until the people get tired of him too.'

Gwen smiled. 'You ain't in favour of Labour then?'

He shrugged. 'They're all the same to me.'

'The wireless says there's crowds gathering in London and bonfires being lit along the Thames,' elaborated Gwen. 'The American servicemen still in this country are celebrating the bombs. No doubt there will be a few of us along with them.'

Just then, Dillys, from across the road, ran in. 'Mummy says we can have a VJ party in our backyard. Can Cynth come?'

'When is it?' asked Pearl.

'In the morning. Dad's put the flags out again.'

'Has your dad said why?' asked Pearl curiously.

'It's the end of the war, ain't it? Britannia rules the waves.'

Pearl knew that all the kids were taught this in school. No one had explained the suffering atom bombs had caused. Instead, the public were awarded a holiday to celebrate.

But Dillys wasn't to know all this. Pearl smiled. 'I'll bring Cynth across tomorrow.'

'Can she come out now?'

'All right. While I do me shopping.'

Dillys and Cynthia left hand in hand. Gwen and Pearl gazed out of the window.

'A party is all the kids are interested in,' Gwen commented. 'And rightly so, as they're just kids.'

'I wonder what the history books will say in years to come?' murmured Pearl.

Once more people were stringing flags of red, white and blue across their houses. Pearl sighed softly. Was she just in a lonely mood without Jim when other people were happy?

'How's your mum and Ruby?' Gwen asked, breaking into Pearl's thoughts.

'I had a letter from Mum. Mr Brewer went to see Ruby. He took her for a ride in the country.' Pearl had been very relieved when the letter came. At least Ruby had been shown some kindness and her mother was very taken by Mr Brewer.

'Now he's the kind of man your sister needs.'

Pearl smiled. 'He always liked Ruby.'

'Why don't you telephone your mum's neighbour?' Gwen nudged her arm. 'Have a word with your sister on the phone. Do you two good to have a natter.'

Pearl wasn't at all certain if that was a good idea. She hadn't trusted herself to phone before as she had been very upset about what her mother had told her.

'Give her a ring tomorrow, p'raps, whilst Cynth is at the party?'

Pearl nodded thoughtfully. She would decide what to do in the morning.

Chapter 30

The August sun made the telephone box very hot. Pearl had to wait whilst Patty ran in next door to get Ruby. As she waited, the children outside were screaming and laughing. Most of the backyards were full of kids. She could hear a piano being played and the sound of singing. All the pubs were hoping for trade.

'Hello, Pearl.'

'Ruby!'

'I'm sorry I ain't written.'

Pearl knew why, but couldn't say their mother had told her about the aspirin. 'How are you?' she asked instead.

'All right. But I'm fed up with looking at fields and cows.'

'I thought you liked the country.'

'I don't without Ricky.'

Pearl held the telephone tightly. 'You'll have to get on with your life.'

'Don't keep on, like Mum does.'

'She's only trying to help.' Pearl had to strain to hear her above the noise outside.

'She says he couldn't have loved me or the baby.'

'Mum wrote that Mr Brewer came to see you,' said Pearl, putting her finger in her other ear, as some noisy young people went by.

364

'Yes, but he couldn't stay long. He had some business to attend to close by. We went for a drive and then had tea at the market. But I was glad when he went.'

'Why?'

'I was thinking of the baby and Ricky.' She began to cry.

'You'll have another baby one day.' Pearl had to shout as the singing and laughing outside grew louder.

'What's going on?' Ruby asked miserably.

'It's VJ day.'

'There's nothing much doing round here.'

Pearl didn't want to stop talking but she had to. 'Ruby, I haven't got any more money to put in. Please try to write.'

'I'll try, but I don't have much to say as nothing really happens.'

'Doesn't matter. Anything will do, just to let me know you're all right.'

Ruby mumbled something just as the pips went and the call ended. Slowly Pearl replaced the receiver. She rested her head on a pane of glass and closed her eyes. She felt sad for Ruby, but what could be done? Life in Abingley was not the end of the world. It could be a lot worse. Ruby had set her sights on country living when they were at Brawton. But now she disliked it. Pearl couldn't wave a magic wand for Ruby, though she was beginning to wonder if she'd been trying to do that all her life.

Perhaps it was the sight of the happy youngsters outside that caused Pearl to turn towards Roper's Way. Twenty-two years of her life and twenty of Ruby's had been spent there. For their Mum and Dad it had been more, as Gran and Granddad Jenkins had lived there since before the First World War. Pearl couldn't remember them, as Granddad was killed in France and Gran died soon after. Aunt Till and Uncle Ted, Aunt May and Uncle Ron, her cousins Betty and Jane and Howard lived miles away. The last time there

had been a family reunion was on her wedding day. What had happened to the closely knit family that once was? The war had broken so many families apart. She found herself entering Roper's Way and hardly recognized it.

There was now nothing left of number twenty-four. All that remained was one wall that held the fireplace. Around it was all rubble. The Sampsons' had disappeared under a mountain of broken bricks. You wouldn't even know a house had been there except for the debris. Other houses along the road had been abandoned too. Once again the looters had stripped them bare.

Slowly Pearl walked up to the debris. Her eyes searched for anything she might recognize. A door knocker, a shelf, a pot or pan, floor tiles, a reminder of home. But there was nothing, only the chimney breast, its bricks slowly disintegrating, large gaps under the broken mantel where the flowery tiles had been. Tiles were valuable in wartime. Someone had helped themselves to them all.

She found herself stumbling up the mountain of debris, trying to balance, turning over the pieces of brick that had crumbled so badly no one wanted them. When she came to the top, she looked over at what was once the backyard. The workmen had begun to remove what was left of the factory. There were big signs on the boards: 'Danger. Keep Out.'

Whatever the reason for the explosion, it had changed the course of their lives. If the factory had still been standing, then twenty-four Roper's Way would have been too. Her parents would still be living there and Ruby might never have left home. She might never have married Ricky. And when Jim came home from war, their lives could have been very different.

She picked her way to the fireplace, once her mum's pride and joy. The mantel was broken and the hearth was blocked by a large object covered in soot.

A hand grasped her. 'You should be more careful, Pearl. This is not the place to go poking around.'

'What . . . where did you come from?' she gasped.

'I've been watching you for some time,' said Ricky.

She tried to pull away her arm. 'Let me go.'

'All right, but you know these bomb sites can be very dangerous. And after all,' he sneered, 'that's all this is now. A dirty, long-forgotten road that even the authorities don't want to be bothered with.'

The harsh words hurt. She looked around for someone, anyone she could call out to. But on this day of celebration the street was deserted.

'Wh-what do you want?'

'It's not *what* I want but who.'

'Leave me alone,' she blurted. 'If the police find you—'

But Ricky only laughed. 'Let them look all they want.'

'Did you steal the money?'

'It wasn't stealing. I am owed more money than I could ever take from this country. Do you know that my so-called employers put me in this ridiculous little room and expected me to add up figures all day?' A coldness came into his gaze as he lifted his deformed hand and banged it against his head. 'Was that how I was to be treated? Like some sort of freak when I fought for this country and I deserved to be acknowledged for what I did. I got nothing. Nothing! We could have been on the other side of the world by now if only you'd listened to me.' He pulled her against him. 'You belong to me, Pearl. You're mine.'

'Stop it, stop it!' she screamed. 'I hate you for what you've done to me and my sister.'

'Ruby is a silly girl,' he growled, his eyes wild and dark. 'I've been watching you and I know that Jim has left you.' He smiled unpleasantly. 'Did he find out about us? Was knowing that I'd made love to you in a way that he never could, the reason he left? Admit it, Pearl, your marriage is over.'

367

'No!' Pearl screamed. 'Jim loves me.' She struggled to be free but he wouldn't let her go. As she screamed he put his hand over her mouth. She closed her eyes and bit the burned skin as hard as she could.

His howl of pain echoed round the street. She turned and fled, stumbling blindly to the Sampsons'. The dust flew up in her face and choked her.

She could hear his shouted taunts and threats as he followed her. Were they never going to stop?

Suddenly there was a loud bang and the ground trembled. She found herself falling, tumbling and turning down to the bottom of the debris.

Gwen was worried. It was half-past one and Pearl had been gone all morning. It didn't take that long to walk to the phone box and speak to Ruby. Although the shop was closed for the holiday, the door was open for Cynthia.

Gwen looked up and down the road. Unlike VE day there were no tables filled with food. Even the bunting seemed to flap listlessly in the breeze. A few women stood on the doorsteps, as the kids played noisily in the back-yards, making the most of the holiday. Once more Gwen's brow furrowed as she wondered where Pearl could be.

Fitz was sweeping in the storeroom. Gwen poked her head round the door. 'Fitz, Pearl ain't back yet.'

He looked up, resting his arm on the top of the broom. It was a hot day and his collar was open under his brown overall. 'She's probably having a gas somewhere.'

'It's a bloody long one, if she is.'

'Might have called in to see someone.'

'Like who?'

Fitz passed his hanky across his sweating forehead. 'So what do you want me to do?'

'Don't know. Wish I did.' Gwen felt a shiver of unease. 'I've just got this feeling.'

'Give her another half-hour. If she's not back, I'll go up to the box. But don't reckon I'll need to.'

'No, probably not,' Gwen smiled faintly. She was probably worrying for nothing, but after all that had gone on with Jim, and bearing in mind his temper, could they have met and had a set-to? No, she was being daft. Returning to the shop, she waited for Dillys to bring Cynth home.

It was almost four o'clock by the time Gwen reached Percy's. The big wooden gate was ajar and she squeezed through, standing breathlessly in the cluttered space. She didn't like having to come here, not after the way Jim was behaving. But it was the only place they hadn't tried. Fitz had gone up to the phone box and come home without any answers.

'Pearl!' Gwen called, walking slowly forward. She moved carefully between the old bedsteads, chairs, horsehair mattresses, clocks, clothes, piles of newspapers, ladders, tin baths and any amount of rags buried under them. 'Pearl, are you there, gel?' she shouted as she came to the ramshackle old cottage that was Percy's home.

The door creaked open. 'Who's there?' a gruff voice said.

'It's me. Gwen Hemsley.'

The old man came out. Wiping his whiskers, he frowned under his cap. 'It's an 'oliday. I ain't buying or selling terday.'

'I don't want to buy or sell. I'm looking for Pearl.'

'What, you mean the lad's missus?' he asked.

'Course I do,' Gwen said impatiently. 'Have you seen her?'

Percy shuffled from one foot to the other. 'No, I ain't.'

'Then I'll have a word with Jim.'

Percy's bushy grey eyebrows rose. 'Listen, if I was you—'

At this Gwen lost patience. 'Listen, Percy, if he's here, then I want to see him.' She tightened the belt on her pinafore. 'Now, which way?'

369

Percy shrugged under his overcoat and pointed to the stable. 'It's open, help yerself. You'll find him in the loft. But don't say I didn't warn yer.'

Gwen hurried over. She didn't care for the muck that horses left behind them, and cared even less for the stink they created in hot weather. But she liked Barney, and as he turned his big head slowly towards her, twitching his ears against the flies, she gently patted his rump.

'Jim, are you there?' she called up the ladder.

Receiving no answer, she stepped on each rung cautiously. Poking her head above the rafters she saw a shaft of sunlight. In the dusty beam a body was stretched out on the straw.

'Jim, is that you?'

No movement came and she clambered onto the ledge. Poking his leg with her shoe, she said fiercely, 'Jim, you lazy bugger, wake up!'

He stirred and turned away.

'Jim Nesbitt,' she shouted again, 'wake up this instant.'

Slowly he lifted his head.

'My God, look at the state of you!' Gwen put her hands on her hips.

'What do you want?'

'Some help, that's what. Get up, you dozy bugger.'

'Go away, Gwen.'

'I wish I could,' she answered furiously. 'I wouldn't waste me time here if I didn't need your help.'

'Did Pearl send you?'

'No, she bloody didn't,' Gwen snapped as he sat up, holding his head. 'Your wife has disappeared. She went to phone Ruby this morning and ain't come back since. Cynth is upset her mummy is gone. You've got a little girl to think of and it's about time you started pulling your weight.'

Slowly he climbed to his feet. Blinking his bloodshot eyes, he slurred, 'Disappeared? Where?'

'Don't know, do I? For Gawd's sake, Jim, where can she be?'

'She ain't just gone out somewhere?'

'I shouldn't be here if that was the case. The girl has got a home to look after. She never goes out without saying where she is. She's as reliable as clockwork, which is more than I can say for you. I'm at my wits' end and you are the only who can help.'

He gazed at her for some while, then stooped to lift his jacket from the boards. In silence he passed her and climbed down the ladder.

Jim was trying to think past the hammer hitting his brains. He held his daughter in his arms, as always the guilt of being apart from her washing through him now he was sober. Gwen and Fitz were good sorts; but after that night when he'd walked out and left his home a wreck, he'd been too ashamed to face them. Now, as he stood in their back room, with their anxious faces directed towards him, he tried to pull himself together.

'So you've been up to the telephone box?' he asked Fitz.

'Yes. Pearl has the number for Syd and Amy's neighbour, for emergencies, like. Thought I'd ring it, ask Ruby if she had any ideas. Ruby wasn't much help, though, more interested in telling me how fed up she was. Said that Pearl had most likely gone for a walk as it was a nice day. And I was more inclined to think that meself at the time.'

'Did you ask anyone on the way home?'

'No one to ask. It's a holiday, ain't it? People are having a tipple or a knees-up.'

It was Ricky Winters who was on Jim's mind; the thought of him being with Pearl. The drink was the only way to stop himself thinking. Had she gone away with him? Had it finally happened, the outcome he had dreaded?

'What I can't fathom out,' said Fitz, 'is that Pearl is a

371

home bird. She don't go out on the razzle, nor does she go without Cynth. She wouldn't have left her today had there not been a kids' party across the road. We told her we'd keep an eye out whilst she was gone. It was just to speak to her sister that she went.'

'Are you sure nothing was said between the two sisters?' Gwen pressed. 'They didn't have a tiff or nothing?'

Fitz furrowed his brow in deep thought. 'Don't think so. Ruby just kept on about how Abingley wasn't the same as the island. That it was lonely in the country, not like the old days at Roper's Way. Nothing else was said far as I can remember. They didn't have no tiff, that's for sure.'

'Roper's Way,' Jim repeated, glancing out of the window to where Percy sat on the cart. The old man had brought him and Gwen back to Pride Place.

Jim smiled at his daughter. 'Now, you stay with Gwen till I get back.' He passed her over, gently pulling her plait and making her laugh.

'Where are you going?' Gwen asked.

'Over to Roper's Way.'

'Why's that?'

'Pearl was talking about it with Ruby.'

'Shall I come with you, lad?' asked Fitz.

Jim shook his head. Would he find Pearl and Winters together there? Was Roper's Way where they met? He was telling himself to keep calm, but the picture inside his brain was of them together, in each other's arms, in a place no one would suspect them of being.

Jim asked Percy to wait for him in the next road and hurried around the corner to Roper's Way. As he strode along, he was barely conscious of the bomb sites and dere-lict houses. Instead Winters' face loomed large in his mind as he stood in uniform at the Jenkinses' house, looking the dog's dinner, and alone in the hall with Pearl. How

could she have betrayed him like she had? She had meant everything to him. What if he hadn't enlisted? Would it have made a difference? Should the blame lie with him for leaving her? The questions and suspicions poured through his mind.

He suddenly realized he was halfway along the street. To add to his confusion, there was nothing he recognized under the mountains of rubble and brick. This was a limbo, a ghost land. What had happened to the lively road he had once known?

Where was number twenty-four? The answer must be, in front of him. He could hardly believe it. He walked closer, narrowing his eyes at the dusty brick. Nothing remained of the house that used to be.

He glanced up and down the road again, trying to remember what it was once like. Then carefully he began to pick his way up to the top of the debris. He found a large crater and beyond this he could see where the factory had once stood. The space was boarded off and had signs to keep out. No doubt about it, this was where the Jenkinses' old home.

A soft wind blew dust across his face. He looked down at the dip and at last saw something he recognized. Six inches of wooden mantel, black and broken. He turfed away the bricks and lifted it, running his fingers carefully over the splintered edge. But where were Winters and Pearl? He'd had the picture clear in his mind. His fingers itched to take hold of Winters. To have the satisfaction at last of revenge. But there was only the wasteland and the dust still rising.

Suddenly there was a sound. Looking round, Jim saw no one. Even the scavengers and looters had taken the day off.

The sound came again. Jim dropped the wood and began to follow his nose. Was it an animal? He slid down the debris and ascended the Sampsons', another shattered pile.

Jim stood on the top. His heart lurched as the moaning became clear. He scrambled towards it and fell on his backside as an avalanche of bricks toppled with him. When he came to a halt he was on all fours. Wiping the dust from his face with the back of his sleeve, he gasped aloud.

'Pearl! Pearl!' he yelled, scrambling towards her, dropping to his knees and throwing aside the broken bricks that covered her still body.

Chapter 31

There was daylight coming through the window, but Pearl didn't recognize the room. Her eyes ached and as she turned her head, that did too. Her mouth was dry and she put out her tongue to lick her dry lips. The starched sheets felt unfamiliar as she tried to sit up but fell back again.

'Doctor!' a voice called.

Pearl lay in confusion, staring up at the ceiling.

'Mrs Nesbitt?' A tall, bearded man in a white coat stood over her.

'Who ... who are you?'

'My name is Dr Taylor and you've been in my care for the past three days. This is the London Hospital and, I must say, we have been very worried about you.'

'Why?' she mumbled. 'What's wrong with me?'

He smiled a friendly smile as he shone a torch in her eyes and made her blink. 'We think you took a tumble on some debris, cracked your head and knocked yourself unconscious. You have a few bumps and bruises that we can't account for, but perhaps you'll be able to tell us.'

'Did you say I've been in here three days?'

'Yes, since last Wednesday and today is Saturday.'

'But who—'

'Now before I answer all your questions,' he interrupted gently, 'I have a short examination to make. We need to make certain your legs and arms work. It won't take long. Just try to relax.'

Pearl closed her eyes again as the nurses came in and out of the room, talking in whispers as they bent her legs and arms and tapped her knees and feet. Why were they doing all this? And what was the pain in her head?

Finally the doctor spoke. 'Well, apart from a slightly raised temperature, I'm very pleased with you. All seems to be in working order but we'll need to keep you under observation.'

'Can I sit up?'

'Yes, the nurse will help you.'

Pearl was grateful for the assistance of the nurse, as when she tried to move she had no strength.

'Is that better?' asked the doctor, studying her carefully.

'Yes, but my head hurts.'

'We did find a very large lump on it.'

Pearl blinked her painful eyes. 'How did I get that?'

'We were hoping you could enlighten us, Mrs Nesbitt. You see, other than what your husband told us, we have very little to go on.'

'My husband?' Pearl stared at the doctor. 'You mean Jim?'

'Mr Nesbitt has been here every day, at your bedside. It was he who found you on Wednesday and brought you here. And you were lucky that he did as a night out in the open wouldn't have helped your condition.'

'But Jim isn't ... he doesn't ...' Pelt felt confused. What was she trying to say?

The doctor looked at her curiously. 'Don't tire yourself for the moment. Your memory will come back, I'm sure.

But I will just ask you a few easy questions before I leave. Can you tell me what year we are in?'

'Yes, nineteen forty-five,' she answered slowly.

'Very good, very good. And your Christian name would be?'

'I . . . I'm Pearl Nesbitt and I live at . . . at twenty-seven A, Pride Place. And I have a daughter. Her name's Cynth. And . . . and . . .'

The doctor pushed her gently back again. 'Well, I don't think we have much to worry about. For the rest of today I would like you to rest and I shall leave you in the capable hands of the nursing staff.'

Pearl wanted to ask so many questions. She watched him walk out of the room. He'd told her that Jim had brought her here and been at her bedside. Could that be true?

But why was she here? Where had Jim found her? And who was looking after Cynth? The last thing she could remember was Dillys, the little girl across the road. Cynth had gone to her party. But what had happened after that?

As she lay there, she tried hard to think. But even thinking hurt.

It was three o'clock and Gwen glanced out of the shop window to Dillys's house. Cynth had gone to play in their backyard and taken her white chalk with her. Dillys was teaching her hopscotch.

Gwen glanced the other way. No sign of Jim. He'd gone to the hospital early, in the hope they'd let him see Pearl. He had been like a cat on a hot tin roof since Wednesday. Granted, he'd not been near the booze since finding Pearl at Roper's Way. And he'd looked after little Cynth like an old mother hen. But he blamed himself for what had happened. Seeing Pearl at death's door had finally woken him up.

Just then Fitz brought in a box of dried-up-looking

greens from the storeroom. 'We'll knock these out cheap, Gwenny,' he told her, ' 'cos if we don't, they'll go off before Monday.' He took the box out in front of the shop and placed it with the others. Glancing up and down the road, he frowned.

'Do you think they let him see her?' Gwen asked when he returned.

'Dunno. Hospitals are funny like that.'

'They let him stay longer yesterday.'

Gwen didn't want to think what might happen if Pearl didn't recover. She was an angel and Jim was only beginning to recognize it.

Gwen served a customer and, as it was late, cleaned the shelves and began to wash the floor. She was on her knees when the door opened. A pair of boots she recognized appeared.

'Jim! Is there any news?'

He had a big grin on his face. 'I can't believe it, Gwen. She's come round.'

'What?'

'She's woke up.'

Gwen dropped the brush and climbed to her feet. 'Oh, thank God.'

'The doctor told me she's going to be all right. But they've got to keep an eye on her.'

'Did they let you see her?'

'No. I'm off to visit later.'

'Do you want a cup of tea or something to eat? I can find you a slice of corned beef and a pickled onion.'

'No, thanks. I need a wash and shave.' He pushed his hands over his face. His eyes were full of doubt when he looked up. 'Gwen, do you think she'll . . . I mean – will she even want to see me?'

'I think your missus will be *very* glad to see you.'

'Can't blame her if she's not.'

'You're her world, Jim. Only you don't know it.'

'I do now.'

Gwen pulled her pinafore across her chest and straightened her shoulders. 'Is there anything I can do to help?'

'Watch Cynth for me till I come back?'

'That's no trouble, ducks. She's been a happy little girl since her dad's come home. You're where you should be now, Jim Nesbitt. You've got your thinking cap on again, and I hope it stays there.'

He nodded slowly. 'I've missed home, Gwen. More than I can say.'

'Well, you'll have to find the right words, won't you? It'll mean a great deal to Pearl to know your feelings.' She wasn't going to let him off the hook. No matter how repentant a man might be, it was actions that counted. But he was a good man at heart. He'd just lost his way for a time, like so many others had in the conflict.

'I've found another lot,' said Fitz, coming in from the back. He dropped the box when he saw Jim. 'Is it Pearl? Is she awake?'

Jim smiled. 'Too right she is.'

'Oh blimey!' Fitz took out his hanky and blew his nose. 'Thank the Lord for that. Any damage done, do yer know?'

'She's still got that bump on her head. She had it when me and Percy lifted her onto the cart. The doctor said she had a few other bumps and bruises. But for the life of me, I wouldn't know where she got them.'

'It was climbing over that bloody debris,' said Gwen crossly. 'What else could it be?'

'Dunno,' Fitz shrugged. 'Something might have fell and hit her.'

'Like what? There was nothing left standing to fall.'

'The only one who knows is Pearl,' shrugged Jim. 'And the doc said she's having a job to remember. Now, I'd better get off your clean floor and get meself tidied up.'

'And, Jim,' Gwen called as he went to walk away, 'give her our best, won't you?'

'Course, that'll be first on me list.'

When he'd gone, Gwen looked at her husband and saw tears in his eyes. She walked across the wet floor and put her arms around him. 'You soft old bugger,' she sniffed and searched for a hanky too.

Pearl opened her eyes, remembering that after lunch, a bowl of hot soup and a glass of water, she had been transferred from the small room to the main ward.

'You all right, ducks?' a voice said from the next bed.

Pearl nodded. 'I must have dozed off.'

'You been asleep a good hour.'

'What time is it?'

The big woman, with rosy red cheeks, laughed. 'Half-past four, and time for a cup of tea if they remember us. My neighbour has just smuggled me in a nice piece of bread pudding. You can have some, if you like.'

'I don't think I can eat any more.'

'Please yerself. But it'd do you good.'

Pearl eased herself up on her elbows. Her back ached from where she had been trying to sit upright, even in her sleep. She wanted to get up but the nurses wouldn't let her.

A man and woman were leaving and waved to the girl in the bed opposite. Was it the end of visiting time?

'By the way,' said her companion, 'a bloke has been sitting on the chair beside you. He was very worried when he saw you kipping. He kept asking the nurse if you was all right. I told him meself that you were, but I could see he didn't believe me.'

'What did he look like?' Pearl asked.

'A bit rough round the edges. He had lovely blue eyes, though.'

Pearl smiled. 'That would be my husband.'

'Said he'd be back.'

Pearl felt very strange. She was trying to remember what happened. Had Jim really come each day to the hospital? She wondered what his feelings towards her were now.

The ward door opened and closed but no one came in. Had he gone away? Once more she closed her eyes. She was very tired and was on the edge of sleep again when she heard a voice.

'Mrs Nesbitt?' A nurse was shaking her.

'Yes? What?' Her head swam.

'Your husband is concerned about you, although I've tried to reassure him that you're only taking forty winks.'

Pearl saw Jim standing there. He was wearing his best trousers and short-sleeved white shirt. His hair had grown a little and he'd parted it on the side and combed it flat.

When the nurse had gone, she smiled hesitantly. 'Hello, Jim.'

He pulled back his shoulders and placed a bunch of chrysanthemums on the bed. 'It's lovely to see you awake, gel.'

'Are those for me?'

'I wouldn't buy 'em for anyone else.'

'Thank you.'

'You know, you're a real sight for sore eyes.'

'Am I?' She didn't know what she looked like as she didn't have a mirror. She felt embarrassed in her starched hospital gown.

'Can I sit beside you?'

'Course you can. The lady in the next bed said you was here.'

'Did she give you the weather report an' all?'

For the first time since she'd been awake she wanted to laugh.

'How are you feeling?'

'I want to get up but they won't let me.'

'The doc says it looks like you took a nasty fall.'

Pearl tried to remember having fallen, but she couldn't get beyond her head aching. 'The last thing I remember is going over to Roper's Way after I'd phoned Ruby.'

'Yes, Fitz went after you when you didn't come home. Gwen came to fetch me from the yard and we put our heads together and came up with Roper's Way. So Percy and me went over.'

'The doctor said I was lucky you found me.'

He moved the flowers to one side and took her hand. 'When I saw you lying there, I thought you was dead. You know what they say, that your life flashes before you? Well, mine did just that.'

Pearl felt as though she'd gone to sleep in one world and woken in another. Jim was his old self, just like he used to be. She felt confused.

He squeezed her hand. 'Oh, Pearly-girl, don't cry.'

'I'm sorry,' she sniffed.

'Listen, we want you to get well. Cynth is fed up with me cooking already.'

She smiled. 'I miss her.' Had he come back home? She didn't have enough courage to ask.

For a few moments they were quiet. 'I wish I could remember,' she sighed.

'Don't try now.'

'I must.' She closed her eyes. 'I was standing looking at the debris. There was just the wall and the chimney. Everything else was ... it was just bricks and dust.' She swallowed. 'Then ... then someone grabbed me.' Her eyes flew open. 'It was Ricky.'

His face went pale. 'He was there?'

'Yes,' she faltered. 'He said he'd been watching me. That ... that he knew you'd left. I tried to get away ... he ... was coming after me. I ran. There was a loud noise and ... I fell.' She burst into tears.

'What's up over there?' the woman called from the next bed.

'Nothing,' Jim called gruffly. He squeezed Pearl's hands hard. 'I should have been there to protect you. Instead I'd got it into me head that was where you and him met. I must need me brains tested.'

'And I should never have gone to Abingley,' she admitted. 'He said if I didn't do as he said, he'd tell you and Ruby everything.'

'So he's still up to his old tricks?' His eyes had grown cold.

'Jim, I've always been faithful to you.'

'I know that, Pearl,' he whispered. 'When I saw you at Roper's Way, all I wanted was to take you in my arms and tell you I was sorry. So I'm asking you now, for another chance.'

'I love you, Jim. But what if he comes back? Will you still trust me then?'

'If the bugger does,' he replied fiercely, 'then you'll have me beside you and nothing he says will touch us. I'll feel like bloody murdering him, but I won't as I've too much to live for now. I've made the biggest pig's ear of me life that a bloke could make, but I promise you this: no one is going to steal any more of *our* happiness. You've got me with you every step of the way and I intend to prove it.'

'Jim, if only that could be.'

It was cooler as Jim made his way home. The late afternoon was overcast and unsettled, and a few specks of rain wet his cheeks. A rumble of thunder caused him to remember the day at the yard when Pearl had told him about Ricky. He'd never known such bitterness inside him. Instead of hearing her out, he'd acted like a jealous fool.

All his life he'd been a moderate man. He'd enjoyed a few beers, but the drink had never really interested him.

Not until he'd let Winters get under his skin so deeply there was no turning back. Well, now he was facing things square on. He'd known when Pearl was lying in hospital that he wouldn't want life without her.

But what would happen if Winters returned? He'd replied that he'd be beside her this time. And he would. But could he really shape up?

Suddenly he stood still, allowing the salty breeze to blow into his nostrils. Was he still Jim Nesbitt, the man who had chosen to fight for his country and prove himself? A man with a passion for life burning inside him? Or was he a shadow of his former self? What could he offer Pearl other than promises? What prospects did he have for the future?

The traffic was going homeward; heavy vehicles, those that were still issued with petrol, lined up with the horses and carts, all moving towards the lifting bridges to wait their turn to cross. The island stretched around him, the Blitz and Hitler's secret weapons having done their work. Bomb craters, piles of debris and mountains of bricks. On impulse he turned towards Roper's Way.

It wasn't long before he came to the wasteland that was once the Jenkinses' street.

'Bit of an eyesore,' said a voice, and Jim turned to find a young bobby beside him. Tipping his helmet back an inch he sighed. 'You from round here?'

Jim nodded. 'My wife lived at number twenty-four.'

'Blimey, she wouldn't recognize it now, would she?' The policeman frowned. 'This time next week they're having this lot away. They're going to build these prefabricated efforts. With all the blokes being demobbed, they need something to tide them over.'

'It puts roofs over heads.'

'That it does. You looking for anything to take? Like a souvenir or such like?'

'No,' Jim answered with a shrug. 'I was just strolling down memory lane.'

'Well, don't stroll over that lot. There used to be an old factory over there. A stray dog got his chips yesterday. Blown sky high, it was. Thank God it was only an animal. The bomb disposal blokes said the Luftwaffe dropped bombs on purpose that had faulty timers. Said it was probably one of them buggers that caused all the trouble in the first place.' He shook his head warily. 'Anyway, be seeing you around.'

'Yes, cheerio.'

Jim watched the young rookie walk down the road, his hands clutched behind his back.

Treading carefully up the debris, Jim stood at the top. His heart raced. In his head, he heard Pearl's words: . . . *just the wall and the chimney . . . There was a loud noise and I fell . . .*

But there was no wall or chimney now. When had it fallen? It was certainly before he had found her. He looked down at his feet, at the small crater.

Slowly he began to lift the bricks, working deeper into the hole. He found more of the mantel and a broken hearth stone. Deep in thought, he paused, rubbing the dust from his eyes. As he blinked, a human arm appeared. For some while, he remained there, too stunned to move as he stared into the face of the man, that in life, he had once so hated.

Part Four

Chapter 32

June 1949

'Mum! I just sold a bit of china that Gwen give me last time we was over the shop,' shouted six-year-old Cynthia as she leaped the stairs of the cottage and burst into her mother's rag-room. Breathlessly she stood before Pearl, her blue eyes as wide as Jim's and her bouncing sandy curls spilling down her back like a waterfall. She was very tall for her age and, Pearl liked to think, very bright. For sixpence a week, after school and at weekends, she worked in the yard and loved it. She was her father's girl, as she always had been.

'Gwen will be pleased when she hears that.'

Cynthia tossed back her head. 'I gave Fitz an 'a'penny for it. And sold it for a bob.'

'You made a fine profit there.'

'I've got more for me 'orse now.'

'Who did you sell it to?' Pearl enquired as she sifted the cuttings of tailor's cloth that Jim had returned with last night.

'Some coster from West Ferry Road that knows Dad.' Cynthia dropped the payment for the china in the big tobacco pouch that hung from the wall. In this she kept all her savings. 'Do I get me tanner yet?'

'Have you sorted out the bottles?'

'Dillys is callin'. She wants to help out, but I don't want to give her any of me money. I'm savin' up for me 'orse, ain't I?'

Pearl left the pile of rags and sat down on the chair. 'Well, you might not get one of those for a while. You'll have to be patient.'

'Dad said I could after Barney.'

'Yes, well, we don't want to wish him away, do we?'

'Course not. I reckon he'll live as long as me. But there's space in the stable for a little 'orse too.'

Pearl laughed and brought her daughter close. 'Listen, clever clogs, if Dillys wants to help out, I'll give her thrupence for her time. How does that sound?'

Cynthia's brow knitted. 'I'll get her to clean the brass for that.'

'It's a dirty job.'

'She don't mind. She wants an 'orse too.'

'She's going to have a job fitting it in her house.'

Cynthia burst out laughing. Pearl loved her laughter, loud and unguarded. No one was ever going to dampen her spirits and that was the way Pearl encouraged it. The East End was a tough place to live, but Cynth was a natural; she had embraced her new life at the yard with a passion.

'Don't want to squash me brother,' she grinned, rolling a finger over the slope of Pearl's belly. 'How long's he gonna be in there?'

Pearl grinned. 'Next month, in July, he'll arrive. Unless he comes early like you.'

'Why did I come early?'

'The stork was flying over this way.'

'I ain't seen many storks around 'ere.'

'Just keep a good look out and you'll see one.'

A small voice from downstairs floated up, calling Cynth. Pearl patted her bottom. 'That's Dillys. Off you go.'

'Can I go out with Dad tomorra?'

'It's Sunday.'

'Are we going to Gran's?' Cynthia frowned, scratching her head as she looked at Pearl.

'If your dad wants.'

'Or I could go to Sunday school. They give us liquorice strips for readin' the Bible. I can read all them funny names

easy-peasy. But they run out of liquorice last time. It was borin' after that.'

Pearl grinned as her daughter ran off. In that respect she certainly took after her mother! No, there was never a dull moment when Cynth was around, as Granny Nesbitt had discovered over the years. Whether it was Cynth's rough charm that had mellowed her, or age, Pearl couldn't be sure. But time had brought a truce.

She was about to stand up when the baby kicked. How surprised she had been when Cynth had turned out to be a girl! But this child was quieter, ponderous even. Would Jim soon have a son?

Her cheeks warmed at the thought and Pearl caught sight of her reflection in the big, rust-pitted mirror Jim had attached to the wall. Her hair was pinned to the back of her head, a scarf across it to keep out the dust from the rags. Her large canvas apron was stretched tight across her bulge and she smiled at the sight of her rosy cheeks and bright green eyes. Behind her she saw the piles of rags and cuttings that were ready for inspection. Over the years she had learned the value of the clothes and assorted wools that were returned on the cart. Rags of all kinds were a totter's bread and butter. She loved working in her large, well-ordered rag-room in the eaves of Percy's cottage. How clever Jim had been to bring the old place back to life after Percy's death. In the space of three years the yard had become a profitable business, and though it was a dirty old trade, there was a good living in it. Jim had put his heart and soul into the legacy he had received; with no family to call his own, Percy had looked on Jim as a son.

Pearl went to the window overlooking the yard. From here she could see Cynthia and Dillys by the yard gates. Cynthia was arranging the rows of old bottles and Dillys was on her knees, scrubbing the brass.

She smiled. It was difficult to believe that in such a short

389

time their lives had blossomed to this. Thanks to Percy, they had begun a new adventure that, during the dark days of war, could never have entered their wildest dreams. She hoped Percy was satisfied with what he now saw as he looked down from a higher place. Perhaps he even smiled at the repainted wooden banner across the gates: 'James Nesbitt, trader in rags, clothing, plants, ferns, china, brass, lead, iron and bottles. Everything considered, bought and sold.'

Just then the clipclop of hoofs rang out. Cynthia ran to the big wooden gate and lifted the new latch. Barney plodded in, giving a whinny and tossing his head. Bringing the cart to a halt, Jim pulled Cynthia up beside him. Soon she had climbed down to Barney and sat astride his back, leaning her cheek affectionately against his dirty brown mane and feeding him a carrot. Dillys, who was eleven, watched enviously. Jim called to her and swung her up beside him. Cynthia clambered back and took the reins, driving the cart into the stable below.

Pearl left her workbench and went downstairs, treading carefully over the rag rug she had made to cover the patchwork of tiles. The cottage was small but adequate – three bedrooms and a large room for their living space, and a scullery and kitchen. They had brought all their things with them from Pride Place so they wouldn't miss their old home too much. Even Cynth's small bed that had once been her cot; this would meet the baby's needs perfectly.

Just then a tall, handsome man with a slight limp walked in the door and came to greet her. The sun shone behind him, silhouetting his muscular figure clad in a collarless shirt, with the sleeves rolled up, and baggy trousers.

'Hello, beautiful.' Pearl felt his warm lips cover hers. She could taste the river's salt and she trembled with pleasure. 'You shouldn't be on your feet, Mrs N,' he whispered as he held her close.

'I've got nothing else to stand on,' she laughed, her fingers smoothing the muscle of his strong arms.

'So, is the kettle on?'

'No, but it will be. How was your rounds?'

A corn-coloured eyebrow lifted, meeting the tumble of sandy grey hair above. 'I've been over the prefabs.'

'Roper's Way?'

'It's a nice little road now.'

Pearl nodded, despite a twinge of sadness. 'I'm glad.'

He cupped her face in his hands. 'I did a trade, a bit of metal for that old washboard on the back of the cart.'

'That was a nice washboard.'

'But the metal's more interesting. Leastways, what it might have been. Come along with me and I'll show you.' He took her hand and led her out to the stable. The girls had fed Barney and he was munching his hay.

Jim unlocked the backboard and nodded. 'Do you recognize that?' He pointed to a plate-shaped object, lying on the pile of rags. He brushed off the earth and held it up. 'This geezer dug it up. Must have been there a good while. But I've seen the like of it before when I was with the council. And many times on the battlefield.' He looked at her. 'And so have you – once.'

Pearl touched its rough edges.

'Careful, it's sharp.'

'What is it?'

'A bit of casing from a shell. The prefab I traded at was number twenty-four. Well, it was once, a long time ago.'

'Mum and Dad's?'

He nodded slowly, waiting for her response. She screwed up her eyes and shook her head.

'Remember you told me when you was in hospital that there was something stuck in the chimney under all that soot? Well, it was this, or part of it. One of them faulty timer devises from the Blitz.'

391

'Are you sure?'

'As sure as I can be. It was what killed Winters, knocked the wall down on top of him and blew you off your feet. Not enough of an explosion to do much damage unless you was standing right by it.'

Pearl gasped softly. 'So that was how it happened.'

'It was VJ day, remember, and no one would have bothered about the noise.' He placed the metal back in the cart and covered it. 'So the mystery is finally solved.'

She shivered. 'Should I tell Ruby?'

Jim frowned. 'Is there any point?'

'She never understood why he was found there,' Pearl faltered, 'under all that rubble.'

'If the only question she is left with is why did he fetch up in Roper's Way, it ain't a hard one to live with.'

'You did the right thing, laying back those bricks.'

'It was either me or the builders,' Jim shrugged. 'But I chose to end it all there and let them find him. His end came as our release and he owed you that much, Pearl.'

She smiled wistfully. 'They say ignorance is bliss. Ruby is happy now, with her Mr Right.'

'Old Brewer ain't a bad sort. He sold the factory for her, didn't he? And bought them a fine house in the country.'

Pearl nodded. 'Near to Mum and Dad as well.'

He took her hands in his. 'She's Mrs Brewer now, leading the fine life she always wanted. She's given our girl her first cousin and the boy is learning to speak the King's English, just as Ruby wanted. Not bad going, on the whole, is it?'

Pearl smiled as she looked up at him. 'But no woman is as happy as I am.'

'I'd give you the whole world if you wanted it. A big house in the sticks and a posh school for Cynth and the nipper. You only have to say.'

Pearl pressed his hands on her tummy. 'Can you see our Cynth warming to a posh school? She's a free spirit, Jim,

and always will be. She loves this island as much as you and me.'

Jim grinned. 'You're not wrong there, Pearly-girl. Why, she can drive that old nag as if she was born and bred to this trade. But I've got a secret up me sleeve. I'm going to get her a pony, a pretty one with long legs and a good head. I saw a nice little filly over at Houndsditch today. A bloke is flogging her off cheap to buy a van.'

'I told her she'd have to wait till Barney went.'

He chuckled. 'Barney has a good few years in him yet. And I want to see me girl riding proper, with a straight back and on a good-looking animal. Going up Rotten Row of a Sunday and showing them toffs what an islander's made of.' He drew her closer. 'Every day counts, Pearly-girl. Why should we wait for tomorrow? You and I of all people should know that.'

Pearl drew his face down and kissed his lips tenderly. She didn't know why their lives were so blessed, or why fate had brought them along this path. For her and Jim, the war had brought heartache and happiness, as it had for so many others. But here in his arms, on the dirty patch of earth they now called their own, no one could be richer in love than the Nesbitts.